MESABI PIONEERS

MESABI PIONEERS

RUSSELL HILL & JEFFREY SMITH

ACKNOWLEDGEMENTS

This book would not have been possible without two amazing people. First and foremost, Russell Hill had the foresight more than forty years ago to imagine a story about the people who came from all over Europe and Scandinavia to mine the iron ore on the Mesabi Range. Though he is no longer with us, I think he would be proud of the finished product. On equal footing is his daughter, Cheryl Hill Gordon, without whom the book you now hold in your hands would not have been possible. Cheryl persevered like Lon Merritt in the novel, digging this story out of the deep well of history, finding the right people to put the story together, and laying the foundation towards getting it to market. Cheryl is an Iron Ranger of the first order, and her father would be proud of what she has accomplished.

The Virginia Area Historical Society has been extraordinarily helpful with research and guidance. Harry Lamppa and Betty Birnstihl spent many hours with me talking over Range history.

Many people read early drafts of the book and gave some excellent feedback and guidance. Jeanne Maki provided some much needed input on Finnish culture and language, as well as some great editorial assistance. Bill Latady at the Bois Forte Heritage Center helped me better understand the Chippewa culture and heritage. I hope I have done right by the great Anishinaabe people. Damian Costello and Christine Bruce helped guide early drafts of the book.

Thanks to my editor, The Threepenny Editor, Sarah Cypher, for her startling insight and for helping the book find clarity.

There stands out there a large block of people, friends and family and strangers alike, who deserve special recognition for the contribution they made to getting this book in print. The Kickstarter campaign that helped fund this publication provided not only much needed seed money but also showed me that I am not alone in the solitary pursuit of writing. Writing is a lonely job, with lots of lonely time spent in quiet rooms. The tremendous support I received helped me realize that I am not alone in my work, not alone in that room. Like the men and women who populated the Mesabi Range in the latter part of the 19th century, these Kickstarter backers have formed a community through which the story of the Range can be told.

Gary & Janelda Silva, Robert Maki & Nathalie Blachere, Nannette Evans, Carroll & Sandy Key, Cynthia Wainwright, Vincent Scarpinato, Robert & Jennifer Darnell, Debbie Eberts, Silas Brown & Katie Saffady, Shirley Xie, Jennifer Sendek, Kevin J. O'Donovan, Kris & Jan Schafer, Evan & Kristin Ray, Amy Baumgartner Akins, Stephane Larochelle & Reiko Cyr, Aaron & Julie Mann, Lee Olson, Virginia Gann, Dan & Vicki Smith, Fred & Carolyn Sweetapple, Louise Jourdan, Sean J.S. Jourdan, Vivian Piper, Jason Kissner, Jak Fak, Jennifer Louis-Jacques, Lucy Gassaway, David & Kaye Green, Robin Kruse, Damian & Katie Costello, Stephen Cooper, Logan Ingalls & Maureen Dubreuil, J. Kevin Smith, Andrew Weber & Heather Kovich, The Gantman Family, Ian & Corinne Rea, Jeffrey Loh & Caroline Chang, Preston & Katie Staudt, Mirna Mohanraj & Gian Ghandi, Julia Aguilar, Mike & Melissa Nicholson, Jason & Julia Kaufman, Sarah Bliss, Gini Dodds, Christie McDowell, Yuan Yuan, Peter Polivka, Ken & Cathy Jourdan, Jeff Yaeger & Katie Baker, Debbie Weiner, Adam Nyhan, Christina Marney, and Soledad Miranda-Rottmann.

My writing and my life would not be where it is today were it not for the support of my family: my parents, Dan & Vicki Smith and Carroll & Sandy Key; J. Kevin Smith; and Silas Brown.

Last but not least, my wife and daughter, who teach me what it is to love and laugh and live.

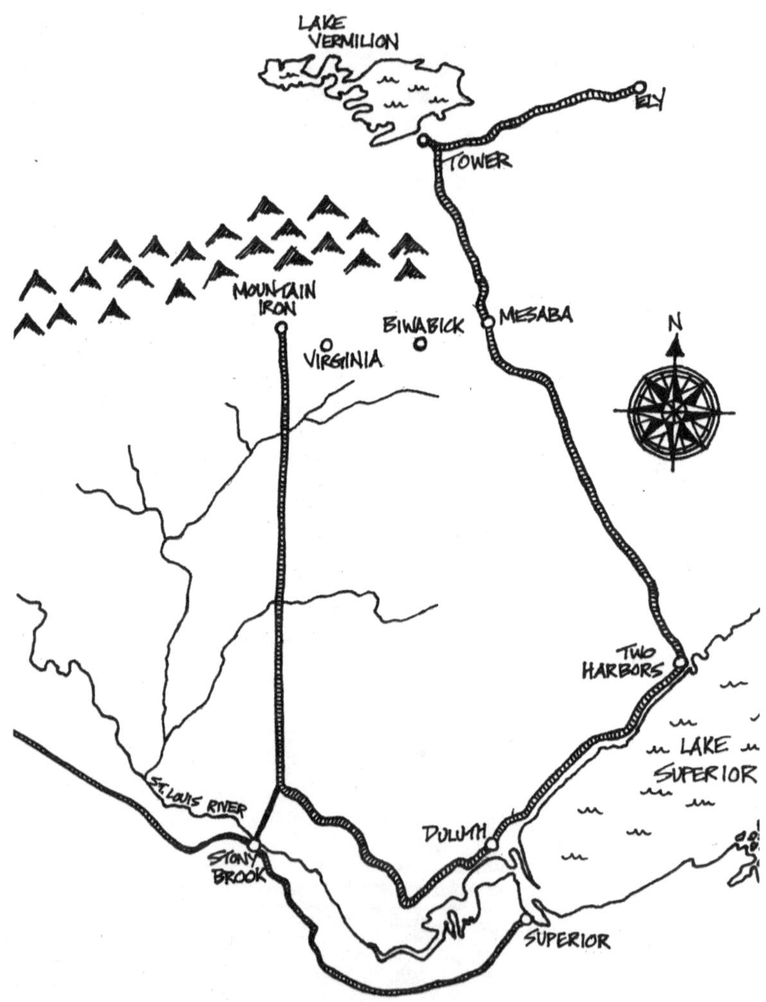

LAKE VERMILION
ELY
TOWER
MOUNTAIN IRON
BIWABICK
MESABA
VIRGINIA
N
TWO HARBORS
ST. LOUIS RIVER
STONY BROOK
DULUTH
LAKE SUPERIOR
SUPERIOR

CHAPTER I

SE ALKOI MOUNTAIN IRONISSA

My sister Delia called and gave me the news. Jo and I left that hot August afternoon, driving from our new home in Battle Lake to Virginia, Minnesota. Jo let me drive. She knew I needed something to do, though we both knew she was the better driver, and I thanked her for that. I managed to find a Brooklyn Dodgers game on the radio and that occupied my mind. I don't know what I would have done if I'd had those five hours to just stare out the window. I had to stay busy, had to keep myself moving. Over the years she must have grown tired of my restlessness, but she never let on.

Delia said it was his heart that gave out. But after Mummu passed in '48 Pappa predicted he wouldn't last more than a few years. He was eighty-six and had been without his Minnie for two years and three days too many.

I brought the fist sized reddish-gray rock Pappa had given me many years before. He had told me it was important, that it represented the land that was here before he arrived, and the way of life that he and so many others worked to create. He told me Leonidas Merritt had given it to him, and I was never really sure if the stories he told were true or not. Pappa was a great story teller.

After we arrived I took a walk by myself along Silver Lake, past the pluming smoke of the city's water plant. Virginia was a big town, the largest of the quad-cities on the Range, and though I was born in Eveleth, five miles to the southeast, this place felt more like home. As a kid I climbed the vermilion dumps of useless overburden at the edge of the mines east of town, playing king of the mountain with Skeeter and The Ruk and Eddie. In the mornings we fished for pike and perch in Silver Lake, and in the evenings we swam in her calm water. It was on the eastern shore of the other lake in town, Virginia Lake, where Pappa had built his first house in 1895. Back then, he didn't have a sawmill to provide lumber; he only had sisu and an axe. When that house burned down in the fire of 1900, he rebuilt farther south. Delia lived there now, and it was still an amazing structure. Yet it wasn't the first he had built on the Range.

As I walked, heat radiated off the streets and the mosquitoes danced like flying thumbtacks, jabbing and biting my exposed flesh. I thought about Pappa and the forbidding area this used to be: thick with muddy bogs and the nightly howl of wolves and hoot of owls. He had grappled with the land from the ground up, had helped start its transformation into the iron ore capital it would become. He turned trees to houses. He helped converge a disparate group of men from diverse cultures into what would become the Range culture. He built not only a life for himself and his family, but for all the families to come after him. He was a leader, a builder, a father. At least, he was a father to me when my own father could no longer fill that role. I missed him already.

⟞⟝◆⟞⟝

The next day Jo and I took the car to see the airshow flying out of the new airport outside of Eveleth. We sat on the metal grandstand and ate popcorn from paper bags while we watched World War II style fighter planes perform aerial stunts over the mines. When the planes landed I managed to bend the ear of the pilot of a Republic AT12 Guardsman with two seats. I told him I had been in the Navy and fought in the Pacific Theater.

"I flew over Germany," he said.

He agreed to take me up, and within five minutes I was strapped into the seat behind him where we were both enclosed in a large glass canopy. He gave me a leather helmet, pulled on his own, and after ensuring I was properly buckled in, zoomed down the runway and into the air. The plane banked left into a wide circle toward the big Eveleth water tower, and then turned back toward Virginia following the state highway that linked the two communities. Again the pilot banked and dipped the right wing, allowing me to view the shallow valley in which most of Virginia lay and the low, rolling hills to the north.

Dark green hills waved across an ocean of pale blue sky. Mines lay scattered among the trees like the pieces of a giant earthen quilt. The Fayal Mine, which started underground, gashed open the earth outside of Eveleth. The deep Rouchleau pit below—the combination of dozens of other mines that, over the years, had grown together—reflected shades of brown, rich purple, bright orange, ribbons of dark blue, and shimmering gold. The pit hugged the eastern edge of Virginia itself, slowly swallowing the Shaw and Franklin locations, which were situated in a sea of pit mines. White puffs rose from the chimneys of railroad engines deep within the mine. The vermilion red dump where I played as a kid was dwarfed by the vastness beyond the airplane's wingtips. Black rivers snaked between ridge lines and vanished in green tunnels of pine, tamarack and cedar. Lake Vermilion far to the north shimmered.

The pilot flew west into the afternoon sun and then dipped the left wing. Below, the deep Mountain Iron mine sat dormant and half-filled with bluish water, plunging sides exposing ocher and rust-colored dirt above the waterline. The land around it was stripped bare, left like a moonscape by the U.S. Steel owned Oliver Mining Company. On it was a single human outpost, a tidy white square where the Pilotac plant would stand—the first step in a process to turn the dumps into usable iron ore. Beyond it to the north, the long ridge of rolling hills marked the Laurentian Divide.

Mountain Iron. The name brought memories to mind that were not even mine—images from stories Pappa used to tell. He was a good storyteller, much more so than my father, who was more concerned with making money than lingering over the past. Pappa came to the range in the spring of 1891 when it was a vast, trackless jungle of pine, tamarack, spruce, ash, maple, cedar and birch punctuated by a stony ridge that resembled the knotty spine of an emaciated giant. The natives called it *nibaad misaabe*: the sleeping giant. It was home to deer and elk, bear, moose, and wolf. The skies were filled with bullfinches, cardinals, and blue jays. Hawks and eagles perched in the high branches. Ducks, swans and geese paddled the myriad lakes and ponds, and herons and egrets stalked through the rushes.

The native Chippewa migrated overland from the shores of the great salt water in the east, what we now call the Atlantic Ocean, and settled on the shores of Leech Lake, Red Lake, *Gichigami*—what the Chippewa called Lake Superior—and the dense forest in between. Once there, they tolerated the French Canadian fur traders who trapped minx and fox on their lands, and bartered with the few white settlers for food and tools. In the summertime the pine bogs swarmed with blackflies and mosquitoes. In winter, snow piled fifteen feet high and the land was as white and as frozen as the arctic.

Back in 1865, when the state was not even a decade old, a lanky land surveyor and merchant named George Stuntz found what he called a "mountain of iron" up near Lake Vermilion. It would take him twenty years, and the work of the Minnesota legislature, before any of the iron he found would be brought to market. Then it was a shrewd Philadelphia lawyer by the unforgettable name of Charlemagne Tower—a giant in coal—who sent geologist Albert Chester to test Stuntz's mountain. Chester reported red gold in the form of 75 percent pure iron ore. Tower invested heavily and built the town that came to bear his name on the south shore of the lake. To get his ore to market, he chopped a rail line through the dense forest. He was seventy-eight when a syndicate of steel magnates and oil men, John D. Rockefeller among them, pressured Tower to sell his mine holdings. It was history that would repeat itself six years later.

For a while people thought that the Vermilion range contained all the usable iron Minnesota had to offer. Experts believed that to get high-quality ore you had to dig under layers of hard rock deep in the ground. The only other natural resource in the state, they said, was wood—lots of it. Huge swaths of state-owned pine forest were leased to the first men to file claim with the land office.

But rumors persisted. Men came out of the woods holding aloft chunks of red-hued rock they had found lying on the ground.

And Leonidas Merritt was one of them.

He believed the iron was there, that it had to be there. He and his brothers, timber cruisers by trade who specialized in finding stands of white pine, discovered chunks of iron ore laying on the ground. While he amassed a timber-based fortune, he continued his hunt for the cache of iron ore he believed lay along the vast *nibaad misaabe*. But even when he brought samples back to Duluth, sacks full of gray clay and hunks of metallic rock, when he showed them his maps with markings pointing to long stretches of land where the compass pointed neither north nor south but straight down into the ground—even then he was received with blank stares and incredulous shrugs.

"It's just surface ore," the mineralogists told him. "Doesn't mean anything."

"That's the washout from some long dried ocean," others said. "There ain't enough iron on the ground to sustain a mine."

Even the United States Geological Survey said, "Not a single deposit of iron ore of such size and character as to warrant exploration has shown up."

Leonidas—everyone called him Lon—and his brothers fixated on the idea that there was iron ore in the woods. Pappa said he thought Lon must have had a little Finn in him to have such determination to achieve a goal that the entire world thought was crazy.

For the Merritts and for mining itself, help came from two fronts. The industrial revolution increased a demand for steel, and America, recovering from the bloody and protracted Civil War, was becoming a world leader in industrialization. America needed steel, and steel needed iron. With an abundance of land, America seemed ripe to take advantage of the age of mineral exploration. Speculation was rampant: where would the minerals come from? Then came Minnesota's Braden Act of 1889, which authorized the state to negotiate leases and contracts for any of its land, for the purposes of mining and shipping iron ore. Suddenly there was a bounty on deposits of ore. Men did not need to dig it out of the ground—they simply needed to find where it lay.

Lon insisted he already knew; he spent his family fortune digging the ore out of the ground. Then he spent another fortune trying to get his ore to market.

It was to this place and in this time that Arthur Maki, Pappa, my grandfather, came into Lon's life. Born Arvid Mäkelä in Jalasjärvi, Finland, in 1864, at a time when Finland was a territory of the vast Russian state, he was the bastard son of a Russian colonel. Raised by his mother and stepfather, Hilda and Matti Mäkelä, he learned carpentry and farming on their small farm until his eighteenth birthday, when he was conscripted into the Russian army. After two years he walked out of camp one dark winter night and kept walking until he reached Helsinki, where he boarded a boat and came to America.

He spent some time in New York before he heard about jobs in the west. He traveled by train, sleeping in freight cars or in haystacks. In Minneapolis he attended a Finnish Lutheran church where he met Minnie. They were married a few months later and together rented a room in a Duluth boarding house run by Hephzibah Merritt, Lon's mother. Arthur helped around the house, fixing walls and repairing furniture, and Lon liked what he saw. He offered Arthur a job.

"When we find the deposits we'll need a good carpenter," Lon told him.

Arthur was reluctant. He wanted steady money, but what Lon was offering was not stable or firm. It was speculation, and that was no better than a bet, as far as Arthur was concerned. Instead he took a job working in the mines around Tower and Soudan. Minnie stayed in Duluth to work at the Merritt Hotel; it was the only time in their lives that they were separated.

Meanwhile, Lon persevered. On November 16, 1890, a German engineer named Josef Nichols sunk a drill in section three of Township 58-18—what would become the Mountain Iron Mine— and found the iron went down six feet. For Lon Merritt, the rush was on.

Lon and Arthur had a lot in common. Both were spiritual men who prayed daily and attended church regularly. Both men believed in keeping the body pure. Unlike most other hardy men of the day who spent their lives in the harsh environments of northern Minnesota, they neither drank nor smoked. Most importantly, both men believed in the power of man, believed that with a strong will and a strong back they could move mountains.

"Come and work with us," he implored my grandfather a second time in early 1891. "We need you."

As Arthur considered it, the look on his clean-shaven face betrayed no emotion. My grandfather was a stoic Finn with the disposition of a three-days-dead walleye.

"You will be in from the beginning," Lon said. "With a share of the profits."

My grandfather's thin eyebrows lifted.

"And the profits will be huge."

Being rich was not one of Arthur Maki's goals. He simply wanted to live without struggle, to live safely and comfortably with his wife always by his side. In this place, in this country, where he had been for nearly five years, he understood that life without struggle meant life with money. For himself, for the big family he yearned to have, that was what he wanted.

"*Joo*," Arthur said. "I come."

There were those who thought that the Merritts were working beyond their knowledge, and it is of some conjecture that had the Merritts "stuck to pine" as it were, they might have wound up among the richest timber barons in the country. Instead, Lon brought a group of men into the woods to sniff out something he believed was there. For Lon, that is almost all it was: belief.

"*Se alkoi Mountain Ironissa*," Pappa used to say when he told the stories of those early days. *It started in Mountain Iron.* He knew very little about iron. Arthur Maki could dig, sure, and while he was creative in the construction arts, he never considered himself a leader. He was a builder, a carpenter. "A doer," he used to tell me. He came to the Mesabi Range to follow orders and find a quiet place to raise his family. He hoped a small mining camp in the woods would be that place.

CHAPTER 2

NIBAAD MISAABE

Arthur Maki gripped a woolen cap in his calloused hands and stared out the window of the lone passenger car. The Three Spot engine had tugged him all this way, through the northern Minnesota woods. Out there was a blurred wall of evergreens and brown ash, and the maple trees were already focusing themselves into blossoming buds. A whistle pierced the rhythmic chugging; a flock of sparrows shot into the swaying trees and vanished.

The train lurched and steel wheels screeched against the rail. Telegraph poles that had whizzed past the windows now loomed and marked time as the train slowed. Smoke and steam billowed into the woods. Ahead the trees thinned and two rows of wooden shacks appeared as though they had been carved from the forest itself—in fact, they had. The train depot, painted green as though it were trying to become part of the forest again, leaned away from the tracks like a drunken miner. A white wooden lettered sign hung over a window: *Mesaba*.

Arthur had last seen this town in '89 on his way to the mines in Tower and Soudan. For nearly two years he slept in the hall of the Northern Flame Temperance Society with fifty other Finns. Every morning he trudged across a dirt field to the mine entrance, wrapped himself in heavy waterproof jacket and pants, took four candles from the supply offered by the foreman—cost later deducted from his pay—and rode the steam-powered cage down into the shaft. The Cornish mine captain, Cousin Jack—Arthur never knew his real name, that was simply what everyone called him—would assign him and three other Finns to a drift where they worked mostly in the dark picking at the soft ore one thousand feet below the surface. It was humid, dank, suffocating work, and Arthur feared the cave would take his life. Every evening when he stepped out of the cage and into the fresh air, he gave thanks.

Tower itself was a lawless place, rife with saloons and gambling and prostitution. Each night as he walked back to the Temperance Hall he passed bar fights and street fights, harassing gangs of drunk Finns and Italians and Slovenians, bands of violent mine guards playing deputy sheriff. He was glad Minnie had stayed in Duluth to have their baby.

As the train shuddered to a stop, the sleeping conductor tumbled off his bench with a thud against the wooden floor. He rubbed his wrinkled eyes and muttered, "Mesaba Station."

The only other passengers in the car were a Finnish woman and her son. The boy, all of twelve, was asleep with his head on his mother's lap. Though a black veil obscured her face, Arthur recognized her. A week before, her husband, the boy's father, had been killed in the Minnesota Mine when the drift he had been working reached a pocket of water and flooded. Twenty-one other men died with him. Arthur was unpaid for the time he spent recovering their bodies and pumping the water out of the shaft. It was then, as he'd been standing beside the line of shrouded figures, that a group of widows came over the rise from the camp, led by the woman on the train. She examined each bloated face until she found the one that was her husband. Later she was given the opportunity to remain in miner's housing if her son agreed to take his father's place in the drifts. The woman had refused, and within an hour a guard had escorted her and her son out of the house they had occupied for more than a year.

In her Arthur saw Minnie and shivered at the image of his wife trudging over that hill to find his body. When he received a visit two days after the accident from Leonidas Merritt offering him a job, he was eager to say yes.

A wind whisked the train's white cloud across the tracks, and into the open door on a gust of cold air.

Arthur slipped his canvas packsack onto his broad shoulders. As he pulled his tool bag from the shelf over his head, metal clanked against metal. He had wrapped his tools well, but still they knocked about. The axe handle he had carved from birch was strapped to the side of the bag and bumped against his leg as he climbed the three steps down to the station platform. My grandfather was a tall, muscular man with roughly cut short blonde hair and even without a cap he had to duck to get through the door. He wore denim pants and a flannel cotton shirt over long underwear that had faded to the dull gray of birch bark. Though the April air was still crisp, he left his fur lined long coat unbuttoned and his gloves stuffed in a pocket.

It was not Lon Merritt who met him that day, but his nephew, Johnnie. As John emerged from the smoke, his pale, dirt smeared face made him appear past thirty. He removed a leather glove and extended his right hand to Arthur, betraying sleeves frayed at the cuffs.

"Mr. Maki," he said. "I'm John Merritt. I'll be leading the party."

Arthur held the man's gaze and then gave a small, quick nod of his head. Like most Finns, he was a man of few words.

"Call me Johnnie. Everybody does." He smiled. The hand dangled, untouched, between the two men.

Arthur stared, unblinking.

"Right," Johnnie said. He slipped his hand back into his glove and turned. Arthur followed him.

Inside the leaning depot, three burly men stood in a half circle around a stove, warming themselves in its sooty heat. Long beards hid faces worn by years of hardened work; even Johnnie had a caterpillar mustache. Arthur was the only one with a smooth shave.

"Gentlemen," Johnnie said. "This is Arthur Maki, our carpenter and builder. Mr. Maki, this is Captain Alfred Wood, Mr. Verne Richardson, and Captain Eustis Gill."

Captain Gill bit the end of his pipe and puffed a mouthful of white smoke. "Tis good to finally meet you, brother," he said. "We've heard much about the Finn who works magic with birch." His beard danced as he spoke.

Verne Richardson smiled broadly, yellow teeth bared around a thinly rolled cigarette. "Please to meet you," he said. He had narrow eyes and wide cheeks and skin the color of ironwood. "I am a timberman myself," he said.

Arthur was glad to see another woodsman among them, but said nothing.

The third man plucked an unlit cigar from his yellowed teeth. "Daylight's wasting," Captain Wood said. His lip curled with a scowl as he turned from the others. "Let's get on with it." He slung his pack over his broad back and lurched out the door. Beneath his big chest his legs were like twigs and with each step Wood looked as though he might topple over.

Richardson lifted his own pack and leaned toward Arthur. "He's tough but fair. Been like that since I met him."

The train whistle blew and pushed out of the station. Arthur thought of the widow and her son and silently wished them a safe journey.

Outside Arthur breathed in the sweet scent of burning pine, the cold and muddy earth, and the fragrance of moist pine needles. This was the outdoors, and for the first time in two years, Arthur felt alive. The future was now an open book and he was finally holding the pen. He had come here, on this wild speculation, in the hopes that here he would get his chance to find something that had been missing since he left his family behind in the old country—some breath of clear sky and stars and cold air, a homeland magic. Maybe if he found it here, and could find a place of his own, too, maybe then Minnie and Ben could join him.

Arthur followed the four men through town. A dozen buildings with false storefronts lined both sides of the street. Signs creaked on rusty chains: Stone Mining Company, Moss Mining Company, Eureka Mining Company, Minnesota Iron, Mallman Iron Company, Tallworth Mining Company, Coopers Copper Mining, Pine River Timber, St. Louis Timber, American Fur Trading Company. Most of the signs were rotting and the log shacks they hung above were empty. Piles of horse manure littered the muddy street. Gritty crusts of snow clung to the northern shadows. Just beyond the end of the street the small town ended where the trees began, as though the little place were simply on loan from the wilderness.

Arthur studied the signs—so many mining companies had come and gone. The only businesses not shuttered here were the lumber companies. It was not the first time, nor would it be the last, that he allowed himself to doubt his dream. Did these Merritt boys know what they were doing? He had to trust them, either way.

At the only livery in town they picked up two wagons and four mules. The livery owner, a slight man with red hair, shifted on the balls of his feet as he called out to them. "You boys are exploring, eh? Going to take de trail?" He cackled through missing front teeth.

Wood said, "Where we go is our own business."

"Ya, ya," the man said. Arthur recognized the Norwegian accent. "I vas yust asking. Be careful of de giant in de hills. Do not vake him." He laughed again.

Arthur thought he sensed something in the man's voice, something he was not saying. Or maybe it was something he was saying. Arthur was a superstitious man. If the Norwegian said there was a giant in the hills, who was to say that he was not right?

Wooden crates with the name Merritt stenciled on the side were already stacked in front of the dry goods store. Wood and Johnnie went inside while Arthur and the others loaded the crates into the wagons. There were sacks of dried beans and flour and sugar and salt and pepper, tins of tobacco and allspice, nutmeg and saltpeter, two barrels of gunpowder. In addition, there were more than a dozen picks and shovels and axes. Three crates of TNT. One of the crates, larger than the others, contained a small portable sawmill. Four crates were labeled nails, another saws, and still another simply Maki. Inside this last were planers and tongs and rulers and chisels and squares and half a dozen sharpening stones.

"Lon said you would appreciate that," Johnnie said to Arthur.

Arthur did not know what to say. He was delighted, but like a good Finn he opted to say nothing at all.

Richardson said, "We have enough here to build a town."

Johnnie smiled. "That is exactly what we are going to do."

Arthur led one wagon while Richardson led the other, both of them following Johnnie to the end of town where the woods began. The little liveryman waved to them as they passed, his mustache dancing as he cackled.

At the end of the street began what could have been called a road. It looked as though a den of beavers had chewed a swath through forest. Hastily chopped trees lay like fallen soldiers along the middle of the trail. Some of the leftover stumps were so tall as to be nearly trees themselves. Slushy snow, melting into mud, filled two deep ruts in the forest floor.

Captain Gill removed his pipe from his teeth and whistled. "Is that our way?"

Johnnie nodded. "Aye, it is."

Wood did not look behind him as he took the first steps into the woods. "The first one who complains carries my pack."

"Come on, then," Johnnie said, and followed.

Richardson guided the mules into the trees, and the wheels of the first wagon became mired in ankle deep mud almost instantly. Gill got behind and pushed while Richardson yelled at the asses to move. "Get up there!"

The animals pushed against the soft earth until finally a wheel caught a rock and the wagon jumped forward, knocking Gill on his face.

Arthur helped the Cornishman to his feet. Gill wiped the mud away with his handkerchief and grumbled, "Why don't we ride these wagons instead of push them?"

Wood squelched through the mud and poked Gill in the chest. "Because these wagons are heavy enough without you lazing in them." He took off his pack and handed it to the Cornishman. "Let's move."

The men hacked at saplings encroaching on the road. They took turns leading the wagons and cutting. They journeyed for only two miles before they came to a stump five feet in diameter in the middle of the road. Purple twilight settled in the trees. Arthur set his pack on a nearby stump, flung off his coat and hefted his axe.

Richardson joined him. Wood chips flew. The two men took turns rhythmically hacking at the stump of knotty pine blocking their way. When they had chopped nearly through, Richardson kicked the stump and it fell with a splat into the mud.

Wood said, "We camp here tonight."

Arthur buried his axe in a nearby stump. Darkness settled around him, but up through the canopy he saw the bright moon, nearly full, etched in the trees. As he unfurled his bedroll he thought of Minnie and muttered a prayer that God watch over his wife and son. "Bring them soon to me," he whispered.

⬦◆⬦

They rose with dawn. After a breakfast of leftover beans, they led the wagons over the now-small stump. Yet within a few miles they came across a hulking mass of gray granite that seemed to grow out of the ground.

"Where did this come from?" Johnnie said.

Gill stuffed his pipe with tobacco. "They come out o' the earth," he said. He lit his pipe and puffed thick smoke into the air. "Churned by the heat and cold."

The jutting boulder had caused the trees to shift, baring their roots to the air, and the underbrush on either side of the trail was thick. There was no way around.

"We've got to blast it," Gill said. "Move everything well back." Using a hand drill, he bore three holes into the center of the rock, from the top and from the sides. Despite the denseness of the rock, Gill worked swiftly. Into each hole he dropped a stick of TNT, tied together the fuses, then stretched the three strands behind the line of the now-distant wagons.

"Have ye ever seen proper blasting done, boys?" Gill said.

Richardson said, "Aye. And I have seen proper blasting done wrong."

"Eustis Gill does naye do blasting wrong." He swiped a match across his boot and touched the flame to the end of the fuse. "Fire in the hole," he called.

The flame sparkled along the fuse, melting a path through the snow until it dispersed along the three paths into the holes. The ground bumped as though a giant had fallen, and a fraction of a second later, the boulder shifted and its backside exploded.

Shards of rock sliced through the trees, away from the wagons. A gray cloud ballooned into the air and rained dust. The concussion spooked the mules, which went wild in their reins.

Arthur covered his mouth and nose, but the deafening blast left his ears ringing. When the air cleared the rock was still there.

Wood was furious. "All that and it's still standing!"

Gill bit down on the end of his pipe and smiled. He walked over to the rock and pushed on it with one hand. The rock toppled over onto the road, a flattened mass that perfectly filled the hole from the blast, creating a bridge. He put his pipe between his teeth, pushed back his shoulders and smiled proudly. "Blasting done right."

The day grew warmer and with it came the bugs. Blackflies and gnats swarmed in annoying clouds around Arthur's head and face. He swatted at them but that didn't seem to do any good. Calmly, Gill puffed pipe smoke around his head, keeping the creatures at bay. Johnnie seemed just as undisturbed, swiping lazily at them as he walked. Arthur pulled his hat low over his ears and buttoned his collar tight.

As they moved deeper into the thick forest, the trail began to vanish amid the underbrush. Arthur felt the canopy of trees crowding over him. Sunlight, blocked by shimmering leaves, flickered through the shadows. He thought of Minnie and wished that he had written a quick letter to her before they left Mesaba. He felt, suddenly, so far from her.

Towards the end of the second day, as the sun fell behind the tree line, Wood stopped. "What's that?" he asked, pointing ahead.

A crouching bear blocked the path, its brown fur blending with the trees. As the men watched, the bear ambled towards them.

"Nobody move," Wood said. He slipped his rifle off his shoulder. The animal seemed to rise up to the height of a man. Wood lifted the rifle and took aim.

"Wait," Johnnie said.

The animal walked closer and in the fading light his fur changed to a lighter color. Arthur saw he had arms, too. Human arms.

Johnnie said, "That's Charlie."

Wood lowered his rifle. "Who's Charlie?"

"Chippewa Charlie," Johnnie said.

The man glided over the rocks and stumps like they were pebbles. As he came closer Arthur could see that the bearskin draped over his shoulders had a head attached. Beneath it he wore a tan leather shirt and leather pants and thick fur moccasins on his feet. As he approached he tilted the head back to reveal long black hair tied in a braid and draped over his shoulder. A wood handled knife was stuck in his belt and a colorful woolen sash lay across his chest.

He and Johnnie gripped each other's left forearm. "*Boozhoo*," Johnnie said.

"*Boozhoo*," the Indian said. He surveyed the group behind Johnnie. His lips turned up in a smile and he spoke in a language Arthur could not understand. Johnnie laughed. The two spoke quietly as the Indian gestured to the west.

Wood bit down on his stick cigar. "Who is this?" he demanded. "Since when was one of them in my party?"

"Charlie is a Chippewa," Johnnie said. "He knows these woods better than any of us. Even me."

"I don't care if he can find iron with his nose," Wood barked. "He ain't on my outfit."

Johnnie turned to Wood. "I hope you learn better to control that tongue of yours. This isn't your outfit—it's mine. I say who's on it and who's not. If you have a problem with that, then I suggest you go back to Duluth." He turned back to the Indian who showed the slightest of smiles and watched Wood out of the corner of his eye. Arthur figured Charlie understood more than he let on, and he wondered if the reason the two men continued to speak in Chippewa was only to keep Wood out of the conversation.

Wood fumed and chomped his cigar. He stared at the two men for a tense moment and then stormed away. Johnnie and Charlie clasped arms again and then the Indian returned to the trees, his bear skin shawl draping down his back.

Arthur watched the Indian go. His quiet stoicism reminded Arthur of the Finns back home, and that alone gave Arthur greater hope for the unknown that lay ahead.

"Let's keep moving," Johnnie said.

"Where's he going?" Gill said. "I thought he was going to guide us through this morass."

Johnnie smiled. "Charlie will be useful in many ways."

Tree stumps and boulders continued to slow their progress, but the mud annoyed them most. It was gray-black and rust colored and it coated everything and everyone. It splattered the wagons, clogged the wheels, stuck to the mules' hoofs and weighed down their boots. Richardson alone seemed unfazed; he caked his face with the stuff to thwart the mosquitoes. Arthur heard Charlie scurrying in the trees, following them unseen.

Soon the sun sank into the horizon. Johnnie suggested they stop for the night and Wood agreed. Richardson and Arthur collected wood for a fire while Gill got the pots from the wagon. Once the fire raged Gill placed a bean filled pot on the hot embers and they sat back to wait. Johnnie scratched in a journal, and Wood studied the map. Mosquitoes and flies swarmed, and the men moved closer to the heat, not for warmth, but to keep the bugs at bay. Crickets crooned. A wolf howled. Through the swaying trees Arthur saw the sliver of the moon, blurry in a distant cloud. He wondered if Minnie were looking at the same moon.

Arthur heard the snap of a branch. He knew the Indian was near.

Gill stood up. "What was that?"

Leaves rustled.

Richardson bolted upright, and Wood grabbed his rifle.

Johnnie held up his hands in an effort to calm the men. "No one panic. It may be nothing."

Arthur stared at the fire. "Charlie," he said flatly.

"Who?" Wood said.

"Chippewa," Arthur said.

Then Charlie was standing next to the fire, holding his rifle in his right hand and his knife in the other. Firelight flickered in his dark eyes.

Startled, Gill fell back and landed in the mud. "Dammit!"

Johnnie smiled.

Wood jammed the butt of his rifle into the dirt. "Damned savage like to scare me to death."

Charlie draped his rifle over his shoulder. Blood dripped off the blade of his knife. He turned and twisted a rope around his hand and pulled. The rope, which Arthur recognized as spruce root, was attached to his waist. Something dragged along the ground. The white-gray tips of antlers appeared in the edge of the light.

Gill said, "Is that—"

Wood interrupted him. "Venison!" He dropped his gun and pulled a knife from his pack. He jumped across the fire and brushed past the Charlie.

Gill grabbed his arm. "What are you doing, brother?"

Wood pulled his arm free. "Cutting off some steaks for us."

Johnnie stood up. "Captain Wood, that is not our kill."

"Look at it. Must be a ten pointer." Wood pointed his knife, glinting in the firelight, at the deer. "He's got plenty for all of us. That savage here can no more eat all of that than you or I could."

Richardson stood next to Charlie. Arthur noticed the similarity in the way the light flickered across their skin. "The deer is not ours to share," he said firmly.

"These savages know nothing about sharing," Wood said. "They use a place up and they move on. They left the east cause they used it all up. We need that meat more than he does. And there are more of us. Why don't we just take it?"

Arthur remained seated by the fire, watching the scene play out. There were plenty of other deer in the forest, but Wood stood his ground by the fire, facing off with Charlie. Richardson and Johnnie each flanked him, taking his side against Wood. Gill kept out of the way with Arthur. It was like the fights Arthur had seen in Tower, a showing of manhood, boys fighting over deer meat.

"I think you may be talking about us," Richardson said.

Charlie loosened the knot around his waist and let the spruce rope fall to the ground. He disappeared into the darkness, his feet crunching on fallen branches.

"See," Wood said, taking a step towards the animal. "He brought it for us."

Johnnie put a hand on his chest. "We are not going to lay into another man's kill."

"Why else would he bring it here?"

"That may be the case," Johnnie said. "But we shall talk with him first."

"We don't know how long this animal's been dead. The longer we wait the more likely it will rot before our eyes." Wood took another step but Johnnie held him back. "Belly's probably already full of maggots."

"We wait," Johnnie said.

Wood threw up his hands. "This is ridiculous. I know all of

you'd like some meat. I've had my fill of beans, enough to last a year."

Charlie reappeared carrying a strand of spruce rope. He looked up into the trees. Arthur stood and looked up in the trees, too. He felt a connection to the Indian and he wanted to help.

"There," Arthur said.

Charlie stepped over the deer and looked up to where Arthur pointed. He tossed one end of the rope over the yoke in the branches. Arthur caught the end that came down and tied it to a thick pine branch Charlie had lashed between the animal's hind legs. Together the two men pulled the rope until the animal hung two feet off the ground, antlers dangling. While Charlie held the rope, Arthur tied the free end around a nearby tree stump.

Charlie pulled his knife from his belt and cut a circle around the animal's throat, then a slit under its skin straight up its belly. The skin seemed to tear easily from the body. He draped the skin over a nearby log. From the animal's groin he pulled out the scent glands which he threw into the woods. Then he sliced a hunk of meat from the hind leg and dropped it at Captain Wood's feet.

Wood snatched the meat off the ground and, using the edge of his knife, scraped away the dirt and mud. He lay it on a log and cut the meat into long steaks, then pulled a pan from one of the wagons and put it on the fire.

"Listen to it sizzle," he said. "Smells like heaven!"

Charlie began to slice the meat in strips which he placed on the skin. Arthur recognized the cuts and stepped into the forest. The flickering light from the fire spread wide enough so that he could see. Thick branches lay across the ground and he turned them over with his foot until he found three that were long and thick and relatively evenly sized. Then he cut saplings with his knife and dragged all of it back to camp. He felt in his element now and sensed the others watching him. He worked surely and swiftly, confident in his actions. A few feet from the fire, close to where Charlie worked, he dug a small hole and created a triangle around it with the three long branches. Then he tied the saplings in rings between them. He cut a long sheet of birch bark from a fallen tree and left pieces near the stand. Using a shovel he scooped up embers from the fire and dumped them in the hole. Arthur carefully draped the strips of meat over the saplings. Shortly the deer was deboned and all remaining meat hung in strips over the smoldering embers. Together Arthur and Charlie covered the structure with the birch bark and used lengths of spruce root rope to tie it closed.

Charlie cleaned his knife using a handful of wet leaves. He folded and draped the deer hide over his shoulder and dragged the bones into the forest. As he passed Arthur he nodded.

Richardson said, "You ever done that before?"

Arthur shook his head.

"How did you know how to do that?"

Arthur shrugged. "Smoking the meat. Is all the same."

Wood took the steaks off the fire. There were five of them in all. He stuck his knife in one and ate it as it dripped fat onto the ground at his feet. "Oh, that is good," he said. "Dig in, boys."

Arthur ladled out a plateful of beans while everyone else took a steak. To Arthur, the kill did not belong to him, and he did not want to take what was not his. The group ate in silence.

Afterwards, my grandfather lay on his sleeping roll and stared up at the tree canopy while firelight danced across the leaves and branches. The smell of smoking meat mixed with the pinesap and wet leaves. The last time he had slept under a sky like this had been more than seven years before, in an army camp in the Cossack mountains. Back then he had awoken with a start while the moon still hung high overhead, and he had quietly risen and walked away into the woods. For a long time he had feared they would find him and force him to return. Now, out here amid the pine and cedar and tamarack, he felt free of that. Then, he had been walking towards a better life. Now, he hoped he had finally found it.

⋇

The trees vanished in a mist that hung low over the ground like rising steam. Arthur, leading a team of mules at the rear of the caravan, stayed close behind the lead wagon so as not to get lost. His boots squished across the wet ground. The air was still and strangely silent. Even the creaking wheels of the wagon seemed remote and distant.

"Call," Captain Wood ordered them, and the voices of the other members of the party echoed through the fog.

"Merritt."

"Gill."

"Richardson."

They had been trekking for two long days, chopping down trees, blasting out boulders the size of small homes. Pulling wagons into mud pits, and then pulling them back out again. Arthur, a woodsman at heart, listened to the sound of the trees swaying. They creaked against one another, speaking to each other as if telling the stories of their lives: how long they had been growing, the saplings that had lost the battle for light in the denseness of the forest. While the men walked Arthur picked out the trees that would be good for house building, the ones that would be good firewood. In his head he was already planning the buildings he would construct, what the kitchen would look like, the eating hall, the public meetinghouse. And he planned his own home, surrounded by trees, fronting a lake where he could build his sauna.

"Maki! You back there?"

Wood's voice pulled him out of his daydream. "*Joo*," he said.

"Jesus Christ, all you got to do is answer," Wood shouted.

"*Joo*," Arthur said again. His moist breath clouded around his face and then vanished into the mist. The caravan continued, but shortly stopped again. Jangling reins echoed back through the line. Arthur shifted from foot to foot to prevent himself from sinking in the mud.

"God dammit," Wood said. Then, "Richardson, Maki. Your turn."

Arthur tied off the mules' lead and followed the length of the first wagon until he found Richardson with the others in a half circle. Blocking the road was the rotting stump of a tamarack tree that stuck out of the ground like a giant's crooked finger. Wood pushed against it as though it might just fall down.

"Too big to go around," he said. "Take it out."

Richardson set at the roots with his axe. "Who cut these?" he said. "This was the job of children and fools, not lumbermen."

While Arthur dug at the earth around the stump, and Richardson attempted to sever the roots, Gill unhitched the mules from the first wagon. He tied one end of a rope to the harness and the other end he wrapped around the stump.

Arthur heard a rumble from the trees. He stopped digging.

Richardson swung his axe into the stump with a thwack.

"What was that?" Wood said.

"Blasting," Gill said. "Smell the powder?"

Richardson said, "I thought we were the only ones out here."

Charlie appeared out of the fog and spoke quietly to Johnnie. Wood stood behind them and ground his teeth around his cigar. Johnnie clapped his hands and turned with a grin. "That's our camp, boys. We're almost there."

With feverish urgency, the men pitched in to get this final obstacle out of their path. While Richardson and Arthur continued to dig and chop around the roots of the stump, Wood and Gill coaxed the stubborn mules to pull the rope. Finally, with a deep splintering sound, the stump broke. They re-hitched the mules to the wagons and walked on. Soon, wafting pine smoke filled the air and the smell of gunpowder saturated the fog. Straight overhead, the swirling mist parted a little, revealing blue sky.

"Leave the wagons," Johnnie said.

⋙⋅◇⋅⋘

They walked single file along a narrow path. The trees ahead vanished in the shifting fog. When they stopped Arthur took in the sight: an area about one hundred yards square, completely cleared of trees. Felled spruce, pine and tamarack, some as long as fifty feet, were scattered around the clearing like spilled matchsticks. White stumps dotted the soil. And next to dozens of piles of reddish brown dirt were holes as wide as a man's shoulders, each marked with a stake and a small white flag.

Up the gentle slope to the north a man dug into the earth with a spade while another man wrote in a small notebook. Beyond them the clearing rose higher still to a rocky ridge where the cloud-heavy sky swallowed the land. Arthur spied a small cabin made from unevenly cut pine logs crookedly disconnected at one corner. A pine bough roof was so poorly laid that smoke wafted from the entire surface as though the building were on fire.

"Hallooo!" Johnnie called.

The man with the book looked up and waved. From the smoking cabin a third man emerged. He was short and fat and his hairy face reminded Arthur of a badger. A ladle dangled from his hand.

"Mind the test pits," Johnnie said as they made their way up the hill.

As they walked, Arthur quickly surmised which of the felled trees he would use for foundations, which for walls, which for roof beams. Some of the logs, he noted, were split or rotted and would only be useful chopped for firewood. He climbed atop a felled birch. The bark was mostly intact and with a knife he was able to peel away a large sheet. Despite the heavy snowmelt, the wood beneath was firm and dry.

The man with the book was Captain Josef P. Nichols, a German-born officer formerly of the U.S. Cavalry stationed at Fort Laramie, Wyoming. He had left military service ten years ago, and after failing to reintegrate with civilization down in Philadelphia, had returned to the frontier on a hunt for gold. When that failed, too, he became a prospector for hire, and now he worked for the Merritts. He wore a black suit and black tie and his shirt was smeared with red dirt. A three-pointed gray beard covered his neck like a priest's collar, and when he walked a bushel of gray hair lifted from his head like the feathers of a rooster. Even without the added height of his hair, he towered over the young Merritt, and he was obviously the oldest one of them out here.

Johnnie approached first. "Hello, Captain Nichols."

The two men shook hands and Nichols folded the book he had been carrying and slipped it inside his shirt.

"You remember Jack Wheeler." Nichols nodded to the man with the shovel.

Wheeler was sturdy and broad-shouldered with thick, heavy arms made for swinging a pick. From his shaven face down to his denim overalls, he was covered with red dirt and soot. Though he slouched as he stood behind Nichols, Arthur saw his eyes twinkle and dance as he glanced at the faces of the new men.

Nichols continued, "Wheeler has been helping me with the test pits."

Johnnie glanced around the clearing. "You have been busy."

Nichols turned. "Let me show you what we found."

"First I want to know: Is this the place?"

Nichols pointy beard lifted when he smiled. "It is huge, Johnnie. Bigger than we could have hoped."

Johnnie rubbed his palms together. "All right." He danced as he turned. "Arthur, you, Richardson, and Charlie get started on building. I for one do not cotton to the idea of all of us bedding down in that cabin. Not even sure if it will stand much longer. Wheeler can help Captain Gill unload the equipment. Captain Wood—do you know Josef Nichols?"

Wood said, "I have heard the name. A pleasure. You will go down in the history books, I hope." The two men shook hands.

Nichols shrugged. "I believe it is the Merritts who will make history."

"Wood will be in charge of the mine," Johnnie said. "Whatever you need, Joe, ask him."

Johnnie, Wood, and Nichols walked down the hill and Arthur and the others retrieved the wagons. While Wheeler and Gill unloaded supplies into the small cabin, Arthur retrieved his tools and got started.

Arthur, like most Finns, knew construction. It was in his blood to build with wood. He had been taught by his father, who had been taught by his father and his father before him. The techniques he used were not new—they were as old as time itself. For Arthur, building a structure with pine logs was as straightforward as fishing, as ingrained as breathing; as easy as looking at a log.

A few feet uphill from the leaning cabin he paced off the floor plan for the new cabin, twenty-five feet by forty feet. While he dug out the slope, Arthur sent Richardson and Charlie to find boulders for the foundation. The two men hefted the stones in place as Arthur sighted them level. They collected felled logs from the clearing and in this Arthur found Charlie most helpful. More than Richardson, the Indian could identify a good log and was even better than Arthur in peeling bark. As Charlie and Arthur marked the useful logs, Richardson began to collect them into groups that could be skidded across the clearing to the building site. Using axes and planers and scrapers, they shaved and flattened those Arthur selected for the base. The prepared base logs were laid on top of a layer of moss and sod that Arthur spread atop the stone foundation. Notches were marked in the adjacent logs, and then cleaned out with axes and chisels. They continued this process, one set of logs laid, notches cut, then planed and set in place, spreading moss and grass between each log row for insulation.

It was laborious work, but Arthur loved it. With each swing of an axe or pull of a saw or push of a planer Arthur felt the fear of being so far from Minnie fade like the mist. He felt alive, as though every part of his being were meant for this. While Charlie peeled the logs—difficult because they had been sitting for more than a month, Arthur guessed—Arthur and Richardson hewed them flat using a special wide-headed axe. With each swing Arthur considered the layout of the building, picturing where each window would sit, the orientation of internal walls, the location of doors. He directed Richardson to carve wooden pegs which would be used to hold the wall logs in place. Once a log was set Arthur would bore a hole through it and the log below, hammer in a peg, and then chop off the protruding end of the peg. By early evening the walls were halfway up. Arthur sat on a log and admired the work. By his standards it was still crude. The walls would need to be flattened on the outside still, and the ends of the logs sawed flush to each other. Still, it would be a good building, strong and sturdy. Tomorrow, with more hands, they would finish the walls and then lay the roof.

As the sun hovered in the west just over the tree line, Arthur left Richardson and Charlie cutting pine shingles for the roof and walked across the muddy clearing to where Nichols and Johnnie were talking over Nichols's notebook.

Arthur said, "We get help with the cabin."

Johnnie turned. His eyes widened. "My goodness, Arthur. You have done a lot."

Arthur said, "Hands on the roof, get it done tomorrow."

The sun fell behind the trees and shadows stretched over the clearing. The fire inside the crude cabin Arthur had seen when he first arrived let off a warm yellow glow visible in the gaps between the rough wall logs. Inside he found the men sitting on the ground on either side of the thick trunk of a pine log. Johnnie, Wood, and Nichols sat on one side, hunched over a map spread on a flattened part of the log, with Gill, Richardson and Wheeler on the other, looking on. Wheeler, the digger, appeared bemused by the talk of the other men. Richardson seemed keenly interested. The scent of venison stew, mixed with the odor of rotting meat, filled the air. The big man in the white frock Arthur had seen earlier now crouched over a boiling pot hanging over a fire near the middle of the cabin. Beyond him, in the corner, flies buzzed around a pile of bones and discarded vegetables. Next to the detritus were sacks of flour, boxes of carrots, bags of onions and potatoes, crates of string wrapped cured ham. Arthur made a mental note to dig a root cellar for the kitchen.

"Ah, Arthur," Johnnie said. "Come, come."

The cook stood up. He was a big man, not muscular like the other miners but simply chubby. The front of his white smock was smeared with blood. His long gray hair hung in loose tendrils over his shoulders, and his gray beard was singed from being too close to the fire.

"You Maki?" he said. "The builder? When're you gonna build me a proper kitchen?" he said.

Johnnie said, "Have patience, Housell. Arthur is working as fast as he can." He turned to Arthur. "Arthur, this is Housell, our cook. Have a seat."

Arthur sat cross-legged on the ground next to Richardson.

Johnnie said, "Is that stew ready? I'm famished."

The others laughed, including Gill.

"I ain't going to serve you," Housell said.

The men got bowls of the stew. Arthur tasted the richness of the sauce, cooked all day over the fire. He missed Minnie's stews, full of the tangy crunch of rutabaga. When she arrived she would want to see a garden behind the kitchen. Arthur envisioned where it would go, and he wanted to get the carrots into the ground soon so they could begin harvesting them by summer. Tomatoes would be nice, too, and perhaps some cabbage. Arthur reminded himself to ask Johnnie for some seed. Maybe that could come with the next batch of supplies.

Charlie came in then, the fire dancing in his dark eyes as he stood at the door.

"Charlie," Johnnie said. "Thanks for joining us."

Housell hissed, "What's a dirty savage doin' here?"

Arthur bristled. He was already fond of the quiet Indian.

"Charlie is an old friend of my family and he is a member of this crew." Johnnie's tone was authoritative and stern.

Housell gaped like a charging moose.

Of the same mind, Wood added, "We got to share food with him, too?"

Charlie stepped to the fire and smelled the stew. "I shared food with you," he said in clear English.

Wood spit out a hunk of potato. "God dammit, I knew he understood me."

Johnnie laughed. "Charlie went to school in Minneapolis."

Gill slapped his knee. "I bet he can scrawl better than you, too," he laughed.

Charlie took a plate from a pile on the floor and wiped it on his pants, then dished out some of the stew. Housell watched him, fists clenched, powerless to stop what seemed to him a gross violation of hygiene. Charlie crouched on the floor behind Johnnie. Arthur watched him balance the plate on his knees and eat carefully with a spoon, a far cry from the table manners of Wood, who scooped up hunks of the venison with his fingers and slurped the sauce out of his plate.

Housell said, "I seen you out in the woods building something." He looked at Charlie who ignored him. "I'm talkin' to you, savage. What're you making out there?"

Charlie, without looking up, said, "*Waaginogaan.*"

"What the sam hill is that?" Wood said.

Housell snorted. "It's one of them indjun huts. Prob'ly gonna bring in a hole bunch of his kind and they'll take more of our land."

"I believe it's the other way around," Richardson said.

"I ain't talking to you."

Charlie said nothing.

"He ain't fit to even answer me." Housell spit bits of food as he spoke. "Good enough to eat my food, but not talk to me nor sleep under the same roof."

Richardson said, "Would you have him?"

"Hell, no. I'll bed outside first."

Wood said, "He's better off out there by himself."

"God damned savages," Housell said.

Charlie finished his food and stood. He took the plate to the fire and set it on a log.

Housell huffed. "Ain't even gonna clean up."

Johnnie said, "Enough. Housell, Charlie is part of this crew. Get used to it. You cook and clean. That's your job. Charlie is a hunter and scout and will assist Arthur with building. Everyone has a job and everyone will do his own job. If you don't like it then you can pack up and start back down the trail right now."

Housell stood before the fire, his greasy hair matted to his sweating head. In the distance a wolf howled. "Bah," he said and turned his back to the men and went to the fire.

The men ate. Charlie crouched against the wall again and watched silently. Wood shifted so that he could keep an eye on him. Metal spoons clinked against metal plates and more stew was dished out. Housell stood by his fire and ate standing up. He alone refused to even sit near Charlie.

When they had all finished, Johnnie pulled a map out of his jacket and unfolded it on the log. "Let's look at what we have." Johnnie leaned over the paper. The legend at the top read *Township 58 North, Range 18 West*. The darkest lines indicated rivers connecting small lakes and ponds. Other, lighter lines, concentric and parallel, curving closer and further, marked the rolling hills surrounding the area. The map was segmented into squares, each one represented by a number on one axis and a letter on the other. "This is us," Johnnie said, holding a pencil at a point near the upper right corner of the map. "This is the area we shall search next." He indicated an area off the map to the northeast. "This quadrant"— he indicated the section where they were now—"to this one"—a square five away from their current location—"and all this land in between." He put the pencil on the map at their location again. "We want to make this our base of operations. This little mountain here." He patted the log and smiled. "It's like a mountain of iron. Maybe that's what we'll call it. Mountain Iron."

"*Misaabe*," Charlie said.

Everyone stared at him.

"What?" Wood said.

"*Nibaad misaabe*." Charlie's deep voice seemed to echo in the small cabin. "Sleeping giant."

Johnnie nodded. "The Chippewa legend."

Charlie explained, "My people believe a giant once roamed these hills, protecting a great treasure. He wandered through the forest until a winter came when the fierce winds blew but did not bring snow. The giant brushed aside the trees and laid down to sleep, and he has slept there since."

Wood smiled. "Sounds like the giant is waiting for us to wake him!"

Gill laughed. "Aye, I can rouse 'im with me blasting powder."

"That giant's gonna make us all rich," Housell added. Everything he said came out with a sneer.

Johnnie smiled. "All in due time, gentlemen. First we need to get the ore out of the ground."

"That will be no problem," Wood said. "Just give me a few good backs."

"And you will have them," Johnnie said. "Based on what I have seen here, I shall wire Duluth informing Lon and Alfred that the next phase of operations should begin. I expect they can have crews up here within a month. Arthur, that gives you very little time. You must build us a town, or as much of one as you can build with the hands you have."

"More hands I build faster," Arthur said.

"I think we can all pitch in to get that first cabin finished tomorrow. Afterwards it'll be you and Richardson and Charlie here. If what you did today is any indication, I have complete confidence that you can build a city in a week."

"How many come?" Arthur asked.

"I would expect upwards of a couple dozen, maybe more. You just do what you can and what you think best."

Arthur nodded. He had never built a town before, but he figured it could not be that hard. It was just a matter of doing the same thing he did today. He was a Finn, after all, and Finns knew how to work.

Johnnie continued. "After we have finished marking for the mine here, within a week at most, Captain Nichols, Wood, Wheeler, and myself will search this area here." He pointed to a spot on the map north and east of their location. "If the markings on Lon's map are even remotely correct, we are on the verge of a massive discovery. This will change everything."

Richardson said, "What about timber for the mine?"

"This won't be like any mine you've ever seen." The joy in his voice excited Arthur. "The ore here is just under the surface. All we have to do is clear away the top layer, which is less than a foot deep in places, and the high grade ore we want is there for us to simply load onto cars and push down to Duluth. Eventually, depending on how deep we go, we shall need to determine how to get the ore out. But we can sort that all out later. For now, we shall concentrate on building a town."

Richardson said, "How will you get the ore to Duluth?"

Johnnie smiled. "Lon and Al are working with the Duluth and Iron Range Railroad. Eventually they shall build a spur to here, I suppose. Let's not worry about that now. Let's get the stuff out of the ground first."

The men said nothing for a few moments as the fire crackled and sputtered. Housell removed a canvas cloth from his pack, revealing a bottle of dark liquid. The cook pulled the cork with his stained teeth and then drank a long swallow. "Anyone want a pull?" he said.

Wood reached for the bottle. "Wondered when you were going to ask." Wood took two long gulps before Housell grabbed the bottle back from him.

"Hey, I only got this little bit."

The others laughed. Housell scowled as he rolled the bottle into the canvas cloth and returned it carefully to his pack. He leaned against the log and lit a pipe.

Johnnie folded the map. "Let's get some rest. We have much to do tomorrow."

Charlie stood, the fire casting his dancing shadow across the wall.

"Good riddance," Housell said.

Charlie stared down at Housell who seemed to shrink under that dark gaze. The fire crackled, and in the distance a wolf howled. Finally, Charlie stepped out of the cabin, ducking as he went through the gap. Arthur felt a kinship with the Indian. In the Army, the Russians had ridiculed Arthur solely because he was a Finn. He was sad at seeing the same attitude here. To Arthur, men were men; their origins were irrelevant.

Bedrolls were unfurled and cigarettes lit. A cool wind drifted through the poorly aligned walls, but it was not enough to whisk away the smell from the little cabin—not only of the men but also of the rotting kitchen scraps in the corner. Arthur took his pack and his roll and stepped into the night. From outside he heard the cook's angry voice.

"God damned Finn ain't even good enough to share our cabin."

Johnnie snapped, "Shut up, Housell."

Arthur looked for the Indian, but Charlie was already gone.

⸺◆⸺

The next day everyone pitched in to finish the big cabin. It had two rooms: a kitchen area in back where Housell would do the majority of his cooking, and a dining area in front, with a wall separating the two spaces. A set of stairs led from the kitchen area to a storage and sleeping space upstairs. This would be Housell's quarters. Richardson set up the portable sawmill, and with the lumber, Arthur was able to lay down a plank floor in the dining hall. This had the advantage of making their eating space much cleaner than it had been before.

With extra hands the roof was on by lunch. Arthur put together a door from the floor plank scraps, and since they had no glass, he hinged wooden shutters over the window cutouts. He made the hinges for both doors and shutters from pine, carved a pin and augured a hole to hold the two parts of the hinge together. The door stuck at first, but Arthur knew that over time the hinge would loosen. He built six long tables with benches where the men, whenever they came and however many there were, could eat. The building had three fireplaces: one in the kitchen to be used for cooking, and two in the dining hall, made from stones that he and Charlie and Richardson harvested from the clearing itself. It was a spectacular building, made more so by the fact that they had it done by the end of the third day.

When the cook saw it he found plenty to complain about. "What about a root cellar? I need a place to keep food cool in summer. What about a window? It's going to get stuffy in here in summer. Am I supposed to sleep up here with the dry goods?"

Even when Arthur showed him the trap door in the floor that led to the root cellar, he looked down at it with contempt. "Humph. It's probably not big enough." He pushed the door shut. "I ordered a stove," he said, walking away. "Find a place for it."

That afternoon Housell moved into the new kitchen. He spent almost all of his time inside, cooking and drinking. Like his complaints, his supply of alcohol seemed unlimited.

After the kitchen was finished, Wood directed Gill, Wheeler, Nichols and Johnnie to begin mapping out the site for the mine itself. Arthur and Charlie, meanwhile, began the process of limbing the logs scattered around the clearing and skidding them to the small sawmill, where Richardson peeled, bucked, and hewed them into usable lengths of lumber.

All the while, Charlie still impressed Arthur. He was a hard worker who never seemed to tire, and could hack the limbs off a tree faster than even Arthur himself. By the end of the first week, while Wood and the others were digging a hole, the three woodsmen had sorted and cleared the camp of all logs. They sorted the uncut logs: those to be used for firewood in one pile, those to be hewn into lumber in another, and finally those logs that would be used to build walls for cabins. The birch had a unique pile as the bark was waterproof and the trunks themselves were useful for more than just building houses.

"Much can be done with birch," Charlie told Arthur. "My people build with birch. We call it *wiigwaas.*"

"*Wiigwaas,*" Arthur repeated.

Charlie showed Arthur how to core out the inside of a birch log and then burn it to make a canoe. "*Wiigwaasi-jiimaan,*" Charlie called it.

For his part Arthur showed Charlie how to build a tar kiln to cook some of the hunks of pine. "Good for waterproofing," Arthur said.

Charlie put down his axe. "Come," he said to Arthur.

"Where?"

"I shall show you," Charlie said.

⋙◆⋘

Charlie led Arthur into the dense thicket of trees beyond the clearing. Arthur's thick leather-soled boots crunched against the earth, the sometimes icy crust, the mud, and the fallen leaves and branches underfoot, while Charlie's moccasins made little noise at all. After about a hundred yards they came to a small natural clearing where moss grew in a gentle slope against a copse of birch trees. In the middle of the clearing stood a domed structure shaped like a bread loaf, about six feet around and six feet tall. Its walls were made from birch bark which was tied together in long sheets. Charlie lifted away one piece of the bark to reveal an opening large enough to walk through. Inside, a skeleton of bent spruce and pine branches and saplings formed arches, criss-crossed by horizontal support bars lashed together with vine roots. The structure was completely enclosed save an opening in the middle above a circle of rocks where Charlie had built a fire pit.

Arthur put his hand against the wall and pushed. The structure did not move. "Good," he said. "Solid."

Charlie said, "*Waaginogaan.*"

Arthur said, "This where you sleep?"

"No," Charlie said. "This is a sacred place."

Arthur nodded. "*Waaginogaan.*" He would remember that.

Charlie smiled. "My name is *Wiigwaasgewinini*. My Chippewa name."

"Hard to say," Arthur said.

"They came into my village when I was a boy and took me and my brothers to live at a school in Minneapolis. They gave us new names. They called me Charlie." He stacked logs over dried grass, pine needles, and birch bark in the stone fire pit and struck a flint. The spark caught the kindling and a thin line of smoke rose and then vanished in the cool air.

"Is that where you learned English so well?" Arthur said.

Charlie blew gently on the tiny glowing embers until he had a small flame that caught the larger sticks quickly. "They told us they were giving us an education, but really they wanted to beat the Chippewa out of us. They cut our hair and gave us clothes and forbid us from using our language."

"I am also not Arthur. I am Arvid Mäkelä. They change it when I come. At the port in New York the man ask me my name. I tell him and he say, 'That is too hard. Is not American name. You want to live in America you must have American name.' I have good Finnish name. It is the name of my *isä*." He tapped himself on the chest, filling with emotion. "I do not want to change but how to say this? If I say no maybe he send me back? The man behind me with his crying baby say to me in Swedish, 'Hurry up. Stop taking all the time.'" Arthur felt his heart pounding. "The officer write it on a paper. It is not my name, but it is now my name, he says. 'Welcome to America,' he tells me. I take my paper and I go and I am now Arthur Maki. This is now what everyone calls me." He took a breath, shocked that he had revealed so much about himself to a man he hardly knew.

"Arvid," Charlie said.

"*Wiigwaasgewinini*," Arthur said.

"Where is Finland?" Charlie asked.

"Across the ocean. It is much like this place with lakes and rivers and trees. And snow. We have lots of snow."

Charlie considered this.

"I was taken from my *isä* and äiti, my father and mother. The Russian army came to my village and tells me I must fight the war. I go but war is not for me. So I sneak away in the night and never look back. Later I find my family has been killed while I am gone. So I leave my home and my country and come here for new life."

The fire grew and with it so did the smoke. Charlie led Arthur out and north through the trees, around a small pond, and up the hill. It took the two men several minutes to reach a rocky outcropping at the edge of a cliff. Charlie waved his arm over the valley below from the southwest to the north. Shadows stretched across the tops of the trees.

"*Misaabe*," Charlie said.

"*Nibaad misaabe*," Arthur said. "You say it before. The sleeping giant."

Charlie smiled. Arthur knew he had impressed the Indian.

The land fell sharply into a shallow valley and then rose slowly to a range of gently sloping hills about five miles away. The valley stretched from a point in the western horizon some thirty miles away to a low ridge immediately in front of them and then resumed its way to the eastern horizon. The trees and hills to their right blocked their view of the valley as it wound its way to the east. Both the valley below and the distant hills beyond were almost entirely covered by trees—birch, pine, tamarack, poplar, ash, maple—as though they were protecting the land from the forces of nature. Silver-blue rays filtered through the arms of the trees revealing small lakes in the valley below. Thin streams of clouds whispered across the deep blue sky.

Arthur was unprepared for the onslaught of emotions which besieged him. The tree-mantled hills were more rugged and forbidding than he had expected—gone was the gentleness he was used to seeing from the ground. A fluid movement seemed to exist between each hill, reminding him of the angry waves that had rolled across the horizon of the Atlantic during his journey from Helsinki to New York.

Charlie swept his arm across the valley to the north and back around again to the southwest. "*Misaabe*," he said.

Behind them, to the southwest, the clearing where they were building a camp lay like an open wound. Beyond camp Arthur could see other bare spots, too, where trees had been felled and clearings made, where smoke rose into the air, by other seekers who had either found or were looking for the red gold of iron: drilling holes, digging pits, clearing land. There was money to be made out there, and people were going to come to make it.

Charlie lowered down on one knee and put his hand on the ground. "*Aki*," he said. He closed his eyes as though he were feeling something in the ground, as though the ground were telling him something. Arthur got down and put his hand on the ground, too, and closed his eyes. He felt nothing but the cold earth.

Charlie stood and pointed to the rocky outcropping on which they were standing and then gestured again at the land beyond. "This place was given to my people by the grandfathers. We came to the land of the giant, where food grows on the water. Soon *misaabe goshkozie*," he said. "Soon sleeping giant wakes."

Arthur looked around again and saw the activity happening. The hill they were standing on stretched out before them to the northeast, and further southwest, according to Lon Merritt, lay a long band of iron ore twenty miles wide and a hundred miles long. Lon had told Arthur they could dig here for a hundred years and never find the end of the lode, and suddenly Arthur understood. This was Charlie's home, his land, and his people were scattered among those trees, wandering in the forest. Soon, Arthur knew, this place would be overrun with people, overrun with white men who would come to seek their fortunes. They would dig up the land and they would tear out the trees. And all that Charlie knew or had ever known would be gone.

"*Misaabe*," Arthur said. He saw sadness in Charlie's eyes and understood it. It was the same loss Arthur felt when he boarded a boat in Helsinki bound for America and watched Finland fade into the blue horizon forever. It was the loss of home, the loss of country, the loss of a sense of place in the world. And yet, Arthur thought, together we can build a home here.

The two men stared over this remote wilderness, surveying all that it was and all that it would become. Like Arthur and Charlie themselves, the land would bear a name that others would give it: Mesabi.

CHAPTER 3

MADOODISWAN

Spring on the Mesabi brought rain. Clouds as dark as Housell's breakfast porridge bubbled out of the south and swallowed the blue sky. A steady drizzle of rainfall created muddy streams that swelled downhill and turned parts of the clearing into a swamp. The test pits filled with red-gray mud and became a hazard. Arthur, Charlie, and Richardson used their picks and shovels to plow trenches that would channel water away from the cabins and away from the mine now being dug. Even so, there was so much water the firewood became soaked and unusable. After Housell complained of being unable to start a fire, Richardson built a lean-to stilted up on three layers of rock under which firewood could be stored.

On the days when the rains ceased and the sun emerged, so too came the mosquitoes, big and fat and hungry. They swarmed every exposed bit of flesh and even managed to crawl under layers of clothes. When Arthur observed that Charlie seemed unperturbed by them, Charlie told him the secret: a poultice made from the horn-shaped touch-me-nots and the stalk of the common yarrow plant. When Arthur rubbed the paste on his neck and arms, the bugs stopped bothering him. Arthur secretly thrilled in watching Housell and Wood swat at swarms of the annoying insects.

Johnnie left for Duluth to help Lon and Alfred raise funds and hire a workforce to come to Mountain Iron. He took with him a letter for Minnie in which Arthur told her about his life in the north woods. "It is hard work here, and though my body is occupied with construction, my mind wanders constantly to thoughts of you," he wrote. "I am searching for the place to build our home, and though I have not found it yet I know it is here somewhere. This place reminds me so much of Finland. I know you will enjoy it here as much as I do. I hope you will be able to join me soon."

He directed Johnnie to give her the wages he had earned so far, forty dollars for the month.

"All of it?" Johnnie asked.

"*Joo, joo,*" Arthur said.

Johnnie agreed. "You are a good man, Arthur Maki. Trust me to see she gets it."

Arthur wandered the clearing and paced the distance between stakes he hammered in the ground to mark foundation lines. He measured the length of the walls by his stride and the distance to the eaves by his height. He imagined each building from the foundation to the walls to the roof to the way the furniture would be arranged inside. In his mind he already saw the mining camp, pictured the way the buildings faced each other and their orientation to the surrounding forest. Each structure was his child borne from his own sweat, and the camp his family. He was beginning to feel that this place was part of him already.

Arthur always worked from a plan, even if that plan was nowhere but in his own head—which it often was. He used to say that building a house without a plan was like chopping down a tree with a knife: it could be done, but it would take a lot more time.

Housell spent most of his time in the kitchen either drunk or cooking or both. He set up a still in the woods near the kitchen and he was stockpiling moonshine, having cooked up a plan of his own: when the miners came, he wanted to make a tidy profit selling hooch. He planted a garden of tomatoes, carrots, onions, turnips, beets, potatoes, rutabagas, parsley, chives, peppers and garlic. He emerged every few days, squinting in the scarce sunshine, with an empty canvas bag and a fishing pole he had fashioned himself out of a long, thin tamarack branch. He wandered up to the lake and, lounging against a log, dropped his line into the murky water. There were so many walleye and pike that even an inept fisherman like himself found himself surrounded by flopping, wriggling fish, and he grudgingly tossed some of the smaller ones back. Charlie took pity on him and brought him a length of spruce root vine.

"What the hell am I s'pposed to do with this?"

Charlie tied the wriggling fish to loops in the rope, dropped the fish back into the water, then lashed the loose end of the rope to a rock.

"Hmph," Housell said. "I could have figured that out m'self. Don't need no savage to help me."

Richardson worked the small sawmill most days, but when he had gone through all the logs Arthur had marked for hewing, he whistled to Arthur and Charlie and the three of them took to the woods. Arthur and Charlie were good with an axe, but Richardson surpassed them both. His broad shoulders and arms as thick as a birch trunk could fell a three-foot diameter tree in a dozen swings. He worked so quickly that he often walked away from a tree before it fell. His cavalier attitude, Arthur worried, would get him hurt.

After Johnnie had left, Arthur discovered that the others in the group—Wood, Nichols, Wheeler, and Gill—were skeptical of iron in the hills and forests around Mountain Iron. Had Arthur paid attention to the world at large, had he read a newspaper or talked to other people who knew about mining and iron, he might have known that the whole world thought the Merritts were crazy.

"What are we doing up here, Nichols?" Wood asked one night after dinner. "You searched the rocks yourself. There ain't no ore out there if there ain't no rock for it to hide under."

"Maybe we haven't looked in the right places," Nichols said, always the Merritts' reluctant defender. "I looked in the hills, yes, but it wasn't until Lon started me digging down here in the valley that I found it."

Wood was annoyed. "That ain't a mine we're digging. It's a hole in the ground. 'Nother five feet and we'll hit the same useless mud we been fighting for weeks. Ain't enough ore there to fill a wagon."

"'Tain't enough blasting for my liking." Gill laughed.

Arthur had been eating quietly with Richardson when Wood turned to him. "What do you think, Maki? Any chance we'll make money here?"

Arthur shrugged. "I no understand mining. I build the camp."

"No point in the camp if there ain't no iron," Wood barked.

"Lon say the ore here," Arthur said, surprised at all the doubt.

Nichols waved his hand. He seemed to be the only one with

faith. "It's out there somewhere. We simply have to dig in the right place. The adventure is in the hunt."

"Bah your hunt," Wood said. "I'm a miner. I come to dig the ore, not wander the woods looking for it where it don't exist."

Arthur thought it strange that Charlie seemed to have the last word. "If Lon says it is there, then there it is." There was a quiet certainty in his voice.

The next day the miners left on their hunt, and Arthur continued planning and building the camp. He felt good about the progress he had made on the village plan. Most of the land was cleared and Richard had already milled stacks of lumber for interior walls. Larger logs had been limbed, peeled, and hewed in preparation for building even more cabins. In the month since they had arrived, Arthur and his crew had built the kitchen and one sleeping cabin. And at least in his head he had laid out the plans for the entire camp.

Arthur was staking the ground for the foundation of a second bunkhouse when he saw a lone rider on a black horse emerge from the trees at the south end of the clearing. From a hundred yards Arthur could see the rider was uncomfortable on horseback. He sat high on the saddle and clung to the reins. With each step he tugged the reins too tight, and the horse fought against the bit, which made the rider compensate by tightening the reins even more. The whole thing was comical—the horse meandered left then right then left again, past the pit and up the shallow hill towards the cabins. Arthur stepped back as horse and rider approached.

"I have been trying to get this horse to obey me since yesterday," the man said.

His long, thin face seemed translucent in the glare of the afternoon sun, and the slanted black bowler he wore did nothing to shade his eyes. He squinted through a pair of pince-nez perched on his nose. Flies and mosquitoes swarmed around his head and he let loose the reins long enough to swipe at them. "God damn these bugs." As he brought his lanky frame off the saddle his foot slipped out of the stirrup and he fell backward into the mud.

Arthur grabbed the reins and put a gentle hand on the horse's snout to calm him.

"Wonderful," the man said. "The perfect end to a perfectly

dreadful day." He struggled to his feet and shook mud off his hands. "That horse has been nothing but trouble since I left Duluth." The pince-nez fell off his nose and he wiped his muddy hands on the horse's rump. "Even my new boots are scuffed," he said. "I told them I was not a field man. I thought people would bring samples to me." He pulled a brown leather satchel off the saddle horn and removed a small white card. "I am Harvey Lewis," he said, handing the card to Arthur. "State of Minnesota mineralogist. I'm looking for Leonidas Merritt."

Arthur held the card. Written in black block letters on the front of it was the word Mineralogist, and beneath that Harvey Lewis. He had not seen anything like it. The paper, he thought, would be enough to start a fire. He said, "Duluth." He wondered what a mineralogist was.

"No, no, I am from Minneapolis, though I left Duluth yesterday. They said horseback was the only way to get here. Dreadful things, horses." He plunged his hands in a wooden trough. The horse shuffled over next to him and began to drink. Arthur tied its reins to a post.

"Lon Merritt is in Duluth, I mean," he clarified for the man.

In the distance the saw began to whine. "Wonderful. Well, then, who is in charge?"

"Captain Wood."

"Wood? Would that be Alfred Wood?"

"*Joo*," Arthur said, then added, "Yes."

"I have heard of him. Army man. Gruff fellow, I believe."

Arthur nodded.

"Good. Excellent. Lead on, sir."

Arthur rubbed the horse's nose.

The man clapped his hands together. "Come on, snap to it. Take me to Captain Wood."

"He is not here."

"What do you mean, not here? Did you not just tell me he was in charge?"

"Yes."

"Well then?"

"He is not here."

"Where is he?"

Arthur pointed east. "Looking."

Harvey Lewis looked to the east. "Looking for what?"

Arthur shrugged.

"Well, who is here?"

"Me."

Lewis took a black notebook from the leather satchel. He licked the tip of a pencil and said, "And what is your name?"

"Arthur Maki."

"And what are you here?"

"Carpenter."

"Of course. Another timberman. Mr. Merritt would never have someone here who actually knows something about iron, would he? Or mining. Well, show me the shaft."

"Shaft?"

"Yes, yes. Where is your mine?"

"Ah, the pit."

Harvey Lewis looked out over the tops of his pince-nez. "Pit?"

Arthur led the way down the hill. The pit was about twenty feet wide by ten feet deep. A rope ladder led down to the pit floor where picks and shovels were left strewn about. A small covered cart Arthur had built to protect the tools from the elements was open and unused. Two piles of dirt marked the pit's southern end. One was the overburden, the soil that lay on top of the loose iron ore. The second, larger pile was the ore itself. Together the two piles reminded Arthur of the rolling hills of the Mesabi he had seen from the ridge with Charlie.

"Here," Arthur said. He pointed at the hole.

"This?" Lewis said. "This is your mine? Where is the headframe? Where is the shaft?" His tone was strained and repetitive, making a point Arthur did not quite understand.

Arthur shrugged. "No shaft," he said. "Pit."

The mineralogist walked around the pit shaking his head. He stopped when he got to the first pile of dirt, the overburden. *Useless* was what Wood had called that pile. "How do you expect to get the iron out of the ground if you do not drill a shaft?"

Arthur shrugged again.

Lewis laughed. "If it were that easy..." It seemed an unfinished thought. He took a small canvas bag out of his satchel and filled it with dirt from the pile of overburden. "This does not look like it is worth much of anything." He filled a second canvas bag from the pile of ore, rubbing it between his fingers. "At least this stuff is heavier. Could be iron in here. See here, is this as deep as your pit goes? Have you tested further?"

Arthur said, "I build the camp."

Harvey Lewis stood up. "Yes, you said. The carpenter." He left the two canvas sacks at Arthur's feet and climbed down the rope ladder that dangled over the side. He swung a pick and it sank into the soft earth, then he scooped the dirt with the shovel. "You've already reached the bottom of the lode," he said. He scooped a handful out of the shovel and worked it with his hand letting the dirt fall through his fingers. "If this is all you have, then what have you?"

Arthur said nothing. It didn't seem like a question that wanted to be answered.

Lewis removed a black book from his satchel and began writing. He paced the length and width of the pit and wrote. He buried his fingers in the dirt at his feet and wrote. He examined the picks and shovels and wrote. He studied the rocks and placed two of the smaller ones in his bag and wrote. Finally he folded his book and climbed out of the pit, rubbing his hands together.

"When will Captain Wood return?"

Arthur said, "I do not know."

Lewis shook his head. "This place is like nothing I've ever seen. How long have you been here?"

"Since April," Arthur said. "Captain Nichols since before."

"Is that Josef Nichols? Now there is a man who knows iron. What would he do with an outfit like this?" Lewis picked up the two bags of dirt and dropped them in his satchel. "Do you have a place I can make notes while my horse recovers from the journey? To be honest, I have no interest in climbing aboard that beast again, but I think I have no choice."

Arthur took him to the dining cabin where Housell was cooking and drinking, a combination the cook liked best of all. It was dinnertime and Arthur was hungry, so they ate. Housell seemed keenly interested in the mineralogist's opinion of the mine, and of the work being done. He opened a bottle of his whiskey to help loosen the government man's tongue.

"Is it useful iron?" Housell asked.

"Well, I'll have to perform tests on the soil, of course. From what I see they have a few feet down of useful stuff. Could even be high grade. Based on the feel and weight I'd say at least sixty-five percent iron."

Housell whistled.

"Sure, it sounds like a lot." He held out an empty cup and Housell refilled it. "But if it doesn't go any deeper than that it's a useless sixty-five percent."

Housell slapped the table. "I knew it! I don't think any of 'em knows what they're doing up here."

"There are rocks further up in the hills there. Those might prove fruitful."

Housell shook his head. "Nichols searched all through that. He didn't find nothing. Had a big row with Lon Merritt about where to look. Lon's the one who made him dig down here."

Lewis swallowed the rest of his third glass of whiskey and laughed. "A pit! How much do they think they can get out of a simple hole in the ground?"

The door opened, admitting a gust of fresh air that partly dispelled the musk of Housell's cooking. Richardson stepped through, and Arthur was relieved to see that behind him came Charlie.

"Oh, good, the natives have arrived," Housell sneered. "Charlie, tell Mr. Lewis here about the giant in the hills." He poured more whiskey and said to Lewis, "Chippewa Charlie here is a expert on local wildlife, including a tribe of big people who wandered these hills. Or was it just the one giant, Charlie?" He laughed.

Richardson said, "Shut up, Housell."

"Mr. Lewis, tell the boys here what you been telling me. About the iron."

Lewis swallowed and swayed a bit, his upper body moving in a circle. "Well, as I was telling Mister Housell here, iron forms under rocks. Big rocks. Have you been to Tower? Or Iron Mountain, Michigan? That is what an iron mine looks like. This here, this place, whatever you call it, this is a hole in the ground." He held out his empty cup and Housell filled it a fourth time.

Richardson said, "But there is iron here, on the ground. I have seen it."

Lewis laughed. "Washout. Rain brought that stuff down from somewhere. Now, you find that somewhere and you might have something—something." He waved his hand in the air as if the iron ore would have to fall from the sky. "All you have here is a hole in the ground. You've cleared a good piece of land. Maybe you can plant wheat?" He looked at Charlie as though seeing him for the first time. "Or corn."

Housell slapped his palm on the table and laughed. The cups rattled. "Farmers," he cried. "That's what they are. Farmers!"

Lewis laughed, too, and raised his cup. "To the farmers," he cried, and the two men bashed their cups together, then drank.

Arthur wondered if the drunk mineralogist was right. Was it worth it, coming here?

"I can cook for farmers, too, don't get me wrong," Housell said. "As long as they pay me I'll keep cooking."

"They've mortgaged themselves," Lewis said. "Word in Duluth is that they've borrowed against future profits."

"If there ain't no iron, there ain't gonna be no profits," Housell said, suddenly sober.

Lewis nodded. "Unless you find the lode this washout came from." He tilted back his cup but it was empty. As he leaned back he fell off the bench and crashed on his back on the wood planked floor.

Lewis woke with the dawn and drank two cups of coffee. He did not speak to any of them before he climbed atop his horse. He looked even more pale than he had the day before. As Arthur handed him the reins he pulled his bowler low on his face and spoke softly, his voice raw. "Tell Mr. Merritt that we shall send a copy of my report to him when it is completed." And with that he cantered the horse down the hill, past the pit, and into the trees.

Housell watched from the doorway of the kitchen. "Farmers." He shook his head sadly and disappeared inside.

Arthur was building walls for the second bunkhouse thinking about farming when he heard the familiar crack and pop of a tree that had finally lost its battle with the axe. Richardson called out,

"Timber!" Groaning echoed through the trees. Arthur had heard the sound so many times in the past week that the yell and the crackling of the pine faded into the background. He kept working. But the second cry that came from Richardson was louder and desperate. Axe in hand, Arthur ran and found the knotty pine Richardson had felled, green needles quivering, sagged against an ash few feet away. White wood chips were scattered among the brown leaves and dirt. He saw no sign of the timberman.

"Halloo!" Arthur called.

"Over here," Richardson said. "Dammit."

He was trapped beneath the felled pine, his right shoulder pinned where the pine and ash trees met. His arm hugged the trunk.

"*Voi luoja!*" Arthur said. *Oh my god!*

Arthur put his back against the fallen tree and pushed the ground with his legs, but the tree would not budge.

"It's too heavy," Richardson said.

Arthur started to go. "I will find help."

Richardson winced. "Everybody's gone." Sweat dripped off of his forehead, and mosquitoes swarmed around his exposed face and arms. When he tried to wave them away he cried out in pain.

But Richardson's cries had attracted one more person—from the trees Charlie appeared. Arthur was relieved to see him. Charlie looked up into the leafy canopy as though it would provide an answer. He then rushed back into the forest and returned a minute later pulling a vine. Arthur scrambled among the underbrush and found more vine, and the two men fashioned a rope.

"We get you out," Arthur said.

Charlie scrambled up the felled tree. Richardson groaned at the extra weight on his shoulder. The two men threw the other end of the rope over the thick branch of a nearby pine and then they took hold of the loose end and pulled. The vine rope ripped at Arthur's hands. It was either blood or sweat trickling down his wrists as he dug his feet into the soft turf and pulled. Finally Arthur felt the tree give. The two men pulled harder and the rope shifted along the lever branch and the felled tree lifted off of Richardson's shoulder. The hurt man slumped to the ground and then rolled out from under the tree. Once he was clear, Arthur and Charlie let go of the vine and the tree thumped back in place.

"Can you move your arm?" Arthur said.

Richardson twisted his wrist.

Charlie put his hands on the shoulder and began probing with fingers pressed into the skin. Richardson screamed and pulled away.

"Do not move," Charlie said. He felt again, fingering the area around the shoulder from his neck to his upper arm and down into his chest. Finally he stood up. "The bone is still intact but it will hurt for many days. Take him to camp. I get medicine." He vanished into the dense underbrush.

Arthur helped Richardson to his feet and together the two men slowly made it back to the dining cabin.

"What the hell happened to him," Housell said.

"Tree," Richardson said. His neck was turning shades of purple and black.

"Shit," Housell said.

"Water," Arthur said.

Housell pointed to the door. "Bucket's outside. I'm not a servant."

Arthur filled a canteen and brought it back to Richardson who drank heartily.

"You're gonna need sompin' stronger than that." Housell went into the kitchen and returned with one of his bottles. "Here."

Richardson took a long gulp.

Charlie burst through the door and gave a handful of leaves and stalks of a small white flower to Housell. "Boil this."

Housell sniffed and corked his face. "Blech! What the hell is it?"

"Boil," Charlie repeated. The tone in his voice had changed. Housell did not question him again. He went into the kitchen with the herbs. The cabin filled with an acidic, putrid odor. After a few minutes Housell emerged with a steaming pot. Charlie pulled the limp greens from the water and spread them out on a cloth. He folded the cloth and wrapped the bundle around Richardson's shoulder.

"It's hot," Richardson protested.

Charlie tied the cloth in place. "The poultice will draw out the pain." He put the steaming pot of water in front of Richardson and said, "Breathe." The injured man took a few deep breaths of the steam.

Dark settled over camp. Housell announced supper. "Fish soup."

"Again?" Richardson said.

"No one says you have to eat it."

He shook the empty bottle. "How about some more of this hooch?"

Housell laughed. "Can you handle more?"

"If I can swallow your soup I can swallow your whiskey."

Housell returned with a half full bottle. He poured four cups of it. He and Richardson were the only ones to drink, and Richardson sputtered and coughed at the first sip. "I take that back about the soup. This stuff is awful," he said.

Housell chuckled down a second cup full. "My own recipe. Told you you couldn't handle it."

Charlie sniffed the liquid then tossed the contents onto the fire. Flames shot out of the fireplace.

Housell glared at him. "That's good stuff you just burnt."

Charlie glowered and Housell seemed to shrink inside himself. The cook grabbed the bottle and poured himself another cup.

After they ate, the four men sat around the fire. Outside was a racket of birds, owls, and the cries of not-so-distant wolves. The wind turned trees into a crooning chorus. Firelight danced across the ceiling, and Housell opened another bottle.

Richardson muttered that it must have killed his sense of taste, and took another turn drinking from it. "I've been cutting down trees since I was old enough to walk," he said. "Never thought I'd lose sight of a fell."

Arthur remembered the cavalier way Richardson had walked away from a tree before seeing it fall.

"I come from just over the border," Richardson continued. "My mother was one of your people, Charlie, from the north. Bois Forte. My father was a fur trader from France. He lived with a band of Chippewa and traded furs with French settlers in Canada. My mother died of starvation when the tribe was relocated to White Lakes in '89. My father took me off the reservation. He said I was white enough to pass and that fur trading would keep me from having anything to do with the Americans who killed my family. Fur trading is hard work, though, and the business of it came to be even harder when iron was discovered up in Vermilion. So I became a cruiser." He laughed. "My real name's LaVerne Riçard."

Arthur looked at Charlie. They were not the only ones who lived under different names.

Charlie leaned forward. He spoke in Chippewa. *What is your Chippewa name?*

Richardson said, "*Wabishkadowe.*"

Charlie nodded. "*Niwiinz Wiigwaasgewinini.*" *My name is Wiigwaasgewinini.*

Housell huffed. "I knew there was sompin' wrong with you." His face glistened in the firelight as he grabbed the bottle from Richardson. "Goddamned savages." He clomped up the back stairs.

Richardson laughed. "Asshole."

Charlie said, "Men like him are dangerous."

"Men like him are all talk. He's a blustering drunk."

Arthur said, "Charlie is right." He had seen Housell's attitude before: among the Russian soldiers and officers who chided the Finns because they were Finns; among the captains and supervisors in Tower who treated miners and laborers like cattle. The idea that foreign was bad just because it was foreign was universal. For Housell, foreign meant the natives who had been here long before his ancestors came to this land. Even Lon Merritt, who espoused a belief in the equality of all men, was taking advantage of a Chippewa population that had already been pushed out of the woods. Housell was poison, and Arthur hoped that the poison wouldn't spread. "Best to just stay out of his way," Arthur said.

Richardson waved his hand. "*La absurdité.*"

⟵◆⟶

Charlie said, "Come."

They helped Richardson to his feet. Outside, few stars were visible in the white brightness of the full moon. Frogs croaked and all around fireflies danced like floating yellow stars. Charlie led them through the trees to the *waaginogaan* and lifted aside the birch bark door. The orange-red embers from the interior fire smoldered in its shallow pit of stones. The Indian took a long pipe from his belt sash and stuffed tobacco into the bowl, lit it, and blew puffs of white smoke around the door.

"The smoke is an offering to the grandfathers," he told Arthur.

Richardson said, "You built a *madoodiswan*."

"Yes," Charlie nodded as he stripped off his clothes.

"It's a sweat lodge," Richardson told Arthur. "Kind of a traditional healing place." He winced as he pulled off his outer shirt and followed Charlie into the *waaginogaan* wearing his long underwear.

The heat coming out of the hut was overwhelming and Arthur was reminded of the sauna behind his father's home in Jalasjärvi. *Isä* had the best sauna in the province, tightly constructed of cedar and pine with a smooth rock chimney. Each Saturday after dinner they would follow the path behind the house to the sauna and, after leaving their clothes in the outer room, would spend an hour or more talking and bathing in the heat. It had been in the sauna that Arthur, then a boy of fourteen, learned that Matti Mäkelä was not his real father, that his father had been a Russian colonel who had raped Hilda Mäkelä. "You will always be my son," his *isä* had told him, and Arthur believed it. Felt it.

Now Arthur hung his clothes on a pine branch and stepped into the *waaginogaan*. The night's chill quickly vanished, replaced with intense heat that was hotter than any sauna he had ever experienced. Charlie helped Richardson sit on the floor and then he crossed his legs and placed his hands on his knees. Arthur did the same. They sat that way for what seemed to Arthur a long time. Charlie began to chant, and then he dropped the door to the hut in place. The space was completely dark save the faint glow of the coals in the fire pit. This was like being in the Tower mines with just a flickering candle holding back the wet, claustrophobic blackness. A metal drum sounded. Charlie's deep, rhythmic voice began to echo. Arthur felt lightheaded. He had not been in a sauna for many years and his endurance was not what it used to be. In the dark Arthur thought he saw movement. Not from Charlie, whose voice came from directly across the stone circle from Arthur, nor from Richardson, who was slumped against the birch bark wall. Something seemed to move in the air through the darkness, shadows of shadows flickering.

Charlie said, "*Wiigwaasgewinini*." Charlie chanted some more in Chippewa, and though Arthur could not understand the strange words he thought he understood the meaning behind them. Charlie said his name and announced himself to the spirits that Arthur felt were in the *waaginogaan* with them. Shadows no longer moved through the air but seemed to be still around them. As though on cue Richardson took up the chant, repeating his name three times, the same rhythm in his voice that Charlie had used in following the drum. The fire crackled and the rocks hissed. The drumming stopped. Arthur heard rustlings in the trees outside.

"Arvid Mäkelä," Charlie said.

"*Joo.*"

"This is a *madoodiswan*. Sweat lodge. We use this to purify our spirit."

"*Savusauna*," Arthur said. "Finnish smoke bath."

"*Savusauna*," Charlie repeated.

Richardson, drunk, said, "Healing place."

Charlie continued, "You are not like the others, Arvid Mäkelä. You seek harmony with the earth and the wind and the trees. The others simply want to wake the giant."

Richardson mumbled, "*Nibaad misaabe.*"

Charlie ignored him. "A long time ago my people were peaceful. We lived in harmony with each other and with the earth. The white man came and gave us things we had never seen. We began to fight over them. The warrior clan emerged and we became our own enemies. We could not live in harmony.

"A young boy went to the elders and asked how he could change this. They told him to take four kernels of maize and walk and eat a kernel each day. At the end of four days the boy sat down and waited. He waited for a long time. Then the *Skawbawis* spirit helpers came and took him to the other side of the Good Sister Moon." He paused and Arthur heard Richardson's slight snore. "The *Skawbawis* placed him in a hut with seven grandfathers. They showed him a seven-colored rainbow and a beautiful tree and each gave him a teaching. When it was time to go, they painted his face with the rainbow and the spirit helpers took him back to where he had sat down. He ate of a plant to regain his strength and then told his people that they must build a sacred *madoodiswan* and offer tobacco and juniper berries and water. The ceremony removes sorrow and grief and heals bodies and spirits."

Arthur pictured the boy carried away to the moon and crawling into a *waaginogaan* just like this one, talking with seven old men, and then returning with news of how to save his people. "It works?" Arthur asked.

"The *madoodiswan* was a gift. It purifies us, but does not remove the temptations that led us to this place. Each of us must go where the spirit leads us. This place can guide our spirits down the path of the seven teachings. My father is *medewi*. Medicine man. He taught me healing. I see in Arvid Mäkelä *bookojichaag*. Broken spirit."

The drum beat began again and then the chanting jumbled in Arthur's head. The heat became stifling and Arthur felt his blood rumble in his ears. He heard beating, and in the darkness saw horses. A dozen of them, with dark riders in red cloaks riding through the field toward his home in Jalasjärvi. There was no reason to run. Yet he watched as the horses kicked up the snow and created their own swirling blizzard. They were Russian army soldiers conscripting able-bodied young men to fight in the Cossacks. Arthur was only eighteen at the time, as able-bodied as they came, but he refused to fight. When they handed him a weapon he dropped it. Beatings did not change his mind. He was locked shoeless in a cold stockade without food and only a little water for seventeen days. His body shriveled and he knew he would soon die. His mind remained sharp, however. He was given a warm uniform and hot food and a gun and taught how to shoot and march and kill. He fought alongside other conscripted Finns until one night, nearly two years after his capture, when he walked out of the camp into the woods and just kept walking. He found a bear den and slit the male's throat, skinned it and kept warm in the fur. The flesh was tough but he ate it. He kept moving, not looking back. He walked to Helsinki, over three hundred miles away, where he got work on a freighter bound for America. Up until the moment the ship left port he feared the arrival of a garrison of Russian soldiers. He watched anxiously through a porthole near the ship's waterline until the boat pushed out to sea.

In the sweat lodge the hoof beats were still beating. It was the drum and the heat and the blood in his ears. Arthur stumbled out of the *madoodiswan* into the cool air and dragged himself through the forest and splashed into the pond. The cold water braced him. He thought of Minnie then, and of little Benjamin, three days journey away in Duluth. He wished they were here to share this journey. Back at the *waaginogaan* Charlie sat outside the door, legs crossed. In the moonlight Arthur saw a smile flash across his face.

"*Nijichaag giige.*" *Spirit healed.*

Arthur sat down. Indeed he felt as though the horses had finally passed him by. As his breathing returned to normal and he found himself, in his mind, back in the sweat lodge, in the *madoodiswan*, he felt the hoof beats recede into the distance. The trees themselves seemed to swallow the sound. And then all was silence.

⬗◆⬖

It was Housell who, after the others returned, told them about the visit by the mineralogist. "Said the stuff in the ground there weren't worth much 'cause there just weren't enough of it. Probably what's left of an old vein that got washed away." Housell laughed, and flecks of fish flew onto the table in front of him.

Wood slapped the table next to the cook. "I told you! This place is worthless. Did I not say it?"

Nichols, across from Arthur, said, "Maybe they have it wrong."

"Bah," Wood scoffed. "You were right the first time. Nothing here. Nothing at all!"

Nichols shrugged. "We can all be wrong sometimes."

Gill shot up and began to pace the room. "Foocking farmers," he said. "That's what he called us. Farmers! I been mining since before that twit was in nappies and he calls me a god-damned farmer!" He poked his finger in the air. "Eustis Gill is nay a farmer, boy. I tell you that."

Wood said, "We've been here for more'n a month and what have we got to show for it? A hole in the ground ten feet deep and twenty wide, and two piles of dirt washing away in the rain. How long you been here, Nichols?"

"Six months, give or take."

"And what have you found?"

"Just the one deposit."

Wood pounded the table again. The cups, and Arthur, jumped. "And is it a deposit? I mean, will it pay?"

Nichols shrugged. "It is ore, yes. How deep, how wide, I do not know."

"And a week traipsing through the forest got us nothing but mosquito bites and blisters."

"Mining's an underground sport, lads," Gill said. "Blast away the rock, tunnel into the earth, and haul it out. That's what mining is. Not this farming."

Richardson said, "What is it about the rock that brings the iron?"

Gill eyed the injured man. "You're a timber man. Ya would nay know about such things."

Arthur said, "But why the rock?" He had worked the mines in Tower, but he knew nothing of the geology of it.

Wood leaned toward Arthur and spoke like a parent. "Good ore, high-quality ore, has to be under rock. It's the pressure that makes it. Over time, the rock pushing against itself brings the mineral out. Without the rock you just have, well, rock. Or dirt. Or nothing."

Arthur shook his head. "I do not understand need for rock to have iron."

Housell laughed. "A damned carpenter thinks he can understand mining. Ha!"

"Arthur has a better connection to the earth than you," Charlie said.

"Now the savage is piping in. Why don't you carpenters go and cut some wood and let the miners talk about the mine."

Nichols said, "Enough. This affects all of us."

Housell was still laughing.

"What're you laughing at, you ingrate?" Wood said.

Housell put a bottle on the table. "I was just thinking about all the money I was gonna make selling my hooch," he said. He pulled the cork and took a long drink, then filled a cup and passed the bottle. Wood and Nichols drank. Arthur shook his head when the bottle passed him. "Afraid of a little nip?"

Gill took the bottle. "Leave 'im alone, Housell. The man does nay drink."

"A man who refuses to drink with you and refuses to shake hands with you is not a man in my book."

Gill downed his tin cupful and refilled it. "Shove your book up your fat arse," he said and cackled. The others laughed, too. Housell turned red, then his mouth turned up in a wry smile.

They continued to drink, and continued to argue. The land was worthless, Gill and Wood declared, and Housell, in his ignorance, agreed with them. "I've got some nice vegetables here for the fall," he declared.

"Anything to improve your cooking," Wood said.

"Not that you'll be here to enjoy it," Housell laughed.

While they laughed Arthur wondered again if his choice to come here had been a mistake. Wondered if he could still find some land to homestead. There were still parcels available, he knew, plots that had been passed over by mineral seekers and timber hunters as invaluable prospects. Farming was a noble thing, to live off the land, not just from it but with it. Not that he knew much about farming. He remembered the way Gill had said the rocks pushed up out of the ground each spring and felt an inner dread at the thought of having to deal with them year after year. Still, the mineralogist's claim and the debate among all of them worried Arthur. Was this place Lon had promised it would be? Or was it, instead, another Tower, another hole in the ground that might, at any moment, flood?

The door burst open. Heads jerked around, and conversation fell abruptly and totally silent. Nearly filling the doorframe was a beast of a man. The late afternoon light shone over the strange pith helmet he wore. He slumped slightly at the waist due to the sack on his shoulders, and his meaty, wool-clad legs were braced on the earth like pillars. Arthur knew that his heft was all muscle, lean and tough like a moose, and when this newcomer entered the dining hall, he filled the room with his presence. He sloughed off the pack and dropped it, smack, against the wood floor. His axe landed with a thud. He arched his broad shoulders and removed his helmet. His eyes, when Arthur looked at them closely, almost glowed from within and made him seem lighter than air. Leonidas Merritt had arrived at his mine.

He dropped his helmet on the table. "All right, who talked to the scientific squirt?"

Housell quickly snatched his bottle off the table and hid it. Arthur stood up.

"Ah, Arthur. Good to see you again. I saw your boy yesterday. He looks wonderful. Growing big now. More on that later. More later. First to business."

"I met Mister Lewis," Arthur said.

"Ah, good. Sit down here, m'boy. Tell me everything."

Arthur related what had happened, and all that Harvey Lewis had said. Lon slapped the table. "Goddamned scientific squirts. They follow a book, walking the earth with their eyes closed. Can they not see what lies before their eyes?"

Gill said, "Aye, but he did look. He looked and saw noothing. Noothing of importance. It's like I told you before, without the slate there ain't no ore."

"You know damn well that's not true," Lon said. "You have seen it with your own eyes."

"Aye, and I know what I know. Iron ore is in the ground. You cannot just dig for it. Ye must blast for it. Down deep, under the rocks. Here be no rock, no shale. Just this dirt lying about."

"It is within that very dirt where the riches lie. All you must do is open your eyes to see it."

The men grumbled. Arthur felt a dread settle in his stomach.

"Nichols, you've looked. You dug up there, all over the horn. You drilled where there is rock, where the shale lies long and deep. You scratched the skin of the giant and what did you find? Nothing. Not an iota of iron lying below that rock. So I came here, myself and Alfred, and we told you to dig down here, down in the valley— that was where the iron waited for us. It took some convincing, but you dug, not where we wanted but close enough, and you found it. It is right outside that door, boys, the biggest lode of iron ore anyone in the world has ever seen. The Gogebic, the Marquette, the Menominee, those will turn into dust while we shall still be churning the iron here out of the ground. Here be one hundred years of it, lying in wait, and it is all here for the taking, all for us. All we must do is step outside there and see it for what it is and dig it up."

Wood waved his hand. "Bah, you're drunk on the lure of it. I've seen it before in the eyes of men who scratch at the earth for her riches. They see the glittering yellow and believe it's gold and spend their lives digging for what turns out to be nothing but pyrite. Fool's iron, that's what you have here."

Housell laughed. Lon glared at him.

Lon unfolded a map and stretched it out on the table. It was worn by use, creases folded and unfolded so often as to be worn nearly through the vellum. Areas of the map were divided into sections separated by grid lines. Rows of numbers—50s and 60s and 70s—blended with other markings. Small x's and other indecipherable notations followed the irregular, wavy lines. The shapes swirled along the length of peaked carets that marked the Mesabi Range of low hills. "Here," Lon said, dropping one stubby finger on the map. "This is us. Look at what you see. It is the line of an ancient ocean lapping at the shore of the Mesabi hills. This area here, where we stand, lies in the midst of that Biblical sea."

"Lon, we've all heard your theory," Wood said.

Arthur leaned away from Wood to distance himself from the mining captain's defiance.

Lon said, "Have you heard it? Have you really listened to it? The iron in Vermilion, or in the Gogebic or Marquette Ranges, all came out of some ancient sea which, as it receded, left behind layers of rock beneath which the iron was formed. This place is part of that same ancient sea. Can you not see it? Here, and here, and here." He jabbed his finger along the swirling lines of numbers and peaks. "If you want to listen to those scientific squirts tell you that none of this is possible, that this place cannot exist, then all I ask is that you open your eyes and look for yourselves. Come with me." He turned and marched out the door without waiting to see if anyone would follow.

The men all stared at the map and then at each other.

Nichols was the first to follow him out the door, then Wood and then Arthur and the rest. Outside, Lon was marching through the field of test pits towards the one that had yielded the cache of iron. He scrambled down into the pit, feet sliding on the loose rock and dirt, and then he sliced a spade into the earth. He lifted a shovel full of the reddish-grey soil. "This is the stuff of dreams."

The men circled the pit and looked down at the hulking presence of Lon Merritt who, despite being more than ten feet below them, still seemed to stand on equal ground. He was the giant of the Mesabi legend. In that moment, with the giant staring up at them, the pit seemed to grow larger, seemed to expand. Arthur saw the whole of the forest then, the trees that were and the trees that were no more, and he saw the place not for what it was but for what it would become, the hole that Lon filled with himself as he grew bigger and deeper and wider and longer. Maybe they would dig and dig and find that the iron continued through to the center of the earth. For my grandfather, and for the others who stood around that pit on that day, with Lon Merritt exhorting them to not believe the experts, not believe the men with knowledge—for what did they know about this land?—the iron was there and it was limitless and they were the men to bring it out of the ground.

By the time he left the next afternoon, Lon Merritt had them all believing again. Believing that anything was possible. He took back with him two fifty-pound sacks of the iron dirt, which he planned on taking down to the iron smelters in Pittsburgh and Cleveland, to convince the people who would buy the ore that it was good ore, worthwhile ore. That the experts did not know the Mesabi Range the way Lon Merritt and his band of brothers knew the Mesabi Range.

He left behind something else that day, too. He announced that the camp had a new leader: Wood may lead the mine, but Arthur Maki led the camp.

CHAPTER 4

NIIGAANIIMITIG

Lon's speech spurred the men of Mountain Iron to quicken the pace of their work. Within a day of his departure, the hole transformed into a deep, wide pit that itself began to swallow some of the other smaller test pits that pockmarked the clearing. Arthur grew excited as he watched the men dig. For Arthur, Lon had cast aside any doubts about the work they were doing here. It was finally more than just an idea. This was becoming a place where the giant was waking, and Arthur was eager to help stir him from slumber.

Johnnie began making trips to Duluth and back twice a week. Captains Nichols, Wood, and Gill, along with Wheeler, loaded food and picks and shovels into packs and trundled into the woods on another Merritt-inspired mission to eke out new caches of ore. Arthur, Richardson, Charlie, and Housell stayed behind to mind the mine and, in Lon's words, "Prepare."

The clearing, now more than doubled in size from the day Arthur arrived, covered the southern slope of the sleeping giant. Charlie helped build the second and third bunkhouses, along with another small building that would become the main office. The five cabins were clustered around a central area on the south side of the clearing. Their orientation was limited in large part by the position of the mine and which direction Wood and Nichols thought it would expand. The last thing Arthur wanted was to have to pull down one of the buildings because someone discovered iron in the ground beneath.

Richardson, despite his injury, could still use a saw and a hatchet, but his injury slowed the pace of construction. Arthur put him to work limbing, stripping bark, buck-sawing the logs into usable lengths, and running them through the portable sawmill. Housell spoke as little as possible to the three of them and spent his mornings alone fishing for walleye or trout at a nearby lake or stream. Each afternoon he would return with a packsack full of still wriggling fish. Arthur made a table near the kitchen where the cook could gut and scale them. Vultures circled, waiting for the opportunity to swoop down and feast on the pile of odoriferous flesh after he had finished. Occasionally Housell would throw a fish head into the air and a cormorant or osprey would dive down and catch it at the peak of its arc.

Arthur made barrels out of strips of tamarack, sealed with round caps made from pine log slabs and coated with his homemade pine tar resin. When Housell cleaned a fish he would stuff it with salt and place it in a barrel and then cover it with more salt, continuing until a barrel held up to fifty or more fish. After a few weeks of curing in the salt, Arthur thought they were good enough to eat straight out of the barrel. For Housell, however, they were better pan fried with salt pork.

Now that the spring rains had stopped, wildfire became a serious issue. More than once, a spark from the kitchen fire or one of the other fires in the clearing snapped away from the flames and begun smoldering in the pine needles and dry wood shavings that lay everywhere. The men managed to put each potential fire out before it spread; still, it was unwise to continue taking chances. Open fires were forbidden, and a big stone-walled fire pit was dug near the mine.

Charlie stayed busy in more ways than one. When he had finished helping Arthur for the day, he set off quietly into the woods and returned each evening, often dragging another deer on a sled made from pine branches and spruce root rope. He converted one of the test pits near the fire pit into a smoker complete with a spruce sapling frame covered with birch bark. He filled the hollow with hot embers from the fire pit so that he had a five-feet-deep pit of smoking coals. He skinned the animal by firelight and draped the long, lean strips of meat over the frame, which he then sealed with birch bark. Once the meat had finished smoking, usually a day later, he packed it in Arthur's tamarack barrels.

"We'll never get through all that," Housell told Arthur. "Goddamned wasteful savage."

"This place will soon fill with men hungry like the mosquitoes," Arthur said. "Meat will sell better than your whiskey."

"Don't count on it," Housell scowled and went back to packing his fish.

After three months of living in the woods, Arthur decided the time was right to build a sauna. Because a sauna required an abundant source of cool, clear water, he looked for a place close to the larger of the two lakes east of the campsite. The lake itself was shaped like a giant's footprint, three points jutting out to the north and a wide base at the south. As Arthur walked around it he imagined the giant clambering through the trees, stepping into the mud the same way Arthur and the others had slopped through it on their way to the camp. On the north shore, a steep bank plunged down to the water. Twenty-five feet from there he paced off a ten-by-twelve area, marking with an axe the trees to be taken out. He paced another fifty feet west and found himself at the edge of the clearing and within sight of the camp. Here he paced the perimeter of the house he would build, again marking with his axe the trees to be felled.

Every night before dinner when there was still daylight to work by, he cleared the land and began digging for the foundation stones.

Housell seemed keenly interested in the project. "What are you building in the woods?" he said one night at dinner.

Arthur dumped a ladleful of stew onto his metal plate.

"Hey, you mute or something?" Housell said.

"Sauna," Arthur said.

"What?"

"Sauna. For bath."

"What in Sam Hill is that?" Housell said. "You want a bath you jump in a river."

"Is Finnish."

"Bah," Housell said. "This ain't Finland. This is America. We don't have time for bathing."

"*Voin kertoa*," Arthur said with a ghost of a smile. *I can tell.*

Housell narrowed his eyes. "What'd you say?"

Arthur sat at the long table across from Charlie.

"You insulting me?"

Arthur ate the stew. It really was delicious. He felt no need to confront its obnoxious cook.

Housell leaned over Arthur, his fists pushing against the table. "I don't take to bein' insulted."

Charlie said, "Back off."

"Fucking savages sticking together. Sounds like something your people thought up."

Richardson stood up. "He said back off."

Housell flared his nostrils like a bull about to charge, his greasy hair matted to his sweating head. From the kitchen a cat hissed. He glared at Richardson. "Bah," he said. He turned his back to the men and went to the kitchen.

The warm nights made the cabins suffocating, so Arthur took to sleeping on a bed of pine boughs under the canopy of stars. The smell of pine tar cooking in the rock-walled earthen pit lulled him to sleep and overcame the noxious odor of rotting fish heads, decaying vegetables, and the rancid meat and bones that the wasteful cook heaped into a pile outside the kitchen. Birds pecked at the pile all day, and Housell was constantly on guard for wolves and bears that followed the scent into camp. More than once Arthur was woken up at night by the sounds of marauding animals feasting on the meal, and then drunk Housell firing his pistol at the shadows. The odor also drew swarming flies and gnats. The poultice Arthur spread on his face and arms helped keep the annoying insects at bay; and at night bats swooped down to feast on some of them, though there weren't enough bats to eat them all.

He wrote to Minnie and told her of his progress with the sauna and of his life in the camp. He was able to express himself better in Finnish. "It is easier to do than to lead," he wrote. "In the doing I have only myself to rely on, but in the leading I must rely on others to do the work I know myself capable of. The work is fulfilling, though, and keeps me occupied so that I do not dwell on how much I miss you. Give Ben a kiss from his father." Johnnie delivered the letters and once a week brought replies from Minnie penned in beautifully scripted Finnish. She wrote of her life in the boarding house, and of how she missed Arthur as much as he missed her. "I look at the moon every night," she wrote, "and think of you."

———◇———

A crescent moon was high overhead early one morning when Arthur awoke to the sound of stumbling in the dark. He sat up. A yellow light bobbed through the forest toward him.

In clear but flustered English, a voice announced, "Anyone awake here?"

Arthur rubbed his eyes. "*Joo.*" He felt like he'd only just fallen asleep.

The light bounced through the trees. "Who's there?"

Arthur said his name. "I am in charge here. Who are you?" It was all he could think to say.

"Oh, there, good, yes, fine," the voice said. The light became larger as it floated out of the trees and stopped short of him. Arthur squinted in the brightness and held his hand up to shield his eyes. "Ah, sorry about that." The light lowered and an unfamiliar figure stood before him. "Maki, is it? I've heard a lot about you. I'm Wilbur. Wilbur Merritt. Pleased to meet you."

Wilbur stuck out his hand. Arthur, standing now on his bed of pine boughs wearing boots and his long underwear, did not offer his hand in return.

"Oh, that's right. Lon told me you Finns don't much like to shake hands. Well, not to worry. We Merritts have our own way of doing things, too." He stepped past Arthur and lifted the lantern. The dim light illuminated his sharp cheeks and heavy jaw. His narrow eyes were shadows, and his lean frame towered over Arthur. "I know every inch of these woods. Been traipsing through here for the past ten years, maybe more. Did not think it was possible for me to get lost out here. But I think I might have been wrong. Maybe it's what you've done to this place. It don't look nothing like what I was expecting it to look."

Arthur was not surprised. This was not the dense forest anymore. For three hundred yards in any direction the trees had been clear cut and the sky feasted upon ground it had not seen since before the Chippewa had made their great migration from the east. Even Arthur did not recognize the place.

The big man turned back to Arthur. His wide jaw was clean-shaven, like the other Merritts', and lifted when a wide smile stretched his mouth. He flashed white teeth. "Lon has told me about you, all about you. Yes, sir. Says you know more about birch bark than just about any Chippewa he's ever known, including Chippewa Charlie. That's saying something. Wish I was here during the day and could see the place better, but I've got no time. No time. Got to get everybody up." Wilbur was smaller than Lon but taller and wider than Arthur, and his deep voice matched his size. He seemed big enough to pull a tree out of the ground with his bare hands. Arthur remembered a story he had heard about Wilbur carrying his injured uncle Cassius out of the woods south of there, carrying him on his back through the swamps and all the way to the St. Louis River where the two men floated right into Duluth. "Need some hands, strong backs, over at Embarrass Lake."

"This way," Arthur said. He led the way to the second bunkhouse where everyone except Housell and Charlie slept. To keep the flying insects out, Richardson had cut one of the fly tents and nailed it over the doors, which he sealed each night from the inside. Then he smoldered yarrow root and goldenseal in the fireplace and let the smoke drift through the building to drive out the mosquitoes. Housell slept above the kitchen, and Charlie stayed in the forest. "Here," Arthur said.

Wilbur walked through the netting, tearing it apart, and lifted the lantern to shine on the four sleeping figures inside. Gill's snoring seemed loud enough to wake even the sleeping giant. Wilbur slapped his hand against the wall. "Hey in here. Up, up." Richardson sat upright, the light reflecting off the knife in his hand. "Whoa," Wilbur said. "No need for cutlery. Get up, get dressed. Hitch the horses, boys. Johnnie's moving east."

Richardson said, "What?"

"No what about it, boy. Shake a leg. We're loading the whole outfit here and moving it over to 3-58-16 by noon tomorrow. Time's a wasting, so hop to it." He walked around the room and kicked the beds. One by one the men grumbled and stumbled to their feet.

Wood said, "What the hell 're you babbling about, Wilbur?"

"Here it is, laid out for ya. Over by Embarrass Lake we drilled down a piece and found good, soft ore, just like here, waiting to be lifted out of the ground. But we only got ten days to make something of it. After that Lon and Johnnie lose the option on the land and someone else'll come in and take it. So we got to move, boys. Shake a leg." He turned to Arthur. "We'll leave Arthur to mind the Mountain while we're gone." He put his hand on Arthur's shoulder. "Anyone else in camp?"

Arthur led Wilbur to the kitchen. Wilbur marched up the stairs. Arthur heard the heavy body of Housell fall onto the wooden floor. "Up with you," Wilbur barked. "Collect yer cook stove and yer gear and meet us at the wagon."

Outside Arthur helped Wilbur hitch the mules to one of the wagons. Richardson and Gill loaded the mining gear, windlasses, pulleys, striking hammers, picks, shovels, and buckets. Charlie arrived with deerskin packs full of dried venison. Housell loaded his small cook stove and pans, as well as a sack of beans, bags of flour, box of salt and pepper, one of the barrels of salted fish, and a fishing pole. Arthur noticed he was very careful with one of his duffels and secured it tightly between the bags of flour and beans. Within an hour the crew was gone. They went along the tote-road, the wagon bumping over rocks and tree stumps that had never been fully cleared. The moon had vanished and the first purple shadows of morning appeared behind the trees. Arthur and Charlie were alone.

Arthur turned to Charlie. "Will you help me build sauna?"

Charlie said, "*Joo.*"

The two men walked back to the area Arthur had cleared. Arthur scratched his crude layout in the dirt and showed Charlie which trees they would use, and the two of them set to work limbing and peeling and then bucking the trees to length. Together they laid flat boulders in the foundation trench around the perimeter and, after ax-hewing the logs, they began building walls, filling in the space between logs with moss.

In two days they had the walls up. Inside Arthur built a stove fireplace using rocks he found nearby. He left a small opening in front for loading wood, and made the top flat on which he loaded loose rocks which would be heated by the stove. The stove itself was more than two feet square, though the firebox inside was less than half that size. The rest of the space was air pockets which would trap the heat long after the fire was extinguished. A rock chimney rose high above the walls. He built a wooden floor and three levels of benches, each row farther away from the fireplace depending on how hot one wanted to get. A wall with a door and small window separated the entry room from the sauna room itself and it was here he shaped wooden pegs and hammered them into the log walls. Together he and Charlie built a ceiling with axe-hewn planks, bracing it with four crossbeams. They then covered the whole thing with a gabled roof topped with pine shingles anchored with pine pins.

Finally, at the lake, they pounded four head-high tar treated pine posts into the water, and over these they built a small dock with axe-hewn planks. Arthur then dropped a short ladder into the water to make it easy to climb in and out. With the sauna complete, Charlie joined Arthur for an inaugural bath.

⸎◆⸎

For the next several days Arthur continued to prepare wood for Richardson's return. Charlie showed up to help Arthur skid the logs out of the woods, but otherwise spent much of his time alone in his *waaginogaan* or hunting for game and curing the meat in his smoker. Arthur kept himself busy, too. He built a covered walkway from the dining cabin to the main sleeping cabin, and then three more connecting the sleeping cabins. He took to fishing in the morning now that Housell was not around, and tended to the garden behind the kitchen. He cooked his own meals—ones that reminded him of home. He managed to make a palatable *piirakkaa* with potatoes and rice and flakes of fish, the whole thing baked in a blackened dutch oven Arthur found in Housell's attic room. In the evenings, before supper, he would light a fire in his sauna so that by the time the sun had settled behind the trees the sauna was hot and ready to use.

Charlie reappeared every night for the sauna. He touched the walls in admiration and tapped the benches Arthur had built. He sat on the high bench, up where the heat was most intense, and closed his eyes. Arthur poured water on the rocks and grew accustomed again to the heat of the sauna. After a time he would go out and walk barefoot across the warm, dry ground and step down the ladder into the waters of what he had come to think of as Footprint Lake. Steam rose off his body despite the hot nights. Charlie followed him to the water and dipped himself, too—the first time, giving a loud whoop. The cool water was a shock to him. Afterwards the two men would slosh out of the lake, dripping water back to the sauna, and spend another twenty to thirty minutes baking in the warmth. He was proud of his sauna, and couldn't wait to share it with Minnie.

The crew had been gone for two weeks and Arthur was just getting used to the quiet. Finally one night Charlie found Arthur eating alone in the dining room. "They come," he said.

"Who?" Arthur said.

The door opened and in walked Captain Wood. "Hello, boys," he said. "Welcome to the party!" He blasted into the room like a giant, stomped his feet, waved his arms. The night was warm and he wore the gear of a summer hike, boots and wool socks and leather pants and a white long-sleeved shirt smeared with gray-red dirt. He tore off his hat and threw it on the table then put his arm around Arthur. "This is a big night, boys. Big night." He gaped at Charlie as though surprised to see him there. "Rest are right behind me."

Arthur went outside to help with the wagon. The others, Gill and Richardson, were unloading gear into the storage cabin. Housell, back bent by a heavy pack, lugged his cook stove along the path from the storage cabin to the kitchen. As he passed Arthur he said, "Get ready, Maki. Your giant just woke up."

Richardson said, "We found it, Arthur."

The wagon unloaded, Arthur unhitched the mules and led them to the lean-to that served as a barn. When he got back to the dining cabin everyone was there, including Johnnie and Wilbur. Housell slouched at the end of the table. Arthur had never seen him so tired or sober. But Wood and Gill were as excited as Arthur had ever seen them. They were all laughing and cheering.

"Maki, m'boy," Wilbur said. "Come in, come in. It's a big day for all of us."

There was a map laid out on the table and all heads were crowded over it.

"Seems to me the best route would be right through here," Johnnie said. "It's a straight shot right down to the Cloquet. The land is mostly flat and stable."

"There's that featherbed swamp I carried old Cash through," Wilbur said. "Got to watch for that."

"A small section, easily dealt with," Johnnie said.

Gill asked the question that was rolling through Arthur's head. "Why not use the Duluth and Iron Range? Will Tower nay give you access?"

"Money will make anyone do anything," Wood said.

"We're putting iron before horses here, boys," Wilbur said. "Shall we get it out of the ground first?"

"If we get it out and it just sits there, what then?" Johnnie added. "We have to find a way to get it to the water. Two Harbors has the docks, so that's the best place to unload."

"Aye, but Johnnie, we are in Duluth." Wilbur slapped his cousin on the back and laughed.

"Tomorrow we shall be in Duluth," Johnnie said. "Tonight we rest."

Wood clapped his hands together. "Rest for the weary tomorrow. Tonight we celebrate."

Gill said, "That's the second grandest thing I've heard all day!"

"Here, here," Wilbur said.

Johnnie said, "Let's not get too excited. There is still much work to be done."

"Come now, Johnnie." Wilbur pointed to the other men. "The fellows here lugged an entire mining camp fifteen miles through the woods in less than eight hours, by God, and then spent two weeks digging in the dirt with nothing but Housell's terrible cooking to keep 'em going."

Housell eyed Wilbur crossly but said nothing.

"No offense, m'boy. I just think we all deserve a little celebration." Johnnie looked around.

"I know you don't drink yourself, Johnnie, but let's give 'em some fun for one night." Wilbur seemed to be excited at the thought of a little of Housell's homemade hooch.

Johnnie was outnumbered in his objection, and knew it.

Wood slapped the table. "Get up there, Housell, and get yer stash," he barked.

Housell seemed to come alive. He hopped out of his seat and vanished into the kitchen and reemerged seconds later with two bottles.

Wood grabbed one out of his hand and pulled the cork with tough yellow teeth. "Grab yer cups, boys," he said. He began to pour cups full of the clear liquid. Housell held onto the second bottle and poured from that one. Wood pushed a cup in front of everyone. Johnnie shook his head, as did Arthur. Charlie did not even acknowledge that there was a cup in front of him. Everyone else lifted theirs high into the air, though—even Wilbur, whom Arthur thought was a teetotaler like his cousins.

"To the Biwabik!" Wilbur said.

"The Biwabik," the others repeated, and they all drank. Housell and Wood and Gill and Richardson swallowed it all in one draft. Wilbur took a sip, then shook himself all over like a dog trying to rid his fur of water.

Johnnie laughed, "Bitter stuff, eh, cuz?"

Gill slapped Wilbur on the shoulder. Wilbur stood a full head taller than the Cornishman, but at that moment Gill seemed the bigger man. "Aye, ye get used to it, brother." He poured himself another cup full.

"This is history in the making, Arthur," Johnnie said, smiling. "The day we Merritts proved it all right. By God, Lon was right!"

"Did you ever doubt him, Johnnie?" Wilbur said.

"If there is a man here who has not himself doubted at one time or another, I'll buy him a case of good Irish whiskey," Gill said. He took another swallow. "Not this fermented horse piss Housell makes."

Wood laughed. "It kicks like a horse, too."

Richardson, drinking too, laughed with the others, as did Wilbur and Johnnie. "Come on," he said to Arthur and Charlie, sitting next to one another and not touching the cups before them. "Drink up!"

Arthur shook his head and pushed his cup over to Richardson who picked it up and swallowed the contents in one gulp.

Charlie put his hand on Richardson's arm and eyed him sternly.

"You are one of us. Whiskey leads to bad things."

Richardson shook him off. "*Midewiwin* doomsayers been preaching that for a while."

Housell swayed behind them, bottle in hand. "Who's not enjoying the celebration?" he said. "Fill that cup again, Arthur." He took a swig, seeming for once not to mind about the drain on his personal supply of hooch. "What about you, savage?"

Charlie pushed his mug off the table. It hit the wood floor with a clang and the whiskey spread like a stain.

Housell's eyes went colder and he sneered. "That's the second time you've wasted my whiskey, savage," he said, and in one motion, grabbed the back of Charlie's head and shoved his face against the table.

Richardson stood up. "Back off, Housell."

"Shut up, mutt. You're no better."

Charlie twisted away from Housell's hand. Housell was a squat, round man and Charlie's long, lean body seemed to tower over him.

Richardson downed another cup of whiskey and stood up, too. His face was bright red. "What did you call me?"

"A savage mutt," Housell said.

Richardson brought his arm back but Charlie grabbed his wrist before he could swing. "No," Charlie said. "Not your fight."

"That's what you people do," Housell said. "You gang up on us. Beat us down with numbers. Slaughter us. Ain't that right?"

Charlie said, "We are at peace with your people."

"Ain't gonna be no peace around here until your kind is gone from this land. This is ours now. When're you gonna get that straight?"

To Arthur, Charlie was the calm one. He stood as still as a tree, arms at his sides, while before him Housell's face squirreled into a knot, his fists tightened, the veins in his temples pulsing. And Richardson, standing beside Charlie, was a grizzly bear waiting to pounce.

"Show me peace," Housell sneered. "Drink with me."

"To not share the peace pipe does not mean war," Charlie said.

Housell looked around the room. The noise of the celebration had stopped and now everyone stared at the cook facing off with the Indian and the timberman.

"That's the kind of cowardice your people have," Housell said. "Too many of us, so you back down. Got to outnumber us to win. Just like at Little Big Horn."

At the mention of the battle, Richardson's suppressed bear came unleashed. He surged forward and dug his good shoulder into Housell's chest. The two men crashed to the floor, Housell landing flat on his back with Richardson on top of him. Housell was fat and slow, but Richardson was hampered by his still-injured shoulder. His blows to the cook's face, while tough, were neither as quick nor as hard as they probably would have been otherwise.

Richardson hit the cook three times, each with his weaker left hand, before Housell managed to slug his attacker with a side punch to his lower back on his injured side. Richardson winced and doubled over and Housell shoved him off with a thrust of his hips. Richardson rolled across the floor and into the wall. Housell got to his feet, wiping the blood off his cheek. He snorted like a bull ready to charge, feet apart, head down. Richardson was slower getting up. He used his good arm and pulled himself to his feet against the wall, but he was still unsteady when Housell lumbered over to him and punched him again in the gut. Housell hit him one, two, three more times, before Richardson managed to pull his injured arm up to block a punch and then swung with his good arm into Housell's jaw. The cook's head snapped to one side and blood splattered against one of the tables. Richardson hit him in the gut. Housell returned with a left cut directly into Richardson's injured shoulder. The timberman howled and Housell hit him twice in the gut, then followed with a right upper cut to his chin. Richardson crumpled. Housell grabbed him by his right arm and tossed him like a doll. Cups scattered as Richardson rolled over the table and onto the floor on the other side. He was on his hands and knees, trying to stand, when Housell kicked him in the chest. The timberman was lifted off the ground and flipped onto his back.

Arthur saw a strange excitement in the eyes of the other men as they watched the fight. He had seen this kind of spectacle as entertainment before, in Tower. It turned his stomach then, as it turned his stomach now, and as he watched the two men fight, and watched Housell set to kick Richardson a second time, he realized with growing dread that he would have to step in and stop it. If for no other reason than he needed Richardson to help stockpile firewood for winter.

Housell reared back with his right boot.

"Enough," Arthur said.

Charlie stepped in then. He kicked the cook's left foot forward. Housell fell backward, his right leg twisting beneath him. His crash rattled tables. He writhed and struggled to get his foot out from under him. Charlie stood over him, fists clenched.

Arthur took Richardson by his good arm and helped him to his feet.

The fire in the corner crackled, and Housell cursed and grunted from the floor. "God damned savages," he shouted. "Gang up on a man!"

Richardson spat blood on him. "You son of a bitch."

Wilbur helped Housell to his feet. "That's enough," he said.

The air seemed to be let out of the room. Wood said, "Bah, just when it was getting good."

Gill shoved a full cup into Housell's hand. "Drink up," he said. "'Tis done."

Arthur led Richardson out into the night, and Charlie followed them. The air was cool despite the warm day. Flies swarmed about their heads, drawn by the smell of Richardson's blood. Crickets were loud in the underbrush.

Charlie said, "He needs heat. *Madoodiswan*."

"Sauna hot," Arthur said.

Arthur and Charlie helped Richardson through the trees. The timberman moaned and his head lolled onto his chest. In the changing room, Arthur undressed and lit a lantern in the small window. Charlie helped Richardson undress and the three men entered the sauna, two of them helping Richardson through the door. Inside the pot of water on the stove was too hot to touch. Arthur added cold water from the lake to cool it off. The heat felt instantly good to Arthur. His skin warmed and beads of sweat began to trickle.

Richardson seemed to perk up, too. "What is this place?"

Arthur poured a little water onto the hot stones and steam hissed. Then he wet a small cloth with the same water and gave it to Richardson with a bar of soap.

"It's hot," Richardson said.

"*Joo*. Sauna."

"What?"

Charlie said, "Like *madoodiswan* that the grandfathers gave us."

Richardson seemed impressed. "You built this?"

"*Joo*," Arthur said. "For bathing."

Richardson winced. In the dim light, Arthur could see the big black bruises forming on the timberman's chest and back. "I've been worse," Richardson said.

Charlie examined the bruises on his chest. "This bad. Broken, I think."

Richardson's breathing was shallow and difficult. He coughed, and when he did he cried out. The cry didn't help the pain. "God damn," he screamed. "I could use some of that whiskey about now."

Charlie stepped outside. When he returned he had some of the same plants he had used when the tree had fallen. He also had one of Housell's bottles. He handed the bottle to Richardson.

"I thought you didn't like this stuff."

"Not for me," Charlie said. He crushed the yarrow in the hot water

"Let that bastard miss one of his precious bottles." There was only enough for a couple of swallows, but it was enough for Richardson. "That's good," he said after he drank the rest of it down. "It'll still hurt tomorrow, but for now it feels a little better."

Charlie tore the leaves on a strip of birch bark and mixed in water to make a poultice. He rubbed the green paste onto Richardson's chest and side and then bandaged him with a strip of birch bark trimmed to fit around Richardson's trunk like armor. Using a bit of spruce root twine he tied the bark in place. "This will help the bruises," Charlie said, "a little."

"Thanks," Richardson said.

The three men sat quietly. Arthur allowed the steam and the heat to penetrate his skin. He closed his eyes and listened to the sounds of the night, the crickets and the owls and the mice scurrying.

Finally, Richardson said, "I need to get out of here. I feel like my skin is on fire."

Charlie helped him through the door. From inside, Arthur listened as they shuffled along the path to Footprint Lake. Richardson, replying to something unheard from Charlie, said, "In there? No way. . . . Is this how he stays so clean looking?" Another murmur and then Arthur heard a splash into the water. A few seconds later there was another. Richardson yelped. Then more splashing as the two men clambered out of the pond. Moments later they were scooting back into the sauna, Richardson moaning and groaning.

"Where did you get the idea for this?" he asked.

Arthur said, "Sauna is part of us."

"Us?"

"My people," Arthur said. "Finnish."

Richardson laughed and then made a sound like he had been punched again. "This place will change a lot," he said through gritted teeth. "We shall all need to grow accustomed to new ideas."

Arthur enjoyed this time of day, for he was finally able to let the dirt and grime of each day pour out of him. The experience was better with others; the sauna had more meaning, more power, when it was shared. He had never thought of this place as his alone, but as a place where they could all go, could all bathe and cleanse themselves, and be a community.

By now Richardson's head was falling onto his chest. Arthur and Charlie helped him to the anteroom, dressed, and walked him back to one of the newer cabins that had yet to be used. From the kitchen they heard the raucous sounds of the celebration still going on. Richardson sat down on the floor and Charlie handed him a canteen. He took a sip and curled his lip.

"What is that?" he said. "Worse than Housell's."

"*Nibewi-mashkiki*. Sleep medicine."

"Not that I need it." He curled his lip and drank down two swallows before handing it back to Charlie.

Arthur laid Richardson down on his own sleeping mat and the timberman was asleep almost instantly. Arthur yawned.

"Rest," Charlie said. The Indian walked out into the night. Arthur lay down on one of the beds he had built, and though there was no mattress on it, he was tired enough that he fell asleep anyway.

⋘◈⋙

It was midday and the sun was shining high overhead. Venison smoke drifted in the late summer heat as vultures circled Housell's moldering heap of kitchen scraps. Arthur was building beds and tables for the cabins, as well as a table for himself. Richardson, moving slowly from his fight with Housell, struggled at the sawmill. Wood, Gill, and Wheeler were digging industriously at the mine itself on the western side of the clearing. The discovery at Biwabik had renewed their energy. Their prospects were exciting again, and Johnnie and Wilbur had gone back to Duluth to report the news and bring back supplies and more people.

Arthur heard a whistle and looked up to see Wilbur, the giant of a man, coming out of the woods at the tote road. Behind him, snaking through the trees, was a line of men, fifty or more, each with a duffel strapped to his back, head low, mud-splattered and weary. They looked like they had they walked all the way from Duluth. Still, an excited murmur arose as they came through the trees, lifted their heads and saw for the first time what had been done here in the woods. One man with bushy gray eyebrows dropped his pack, knelt, and grabbed a fistful of earth. Arthur put down his chisel and went to Charlie who was stacking dried venison on a stretch of leather. "They come," he said.

Charlie stood and looked down at the men streaming into the clearing. After a moment he turned to Arthur and said, "Giant wakes." He folded the venison pouch and hefted it over his shoulder and walked away toward his *waaginogaan.*

Wood and Gill stopped their digging and clambered out of the pit.

Wilbur, with a hulk of a pack clanging against his giant frame, wandered away from the mass of men. "Arthur, m'boy," he said opening his big arms. "The crew has arrived."

Behind him wagons lurched and rattled out of the woods. Arthur counted a dozen in all, each piled high with crates, barrels, canvas sacks, bags, picks, and shovels. There was a cage of chickens, a rooster, seven hens, a line of pigs. Four cows trailed behind one of the wagons. Fresh milk! Arthur thought. One wagon contained nothing but sacks of flour and barrels of salt and pepper. Crates of tobacco were piled on another. One barrel was marked lard. There were sacks of cured ham, potatoes, apples, carrots, and onions. Mining supplies filled other wagons: boxes of dynamite and gunpowder, steel mallets the size of Wilbur's head, and an anvil. Arthur saw all this equipment and supplies and hoped he'd built enough cabins. He had only been thinking about people, not storage.

"Should be enough to get us through winter," Wilbur said. "Johnnie was a day behind us coming out of Duluth with another crew heading for Biwabik." He handed an envelope to Arthur on which was written Arthur's name. "It's all in the letter. I'll meet you up at the camp. We can decide which is going to be my store!" He slapped Arthur on the shoulder and disappeared back into the crowd.

Arthur opened the envelope and withdrew two sheets of paper. The first was written in English in a handwriting he didn't recognize. The second was a delicate Finnish script he knew immediately.

> Dearest Arvid,
>
> Ben indeed misses you, as do I. He grows big-
> ger every day, and more wild. He is in need
> of a father. Lon says he hopes soon fami-
> lies will join the crew in camp, and that I may
> be among the first to come. I do hope so.
>
> Men arrive in Duluth daily by train and boat. Lon
> has set up a recruiting office near the depot and
> hires them as they get off the train. Most of them
> do not speak English. I have heard a spattering of
> Finnish and some Swedish. Lon says he likes to hire
> Finns because they work hardest and drink least.
> He is mistaken if he thinks all Finns are like you.
>
> Ben wakes and I must get back to the kitchen to
> prepare supper. I eagerly await your next letter.
>
> Love,
> Minnie

Arthur held the letter close to his chest. He could picture Minnie sitting at her little writing desk penning it. The paper even smelled like her. It was time to ask if he could move his family here. Soon, he knew, the hill would swarm with miners and laborers looking for work, and neither Lon, nor Wilbur, nor Arthur himself could stop them from bringing their wives and children.

He folded the letter and placed it carefully in his pocket and then looked to the second paper.

Dear Arthur,

John G. Cohoe, an old friend and fellow seeker of iron ore, has agreed to lead this first wagon train of supplies to Mountain Iron and assist Captain Wood with mining operations. I have instructed Mr. Wood to give you full freedom in the planning and construction of buildings to house the workers that have come with this supply train and more that will be coming in the weeks ahead. He will provide you whatever assistance you need.

While I must remain in Duluth to handle matters at this end, and my nephew Johnnie has gone to the new mine at Biwabik, we ask that you continue to supervise the community that will serve as housing and headquarters for the Mountain Iron Company. I must emphasize that mining operations are to be separate and distinct from the development of the community, and that you are the arbiter in all community affairs.

We shall need a main building as mining office, with the interior subdivided into four separate spaces. In addition, my nephew Wilbur has accompanied this train of supplies for the purpose of establishing a store. If you have not already done so, please construct a building suitable for his needs. Wilbur can supply you with his requirements.

Mr. Leonard Halley has agreed to join the Mountain Iron Company to take over operation of the sawmill. I have known Mr. Halley for many years and vouch that he is a loyal and trusted friend and business partner. His wife and niece have accompanied him and are willing to assist in any way you see fit to utilize them.

> Mr. Cohoe will provide you with an inventory
> of supplies that have been sent with this wag-
> on train, as well as an accurate head-count. It is
> our hope that these supplies should see you and
> the men of Mountain Iron through the winter.
>
> God bless you and your family. I remain,
> Respectfully yours,
> Leonidas Merritt

Arthur put the letter inside his overalls. He watched the more than fifty men climb the hill and made quick calculations. There were enough sleeping cabins, though not enough beds. He would need to build a barn to house the horses and other livestock. He watched Housell let the chickens out of their cages. Arthur would need a coop for them first. He figured the amount of timber, logs and lumber he would need for new construction, including a house for himself, how to divide the inside of one of the buildings already made, which of the bunkhouses would be best for a store. The figuring in his head wasn't hard to do.

Wilbur and Cohoe—with the gray caterpillar eyebrows—were coordinating the wagons up the hill. There were a lot of wagons being pulled by a lot of horses, and the place suddenly took on the appearance of a village. Men were everywhere, smoking and grunting and yelling. Hooves pounded into the dirt; dust rose and settled. The gnats and mosquitoes began to swarm even more intensely around the flood of new, warm bodies. Horsetails swished and lashed at them. The men slapped at their necks and cursed in various languages. They were, to a man, dirty and covered in the grime of the tote road. Arthur wondered if any of them was Finnish. From a distance it was hard to tell, and without actually speaking to them, he might never know.

"Hallo," a voice called out. A covered wagon stopped next to him, the horses whinnying, harness rattling. The man driving was big, bigger than Wilbur Merritt, round and tall. He smiled through a big beard. He lifted a wide brimmed hat off his head. A thin black tie was pinned to his white shirt. "Are you Mr. Maki?"

"*Joo.*"

A woman sat beside him, just as tall, with a round bosom covered in cotton ruffles. Despite these, her sharply angled face, large nose, and deep, wide-set eyes gave her a mannish appearance. She looked as though she could best any of the new arrivals in digging ore out of the ground. Yet there was also a tenderness about the way she folded her hands in her lap and smiled down at Arthur through closed lips.

"I'm Leonard Halley. This is my wife, Frances."

The woman nodded. "Pleased to meet you, Mr. Maki."

A young woman—Arthur guessed she was no more than eighteen—peered out from beneath the cover behind them. Her blonde hair was tied neatly behind her head, and piercing blue eyes highlighted her soft, round face. The resemblance between her and Leonard Halley was unmistakable. As she surveyed the camp she seemed filled with a mix of wonder and boredom.

"That's our niece, Virginia," Halley said. He stood and looked around the camp. "You have been busy, haven't you? Done some fine work. Fine work." The wagon bounced when he plopped back onto the buckboard. The horses stomped their feet, impatient to get the harnesses off.

Frances said, "Let us get settled, Len."

"Yes, you are right. Good to meet you, Mr. Maki. We shall talk soon."

Arthur nodded and waved in parting, but as the wagon's horses plodded forward up the hill, the girl continued to peer out from inside.

Arthur walked among horses and wagons and men and heard five or six different languages. Though none was Finnish, he recognized some Swedish and Norwegian. Most of them, he guessed, had only recently arrived in America, and he wondered how many had been given new names, how many were running away from something, and how many were simply looking for a better life. Some of them probably had mining experience, but most of the new arrivals had never gone into a shaft or dug a drift or picked at hard rock looking for the smallest bit of precious metal. And even if they had, this would be new to them for here there was no shaft, no drifts, no cages to take them deep into the earth.

He found Wilbur at the head of the line of wagons. "There," Arthur said pointing to the westernmost of the five buildings. It was the most recently finished and though Arthur had planned it as a bunkhouse it could also serve as a general store. He wondered, though, why the camp would need a store. Weren't all the men's needs going to be met by the Merritts? But he realized, too, there were personal effects that the mine wouldn't supply, such as books and paper and pens to write to loved ones, copies of the bible, soap—it made sense to have a store.

"Let's take a look," Wilbur said.

Arthur led the way. The five cabins were clustered around a central building, the kitchen. There were paths that led from one to the other, and three of them had coverings to protect the path to the kitchen during the snowy winter. The door swung easily on leather hinges.

Wilbur said, "We have iron hinges and locks with us."

The inside of the cabin was a fifteen-foot-long empty room. The fireplace at one end had been built from rocks quarried from the clearing.

"This'll do fine, Arthur," Wilbur said. "I'll need some shelves along both long walls here, all the way to the back and all the way up to the ceiling. And a counter of a sort from here to here." He paced halfway down the room. "And maybe a shorter one there, by the door. And a ladder to put stuff up high."

Arthur made mental calculations. He would need lumber quickly to get this done fast.

Wilbur rubbed his hands together. "This is a very exciting time, Arthur," he said. "We are all poised to make a lot of money."

⟫◆⟪

Housell was unhappy, as usual. But when he found himself with three wagonloads of supplies, ten head of cattle, a dozen chickens, half a dozen pigs, a couple of goats, and almost five times as many hungry men to feed, he became very vocally unhappy.

"How do you expect me to do all this myself?" he yelled. He and Arthur were in the dining hall of the cookhouse. "In one day you double the mouths I'm to feed and expect me to perform miracles? I'm a cook, not a god damned witch."

Arthur did not like Housell. But now that he was in charge of the camp facilities he had to deal with the man, had to figure out a way to manage him. Arthur said, "This is your job. To cook and to organize."

Housell poked Arthur in the chest. "Listen up, you fickle Finn, going out into the woods and sitting in your little fire box all night. Don't you come in my kitchen and tell me what my job is or how to do it. I been doing this longer than you have, and for a lot more folks 'n you. Better folk, too. Merritts picked me because I cooked for the army during the war. There weren't none of these foreigners taking up space in my kitchen. Slags and Krauts and Weegies and you fuckin' Finns always sticking your high noses in other people's faces. After the war I was with the cavalry and saw more blood 'n you'll ever see, that's for damned sure. Fightin' them god damned savages that you got hanging around here like old buddies, like you been raised together or something. So I got news for you, Ice Monkey. In my kitchen, I'm the boss. You don't get to tell me what to do. You get me some people in here to help out or they ain't gonna be no supper, no breakfast, no nothing."

Housell turned and stormed up the stairs. Arthur looked around the room. The kitchen fire was lit but there was nothing on it, nothing cooking. Outside, three wagons sat full of goods that needed to be brought in and sorted, stored, stocked, and marked as received; tallies to be made of what supplies where available so they could make sure there was enough to last through winter; and most important, a meal had to be cooked. A big meal.

Through the front door of the cabin stepped Mrs. Frances Halley. With her hat on she had to duck to get through the door. Her entrance was preceded by her ample bosom, which was held up by a corset. Behind her came Virginia, her blonde hair now tied in a braid and covered by a blue bonnet. Virginia was shorter than her aunt, young and slim. While Frances covered her arms to her wrists and wore gloves, Virginia's sleeves extended only to her elbows and her hands were uncovered. Her young face was almost translucent, as though it had never seen the sun. She kept her head slightly down, looking out at the world with a sly grin.

"Excuse me, Mr. Maki," Mrs. Halley said. "I am sorry to bother you. I could not help but overhear the trouble with—Mr. Housell, is it? I understand his predicament. In fact, in coming with my husband, I expected that we—my niece Virginia and myself— would need to include ourselves in the workforce. After all, one cannot build a town on one's own, can one? Nor can one expect

Mr. Housell to cook for a community of this size on his own, not with all the other duties he has to perform." The girl, her hands together at her waist, kept her head down and her eyes focused on the back of her aunt's legs. "We are more than happy to put ourselves to work in the kitchen."

Arthur stammered, "Uh, Mrs. Halley, I would talk with Mr. Halley first."

"Please call me Frances. And don't worry about Len. He will not object." She moved around Arthur and called up the stairs. "Mr. Housell? Are you up there, sir?"

The fat cook clambered halfway down the steps and poked his head from under the ceiling beams. "What?"

"Ah, Mr. Housell. I am Mrs. Frances Halley. Frances, if you please. This is my niece, Virginia. We heard that you have your hands full, and, as it happens, we are in need of an occupation. As we are both well versed in the culinary arts we shall be glad to assist you."

Housell came the rest of the way down the steps and stood before Frances. She towered over him, her bust level with his greasy eyes. He looked from the older woman to the younger and licked his lips. "Could use the help."

"It is settled then," Frances said. "Come, Virginia. Let us get started." The two women swept through the room and disappeared into the kitchen. Housell watched them go then turned to Arthur.

"That's more like it, Maki. I think I might like this." He rubbed his hands together and then followed the women.

Briefly Arthur wondered what Housell might be capable of and made a mental note to be sure neither of the women were alone with Housell. Then, he figured too that Frances Halley was big enough to handle three Housells, and so he left them to work out the details amongst themselves. For now, at least, the cook seemed satisfied.

⋘⬗⋙

By early September, the nights had begun to cool considerably and as Arthur made his way through the dark trees towards his sauna, he shivered. He smelled the pine and tamarack before he saw the thin tendril of smoke drifting out of the chimney. The moon, high and full, spread dim white light across the dark path. Tree ghosts danced in the shadows. As he buttoned his coat he thrilled at the idea of the coming winter. How it would be like home, in the woods, with the thick, soft snow muting the sounds of the forest. Walking through a snowy wood was like walking through heaven, Arthur thought. It would be even better when Minnie came.

He was surprised to find Charlie sitting in front of the sauna. After the arrival of the new miners, the Indian had virtually vanished.

"*Hei*," Charlie said. His black hair shone in the moon's white glow.

"*Boozhoo*," said Arthur. He stepped into the sauna's anteroom, undressed and stepped inside. The hot air blasted his skin and he felt himself almost instantly relax. Charlie came in shortly after. Naked, Charlie was as pale as Arthur, and if not for his black hair he could pass for a Finn. In the sauna, skin color did not matter. In the sauna, they were all the same. Stripped of clothes, uniforms, the dressings of society, all humanity was equal.

The hot rocks in the corner hissed angrily as Arthur dribbled water over them. The men sat for a long time as the heat surrounded and engulfed them. Arthur took a fan of birch branches from a pail of water and began slapping his back and legs with it. The effect was both cooling and stimulating. The slap of the *vihta* quieted the crickets around the building.

Charlie spoke first. "I am going."

"*Joo*," Arthur said. He had been expecting this.

"Mountain Iron crowded," Charlie said. "These people are not my people. They are different and they do not like the differences. They want sameness. The same homes, the same land. This place, this sleeping giant, cries out as the people here tear it up. I am only one man. I cannot stop them. I cannot watch the giant be picked away one shovel full at a time."

There was sadness in the way Charlie spoke, a loss Arthur could only guess at. This would be the second time the Chippewa would lose the forest, Arthur thought, and this time it would be final. When the sleeping giant woke, there would be no putting him back to sleep.

"You go back to the lake?" Arthur said. He felt the loss of his friend. Charlie was the first person, aside from Minnie, with whom Arthur had truly connected. Mountain Iron would not be the same without him.

"First to Duluth. My father is there. I will bring him home with me. Together we shall return to our people."

"When will you go?"

"Tomorrow, or the day after. I have no reason to stay longer."

Arthur felt drops of sweat pooling on his skin. He lashed at his arms and legs with the *vihta*. He made a decision. "I will send for my wife and son to join me."

"Good," Charlie said. "You will be happy."

"*Joo*, yes. But I worry about them. The road is long and the journey hard. Minnie needs a guide."

Charlie said, "I would do this for you, Arvid Mäkelä."

Arthur breathed out. "I would go to Duluth myself, but I cannot leave, and I do not know when the next supply train will come for her to join."

"I will bring her."

"Thank you," Arthur said.

"You are unlike most *gichi-mookomaan* I have known. All others not ask Wiigwaasgewinini, they tell Wiigwaasgewinini."

"Thank you," Arthur repeated. He held the *vihta* out for Charlie who shook his head.

Instead, Charlie said, "I had a dream. I was walking through the forest for many days, unable to stop, without food and water. Finally, I stopped and fell down. I lay in a bed of brown leaves. The grandfathers came out from the trees. They sat around me and sang a song to me. Each of them gave me a lesson, one in making a boat, another in how to create rope from the spruce root. They gave me a word and told me I would know when to use it. Now I understand it. The word is you, Arvid Mäkelä."

Charlie retrieved a pouch and opened it. From it he removed a handful of tobacco which he tossed onto the hot embers inside the stove. They sputtered but did not burn. The sweet, stinging aroma brought tears to Arthur's eyes. He coughed. The heat felt suddenly more intense. The Indian began to chant, his deep voice a singsong that filled the room like so much tobacco smoke. Arthur closed his eyes and four men emerged from the darkness. They were old men, with long white hair and clean, wrinkled faces. Their eyes danced with the light of the orange embers. They sat in a square around Arthur and Charlie. Each of the old men carried a lit pipe and they smoked and blew the smoke into the air above the stove. Each sat with his legs crossed, his tan taut skin glistening in the heat.

Charlie's voice was the only one Arthur heard, though the other four men moved their lips, too. In the quiet echo of the night Arthur heard one word repeated, each of the men saying it alone, and then together, over and over. *Niigaaniimitig. Niigaaniimitig. Niigaaniimitig.*

Arthur felt himself grow faint. The pungent aroma of tobacco lightened his head and he felt himself swoon. Behind his eyes he saw two more people emerge from the darkness. His *äiti* and *isä* stepped through the door, smiled at Arthur, and sat on either side of him. She had a neat blonde braid draped over her shoulder, and her bright blue skirt swooshed across the wood floor. His father held the small hatchet he had given Arthur for his fourteenth birthday. Arthur had lost the hatchet the day he was conscripted into the Russian army.

They took seats on either side of him and began chanting the same word.

Niigaaniimitig.

Niigaaniimitig.

Niigaaniimitig.

Smoke filled the sauna and the swoon grew to feel more like a detachment from his body. He leaned left and his mother pushed him right. He leaned right and his father pushed him left. He rocked forward and felt their hands on his arms holding him back. The moment seemed to drag forever, and then the smoke drifted to reveal the trees above, and Arthur saw stars shining in the darkness above the canopy. He was staring up at the swaying boughs, the bright moon casting gray light across his face. The trees lined up around him, the birch and the tamarack and the ash and the spruce and the maple, like guardian soldiers. He heard the word, echoing and repeating—

Niigaaniimitig.

Then he was wet, in the water up to his neck. The guardian trees closed the sky and blocked the moon. They reached down and pulled him out of the lake and dropped him on the shore. He dripped water into the mud and he swayed with the trees until he fell forward and put one foot out just in time. He caught himself and stepped with the movement of the tall pines and the twisting tamarack and the strong ash. Their low branches brushed his path clear of debris. The trees led him back to the sauna where he heard a drum beating and that word chanted—

Niigaaniimitig.

He felt goose bumps on his arms as he was hot and cold at the same moment. That was the joy of the sauna. To be all things and all places all at once. He went inside and sat on the bench and stared across at Charlie, legs crossed, hands on his knees. Arthur felt the heat of the sauna again, took a breath. The smoke was gone, the four old men gone, his parents gone. Just the two men faced each other across the dimly lit sauna while the hot rocks sizzled.

Charlie said, "What did you see?"

"Four men," Arthur said. "And *minun vanhemmat*. My parents."

"Good," Charlie said.

"What happened?"

"The Naming ceremony. Four grandfathers from four directions came to me and told me your name. I am not medicine man, but my father taught me. You are Chippewa now," Charlie said.

"*Niigaaniimitig?*"

"This is your name," Charlie said. "Leader of trees."

"*Niigaaniimitig*," Arthur said again and breathed in the heat.

CHAPTER 5

NIBOWIN

Maria Maki, née Riiski, dropped two eggs in the skillet with the steak. The pan sizzled and the eggs turned from clear to white almost immediately. She pulled the pan off the hottest fire on the stove, sprinkled the eggs with salt and pepper, and then covered the pan while she buttered toast.

"Minnie, Mr. Lappala is waiting for his steak and eggs," Hephzibah Merritt called from the next room.

Minnie wiped her hands on her apron and scratched her neck. The tight-fitting collar on the blue dress she wore might have been in fashion, but that didn't make it comfortable. It was too plain, the bodice was too tight, and the folds of the skirt too wide for practicality. Still, Mrs. Merritt had asked her to wear it, and therefore it was her uniform.

She took the lid off the pan and flipped the steak onto a plate, then turned the eggs over onto the steak. Turning from the stove, she went out through the swinging door and through the pantry to the dining room. Mr. Lappala, broad-shouldered and big-nosed, sat with knife and fork in hand. He was the last of the guests to get their breakfast for the day. His white hair hung in clumps from his head, and his ironically long ears were almost totally deaf. She set the plate in front of him and before she could step back he had already cut off a huge chunk of meat and shoved it into his mouth. Minnie nodded politely and returned to the steaming kitchen. When she closed her eyes she could imagine she was with her father and mother back in the sauna in Eräjärvi, where the sky seemed always blue and the water always clear.

Benjamin cooed from the doorway and began banging a spoon against the wall. Minnie took it from him without a word. He was a cute boy, and the spitting image of his father. But life with a two year old, by herself, was difficult. Mrs. Merritt helped, as did the other ladies who worked in the boarding house. But still, Benjamin needed his father. And she missed her husband, missed his warm embrace. She reached out and picked up her son and smiled at him.

"Mama," he said.

"*Äiti*," she said.

The boarding house was a safe and secure place to live, and nice enough. And there were a lot of good women here. Mrs. Merritt—Hephzibah—was kind and patient and tender both with Minnie and Benjamin. But Minnie was forced to do what little she could to create a Finnish connection, and told him stories at night in Finnish and read to him from the Finnish bible she had brought across the ocean. This was life, and while she wished for some things, she was mostly happy.

From outside came the familiar wail of a horn indicating another ship coming into harbor. So much industry, she thought, and such a crowded, dirty place. The summer sky filled with smoke. Streets were littered with trash and filth, and the alley behind the house was basically an open sewer. She wondered how anyone could live like this, could want to live like this.

Lake Superior in winter was windy, treacherous, and icy. In summer, the harbor clogged with hulking cargo vessels carrying timber and oil and other cargo to and from Cleveland and Chicago. Minnie was surprised by how careless people were in keeping cargo out of the water—so much of it spilled into the lake that the water by the docks was tinged black.

Benjamin seemed to like the spoon in his hand, so she put him on the floor and gave him a small pot to stir. The pot was empty, but Benjamin didn't know that, or at least didn't care. He smiled when his mother handed it to him and then began to clang the spoon around the pot. Minnie smiled. Arvid would be happy when he met his son for the first time, she thought.

She stepped through the pantry, grabbed a pot of coffee, and went into the dining room where Mr. Lappala was finishing his eggs. "*Kahvi?*" she asked him in Finnish. He nodded. She filled his cup and took his plate back to the kitchen.

Some of the miners who passed through Duluth, either coming from Tower or heading to it, spoke very little English. Most, none at all. That was a benefit to having Minnie in the house for Hephzibah: She could appeal to a wider range of guests than just the English-speaking ones she had always catered to, and it furthered her reputation as being a welcoming, safe, God-loving household.

The guests were generally quiet young men who worked hard and sent all the money they could to their families back home. Yet Duluth was a wild place still. Eight months out of the year young men came through on trains or boats or wagons, and visited the dozens of saloons that catered to adventure-seekers. For many of them it was the first time they had ever had a drink in their lives.

When word spread about a new iron discovery northwest of Duluth, the speculators began to come through. These were rough men with little more than a shovel and a crazed belief that each of them would find a pot of iron and would make a fortune. Many stayed just one night in the boarding house, for they were all on their way to something else, something bigger, something better; the Merritt boarding house was just a way station, a pit stop, on the way to the riches men sought in the northern woods.

Hephzibah, a temperate woman who raised all her children under the guidance of the Old Testament, believed many of these men were destined for ruin. Minnie did not see the world quite so cut-and-dried, but she did appreciate the temperate nature of the Merritt boarding house.

She took the plate to the kitchen and washed it in the soap-filled sink, then wiped it dry with a cloth. "*Lähetään*, Ben," she said. *Let's go.*

He followed behind as she climbed the back stairs and went along the stairwell landing to her room. It was just big enough for a bed, a small dressing table and desk, and a wardrobe. Arvid had built the wardrobe, and when Hephzibah saw it she asked him to build one for each of the guest rooms to replace the paper-lined shelves mounted to the walls in each room. Minnie both loved and hated the wardrobes—they reminded her both of Arvid and of his departure. It had been the construction of the wardrobes that had brought the attention of Lon, which had been the beginning of Arvid's trek north and their long separation.

Minnie put Benjamin up on the bed and then turned to the dressing table. A small mirror hung on the wall above the water bowl. She reached behind her head and pulled out three pins that were holding two long braids in place. Then she untied the braids. Her white-blonde hair fell over her shoulders and down her back. From the dressing table she took a porcelain brush that had been her mother's, the black bristles the same ones that had brushed her mother's hair on the night of her parents' wedding. It was all she had left to remind her of them.

Maria Riiski had come to America with her parents when she was just sixteen years old, back in 1886. They had come through New York, but Paavo Riiski had saved enough money that they got immediately onto a train bound for the west, and they had not stopped moving until they reached Minneapolis. It was there that hardship became disaster. They had used all their money to get there, and found themselves penniless in Minneapolis in November. Paavo Riiski took work in one of the flour mills operating on the banks of the Mississippi. Hilda Riiski found a room in a boarding house that was cheap enough for them to save money. Minnie's mother got a job as a barmaid in the saloon attached to the rooming house, and Minnie herself helped in the kitchen.

They worked throughout the winter and in the spring Paavo Riiski rented a horse and rode west. Forty miles outside of Minneapolis he found a piece of land to homestead. He staked his claim and registered it at the land office, and then Minnie and her mother joined him on a journey to the land they would call home. Paavo built a temporary sod cabin covered with grasses, which would serve until he could build a larger, more permanent home.

The opportunity never came. One month after they arrived, as the three of them were in the fields digging rocks out of the earth in preparation for planting crops, the sky turned an eerie shade of green. Balls of ice pelted and bruised Minnie's arms and face and splashed in the troughs. Paavo led them into their sod hut and forced Minnie under the heavy bed for protection. Pressure built up in Minnie's ears. Lying on her stomach, she looked out across the floor of the room. Her parents huddled together in a corner. Her mother asked, "What is it?" Her father said he did not know. Then Minnie felt a wall of pressure sucking at her and then the walls of the hut were ripped apart.

Instead of staring across the dirt floor at her parents, she stared across the dirt floor at the field. She screamed, but the sound of her voice was lost in the wind tearing at everything. Debris filled the air, shards of wood, chunks of the sod exterior of the cabin. Seconds after it started, the sound ended. All went quiet.

Minnie crawled out from under the bed to find that almost exactly half of the house was gone, as though an unseen hand had sliced right through the middle of the cabin and taken away the side where her parents had been crouched.

She was miles from the nearest farm. Cold and hungry and scared, she called out for her parents, but they did not answer. One moment she had seen them holding each other and the next moment they were gone. She searched, walking the land, calling out their names. All she got in return was an eerie silence. Not even birds chirped in the aftermath of the wind that ripped apart her life.

She built a fire and, finding a bag of flour, managed to bake some bread. For two days she searched, walked in every direction for an hour and then back, always calling for them, watching the ground for them. Near the end of the second day she saw something in a shallow valley southwest of the cabin. When she got closer big black birds with wings as long as she was tall, jumped away. She did not recognize the body—most of it had been eaten away—but she knew the dress the body wore.

She began walking east that day, back towards Minneapolis. She walked until the stars came out and she stumbled over a rock and then she slept. When the sun crept up she stood and kept walking. Eventually she found a road, two dusty ruts through the long fields of grass, and she followed that. Soon a wagon came up behind her. A man in a black suit with a white shirt was driving. He stopped and spoke to her. She was disoriented and tired and saw his lips move but could not understand him. He spoke again. This time in Finnish. Her clothes were tattered, but she carried with her the porcelain brush she had picked up from the wreck of her home.

"There was a great wind," she told him. "My parents are gone."

He nodded. "Where are you going?" he said, in English.

"Minneapolis," she said.

"I can take you," he said.

He made a bed for her in the back of the wagon using a blanket. She lay down and fell asleep with the rocking of the wagon. When she opened her eyes she was lying down on a real bed. A man stood over her. It was the pastor at the Finnish Lutheran Church her family had attended for the six months they were in Minneapolis.

"Child," the reverend said. "What happened to you?"

She told him the story, of the homestead and of the wind that came and tore half the house. Of searching for her parents, and of the birds flying away from the dress in the grass. The pastor gave her a bed in the church where she lived until she met Arvid six months later at a church picnic.

❯◆❮

Minnie tried not to think about her parents. After she recovered from the shock of their loss, she knew that what they would want was for her to move forward, to live her life. Still she knew she could never live on the prairie again, and when she met Arvid, she told him that the only place she could live would be in the woods or in the city. Arvid had agreed; he wanted to live in the woods.

It was the shared past of losing parents that connected the two of them. Arvid feared his past and had been trying to run from it. Minnie, saddened by it, refused to dwell on her loss, though, and refused to let it affect the rest of her life.

Minnie was on the one hundredth brush of her hair when there was a light tap on her door.

"Yes?" she said. She spoke English as much as possible.

"Minnie, dear," Hephzibah said. "There is a man in the parlor to see you."

She stood and opened the door. Hephzibah, at nearly eighty years old, was thin and had skin as fragile as onion paper, but she maneuvered about the big house with the energy and confidence of a woman half her age.

Minnie said, "A man? Do I know him?"

Hephzibah smiled and gently patted Minnie's arm. "Do not worry, dear. I know him. Please, come."

She left her door open so she could hear Benjamin if he began to cry. As she descended the steps, she braided her blonde hair and wrapped it into a proper bun on her head, then donned a bonnet that was hanging on a peg by the kitchen door.

Hephzibah led her to the front parlor, a beautifully appointed room with two red velvet couches that faced each other in front of a fireplace. Drawn curtains kept the sunlight from damaging the furniture; four kerosene lamps in the corners glowed to compensate. An Indian stood in a darkened corner.

Hephzibah, sensing Minnie's surprise, said, "This is an old friend of our family. Charlie, this is Mrs. Maria Maki."

He wore leather pants and a brightly colored woolen jacket and his long black hair was tied in a neat braid. His wrinkled face belied no emotion, and his eyes were dark and unblinking. "*Hei,*" he said. "*Minun nimeni on Charlie.*" *My name is Charlie.*

Minnie caught her breath. "*Puhutko suomea?*" *Do you speak Finnish?*

"Niigaaniimitig teach me."

She turned to Hephzibah. "I do not understand."

Hephzibah shrugged. "Neither do I, dear. Charlie, what do you mean?"

Charlie produced a folded letter. "Niigaaniimitig," he said. "Arvid Mäkelä."

Minnie crossed the room to the bright lamp on the desk and opened the letter. She recognized the handwriting.

Dearest Minnie,

I am glad that you are being treated well at Mrs. Merritt's boarding house. The roomers there are lucky to taste your cooking. Have you made them your *kalakeitto*? The cook here, Housell, makes his own fish stew, but it pales in comparison to yours.

Mountain Iron grows. We now have about sixty men in camp, though Lon has assured me that more men will arrive soon. I should hope there will be some Finns among them, as only a fellow Finn would appreciate the starkness of this place. It is just like home. Lon has put me in charge of the camp. I am, at times, overwhelmed, but so far the work has kept my mind from dwelling on how much I miss you.

I believe it is time you and Ben joined me here. When you arrive there will be work in the kitchen. I am including a list of provisions we shall need, and you may add whatever goods you would require. Charlie has become a good friend to me and has agreed to assist you in any way you need, including guiding you on the trail to Mountain Iron.

I miss you terribly and eagerly await your arrival. The trees sway in a gentle breeze, and as they rub together I swear they speak your name.

With love,
Arvid

There was a second page to the letter, containing a list of items that she was to obtain: horse and wagon, winter clothing, flour, spices, seeds for the garden, pots and pans, cutlery, plates and cups, knives, other assorted goods. She held the letter and the list close to her chest. Finally! she thought.

Hephzibah said, "What does it say?"

"It is from Arvid," she said. "He wants Ben and I to come." She turned to Charlie. "When can we leave?"

Charlie, unmoving, occupied the space as though the room was not there. "Tomorrow, if you are ready."

"I may be able to be ready tomorrow." She again read down the list. There was a lot to buy, and in two years in Duluth she had never been to the market. "If I can obtain all this." She wondered, too, if all the money Arvid had been sending to her would be enough.

"We go when you are ready," he said.

She turned to Hephzibah. It struck her that she should ask for leave from her job.

As though sensing Minnie's inner voice, Hephzibah smiled. "You will be hard to replace, Minnie, but I shall not keep you here another day. You are free to go when you wish."

From upstairs she heard Benjamin cry. She waited. After a moment he quieted again. "He does that sometimes. Cries and then goes back to sleep. Bad dreams maybe."

"Dreams are gifts from the grandfathers," Charlie said. "They tell us much."

"I have dreamed of the woods for days," she said.

He looked down at her. "Tomorrow, then."

"And if I'm not ready?"

"Day after," he said.

She looked at the list Arthur had sent. She would need time to get everything. If she started now she might be ready in a few days. "I'll need time," she said.

Hephzibah said, "I'm sure Charlie can help with your purchases."

The idea of wandering through town with this strange man worried her. It felt improper, as though she were being somehow unfaithful. She had heard, too, the stories: The natives were savages and killers and drunks and liars. They burned down homesteads and stole children from their parents. They killed men and raped women then took them for their wives. They refused to remain on the reservations and fought with the military who were protecting settlers. They drank until they fell down in the streets. They had to be controlled, corralled, imprisoned and fought. Yet here was one who had befriended her husband, who was a friend to Mrs. Merritt. Who had learned Finnish, if even a little bit. If ever she could trust an Indian, wouldn't it be he?

"Would you help?" Hephzibah asked him.

Minnie felt Arvid's letter crinkle in her hand. He would not have sent this man if he did not trust him. The quiet Indian was so still Minnie thought that if she closed her eyes he might disappear. As though he were not there at all. He seemed uncomfortable in this place. He stared at the room as though it were a foreign language or a strange country in a far away land. As foreign to him as the woods of Mountain Iron would be to her. And then at once she saw it. She understood the similarities between them. He was not a savage to be feared. He was a foreigner, just like her, in a place he understood no better than she. Once she saw that she knew she would get along with this man who would take her to her husband.

She looked at him eagerly, her eyes searching his blank expression. "I know that you must prepare yourself. I only ask for a few hours."

Finally he nodded. "I return tomorrow."

And then he walked through the parlor and out the front door.

Minnie turned to Hephzibah. "He will return?"

Hephzibah nodded. "He is a good man, dear. Trust him. Now, let us go and pack your things. You have a long journey ahead of you."

⟢•◇•⟣

Charlie arrived at ten the next morning as Minnie was finishing cleaning up the kitchen from breakfast. She changed quickly into a pink-and-white-checked gingham dress with matching sunbonnet she had made from fabric Hephzibah had given her. Downstairs she kissed Benjamin goodbye and thanked Mrs. Merritt again for agreeing to watch him for a few hours. She found Charlie on the front porch staring out at the rain.

"*Hei*," she said.

"*Hei*," Charlie said.

She wrapped a woolen rain shawl over her shoulders and clasped it at her neck. On a clear day she could see Superior across the bay. Today the rain brought a gray ceiling down over the dirty, putrid city of Duluth. Even after three years Minnie did not like the place. When it rained, Duluth's streets became a river of fetid mud and human waste flowing down the ditches toward the rail yards, where it was channeled into the bay. White steam and smoke from trains crept along the water and drifted into the massed rainclouds.

As Minnie and Charlie stepped off the porch and made their way towards the shops on First Street, she avoided the deep puddles while Charlie walked a straight path no matter what stood in his way, wading through mud and sewage and rainwater runoff.

Minnie pinched her nose against the smell but Charlie seemed not to notice. "Did my husband teach you Finnish?" she asked.

"*Joo*. What he not teach me I learn with my ear."

"You learn well."

"To survive we must all learn."

"What is your real name?" she said.

He stopped. Rain drizzled down his face from his wet hair. "Wiigwaasgewinini," he said. "People here, they not understand.

They call me Charlie.”

She said, “It does not roll off my Finnish tongue easily. Wigwasgewinini.”

He walked away from her. “You call me Charlie. It is easier.”

She doubled her pace to keep up with him. “What was that you called my husband yesterday?“

He said, “Niigaaniimitig.”

“What does it mean?”

“Leader of trees,” he said.

They turned on First Street where they were greeted by a mass of men coming off the train that had just pulled into the depot— men in denim overalls and wool pants, or in rubber rain gear and leather Mackintoshes. Carriages pulled by horses lined one side of the dirt street, taking on the wealthy passenger who could afford a dry carriage ride to their stately mansions in the Heights. The rest of the men carried their possessions in duffels thrown over shoulders or packsacks hung heavy off their backs, mercy straps mercifully unstrapped. Those who had experience brought tools—picks and shovels and maybe an axe lashed to the packsack. Others, the ones who had not only just arrived in Minnesota but probably just arrived in the United States, carried small duffels that sagged around the empty space inside. This was the influx of workers: timber beasts, lumbermen, dockworkers, diggers, loaders, builders, and, most important, miners. Word was spreading about the Merritt discoveries, and Duluth was the gateway to a new iron range.

Charlie did not stop to look at the newcomers, as if he already knew the greed and callousness he would see in their faces. He walked with purpose, straight to the door to Marshall’s General Store. Inside a balding man in a white shirt and black tie pressed his belly against the counter. His skin and face reminded Minnie of a pig’s. From her blouse she removed the list Arvid had sent. The money he had been sending her was wrapped in a sheet of butcher paper and stuffed inside her corset. “I have a list of items,” she began, but the shopkeeper cut her off.

“Is he with you?“

She looked up from the paper in her hand. Charlie was a statue behind her, hands at his sides. “Ch-Charlie?” she stammered. “Yes.”

“I don’t allow them in m’store.”

"Them?"

The fat man leaned back. His upper lip curled as though he were smelling the sewage outside. "Them's savages."

"I do not understand."

"I'm just sayin' I'll get your stuff but he's got to go." He glared past her and raised his voice as he spoke to Charlie, pointing at the door with a pudgy finger. "You understand? I help the lady when you get out."

Minnie folded the list along the creases that were already there. She slipped it inside the cuff of her sleeve. "No need," she said. And then she walked out the door. Outside she followed the boardwalk. She did not need to look to know that Charlie was behind her, that he would be behind her, that he would not leave her side until she was safely with Arvid.

A crowd gathered in front of a building across the street. A clapboard sign mounted on a wooden porch read Biwabik Mining Company.

"Biwabik," Charlie said. "Lon honors us."

"Is that how they treat you?" she asked him, but he said nothing and the blank expression on his face gave her little clue as to his inner thoughts.

Three doors down she entered Miller's Dry Goods. Charlie followed her inside and again stood like a statue behind her. The man behind the counter was a wisp of a man with a gray beard. He drummed his bony fingers on a case of guns and knives. "Can I help you?" Flecks of tobacco stuck between his teeth.

She removed the list from her cuff. "Can you fill this order?"

He took the paper from her and read it. "I have all this, yes, ma'am." The spittoon on the counter rang. He narrowed his eyes. "You take all this now?"

"No. I come tomorrow with wagon," she said.

"I'll have it ready. Shall I expect you or him?"

"Either of us," she said.

"Yes, ma'am."

"Would you need money now?"

He shook his head. "On delivery."

"Thank you," she said.

She walked to the door. The shopkeeper said, "You ever want to sell him you let me know. I could use something to clean the barn."

She stopped at the door. "I do not understand."

"God damned town is filling up with foreigners. Don't mind you folks so much, but these savages just got to go—"

But Minnie was already striding across the planked floor. She snatched her list out of his fingers. "Is there no one in this horrid city who has anything but hatred in his heart?"

She stormed onto the boardwalk. A waterfall poured off the eave and drizzled down into the sewer ditch below. Charlie followed her.

"You are nothing like Arthur Maki," Charlie said. "Niigaaniimitig keeps voice low. You speak what your heart says."

She wiped her eyes. "And you are *itsepäinen*. Stubborn, like the mule."

He smiled. "We begin to understand. Like the eagle and the bear."

She shook her head.

"The eagle sits high in the tree. He watches the ground for prey. Waiting. He does not move, watches and waits. He may wait for days. Then he sees the mouse and quietly he spreads his wings and flies down from the tree. The mouse only knows what has happened to him when he is in the air.

"The bear needs no sneak attack. The bear rises on two legs and cries out, teeth bared, claws long and ready. The bear chases her prey. She lets it known that she is there, hunting, attacking. Hungry. This is how she protects her den and feeds her cubs.

"The bear and the eagle. Both must eat to survive."

Across the street the line of workers outside the iron company office building stretched almost all the way back to the train depot.

Charlie said, "They come to Mesabi. To wake the giant."

"Giant?"

"The giant in the hills."

"Do you mean the iron?"

"The giant sleeps in the hills. Those men—" he pointed to the line of men— "will wake him. When they do the land will change. It will no longer be a place for me. So I go back to my people."

"Will you not go with me to Mountain Iron?"

"I go with you, then go on. My home is beyond Mesabi."

They began to walk. "I still need supplies," she said.

He led her along the muddy alley between the buildings.

Second Street had no walkway, just a graded road with an open sewer pit. He let her into a drab, damp storefront. Gray light drizzled through a grimy window. A leaky roof had ruined the warped floor. The rotting shelves were bare of goods save a few tins of tobacco. The earthy scent of moss filled the room like smoke. A book sat opened on a wooden podium, a white-and-blue-striped shawl hanging from the corner of the tabletop. From behind a curtain a man emerged. A black box was strapped to his head, and a black strap stretched down and around his arm. A brimless cap barely covered his balding head, while his beard stretched to his chest. When he saw Minnie and Charlie his eyes seemed to pop out of his head.

"Charlie!" He stretched his arms wide. "*Boozhoo, niiji. Biindigen. Biindigen!* Come, come!"

A flicker of a smile crossed Charlie's face. "*Boozhoo*, Eli."

The two men shook hands.

"You have come to visit me again. And you bring a friend. Hello, hello. I am Eli Samuels." He offered Minnie his hand. His skin was warm and dry.

"Maria Maki," she said.

"So pleased to meet you, Mrs. Maki. You must be quite shocked with my appearance. I assure you this is not the way I dress normally."

Charlie stepped over to the podium. "You read your book?"

"Yes, Charlie, yes. I read my book today." His face crinkled when he smiled. "Charlie has joined me in reading from the Torah many times. He is a good man."

Minnie said, "I am starting to see that."

A gust of wind blew a sheet of rain against the glass. Water spurted through cracks between panes and in the wood. "Oy, this rain." He threw a canvas sheet over the window well as though this alone would stop the water. "My windows are like the colander. My wife tells me to repair it, but I tell her, I am a shopkeeper, not a carpenter!" He laughed and Minnie couldn't help but laugh with him. He dropped the cloth to the floor and stuffed it against the wall under the window. "That should soak up much of it. Now, you did not come here to hear me kvetch. How may I help you?"

Charlie said, "We need supplies."

"Of course, my friend, of course. Anything at all. Let me get this off." He unwound the leather strap from his arm and removed the box from his head, setting the apparatus on the rotted counter. From a pocket of his suit jacket he removed a small notebook and a pencil.

Charlie nodded to Minnie. The list had been crumpled in her hand. She straightened it as best she could and handed it to Eli.

"Mm-hmm, yes. I can get these things. Not today, though. As you can see I keep very little here. Tomorrow, perhaps?"

She said, "Tomorrow is fine."

"Good, good," the little man said. "I will take good care of you."

"Thank you," she said.

"Any friend of Charlie's is a friend of mine."

"*Nimiigwechiwi'aa*," Charlie said.

"You are most welcome, most welcome," Eli said. "May I ask, where are you going?"

"Mesabi," Charlie said. "They call the place Mountain Iron."

"Ah, the iron giant. Seems to be a lot of activity up there." He folded the list and placed it in his breast pocket. "I have seen the men coming off the trains. And I have myself outfitted more than one expedition. They are all looking for the next Biwabik."

"You have heard?" Charlie said.

"The whole world knows, my dear boy. The talk at the Spalding is Mesabi, Mesabi, Mesabi. You'd think everyone was turning Chippewa the way they throw the word around." He laughed again. As he talked he waved his arms around his head as though the mere thought of iron excited him. "It can only mean good things for this area. They say the ore there is purer than any found in Vermilion. And that it can be mined with nothing more than a shovel."

Charlie nodded. "I have seen this," he said.

"Then it's true!" Eli said. "There is much money to be made there?"

Charlie nodded. "Yes. Much."

Eli smiled. "Maybe I should invest. We have some money stashed away." He stroked his beard. "I will talk to my wife. She is in charge."

Charlie said, "We return tomorrow."

Eli stared thoughtfully out the window as the rain continued to fall. "Yes, yes. Tomorrow."

Past the saloons and hotels, they came to a stable. Smoke billowed from a sheltered fire pit outside. A big man, round belly, black beard and mustache, brought a red hot horseshoe out of the fire, set it on an anvil and banged it with a hammer. He beat it twice then turned it over and hit it again. Then he dipped it in a bucket of water.

The man pulled off a pair of goggles.

"*Guten tag.*"

Charlie said, "We need horses and a wagon."

"*Pferd und Wagen?*"

Charlie held up two fingers. Was there any language this man didn't know a little of, Minnie thought?

"*Zwei pferd?*"

Charlie nodded.

"*Kommen,*" the man said.

Charlie turned to Minnie. "He wants us to go with him."

His barn had more than two dozen stalls lining both sides, including more than a dozen horses. He motioned for Minnie and Charlie to follow him into one of the stalls. The two horses were huge beasts, standing at least two feet taller than the liveryman himself, and he was already at least a foot taller than Minnie. The horses were both brown, one with a white patch between his eyes and down his nose. The other was all brown except for a patch of black around his left eye.

Charlie ran his hand along first the horse with the black eye. He felt each leg and examined each hoof. When he was done with the first he moved to the second one, and again he ran his hands along the horse's flanks, and then down each leg, examining closely each hoof. When he was done he said, "Needs a shoe." He lifted the hind leg and the stable owner bent down and looked.

"*Ja, ja.* I fix."

Charlie looked at Minnie and nodded.

Minnie said, "How about a wagon?"

He showed them two buckboard wagons parked behind the barn. Charlie examined each wagon carefully, looking at the wheels and the axle between each. Minnie watched him from within the barn, while the owner stood in front of the wagons, rain drizzling down his back. When Charlie was done, he put his hand on the wagon on the right. He motioned a half circle with his hands and the tall man nodded. Charlie seemed to like this one. He pointed to a field of cows in the rain and held up two fingers, then pointed to himself. The stable owner nodded. "Tomorrow?" Charlie said. The stable man nodded again.

Charlie turned to Minnie. "Good wagon. He cover it for you. Protection from rain."

"Why did you point to the cows?" she said.

"Cows for me. For my home."

"I had hoped we could leave tomorrow."

Charlie shook his head. "If done early, maybe."

Minnie and Charlie walked side-by-side down an alley and back to First Street. She felt lighter as she walked. Everything was done, and now all she needed to do was load all her things into her new wagon and drive north. Charlie strode purposefully next to her. All her trepidation of the day before washed away with the rain that continued to fall. It had all gone so much more smoothly than she expected, and now all her thoughts were of seeing Arvid again.

A line of men waited outside the Biwabik mining office. As one man exited, clutching a paper ticket in his hand, another entered. Now that a job had been found, it was time to get to work, and once a man exited he made his way back to the train depot. Some turned the other way, towards Duluth, and stopped inside the nearest saloon to celebrate.

She and Charlie walked past the saloons and hotels, most of which were nothing more than brothels, the rooms rented by the hour. Cheers erupted from within; music clanged from tinny pianos. Glass broke. A man stumbled backwards out of one of the saloons, pants around his knees. He tripped at the top step and landed on his back in a puddle of mud. A man in a white apron came out and yelled, "Don't come back 'til you can pay, you fucking bum." A woman in a red and black dress took one step out the front door and looked down at the man in the street then threw a bottle at his chest. He lay down in the mud, rain pelting him.

Minnie stayed close to Charlie. She didn't trust men who drank. They were rude, rough and, sometimes, dangerous. She was glad to be leaving this place behind, this barroom of a town.

As they passed the swinging door of a saloon a man stumbled out and bumped into Minnie. "Pardon me, ma'am," he said, lifting the tip of his broad brimmed hat. He wobbled backwards and ran into another man emerging. The two men had the same gray eyes and crooked nose, and looked like brothers.

"Watch where you're walking, Ned," the second one barked.

Charlie took Minnie's arm and pulled her quickly to his side.

"I was just trying to get out of the way o' this pretty lady," Ned said.

Beneath each of their long leather coats Minnie caught the glint of silver revolvers strapped to their belts.

"Why didn't you say so?" the second one said. "Pardon my little brother, miss. He can be a rude cur at times. Our mother beat him too much." He laughed, his mouth full of black teeth and gaps where teeth used to be. His breath reeked of whiskey.

Ned slapped his brother on the arm. "You cut it out, Danny. I can whip you any day."

Charlie pulled Minnie and they began to walk away. But the brothers followed them.

"We didn't mean to drive you off, ma'am," the one called Danny said.

"Hey," Ned said. "I seen her first."

"Shut up," Danny said.

Charlie moved faster and Minnie moved with him. Charlie told her, "If we get separated go to the mining office. Biwabik. Look for Lon."

"Don't leave me," she said.

Ned jumped off the boardwalk and splashed through the mud to get in front of them. "Hey, I was talking to you, pretty lady," he sneered and took hold of her wrist.

Charlie grabbed Ned's arm and pulled him off of her. Minnie stepped backwards and bumped into Danny.

"Hey," Danny said. "My brother was just tryin' to be friendly."

Charlie turned to her. "Go."

"No one's talkin' to you, savage. We was talking to her." Danny backed Minnie against the wooden storefront, his dirty face in hers. "Savage there seems to think he owns you. How much did he pay?"

Charlie let go of Ned and pushed Danny away from Minnie. The two men sprang at him, each one grabbing an arm. Charlie tried to twist free, but the men wrenched his arms until he collapsed to his knees.

"Got him," Ned said.

"Let's go teach this boy some manners," Danny said. "Your kind done killed enough of my friends, I think it's time to get a little retribution. As for you, ma'am," he added. "My brother an' I will make sure he don't bother you again."

The other one cackled. "Then we can come back and get our ree-ward."

Pulling at his arms, the two men led Charlie down the alley.

"Go," Charlie said again.

Minnie barely had time to register what was happening. Ignoring Charlie's plea, she turned to the small crowd that had gathered. "Help, someone!" she pleaded. "Those men are dragging him away."

A man in a gray suit and crusher said, "Best to just let them have him. At least you are out of their sights."

"What will they do with him?" she said.

But the man just shrugged and walked away.

The men in line at the mining office had begun to pay attention to what was going on. Minnie rushed across the street. "Help, please, Mr. Merritt," she called. "Come quickly."

In the alley, Charlie let the two brothers push him toward the brick-walled saloon. Then he yanked himself free of Ned's grip and swung the younger man into the older one. The two men careened into the wall and then down into the mud. Minnie's breath caught in her throat—Charlie stared at them for half a second, as though expecting them to get up, and when they did not he disappeared around the corner.

Lon Merritt emerged from inside the mining building. Minnie rushed to him. He wore a vest and the sleeves of his white shirt were folded up to his elbows.

"Mrs. Maki?" he said. "Was that you?"

Panting she said, "Charlie."

"Chippewa Charlie?" he said.

She nodded. "Two men." She turned. In the alley Ned and Danny were gone. She scanned the street. A dozen miners were making their way back to the train depot. Suddenly, Minnie spotted Charlie emerge from between two buildings and try to blend in with the crowd. He stood taller than most everyone else, and he was the only one with leather clothing and long black hair.

"There," she said, pointing. He was a hundred yards away moving swiftly toward the train depot.

Lon called, "Charlie!"

Ned and Danny came from behind another building then and began scanning the crowd. They were both covered in mud and if not for the frantic and angry look on their faces Minnie might have thought the scene comical. They eyed the crowd.

Before she could stop him, Lon called again, "Charlie!" He started along the street toward the depot.

"There," Ned said, and the brothers began to chase after the Indian. Lon moved swiftly, but he did not see Ned and Danny closing fast. Ned jumped down from the sidewalk onto the street while his brother ran along the boardwalk, knocking over anyone in his way. "Move, move!" he shouted as he ran.

Passersby stopped and turned to look. Only Charlie continued to walk. Ned caught up to him and spun him around. Minnie caught the glint of steel as Charlie brandished his knife.

Lon broke into a run.

She saw the flash of the muzzle and the smoke rise from the gun before she heard the shot.

Charlie froze for a moment, then crumpled.

"Charlie!" Minnie shouted.

The miners and other men who had gathered to watch moved away quickly, afraid to be caught at the scene of a murder.

Danny darted through the crowd. He pushed his little brother back and then knelt down next to Charlie. Minnie watched as he rifled through Charlie's jacket and pulled out a wad of bills and showed them to Ned, then flashed the money to the crowd. "Damned thief!" he announced.

Ned stood back and stared down at the body in the mud, gun dangling from his finger.

Then Lon was there. He brushed the two men aside like flies

then knelt over Charlie. When he stood up there was blood on his hands. He reached for Ned but the young man lifted his gun. Danny flashed the wad of bills.

"*Voi luoja,*" Minnie cried. *Oh my god.*

A sheriff appeared in a big brown hat, gold star on the collar of his brown Mackintosh. He pushed the three men away from the body and then knelt down. After a moment he stood up and held out his hand. Danny handed over the money. The sheriff flipped through it and then handed the wad of cash back to Danny. Then he pushed his hat up on his head and stared down at the body in the street. Lon spoke, pointing to Minnie standing in front of the mining office. Danny shook the wad of cash again. Lon took a step toward Danny and the sheriff stopped him. Finally, the sheriff shook his head. The sky darkened then and rain again began to fall. The sheriff walked the two men away, leaving the body in the street. Lon removed his vest and laid it over Charlie's face. Then he walked through the rain back to Minnie standing in the doorway of the mining office. His shirt and pants were wet.

"Come inside. I think we have some coffee." His voice was hollow, like the echo in a mineshaft. He brought her upstairs and led her to a small office. Minnie sat in a plain wooden chair in front of a desk. Her dress was wet and she shivered though she wasn't cold. Lon smeared his bloody hands on a handkerchief. Minnie stared at it as he folded it and stuffed it into his pocket. "*Nibowin,*" Lon said. "He is dead."

"What happened?"

"They say he stole the money. That he was running away."

Minnie shook her head. "It was his money. He was helping me," she said. "Those men attacked him." She felt her heart beat faster with the rage.

Lon nodded. "People here hold a lot of prejudice against the natives. They think they know, but really they fear what they do not understand."

"What about those men? What will happen to them?"

"Probably nothing. The sheriff believes them, I think."

She stood up. "But I saw them!" She slammed the desk top.

Lon shook his head. "I do not think there is anything that can be done," he said.

Minnie began to sob. She looked down at her dress, as if the answer to it all were there, in the patterned mud that stained it. The hatred of this city, of this place, lying in the street outside.

Lon sat down and stared across the room. "Charlie was a good friend. I have known him since I began cruising for timber more than fifteen years ago." His voice trailed off.

She felt her outrage drift away like a feather. "I'm sorry," she said. Slumped in his chair Lon Merritt seemed smaller somehow, as though the giant she had always known him to be suddenly became a man. She knew how he felt. She was reminded of when her parents were swept away, of the shock of their disappearance. There was no chance to say goodbye. Death was like that, she thought.

And then at once her stomach felt empty and she fell into the chair. She thought of Arvid, and she wondered how she would get to him now that Charlie was dead. How would she find the camp? With the fear came a wave of guilt. A man lay dead in the street and all I can think of is that he won't be able to help me? I am no better than those men out there, she thought, no better than the men who gunned him down.

Lon said, "I know of your plan to move to the mine. Charlie was going to take you?"

She nodded. The pit in her stomach grew.

"I have a supply train going in a few days. I'll make arrangements for you to join it."

She began to cry. "Thank you," she said.

Leonidas Merritt stared across the desk at her, his face in shadow. "We must go on," he said.

CHAPTER 6

YSTÄVÄ

Arthur wiped sweat from his forehead and then swung his axe again. He had hit a knot in this tree, and his axe had grown dull. The day was warmer than a late September day should be, a warm fall sun beating down on the ever-expanding camp and mine clearing, and he was working in just his undershirt and overalls. The yarrow poultice was no match for the day's blackflies and mosquitoes.

He brought the axe down at an angle and chips of white ash sprayed the muddy ground. Sweat dripped off his forehead but he did not pause his axe nor did he tire. Normally Arthur loved felling trees. It was relaxing work that freed his mind from worry; the only thing he thought of was the swing of the axe. He had always been strong and could chop at trees all day—but at no time in his life would his strength be greater than it was on these range-clearing days.

Today was different, though. Today his mind wandered. As he heard the tree give its familiar creak he stepped back to check his line and thought of Minnie and Charlie. His friend had gone to Duluth two weeks ago. The journey to and from Duluth might take several days, a week at most, so Arthur had figured that Minnie would have arrived by now. But still there was no sign of her. The mail from Duluth, brought by Wilbur on horseback, brought no news, either. The last message Arthur had received from Johnnie said they should expect another train of supplies and men to arrive in September. Maybe Minnie would be with that group.

"Timber!" Arthur called, and he pushed the tree with one foot and the eighty-foot trunk, as big around as Housell's belly, crashed against the forest floor. Using a smaller hatchet and a billhook he limbed the tree, working quickly to have it ready for skidding to the sawmill storage lake a hundred yards away. That sawmill whirred and ground and screamed from sunrise until sunset and for the most part drowned out the other noises in town, except the occasional dynamite blast set off by Captain Gill.

Leonard Halley turned out to be a jovial fellow with broad shoulders, wide face, and big personality to match. He took over operation of the sawmill from Richardson with a smile. "You picked a great place for the mill," he said. "The water makes for easy operation. And you've got so many logs in there I may not get through them all before winter sets."

Richardson's shoulder was still in a sling, and so he became Leonard's assistant at the sawmill. He lamented his useless right arm, and at night Arthur would often find him wandering drunk in the woods. Arthur helped the lumberman to the sauna where the heat cleansed them both. One night Richardson, lying on his back with his arm dangling like the broken branch from a felled pine, said, "I'm not getting better. The pain is still there. I can't swing the axe like I used to."

"You are great help at the mill."

"Barely. I need Halley to help me with the larger logs most days."

Arthur said, "You will get better in time."

"You are a good man, Arthur. I look forward to meeting this wife of yours."

"She is beautiful and kind. I have not seen her in two years. I have never seen my son."

"How old is he?"

"Two and a half years."

"He was born while you lived in Tower?"

"*Joo*, yes."

The charred embers of the fire popped and the rocks sizzled when Arthur poured a little more water. Richardson stood and swayed on his feet. "When the next group of workers come I may not stay," he said.

Arthur said nothing. He had been expecting the news. "Where will you go?"

"With Charlie back to our people. My people." He went to the door. "Maybe it is the work, the giant waking." He shook his head. "I feel like I lost something here. Like some part of me is gone."

Arthur understood the feeling. The hillside was becoming increasingly bare of trees, a result of all the wood needed for building the camp and clearing space for the mine. But there was something more changing out there, something deeper. The character of the place was changing, too. It was crowded, and noisy. The sawmill buzzed most days, and the mine churned all day and all night. Every couple of days Gill set off a blast that shook the buildings. During mealtimes the men no longer talked together; they had formed groups, cliques of men who spoke the same language and didn't converse with the others. Maybe for Richardson it was the same thing that Charlie felt, that the giant was waking up and as he did he shook the soul out of the land.

Arthur said, "You think you find this part of you with your people?"

Richardson opened the door. "I hope so," he said, and went into the night.

The work continued. Together, Richardson and Halley churned through the logs that had been stacking up in the lake and spilling over the banks. Big hunks of white pine dripping murky water entered the mill, and long, flat lumber exited. Arthur had so much lumber he was able to complete Wilbur's work on the store in just a few short hours. Next, he started building a headquarters office, as the original building was turned into a bunkhouse with the arrival of the first batch of miners. Working alone, though, was slow—both Charlie and Richardson had been irreplaceable laborers.

It was Wilbur who, seeing Arthur struggle with setting a foundation stone, urged him to go to Wood.

"Can't do it all yourself," Wilbur told him. "Plenty o' boys out there can help you."

Arthur found the mining captain standing on the edge of the expanding pit. Below, a group of Irish miners were picking at the soft red ore. "Not like that," Wood barked. "It ain't coal you're clawin' at." He jumped when he found Arthur standing behind him. "Mary and Joseph, Maki, you liked to scare me out of my skin. What is it? And when're you gonna finish my office? I'm tired of working in that foul armpit of a dining hall."

"I need hands," Arthur said.

"Aye, don't we all." He called two husky Swedes over. "Take these. If you can get 'em to lift a shovel you'd be working miracles."

Henrik and Nils Lundgren were brothers from Haparanda, Sweden, just over the border from Finland. Despite the proximity of their homeland to Arthur's, they refused to speak Finnish with my grandfather; they held the stubborn belief that Finland was still part of Sweden, and would always be part of Sweden, and that all Finns should speak Swedish. Arthur did not speak Swedish, but he understood it enough that he and his helpers could communicate haltingly. The brothers Lundgren had gotten off a boat in New York only one week before arriving in Mountain Iron, had come to Minnesota because of a letter they had received from a cousin who worked in Tower. When they got off the train in Duluth, they had stopped at the first iron mining company office they saw—Mountain Iron Company—and after signing with Lon had been dispatched on the wagon train leaving the very next day.

Henrik was the elder one, a stout Swede with a thin, wiry mustache, white-blonde hair and red cheeks. He was cheery but lazy. Nils was no better. He followed his elder brother like a cat follows its mother. Henrik did all the speaking for both of them, and his deep voice let out mostly guttural acknowledgements of instructions that Arthur gave them. Still, help was help, and they excelled at doing exactly what they were told to do—even if they did nothing of their own volition.

The three of them finished the headquarters building in three days.

The front door, attached with iron hinges brought up from Duluth, opened onto a front office big enough for a couple of clerks. Two other offices were in back, off a short hallway. Arthur had built desks for the spaces using leftover lumber. They were nothing more than lengths of pinewood stretched over skirt beams and supported by split pine logs, simple and sturdy. When Arthur showed the space to Wood he was thrilled. He claimed the back room for himself and told Arthur that he should have the front office.

"You are in charge of the camp," Wood told him by way of justification. "Just as much as I am in charge of the mine."

Arthur moved into the office, and work seemed to never end.

While Wood either stayed at the mine or stayed in his office, Cohoe came to Arthur constantly with construction requests for trellises and trestles, scaffolding and skids, pulleys and pallets, anything to make hauling and storing the ore as efficient as possible.

"Damn thing gets deeper every day," Cohoe told Arthur as they stared at a map of the pit. It included a topographical estimation of both how wide and how deep the mine would eventually go. It was all estimates. No one, not Cohoe or Wood or Nichols or even Lon Merritt, knew how far down the iron went. And so came the most frequent request: "We need taller trestles."

For the first couple dozen feet or so, the ore was easy to shovel, but as the workers got deeper they found harder rock mixed with the loose earth. Two weeks before, Arthur, with the help of the Swedes, had built a fifty-foot support for the diamond drill that Wood was using to break up some of the hard gray rock that clogged the pit. As the pit grew deeper the scaffolding needed to grow with it. While the mine continued to expand outward, Wood bored with the drill as deep as it would go. "The lode must go straight to the center of the earth!" he shouted when he came back to the office.

They used hand drills to make dozens of smaller holes around the main vein. Gill detonated dynamite in these holes, and once the dust settled, the laborers went in with shovels and picks, separated the ore from the rock, then carried and pushed both out of the pit in buckets and carts. The piles at the edge of the mine, one of high-grade ore and the other the useless overburden, grew daily.

"The grade is getting too steep for the men to push the ore by hand," Cohoe said as they stood over the map in Arthur's office. "We need scaffolding built along the ridge here to here, and retaining walls to buttress the sides. I'm thinking steam-powered winches and a system of pulleys so we can lift out buckets or carts that way."

Arthur stared at the plan of the mine. "Lines are elevation?"

Cohoe nodded. "The closer the line, the steeper the climb."

Arthur examined the entire map. This type of mining, without tunnels and shafts, was new to everyone. Cohoe had been mining a dozen years and had never mined like this. Gill, who claimed to have been born in a mine, had a hard time getting used to blasting on the surface instead of inside a shaft. From what Cohoe told

Arthur, no one had ever before attempted to pit mine on such a colossal scale. The newness of it meant they scratched their heads a lot trying to figure out what they were doing.

"What about there?" Arthur pointed to the other end of the pit on the map where the lines were spread further apart. This was the western side of the pit where they had yet to begin serious excavation. "The grade is more shallow?"

Cohoe looked closely. "Yep," he said.

"Why not rail?" Arthur suggested. "Small train engines haul the ore out that way, up the easy grade."

With a protractor Cohoe scrawled lines and marked numbers on the map. He made measurements and calculated figures. Finally he put down his pencil. "Arthur, you are a genius!"

"No, no," Arthur said. "I see what I do not know I see."

Cohoe rushed into the back office to tell Wood, who sent one of the laborers on horseback to Duluth with a message for Lon that read, "Rails, ties, and spikes." The reply was just as short. "On the way."

Arthur was disappointed to hear nothing of Minnie or Charlie in the note. Surely Lon would know where they were and more importantly would tell Arthur when to expect them.

Still, in anticipation of Minnie's arrival, he began to plan and build his own home near the sauna on the edge of the clearing. It was a simple and sturdy house built of thick pine logs hand-limbed and hewn. He felled his own trees and used his own tools, refusing even the offer of nails from Wilbur, to make a house he could truly call his own. He imagined Minnie's joy at seeing what he had constructed for her. She would smile and wrap her arms around him. After two years apart, he was ready to start living with his wife.

With the Swedes Arthur built twenty new houses. Ten were single- or double-family homes, for men whose wives accompanied them in the woods, the rest dormitory-style designed to house ten men each. The houses were all built in a square, each facing the kitchen, which also served as a central meeting place. The kitchen was by far the largest building in camp, and it had the largest stove, big enough to accommodate four-foot logs. Arthur built more covered walkways between a few of the houses, and to connect the headquarters to the kitchen.

The men at the pit watched the tote road anxiously. Arthur was not the only one eager to see his family. He overheard Nils telling Henrik about his wife arriving with the next wagon train from Duluth. Haltingly, using pictures drawn in the mud, Arthur convinced both Henrik and Nils to help him finish his own home, in exchange for dibs on one of the single-family homes. Even with the deal, their laziness shone through. If he did not specifically tell them something to do, he found them idly sitting on tree stumps, smoking.

On Sundays Arthur took the day off from camp work. He prayed quietly in the woods, and then spent the rest of the day working on his house. By early afternoon the Swedes would join him and work progressed at a steady pace.

Captain Gill talked excitedly about his own wife, whom he was sure would be with the train of supplies. "Aye, she misses me greatly," he said at dinner one night. Wood had just ordered Housell to bring out his secret stash of whiskey. After the liquor had been poured, Gill raised his glass.

"To the women," he said. "May they bring us back from the edge of the pit!"

The other men cheered, most not because they understood him but because there was drink in their hands which dropped fast to their bellies.

During the days there was always more to do, so much more to do for everyone. The wood left over from constructing a dorm would be either used to make furniture, or piled near each of the homes as winter firewood. Halley kept the sawmill buzzing; lumber piled up inside a protective lean-to Richardson had fashioned. Frances and Virginia Halley helped Housell not only with cooking, but they also tended the garden and maintained the livestock. Horses were corralled on the western end of camp, and Arthur built a watering trough by carving out a birch tree, which Richardson sealed with fire. The smithy was built near the barn and two Norwegians worked there most of the day making and repairing tools and shoeing horses.

Each morning Arthur woke at dawn and walked to the head of the giant, stood on the rocky horn, and scanned the tree line to the south and east for signs of smoke or travelers' campfires. The woods of the Mesabi were filled with tendrils of smoke, and from up here he could see where new swaths of trees had been felled. The land was filling up now with explorers and prospectors searching for the iron that would make them as rich as everyone now thought the Merritts were destined to be.

After looking for the wagon train, Arthur went to the kitchen where, if it was a good day, Housell would have woken early and prepared breakfast. Most days, though, the cook was still snoring off a night of binge drinking with the Cornish and Irish miners, or was squatting outside the kitchen, smoking his little cigarettes and drinking his whiskey while Virginia and Mrs. Halley began the meal. Or if the women were occupied elsewhere, Arthur fought off the mewling cats who seemed to multiply every day, start a fire for making coffee, eat a little bread with honey. Some days Mrs. Halley—Frances—came in and fried him a couple of eggs.

"You miss your missus, I'd imagine," she said. "I'm sure it'll be any day now. I don't think my Len could survive without me near him. He wanted to come here alone, said he thought this place would be too wild for me and Virginia. Ha! He doesn't know wild. He keeps trying to protect me. I tell him, Len, dear, I don't need protection. Don't you remember where you found me?" She laughed quietly as she put a plate of egg and potato hash and thickly sliced bread on the table. "I'm a frontier girl. I can take care of myself."

She brought a pot of coffee over and split it between two mugs— one for herself, which she drank black. "I heard Len talking to Wood about how many more men they expect. Up to a hundred more. I sure hope more women come, though. Honestly, it is start- ing to get a little lonely around here with just Virginia and myself. Be nice to have someone else to talk with other than that leering drunk." Her body bounced when she laughed. "Oh, don't look so worried, Mr. Maki. Housell doesn't scare us."

She took Arthur's empty plate and bid him a good day.

The morning was clear, the blue sky like a thin sheet of ice skimming the tops of the pines that ringed the camp. The leaves were beginning to change color and the circle of trees would soon blossom into a rich, bright fire. Fall would bring cold nights, a crisp chill in the morning air, and a thin layer of white frost over the churned up piles of ore and rock. Arthur had finished his house the day before and he was excited to find out how well it held up in the cold.

At the blacksmith shop Arthur found the two axes he had left the day before leaning against a tree stump, sharp as knives. He liked to spend a few hours in the morning felling or bucking. It was a way to warm up and ready himself, physically and mentally, for the day ahead. By midmorning he had bucked a cord of crooked pine logs, unsuitable for construction, into firewood that he stacked into the woodshed behind the kitchen. By then the Swedes were awake and he showed them the felled trees in the woods that needed to be skidded to the sawmill.

As he was walking back to the headquarters building, he heard a cheerful cry. And then another. He dropped his axes and broke into a trot toward the mine. He was excited--this might be them! As he came into the clearing he saw a few wagons coming out of the woods from the tote road. Wood was already there, as was Wilbur who wiped his hands on his white apron and then clapped them in the air.

"Yippee!" he shouted. "The winter cavalry has arrived!"

The lead wagon was driven by a man Arthur had never seen. The black bowler perched atop his narrow head matched his suit and stringed tie. His lean face and neat mustache concealed the fact that he had spent probably the last four days driving a train of wagons through dense forest and swamps. He could not hide the mud, though, which caked the wheels of the wagon up to the bare wooden sides.

The driver pulled the reins and stopped the wagon next to Wilbur just as Arthur approached.

"Staying off that knee this time, eh, Cash?" Wilbur said and laughed.

"Good morning to you too, Wilbur," the driver said. "Captain Wood, good to see you again."

"'Lo, Cash. Bout time you got here."

Cash looped the reins on a peg and jumped down from the buckboard. A line of wagons, more than a dozen in all, began to stream out of the woods. Workers dropped their shovels and lined the path as the wagons rolled into camp.

"You must be Maki," Cash said. "I've heard a lot about you. All good, all good. I'm Cassius Merritt. The boys call me Cash." He was older than Wilbur, and walked with a slight limp.

"*Hei,*" Arthur said. He looked down the line of wagons but saw no sign of Minnie or Charlie.

Cash smiled. "A man of few words. I like that." The horses clomped on the dusty ground and the wagons were beginning to line up. He squinted into the sun as he eyed the clearing. "My, you boys have been busy. I've more'n a hundred men with me, all ready to work—which should be good news to all of us." He slipped his gloves into his pockets and pulled a sheaf of papers from inside his jacket. "We also have most of the supplies you requested, including rail and ties. A few of the larger items were being shipped to Mesaba for us to retrieve at a later date. You had requested stoves, Mr. Maki? They are at Mesaba Station. Or they will be. We have supplies that need to go to the mines, and we have stores for the kitchen and the general store. Dry goods, canned goods, foodstuffs. Should be enough to get us through winter." He handed the papers to Arthur. Each page was headed with a wagon number, a name of a driver, and a list of contents.

Arthur masked his disappointment and focused on organizing the supplies. He directed that the foodstuffs be taken to the kitchen in the middle of the square of houses. He pointed out headquarters, and the supply and storage buildings. Each driver nodded and then followed his directions without a word. These men knew they were here to work. Walking between and beside the wagons were more workers, more than a hundred in all. One of the sheets listed their names. Arthur recognized the Swedish and Norwegian names immediately, and a few Finn names, too—though not many. There were also Irish and Cornish among the newcomers, another Gill, and a dozen Smiths. None of them spoke when they passed Arthur; they simply followed his directions to the kitchen or to one of the bunkhouses. Behind some of the wagons were cows, half a dozen in all, as well as more pigs and hens. Dogs barked as they ran into the clearing, chasing the herd of cats. Two wagons with rails and ties were sent to the mine. Once they were emptied, Arthur directed ten of them to re-hitch and drive back to Mesaba for the stoves and any other supplies still there.

No more wagons were listed.

Yet one wagon remained, coming late out of the woods, the driver stooped and hidden beneath a gray shawl. He might have been asleep. Arthur looked around for anyone who would be with it—his wife, his son, Charlie himself. But there was no one—just the wagon. His heart sank. Charlie had failed him.

Mud was splattered against the canvas cover. The reins were draped over the buckboard. There were two horses pulling the wagon, and Arthur mechanically grabbed the harness and began to lead them back up the hill.

"You are working the mine?" he asked.

"Arvid?" the driver said.

Arthur turned. The driver pulled back the shawl. Minnie! Arthur dropped the reins and lifted his wife off the wagon. Her face was thin, her eyes dark pools.

"Arvid," she said again and fell against him.

He put his arms around her and held her. He had waited for this moment for so long. Her hair smelled of roses and violets. She was thinner than he remembered, and smaller. He lifted her chin. The smile on her face was as broad as Lake Superior and, to Arthur, more spectacular.

"I have missed you," he said.

Her eyes welled with tears. "And I you."

"Ben?" he said.

She tilted her head towards the wagon. A small face poked through the front of the canopy. Arthur lifted him out and placed him on the ground, too. The boy wore a tiny gray suit and britches and he looked every bit the American Arthur had hoped he would be.

"*Hei*," Arthur said to the boy.

The boy smiled shyly and hugged his mother's leg.

She said, "This is your father, Ben. *Isä*." The boy hugged Minnie tighter and buried his face in her skirt. She smiled at Arthur. "Give him time."

In Finnish, Arthur said, "I was worried. I expected you weeks ago."

Her face fell a little. She spoke to him in English. "There was trouble."

"What trouble? Were you hurt?"

She shook her head.

"Where is Charlie? Why did he not return with you?"

"Leonidas made arrangements for us to join this wagon train." Her voice caught in her throat. "Charlie—" she began, then she shook her head. "I cannot speak of it now, Arvid. I am too happy to see you." She put her head against his chest and her arms around him.

"Ja inä ikävöin sinua." I missed you too. It felt good to speak Finnish again. After a moment he took her hand and together the three walked up the hill towards the edge of the clearing. He had not realized until this moment how much he missed his wife. For the moment he buried his worry about Charlie. "Come. Let me show you your new home."

They held hands as they walked. Arthur's excitement came out in a flurry of words. His native Finnish had been held inside for so many months, and he found himself disgorging it all on his wife.

"This is the headquarters building, where I have my own office," he said. "And that is the kitchen. We built that in our first days here. That woodshed behind it was the combination cookhouse and sleeping cabin when I arrived. The store is there. Wilbur sells many things, and he takes no money for it, though he does subtract what the workers buy from their pay at the end of the month. That is normal. Those are the bunkhouses. Most of them have only been completed within the last few weeks, in anticipation of your arrival. Well, not your particular arrival, but we have been expecting this crew of men for some time."

Behind them the camp was a party, welcoming the new workers. Arthur heard cheers and laughter as they welcomed friends and family, new arrivals not only to Mountain Iron, but to America.

"It has been so quiet here these months, like being an explorer. Like being home again. Now it is like we have moved to Helsinki."

She laughed. "Arvid, this is so quiet compared to Duluth." At the mention of the place she bowed her head.

"What is it?" he said.

She shook her head.

Ben ran ahead of them along the path Arthur had worn through the prickly underbrush. A dog trotted after him, which made him laugh and then trip on a root and fall. Minnie let go of Arthur's hand and ran ahead, but by the time she got to her son he was already up and running again.

"He is a strong boy," Arthur said.

"Willful," she said.

"He will have space here. But he must stay away from the mine. It is dangerous there. Explosions that rattle the houses. Rock and ore that slide off the mounds. When it rains water flows quickly like a wave and can wash one into a river of mud. The workers are rough men who work quickly. If a child were to appear in the mine they might not see him in time."

Minnie smiled. "Already you worry too much."

They went through the trees to the house Arthur had built. It was a two-story log house, with a sloped roof shingled with hand-cut pine. Smoke drifted out of the stone chimney from the fire he had left smoldering that morning. Looking out over the front porch were two small square windows paned with glass. A minor expense, he considered, for his wife to be able to look out into the trees.

The front door opened on iron hinges, and a wooden latch locked the door from the inside. The long front room was empty save for a table and bench Arthur had built. A stone fireplace, embers glowing, kept the room warm. At the back, a doorway led to the kitchen where Arthur had built a wooden table against one wall. A pipe fitted into the ceiling marked the location of the stove. A ladder led from the front room to an upstairs bedroom open to the floor below save for a hand carved wooden banister. A bed, wide enough to sleep three, sat in a corner of the room, with a crude straw mattress atop.

Minnie cupped her hand over her mouth. "Arvid, it is beautiful," she said. Still, there was a nervousness to the way she looked through the rooms of the house, the way she eyed the kitchen, as though at any moment a ghost might burst through a wall.

He beamed. "It is just a house."

Ben, agile for a boy two-and-a-half-years-old, climbed the ladder to the second floor. He wrenched off his coat and pushed it over the rail and watched it float to the floor below. Arthur hoped he had built the rail tall enough. The dog that had followed them up the hill and through the woods bounded into the house and barked.

"I will build more furniture," Arthur said. "A bed for Ben and more chairs. The stove will be here soon. And the mattress is lumpy and uncomfortable. You can make a better one. For now, at least we have our own home."

He held her. It had been so long since he had seen her, so long since he had held her, that he did not know how he would feel. If he would feel close to her anymore. But now that she was here, now that she was in his arms, that fear seemed to vanish. For two years he had carried loneliness like a useless, dull axe. It had weighed him down. Now the axe was sharp again and he could cut down the trees that had surrounded him. Now that she was here, in their home, in his arms, he knew he would never again let her out of his sight.

"Oh, Arvid," Minnie said. She pressed her face to his chest. He sensed her distance, as though she were not completely here with him. But he wanted to give her time.

They unloaded the wagon of all the goods he had told her to buy. Sacks of flour and barrels of salt and pepper went into the kitchen along with boxes of cardamom, cinnamon, and allspice. Boxes of seeds, along with bags of turnips and potatoes, went into the root cellar. Upstairs, Minnie showed Arthur the bolts of fabric she had bought for sewing winter clothes and bedclothes.

Ben clambered up the ladder and hugged his father's leg. "Papa!"

Arthur told the boy, in Finnish, to go downstairs and play. He stared blankly up at his father. Minnie said in English, "Go play, Ben." The boy smiled and darted down the steps. The dog followed him.

"He has not learned Finnish?" Arthur asked.

Ignoring him, Minnie laid a floral quilt over the straw mattress and spread her fingers across the fabric. "Mrs. Merritt gave us this quilt." She refused to meet his eyes.

Arthur lifted her hand to his face and pressed it to his cheek. Tears welled in her eyes and she put her head on his chest. Together they fell onto the bed, holding each other.

Finally, Arthur said, "Will you tell me where Charlie is? Did you not see him?"

She began to cry, her shoulders heaving. He held her and within a few seconds she took deep breaths, wiped her eyes and pulled away from him. "I am sorry," she said.

"You have done something wrong?"

She shook her head. "For my tears."

"I have missed you, too," he said.

"No," she said. "It is more. It is Charlie. I saw him, yes. He brought me your letter and he helped me find the supplies you requested."

"Then he returned to his people," Arthur said flatly. He could not hide his disappointment.

She lowered her head. "Arvid, Charlie is dead."

"What?" He sat up. "Dead?"

She looked at her hands.

"How?"

She told him the story, how Charlie had found her and delivered the letter, how he had helped her the next day shopping. As she spoke, he imagined Charlie leading Minnie through the streets of Duluth. His lean, dark features would have seemed so strange in that crowded place. He pictured the little shopkeeper and was not surprised that Charlie would make friends with just such an outcast. Charlie seemed to gravitate towards those on the fringes, towards those who didn't fit in. Like Arthur himself.

Her voice broke when she spoke of the two men who stumbled out of the saloon and attacked them. "I did not know men could be so cruel," she said.

Arthur stood and went to the window.

And then he thought of his Russian commanders. They had beaten him and ridiculed him and locked him up for refusing to fight. For standing up for himself. For being Finnish. After he left his post he walked back to his village in Finland and saw the burned shell of his old home, the charred ruins of the sauna by the lake. An old man pulling root vegetables from a neighboring farm told him of the couple who had refused to pay the tax that supported the fight that had taken their son from them. The Russian colonel had ordered the couple killed, their land burned. The ground was still fallow, the old man told Arthur. The rage and anger and sadness had welled up in him, and he had pulled it all back, had buried it deep inside. The anger had fueled him on the long walk to Helsinki.

Minnie stood behind him. "Charlie did what he did to keep me safe," she said.

Out the window Arthur saw the sauna that Charlie had helped build, and somewhere beyond was Charlie's *waaginogaan*. In the other direction the camp that he and Charlie had built was coming to life. Charlie had wanted to go back to his home and his people, and now, Arthur supposed, he was—Charlie was moving on to the grandfathers. No, not *Charlie*, not anymore. *Wiigwaasgewinini*.

Arthur began to cry. His friend had not failed him. Had in fact given himself to save what for Arthur was the most precious thing on earth: Wiigwaasgewinini had sacrificed himself to save Minnie. Arthur turned and held Minnie and cried. He cried for Wiigwaasgewinini, yes, but somewhere deeper he knew he cried for himself, for the loss he would feel for the rest of his life. His friend was gone. Arthur would never again see him, and his own children would never meet the man who had saved their mother. The man who had given the full measure of his life not just for the woman, but for the man who waited for her in the woods.

In the distance Arthur heard the cheers of the camp, the celebration of new arrivals. The sawmill was silent for the moment. "What happened to him—his body?"

"Mr. Merritt told me he would care for Charlie, that he knew his father. Arvid," she said, "why would anyone do such a thing?"

He said, "I do not understand why. It is the way of the people here who fear difference. Who hate just to hate."

"He was a good man. You were right to trust him."

"I saw enough bloodshed in Russia to never want to see it again. I thought this place, out here, would be safe from all that. I wanted to come here so that we could live in peace, not live again with that kind of hatred."

She touched his cheek. "It is everywhere. You cannot hide from what is in all of us."

Downstairs Benjamin laughed. Arthur wiped his face with the sleeve of his shirt. "We must go on," he said.

She nodded. "It is what we do."

"Mama?" The boy peaked out from the top of the ladder.

"*Äiti*," Minnie corrected him.

The boy smiled and climbed up. He pointed to Arthur. "*Isä*," he said.

Arthur smiled. He picked the boy up and, in English, said, "Ben. My son." An anger boiled inside him. In Finnish he said, "You will learn better. Here we will make the world better for all children, Finnish and Swedish and Cornish and Italian. Teach them we are more than our differences; we are who we are because of them."

The boy giggled.

"This is your home now," Arthur told the boy.

Minnie said, "I shall unpack and organize our things."

"There is work you must do in the kitchen," Arthur said, as though giving her an order. "There are many men to feed. Mrs. Halley and her niece Virginia are there, and you must help, as well."

Minnie said, "Of course. I do not expect to come here and not work."

"Good," Arthur said. "Be cautious. Housell, the cook, he can be a *paskapää*." *Shithead.*

Minnie said, "Arvid!"

Benjamin repeated, "*Paskapää*." Arthur smiled as the boy wriggled free and disappeared down the ladder.

He took Minnie's hand in his. Despite the terrible news, he was glad to be together again. As a family. Glad to have her wisdom and her words close to him.

Arthur said, "Thank you for telling me about Wiigwaasgewinini."

She nodded. "To see it," she said. "That was terrible."

"I know," he said. And he turned again to the window and stared out at the forest so she could not see the anger in his eyes.

Arthur had to tell Richardson. He walked along the northern edge of the pit and across the clearing. This place was filled with so many memories of Charlie. He found himself, with each step, unable to forget that his friend was gone forever. He wanted to be over his anger. But the world was rough, like the hacked stump of a felled tree, and he felt like the tree had fallen on his chest.

He heard the familiar whine of the sawmill before it came into view on the bank of the lake. Richardson was manning the table, which pushed the logs through the whirring band blade. Cutting each plank took long minutes of intense concentration. At any moment the band saw could break, the log could splinter, a knot could jam the machine. Richardson had been using this mill by himself for months and he was adept at all its faults and idiosyncrasies, but Len Halley was in charge of it now and he had wanted to ensure no one got hurt. Arthur had assigned the Swedes to help when they weren't busy with other construction tasks. Today, they were at the mill. Nils, the younger brother, eased the long planks of cut lumber onto a side conveyor, while Henrik lounged on a stump behind him, smoking a cigarette. Saw dust, coarse and fine, clogged the air. On the ground around Henrik were scraps of pine wood, slivers of logs cut or torn loose, branches and pine needles, weathered and dry.

Arthur seethed. Charlie would never have sat around smoking. Charlie would be busy; Charlie would be working. He marched up to Henrik and snatched the cigarette out of his mouth and tossed it in the lake. It floated between two logs momentarily and then vanished as the logs rolled against one another.

Richardson finished the cut and pulled a lever. The wheels of the mill slowed as the belt that attached the saw to the waterwheel stopped. Nils eased the board onto the table and moved it to the stack of lumber. The field was quiet. Arthur heard the screech of a hawk.

Henrik stood. He was half a foot taller than Arthur. "What is wrong with you?" he said slowly, with growing menace.

"The sawdust will burn," Arthur said with authority.

In Swedish Henrik said, "The worst kind of Finn is the abstinent one."

Arthur faced the Swede. Infused with the confidence of having spent the afternoon speaking his native language, he spoke Finnish. "At least I am a Finn."

"There is no Finland. It was nothing more than a shield for Sweden, and when Sweden was done with it, we gave it to the Russian dogs as a bone." He rocked back on his heels and laughed.

Arthur filled with anger at Henrik's world of hate, a world that had taken Charlie away. Men like Henrik had been pushing Arthur for too long. Arthur was ready to push back. He punched the Swede in the cheek. Henrik's head snapped back and, already off balance, he fell backwards into the woodpile. Nils came to him and tried to pull him up but only succeeded in losing his own balance and falling over. If Arthur hadn't been so angry he might have seen the humor in it. As it was, Arthur stood over the Swedish brothers clenching and unclenching his fists as they scrambled to their feet.

Richardson was behind him suddenly. "Come," he said and began to lead Arthur away.

"You are a farmer!" Henrik called derisively.

Arthur turned and stared down at the Swede. "I am your boss," he answered. "Get to work."

Arthur and Richardson walked towards the mine, feet crunching wood chips and fallen leaves. Arthur felt his heart sink the further they got from the sawmill. He had not struck a man since he had been in the army. Violence was not in his nature. He felt both ashamed and empowered, strong and weak.

"Never knew you to be a violent man," Richardson said. Then, when Arthur did not reply: "He's going to come after you."

Arthur's palms were sweating. The bones in his right hand felt bruised. "Let him. I will put him back into the mine. He will be carrying buckets all winter."

Richardson laughed. "If this is what having your wife back does to you, I like it!"

They moved along the path behind the buildings, neither leading nor following. It was as though they were both drawn to the pit being opened in the earth. The mine, after all, was why they were there. It represented their reason for being, their every thought for the past and present. It was amazing, Arthur considered, what man could do, what they had done. That he and two other men cleared an area of land a few hundred yards square, built the camp, prepared a place where more than a hundred men could dig the earth out of itself. Arthur thought it made sense that this was the place where he would tell Richardson about Charlie.

Ahead, a group of twenty or so workers pulled a rope attached to a pulley on the trestle that he and Richardson had built. They were raising a load of ore. Wood barked orders and the men moved, half going to the edge of the pit. One took a long pole with a hook at one end and grabbed the rope while the others behind him helped pull the cart to the edge of the pit. Once there, the cart was tipped over and the red dirt spilled. Four men then leveled the cart and pushed it back over the pit, while the rest of the men slowly lowered it. A group of Irish workers in oilcloth coats and pants shoveled the spilt ore into wagons which were then pushed to the stockpile just west of the pit. It frustrated Arthur that the operation was so inefficient.

Richardson said, "This place got crowded."

"Yes," Arthur said. "Many people."

A cool breeze blew from the north, and Richardson shivered. "Look at it. When we came here it was an area a hundred yards wide maybe, and the rest was nothing but trees. You couldn't see anything but the trees. And we made this place." He shook his head. "I am torn about it. Part of me looks at what we have done and sees a land torn apart, a land ripped up and leveled. This is not the land the grandfathers foretold.

"In dreams my mother has told me of the future, of the earth burning, the ground melting. She has shown me birds of metal and iron horses that need no tracks. My mother tells me this all comes from here. She tells me Mesabi will give this to us. What was it Charlie said? Sleeping giant wakes? My mother said something else. *Wapaa' mesabi.* The giant wakes because we disturbed him."

Arthur felt his nerves begin to fray. As Richardson spoke, he thought of Charlie and of the direct way he confronted people. If only Arthur could be like that.

"But another part of me sees this as an example of human ingenuity. What is the land if not for us to use? We should mine it for everything we can, because otherwise we shall stay in the *waaginogaans* of the grandfathers forever. The old ways are dying. They cannot survive this new world, this new place. My people, Charlie's people, we want to live in peace, but we want to live in peace in our own way, as though we are still the only ones living. Coming from both peoples, I see the world through two sets of eyes. From the eyes of the grandfathers, and through the eyes of your people. Maybe a day will come when the old ways will return. Perhaps when there is nothing left to take from the land." His voice trailed off sadly.

Arthur waited for Richardson to finish. He did not want to be the bearer of this news.

"I am glad Halley's here," Richardson said. "It is time for me to leave."

Arthur was not surprised at the announcement and relieved at the change of subject. "Where will you go?"

"North, to my village, with Charlie. With winter coming I shall be of good use to my father setting and watching his traps."

At the mention of the name, Arthur bristled. He took a breath and steeled himself. In the pit the workers were raising another cart of ore, spilling it onto the ground. "Charlie is dead," he said.

Richardson turned. "What?"

Arthur looked at the ground. His worn boots were caked with red dirt and white sawdust. Haltingly he said, "In Duluth. He was walking and two men shoot him in the back. My wife, she sees. She is terrified."

Richardson closed his eyes. When he opened them again they were red. He looked out over the pit, at the men below digging for iron. "What men?" he said.

Arthur shrugged. "Two drunk men, that is all she knows."

"Soldiers."

Arthur said, "She does not mention uniforms."

"That's not what I mean. They were ex-cavalry soldiers, probably. Like Housell. They believe all of us, we who were here first, the Chippewa and the Lakota and the Sioux, that we are all savages incapable of living peacefully, and need to be destroyed." His face tightened. "Men like Housell know only hate. God damn him."

"Housell was not there."

"He didn't have to be. It was men like him who killed Charlie and killed my mother and who fight every day to kill us all." He rubbed his eyes with the heels of his hands. "He was a good man."

"He was my friend." Arthur fought back tears. "In Finnish we say *ystävä*. He was more than friend. He was *sukulainen*—my kinsman; he was *veriveli*—my brother of the blood. This is forever."

Richardson mixed French and Chippewa. "*Il étiat mon beshwa-jï.*" *He was my friend.*

A hawk screeched above them. As the two men watched, the hawk circled twice, then swooped down in an arc towards the field behind the pit. The hawk extended its claws and pulled back its wings, slowing as it skimmed the ground, dipped, and shot back into the sky holding a wriggling field mouse.

Richardson said, "Don't let this place be filled with hate. Don't let it become a place where Housell and men like him gun other men down in the street. The sleeping giant wakes. Let him wake at least to a peaceful people, if not a peaceful land."

Arthur winced. He wanted to make this place better than Tower, wanted it to be peaceful and egalitarian. But he felt he was failing at it. "I do not know how I can do this," Arthur said.

Richardson turned to him. "If anyone can, it is you."

They watched the hawk circle again, its prey eaten or fed to its young. Clouds were moving in quickly from the north, a cold wind blowing. Soon winter's cold would bite them all.

"Where is he?" Richardson said.

"Who?"

"Charlie."

"His father bring him from Duluth. On the train."

Richardson nodded. Without another word he walked back to the sawmill. He got about halfway there and then stopped and looked up in the sky. Above his head a line formed, blue to the south, gray to the north. Two fluttering leaves landed at his feet. Richardson stared up and then, as though he had made a decision, and as though the answer for him was written on the sky, he turned and walked towards the camp.

Arthur followed him.

Instead of going into camp, Richardson continued walking, following the worn trail that led along the edge of the pit, past Irishmen pushing carts down the hill toward the pile of ore, past Gill checking on his explosives, along the path where they had emerged from the trail months before. There Richardson disappeared into the pine and spruce and tamarack trees.

He was going home.

Housell emerged from the kitchen and clanged the dinner bell. The sound echoed off the trees and the wind and the clouds. From somewhere far away Arthur heard an explosion and he turned to see balls of smoke drift lazily into the gray sky. Another mine somewhere, more people digging for more ore. Arthur hoped he could do what Richardson asked. Though he knew he could not change others, he knew he could change himself. He could be the person of peace. He could—and would—make sure that when the giant woke, that it would look down and see at least one peaceful person, one soul who lived not for hate but for peace. Maybe he could not change the Housells of the world, but he could ensure that he himself would not be one.

He walked up the hill to the sawmill. Henrik and Nils were lifting a log onto the table. They stopped when they saw him. Arthur stepped up to Henrik and the Swede eyed him suspiciously.

In Swedish Arthur said, "I should not have hit you."

Henrik stood up. Arthur met his eye. If Henrik wanted to hit him, Arthur would let him. The two men stared at each other for an awkward moment. Then Henrik nodded.

Arthur helped them lift the log onto the table, then he walked back down the hill towards camp. From the north the gray sky opened and a shaft of yellow-white light shined down on the vast field and highlighted stacks of curing white pine. He saw the new town he would have to build there, because this place was too close to the pit which would grow into this location. But maybe, he thought, a town could be made here. A town like Duluth but better. For good people. For families. The sunshine came down on a vast part of forest that had yet to be cleared and the bell rang and Arthur heard a voice in his head. He didn't know if it was Charlie or Richardson or God speaking to him, but he knew what the voice told him. He fell to his knees in the mud and closed his eyes and prayed to God to give him the strength to be the kind of man Charlie was, to be as wise and as strong and as brave. If he could be only half the man Charlie was, he prayed, then maybe, just maybe, he would have lived his life to the fullest.

As he prayed the light shining from the hole in the clouds moved, and soon the chill had left his arms and the warm air embraced him. As he let go of all the tears, and the fear, and the anger, he felt himself become lighter.

And then the sun moved away, and he was hungry. He stood and walked to the kitchen.

—⋖◆⋗—

The new group ate in the dining cabin. Cassius Merritt, Cohoe, Gill, and Halley all sat at one table together. The rest of the men took seats wherever they could find them, and that often meant they huddled in groups of similar language. The Norwegians had pushed three tables together and refused to let anyone who was not Norwegian sit with them. Two dozen Cornish miners, thick black mustaches on their gaunt faces, took over a corner of the room. They muttered together in a dialect of English that Arthur could barely understand. The Irish laborers laughed and tossed insults at the Cornishmen. A smaller group of guttural-accented Germans laughed together as they devoured their dinner and, as a group, passed back through the line to get a second helping before most of the others had even a first.

Arthur was pleased to see a group of seven Finnish men eating quietly in one corner. He stopped at their table on his way to get dinner for himself.

"*Hei*," he said.

"Halloo," the men said, looking up from plates of wild rice and venison stew. They had young, clean-shaven faces. Arthur thought they could be mistaken for brothers.

"I am Arthur Maki," he said in Finnish. "I am glad to hear a familiar tongue in this place."

One of the men, an older one, laughed. "We, too, are pleased to see a Finn leading here. My brother and I—" he nodded to the man sitting across from him, a mirror image of himself—"came from Iron Mountain in Michigan where the Finns are used like cattle. Perhaps here we shall be treated like men."

The other Finns nodded and almost collectively murmured, "*Joo, joo.*"

Arthur said, "The Merritts treat all of us as men."

"I am Kaarlo," the man said. "This is my brother, Tapio."

The other men introduced themselves. Arthur would not remember most of their names. But he was glad they were here, and he told them so.

"I have already a sauna," he offered.

Kaarlo dropped his fork and stood. "Is it ready?"

"*Joo, joo,*" Arthur said.

Kaarlo put his arm around Arthur's shoulders. He was a big man, broad shouldered, and he smelled like the forest. "Does anyone else know about this sauna?"

Arthur looked around the room. It had never occurred to him to keep the sauna a secret.

"Let's not let any of the others know," Kaarlo told him. "We don't want the Norwegians to dirty it."

Arthur said, "The sauna is for everyone who wants to use it."

Kaarlo patted him on the shoulder. "On Saturday for the Finns," he said. He sat and turned to his brother. "Think of it! A sauna!"

Arthur went to the kitchen where he found Housell sitting on a stool in the corner, drinking from a bottle he held by the neck, and directing Frances and Minnie. They were stirring pots and frying meats. Virginia chopped vegetables at a table. A fourth woman washed dishes in a metal sink built against the back wall of the kitchen. Benjamin poked his head out of a corner and smiled, then ran to Arthur who picked the boy up.

"Papa," the boy said.

"*Isä*," Arthur corrected.

"Maki!" Housell said. "This is more like it." He spread his arms. "A kitchen full of beautiful women and I don't have to lift a finger!" He wobbled over to Arthur. "Your lady there is not only a good cook, but she's easy on the eyes, if you get my meaning." He held out the bottle for Arthur to take a drink. Arthur pushed him away. "Ha-ha," Housell said, stumbling backwards. "Your loss!"

Arthur went to Minnie. "Are you okay?" he said in Finnish.

She nodded. "He is all words. There is no bite in him."

"You are wrong." He was thinking of Richardson. "I have seen his bite."

Frances came behind them. She smelled of pine and salted fish. "Your wife is quite the cook, Mr. Maki." She lowered her voice. "Please do not worry about Housell. He is a drunk. I have known men like him my whole life, and have dealt with much worse." She patted Arthur gently on the shoulder. He felt like a child in her presence. Benjamin held out his arms and she took the boy from Arthur. "I promise, Mr. Maki. Minnie and Ben here are in good hands with me. I won't let anything happen to them. Now, have you met Mrs. Gill?" She led Arthur to the woman washing.

She was broad shouldered and meaty, and wore a permanent scowl. Loose wisps of tousled black hair spread like the quills on a porcupine. When she spoke it was with an accent so thick Arthur could barely understand her. She made a greeting and held out a wet hand. Arthur nodded. Recognition dawned in her eyes, and she said something else that vaguely sounded like a different form of greeting. She plunged her hands back into the soapy water.

Frances said, "I want you to know that the kitchen is under great care." In the corner Housell slipped off his chair and fell onto the floor. He broke out in a great laugh then took a swig of whiskey from the bottle in his hand. "Despite the presence of Mr. Housell." Benjamin cooed and went to his mother. "Now, please, Mr. Maki, go eat."

Back in the dining room, plate of food in his hand, Wood waved him over. Arthur glanced around the room. While it would be nice to sit with the Finns, he knew that his role in the camp meant he had to be involved in discussions going on at the head table. He sat at the end of the bench, across from the rather large Mr. Halley.

"You have done a magnificent job with the camp," Cassius Merritt said. "I shall send a full report back to Duluth. I know Lon will be pleased with what he hears about this place."

Arthur said, "There is still much work to do."

Wilbur threw back his head and laughed. "That's what I love about the Finns." He slapped his hand on the table. Plates bounced. "Never take well to compliments."

Cassius changed the subject. "Now, the mines. Wood, you made remarkable progress with the little that you have had to work with here. Ore is piling up. That is what we like to see. I shall be off to Biwabik tomorrow to check on operations there. Which reminds me: Halley, the mill needs to provide lumber for that operation as well. We shall have regular supply runs between the two locations."

Halley said, "Captain Nichols has already sent orders."

"Excellent. Captain Cohoe, you are continuing your explorations?"

"Yes, sir. We are moving methodically west and south, digging test pits and taking samples as we go. I have them labeled in the office and ready to send to Duluth for testing. As we discover a new deposit, we send a man to the land office in Duluth and stake a claim to the property."

"Good, good," Cassius said.

"Cash, if I may?" Halley said.

"Please."

"We don't want to spread out too thin, do we? I understand the taxes the state takes off these mining leases is hefty, and they tax whether the ore gets mined or not. Is that so?"

"My brothers handle most of the financial end of the business," Cassius said. "I would have to check with them."

"My only point is that having all this iron does us no good unless there is a way to get it both out of the ground and to market. Right now, from what I can see, the iron is just getting piled up."

Cassius said, "Obviously it'll have to be railroad. There's the Duluth and Iron Range, and to use it we only have to build a spur into Mesaba Station. Lon is negotiating with them now for a fair fee. The docks at Two Harbors are more than equipped to handle the loads we'll drop on them."

Gill spoke up. "All you Merritts sound the same."

The men around the table laughed. Including Cassius and Wilbur. Cassius said, "Yes, Captain Gill, I suppose we do. It's what happens when we all feel as strongly as we do."

The room grew noisier. Plates clinked against plates as Virginia and Frances walked around the room collecting empty dishes and cutlery. Now that eating was over, the men's mouths were free to talk, and talk they did—loudly, and in many different languages. There was an excitement in the air that Arthur could feel. Everyone in the room knew that tonight was really the beginning, the start of something grand. The men here were going to start the real work of mining all the iron that lay just outside the door. These were the men who would wake the giant.

Wood and Cassius spoke quietly, and then Wood went to Frances and whispered to her. Her eyes widened and she scuttled into the kitchen. The mining boss then climbed onto a table and held up his hands. "I've got a couple things to say."

The men in the dining room kept talking.

"Give us yer ears!" Gill shouted.

Wilbur said, "Shut it!"

Wood slammed his boot on the table. Cups clattered to the floor. "I've asked for your ears and I'll get 'em. Listen up!" The room quieted and eyes turned to Wood. In the corner the fire crackled. "That's better. You've all taken the long road gettin' here and most of you've been working hard these past days gettin' settled and gettin' up to snuff on how we been doin' things. I ain't a speech-makin' man like Lon, but I speak for Johnnie and Cash and Lon when I say thanks to all of you. Now, there's a lot still to be done here. We got a long way to go. But for tonight we got somethin' for ya. If you still got your cup I suggest you empty it."

Frances emerged from the kitchen, her long arms wrapped around a small straw-filled crate, which she set on the table. Virginia was with her. Someone whistled, another cheered. Virginia smiled and pushed her hair away from her face. Halley stood up and the catcalls began. Frances scowled.

"If you boys want some of this, I'll expect you to hold your tongues," she said. The room fell quiet again.

She lifted out two bottles of whiskey and handed them to Virginia who carried them to the nearest table. The bottle wasn't opened, though, and as she struggled to get the cork out one of the Irishmen took the bottle from her and yanked the cork out with his teeth. Whiskey spilled over his shirt and the other men at the table cheered. He took a long swallow from the bottle and then passed it to the next man who filled his mug and passed it along. Frances passed bottles around the other tables and within minutes each man had whiskey in their mugs. It did not take long for most of them to be drunk.

When a bottle came to his table, Arthur did not take any. Cassius, too, shook his head. Wilbur, the youngest Merritt, stared at the bottle for a brief second, and covered his cup with his hand. Gill, Cohoe, Wood, and Halley shared the bottle among the four of them.

The room erupted into song and laughter and a joyful celebration. The Norwegians danced on a table, and the Cornish and Irish men began to sing. The Finns stayed together at their table drinking straight from the bottle. Henrik and Nils celebrated the arrival of more Swedes, though Nils seemed more subdued since his wife had not arrived as expected.

The Germans were quiet. One of them, a bearded man with a weathered face and a cap on his head, leaned over to Arthur.

"*Jeder Bier?*" he said.

Arthur shrugged.

"*Bier,*" the German said again and mimed drinking.

Arthur shook his head. There was no beer.

The German turned back to his friends and said, "*Nein.*" As a group the Germans stood and filed out of the room. The bottle they left on the table was snatched up by the Swedes who added it to the one bottle they already had.

Gill said, "Now this is a celebration!"

Arthur did not feel much like celebrating. Amid the clamor and joy and drunken revelry of the night, he sat alone in his thoughts. He could only imagine Charlie lying face down in the muddy street, rain falling on him.

He stood. "Excuse me," he said.

Cassius nodded. "Of course."

Arthur moved down the long line of tables. He felt a hand on his arm. Kaarlo offered him a bottle.

"Drink with us," he said in Finnish.

Arthur shook his head.

"Come. We are friends."

Arthur said, "I do not drink."

Kaarlo stared at him for a long moment as though trying to read something in his blank expression. But sometimes not even Minnie could read him. Finally, Kaarlo let up his hand. "We are not all the same," he said. He turned back to the table with the other Finns.

Arthur went out the door and into the night. Once the door closed behind him the singing and the voices and the yelling seemed to fade into a distant dream. The dark night spread out before him like a still lake, ripples of moonlight shimmering over piles of rock and stacks of white pine waiting to be burned for firewood. He smelled pine trees and leaves and the wet earth. The air was moist and its chill made him shiver. He set a fire in the sauna and then he walked for a long time until the sounds of the revelry became part of the calls of the forest, a different breed of cricket chirping, another kind of owl call. Finally he walked back to the cookhouse and went through the back door into the kitchen itself. Minnie and Mrs. Gill washed dishes while Frances wiped down tables and cleaned up leftover food. Housell was nowhere to be seen, neither was Virginia.

"Where is Ben?" he asked in Finnish. She looked up. He climbed the stairs and found the boy in Housell's bed. He scooped the sleeping child up and carried him downstairs.

"Come," he said.

Minnie turned to Frances who smiled and nodded. "It's all right. Go."

Together the family Maki walked through the darkness, up

the hill and along the path to their home. Arthur laid the boy at the foot of their bed and then led Minnie to the sauna. They undressed in the first room, hanging their clothes on the hooks by the door, and held each other like husband and wife for the first time in a long time. Afterwards they entered the sauna chamber. Arthur felt his skin tingle as sweat trickled over him. The orange glow of embers was the only light as Arthur and Minnie laid together in the hot room.

CHAPTER 7

By October the trees that ringed the clearing became a firestorm of color: the molten amber tamaracks, the burning orange birches, the fiery red maples, the sun yellow ashes. The morning the sun burst over the horizon as Arthur strode through camp, surveying all he had done. The clearing was about four hundred yards square now, the only clump of trees still standing within sight of camp were the ones surrounding his little house. Camp was more like a little town now, and with the addition of Wilbur's general store the idea that this place might be becoming a community finally began to take hold. The sawmill whirred from sun up until sun down. With all the buildings constructed, and with Richardson gone, Arthur sent Henrik and Nils to work full time with Halley at the mill. If he ever needed help, he called for Nils, who was the happier of the brothers and the easier to get along with.

There was something in the air that tingled. It was a cool morning, and the early sun cast long shadows across the rutty street. A thin film of smoke settled over the camp, drifting out of the cabins' fireplaces. The smoke hovered near the treetop line, held in place by an invisible chill. Arthur shivered and walked on. He left the house in such a rush that he had forgotten to take his jacket after one of the miners had banged on his door earlier to tell him he was wanted at camp.

An orderly line of workers stretched from the front door of headquarters and down the quiet street towards the mine. They were dressed in their Sunday clothes: thick leather boots, denim pants with suspenders or denim overalls, white shirts buttoned at the wrist. Each man wore a hat—wide floppy planter hats; narrow brimmed bowlers; stiff sombreros; fancy fedoras. The Italians wore suits with button-downed jackets and thin black ties. The Cornishmen were even more nicely dressed, ties and clean boots with black suits and crisp shirts.

Arthur walked up the line, feeling embarrassed of his own overalls. Splotched with black pine tar, they smelled faintly of the woods and of the red earth that was piling up around the pit.

Housell, a man for whom the outdoors was an insult, did not wear a hat. His hair was combed and slicked back with what smelled like rancid pork fat. He wore blood stained brown gingham pants and a ribbon bow tied under a dirty collar. "Probably gonna tell us to pack it in, ain't nothing here after all," he laughed from the front of the line.

One of the Cornish miners turned to him. "Ditch diggin," he said. "Foocking diggin' ditches. With piles o' dirt to show for it."

He recognized most of the miners, but he did not know their names—they were nameless workers, as the Cornishman said, digging a hole into the earth, all day, every day.

Inside headquarters, the front office was full of boxes of paper, rolled maps stacked in cubbies built along the left wall, and shelves of survey books. Straw packing from stacked wooden crates littered the pine board floor. This was the nicest floor Arthur had built in camp; the boards were hand-grooved to fit neatly against one another. Even still, two boards in the middle of the room were bowed. Arthur would either need to nail them down or replace them completely.

Voices rumbled from the back office. Arthur recognized Wood's wheezing drawl.

"Ain't no inefficiency," Wood said.

"No thanks to you," another voice said. "Using rail to get the ore out of the pit was Cohoe's idea, I believe."

"Don't mean I ain't running the place. I know how to get men to do what needs to be done, is all."

"I have heard you hardly leave your office here. Except to go stand on the edge of the mine and yell."

"You gonna tell me how to run this place? That what this is about?"

"Captain, I am not about to tell you how to do your job. I simply ask that you work towards running the mine as efficiently as possible. Using bucket lasses to haul ore is not a model of efficiency. We need tonnage, Captain. Tonnage."

"Doing the best I can with the men I got. You send more men and I'll dig more ore. We ain't got no way to get the ore off the mountain anyway, except by horse and buggy."

"I recognize that. However, you must be aware of the limitations of our financial situation and work as best you can with what you have."

"That's exactly what I've been doing."

Arthur knocked on the door.

"Come," said the voice that was not Wood's. Arthur entered and found Leonidas Merritt behind the big desk. Arthur had not seen him since July; he looked out of place in a black suit with a wide lapel, his stiff collar turned to expose a black silk tie. His close-cropped black hair was graying at the temples, and his ashen face seemed older somehow. Wood stepped backwards away from the desk as Arthur approached.

"Ah, Arthur," Lon said, his wide, thoughtful eyes brightening. "So good to see you! Captain Wood and I were just discussing some details of operations here."

Arthur nodded.

"Well, I best be getting on," Wood said, backing toward the door.

Lon turned back to him as though only just remembering that he was there. "Ah, yes, yes. As for your request for more manpower, that is an issue best shelved for spring. With winter approaching, sending more men up here would be a waste of both money and supplies."

"No need to stop work just because it gets cold," Wood said.

"In a traditional underground mine that may be the case. The ground here, however, will freeze."

"Can't get that cold."

Lon smiled. "Before spring comes again to Mountain Iron the air will be colder than February in Finland. Am I right, Arthur?"

"*Joo*," Arthur said.

Wood scoffed and turned on his heel and left.

Lon rose and put his hands on Arthur's shoulders as though admiring a son he had not seen in a decade. Arthur felt important.

"Come, come, sit." He gestured to the wooden chair Arthur had made as he returned to the seat behind the desk. "You've done a marvelous job with this place. Spectacular, really. And these chairs." He rubbed his hands along the armrests. "Beautiful craftsmanship."

"Thank you," Arthur said.

"Ah, and your English is getting better, too! Wonderful!"

"My wife helps."

"I'm glad Minnie made it here with the supply train. Tragic about Charlie. He was a good man and a good friend."

Arthur lowered his head. He found it hard to talk about Charlie.

"We can take comfort knowing that his soul is with the Lord now." Lon put his hand over his heart and looked up at the sky. "I had hoped that kind of tragedy was a thing of the past. But men will be men. It is not for us to judge them."

Arthur understood the sentiment, though it did not make him feel the pain any less. Lon was a religious man, and though his words had depth they felt empty because Charlie's death was empty. No matter what Lon said, Arthur thought, Charlie's death was without meaning or purpose.

"I miss him," Arthur said.

"I know you do, m'boy. But it's onward and upward, I always say. No sense getting mired in the bog." He slapped the desk. "Got to say, Arthur, how pleased we are with what you've accomplished. Considering what you had to work with your progress has been nothing short of remarkable. I knew we were right to bring you on board." He paused and took a breath. Arthur felt relieved that Lon had changed the subject. "I have to tell you: our prospects here are tremendous. We have two mines in operation, here and Biwabik, and we have leases on hundreds of other parcels. The assays say over sixty-five percent pure iron! That's better than what comes out of Soudan." He clapped his hands together and laughed. "One could say we are sitting on a gold mine. Mountain Iron is our test pit, as it were. It is here that we started and it is here that we shall learn to develop the techniques needed to bring this ore to market." The chair creaked as he leaned back in it.

"It is also here that we shall find the challenge the hardest. This is a difficult country, with swamps and bogs and stands of pine so dense walking through them is like entering a tunnel. The bugs that fly about our heads now are a nuisance, but they won't kill us. The bogs that we fall into may dirty our clothes, but they are unlikely to drown us. The trees may cloud our vision of our surroundings, make us blind to where we stand, but they also shelter us from the elements. The bitter cold winters can freeze a man in minutes. But we are seasoned men, Arthur, hardened men, well equipped to deal with these challenges."

This was the Lon that Arthur knew, the man full of his own self-worth, who loved to hear himself speak. Always positive, always motivating.

"There are other men, however, men not as hardened, men not as seasoned, men not as rugged, as we. They exist in other places, sit behind desks that are not as beautiful as this one but cost ten times as much. Through windows bigger than that one they stare at concrete forests, at brick bogs, and steel trees. They have cold, thin hands and use pens to try to control us. They want this place for the money it can make them, damn the rest of us. We are chattel in their stockyards, nothing more." He stood and came around the desk, leaned against it and looked down at Arthur who felt small in comparison.

"But we want to change that, Arthur. We want to keep control, here, in Minnesota, to share the wealth of this place with the people who work it, the men who mine it, the women who will rear children here. We want this to be a place of pride for all Minnesotans, for those, like you, who have labored so hard to live with the knowledge and the satisfaction that the work you have done has not been in favor of an unseen hand in an unseen place, but has in fact been for your benefit and for the benefit of your children and your children's children. That is what my brothers and I want for this place."

He paused and let the words settle like smoke from one of Gill's blasts.

"In order to do that, in order to succeed in this venture, we need your help. It comes down to money, m'boy. We have to get a railroad here to move our red gold to market. Carnegie and his man Frick brushed me off like a speck of dust on their lapels. So I made an agreement with the Duluth and Winnipeg Railroad to carry our ore to Allouez Bay in Superior." He smiled proudly. "We only have to build to Stony Brook to connect. The beauty of it is in the simplicity, for the line is straight and downhill all the way. An engine pulling twenty fully loaded freight cars would only have to be nudged out of Mountain Iron."

Lon brought his face close. The little black hairs coming out of his nose quivered, and his breath smelled like milk. Arthur leaned away, taken aback by the sudden closeness.

"In order to do this we need operating capital. Lots of it. Every man who can spare some of his salary for the good of the company will be greatly rewarded."

"Are you asking the men to work for nothing?" Arthur said. The words came out before he could think about them.

Lon leaned back and waved his hands. "No, no, m'boy. Nothing of the sort. In exchange for the layout of back pay, we shall give each man stock in the Mountain Iron Company, and additional stock in the Biwabik Iron Mining Company. As the value of the company rises, so too shall the value of the stocks."

Arthur shifted. It still sounded like Lon wanted the men to work without pay. "I do not understand the stock."

"Nothing to understand, m'boy. Nothing at all. Just like cash money except it grows in value." Lon went back to the chair, opened a small black notebook, and began to write. "Say right now the company is valued at three million dollars—" He jotted down the figures as he talked. "—and we have thirty thousand total shares. That makes each share worth about a hundred dollars. Are you with me?"

Arthur nodded.

"Good. So, in exchange for back pay of, say, three hundred dollars, you'll get three shares of stock. That's today's value. But once people start to see what's coming out of the ground here, once they understand the lode we're sitting on top of, the value of that stock will surely rise. Which means that tomorrow the value of the stocks could be two hundred dollars, or three hundred." He wrote the larger numbers on the page and turned the book so Arthur could read them. "Your pay will itself earn more money. Understand?" He twisted the cap on his pen and watched Arthur intently.

To Arthur they were just numbers on a page. What mattered was what was in the hand, what was in the pocket. "What about families?" he asked. "Many of the men send money home. How can they send home these stocks?"

Lon folded his hands together and took hold of Arthur's gaze with his own. Arthur felt comforted by the seriousness in his voice. "Arthur, you know how much family means to me. I would never put anything between a man and his family. For supplies the men will have full access to the company store. As for cash, loans can be made based on the future earnings of the stock." He smiled. "Interest free, of course." Lon put his hands on the desk. "What do you say?"

Arthur was confused. "Me?" Weren't they talking about the miners who worked in the pit?

Lon nodded. "I am asking our supervisory team first. You men are the leaders, and where you go the others will follow. Wood has already agreed, and so have Cohoe and Gill. Those are men who believe. Do you believe in what we are doing, Arthur?"

Arthur stared at his hands, fingers swollen from constant use, palms calloused. Lon's explanation seemed logical. Still, he felt uncomfortable. It all seemed so complicated. More complicated than he was interested in trying to understand. He was a carpenter, not a businessman. Minnie had a better head for numbers, for calculating figures, than he did. His mind worked in pictures. If he wanted to build a house, he imagined the house in his head, every roof beam, every wall log, every floor joist. He pictured the way the corners of the walls came together like teeth, pictured how they grooved, and knew instinctively how to make the grooves match. He used no math in these calculations; it was all pictures in his head. But this talk of numbers and stocks and capital—it gave him no pictures. All he saw was the pit expanding and expanding until it swallowed all the buildings he had built, until it swallowed the town he had built, and then, still hungry, it would continue to grow. He saw himself throwing pieces of paper, the shares he was being offered, into the gaping maw of the pit, and the pit chomping at his heels. Always hungry, always gobbling more and more.

Lon said, "Each of the men outside will get a similar offer. You and they are the groundbreakers, Arthur, the pioneers. You forged this place, you and those men, and for that you will be rewarded. What I'm offering you is something more than money. It's more than a job. I'm offering you a home. A piece of tomorrow, Arthur. I'm offering you the future."

Now that was something Arthur could understand. He had

come here to build a home, to build a family. Was that what Lon was offering him? The chance to have the future he had been dreaming about?

"Of course you should think it over and talk to Minnie. If she has questions, I shall be here until tomorrow." Lon rubbed his hand along the armrest of the chair again and smiled. "I wonder if you can do me a favor while I'm here?"

"*Joo*," Arthur said.

"Can you make me one of these chairs?"

Blasting was becoming more common at the mine as they dug deeper and wider. Rocks and boulders had to be broken apart and carried out of the pit by hand. Tree stumps and their roots spread like spider webs through the precious iron ore. Heavy equipment would come only a few years later, so in these early days of Mountain Iron, hands and horses and dynamite did the heavy work. If it couldn't be tugged out with a rope, or cut out with axes and saws, then Captain Gill was there with his Cornish *brothers*—to Gill everyone was a brother—to blast it apart.

"'Tis marvelous to watch some of nature's toughest creations blown to bits," Gill said one afternoon during a surprise visit to Arthur's office. "I've been blastin' since I was a wee lad helping me pa set charges in the drifts back in Cornwall. Those were real mines, mind, not these ditches. Not that I'm complainin'. I lost me brother in a shaft collapse."

Watching the blasting was a ritual for Arthur and Benjamin. They would stand at the rocky ridge over the eastern edge of the pit and watch the ground burst open. Together they had seen numerous blasts, and each time they thrilled at the sight of the cloud of dust ballooning out of the ground like the earth was inflating.

For all his pyrotechnical enthusiasm, Gill was a man devoted to safety. He had rigged a bell to the top of a trestle that could be heard throughout the clearing. Gill called it his warning bell, and it was rung each time there was to be a blast, usually during a shift change. While the crew were in the dining hall, either preparing to go into the mine or having just left it, Gill and his brothers packed augured holes with sticks of dynamite, set blasting caps, and ran fuses.

Gill shook his head. "Enough blubberin' over the past now. The mine needs more wood, lad. A lot more. The walls are slippin' and every time I blast, they slip a little more. Men down there could be buried alive if we don' shore it up."

"Captain Wood can talk to Halley," Arthur said.

Gill shook his head. "Bah, Wood. That one can no more run a mine than I can build a house. He's got no sense of the big picture. He stands 'round barkin' orders without thinkin' just to show he's in charge. Cohoe is the real leader here."

Arthur agreed but said nothing. He was surprised to hear Gill talk of Wood that way.

"You talk to Halley and get us more wood. 'Tis dangerous business, and folks best be treatin' it so." With that Gill walked out, muttering to himself as he went.

The news that Gill, too, thought Wood was a poor mine captain made Arthur feel better about his own feelings over Wood. The man spent most of the days in his office, studying maps and survey reports. When he did come out it was to yell about something, usually something that he knew nothing about. Or to get excited about something that wasn't very exciting at all. Wood, like Arthur and the rest of the men, had taken Lon's stock certificates in lieu of pay, but Wood complained louder than any of the workers about it. Nagging Arthur, too, was the Housell question. Wood had taken Housell's side over Charlie, and Wood had been the first, really, to label Charlie a savage. Arthur had never really liked Wood, and he guessed he was glad to hear that someone besides himself felt the same way.

Cohoe, Arthur thought, would be a much more effective leader.

A few nights later Arthur heard Gill's warning bell. He rushed to the kitchen and picked up Benjamin. "Come," he said. Father and son rushed past the people filing into the dining room, and crashed through the waving grasses and along well-trod paths as the sun set behind the western wall of maple. Blood red leaves glowed.

When the men below had finished setting the charges, they unwound coils of fuse until they were together beneath the bell trestle. They climbed out one at a time using a rope ladder and left the final fuse for Gill to light.

The Cornishman rang the bell again, then called out, "Fiiirrrre in the hole!" He lit a match and touched the end of it to the fuse. Sparks danced down the side and across the floor of the pit. The fuses had been measured so that when they split off, the spark from each fuse disappeared into the blasting holes at the same moment.

Benjamin took his father's hand and squeezed.

Silence settled for as long as it took Arthur to hold his breath, and then a line of earth beneath the mine rose up all at once. The ground beneath them rumbled and Arthur feigned falling over. Benjamin giggled and plopped down next to his father. Arthur loved playing this game with his son. Arthur covered the boy's ears as seconds later the thump of the explosion reached them. In the pit, the earth collapsed into a crevasse.

Then something unusual. A ball of fire shot out of the gray cloud of dust. The whistling fireball flew above the tree tops and was briefly illuminated by the bright setting sun. It was a tree stump, probably five feet wide, hovering in the ochre twilight like a hawk hunting for prey, tail-like roots thrashing.

"Look at her fly!" Gill shouted. He jumped up and down as though he had just performed a feat of magical wizardry.

Benjamin screamed with glee.

Arthur stared transfixed as the stump arched across the sky. The whistling became a battle cry as the stump-hawk found its prey: it was heading for the dining hall. Men who had been standing outside the kitchen saw it, too, and began to scatter. One of the Irishmen shouted a warning into the dining hall and more men began to stream out. But there was little time for anyone to get anywhere. With ferocious speed the stump crashed through the kitchen roof. Wood splintered as the roof broke open.

Arthur covered his mouth. "*Voi Luoja*," he whispered. *Oh my God.* Minnie was in the kitchen. He scooped Benjamin into his arms and ran. Blood pumped in his ears and he heard his feet crashing through the underbrush. After all that time apart, after all the waiting, would he lose her like this? An eerie quiet followed the stump tearing open the roof. He didn't hear cries for help or screams of agony.

Men scrambled out of the dining room door as Arthur fought

his way through. Dust filled the room and though the roof seemed to have crumbled, the ceiling was intact. The door to the kitchen had come off its hinges, and the stairs leading to Housell's upstairs room had buckled. Inside the kitchen, a cloud of dust and smoke made it hard to see anything. Housell was already pouring water on the fire. There was wood everywhere, long boards and slivered shards. Clods of mud fell from the broken ceiling. There was a crater in the floor where the stump had landed and broken through to the root cellar.

"Minnie," Arthur coughed into the dust.

"Here," she said.

The hole in the roof pulled the smoke out quickly and he found Minnie crouched next to the crater. "Are you hurt?" he said in Finnish.

"No," she said.

"Mama!" Benjamin cried. Minnie reached out and took the crying boy and held him close.

Then Arthur saw Mrs. Gill lying on her back next to the stump. Kneeling over her were Frances and Virginia. Mrs. Gill was covered with dirt, her face scratched and bleeding, and her whole left leg was twisted outward awkwardly. "Is she pinned?" he said.

Minnie shook her head.

"Dear lord," Mrs. Gill screamed. "Have we dug so deep that hell's fires 're raining down on us?"

Arthur examined the hole. The stump was lodged into the ground and Arthur could see that Mrs. Gill was not beneath it.

Frances tried to comfort the woman. "You'll be all right, Nessa."

Mrs. Gill said, "The bloody ceiling came down on me."

"I do not think it was the ceiling," Frances said. "Let me look at you." She put her hands on the hurt woman and when she touched the twisted left leg Mrs. Gill let out an awful cry. "All right," Frances said. "I think you've broken your hip."

Mrs. Gill shouted, "You've got that the wrong way 'round. 'Tis not me that's broken it."

Frances said, "Well, dislocated it, then."

Gill stumbled through the back door. "My lord, is anyone alive in there?"

"Here," Frances said.

"Oy, thank God." He stepped gingerly over the fractured bits of wood and tree stump and food that had sprayed all over the kitchen. When he looked down at his wife he let out a gasp. "Nessa, dear God!" He plopped down and took his wife's hand. "Speak to me, Mother. Tell me you're unhurt."

Frances said, "I think it's her hip."

Mrs. Gill said, "Eustis, what did you do?"

Gill put his hand there and his wife screamed. "Oh, Nessa. We'll get you out o' there."

Arthur tore the kitchen door off its leather hinges and with the help of three of the men they lifted the injured woman and brought her into the dining room. She screamed loud enough to wake the dead in Duluth. Arthur shook the support beams to satisfy himself that the entire building wouldn't collapse.

Frances leaned over Mrs. Gill and examined her more thoroughly. "I've got to set the leg," she said. "You'll want to hold something."

Gill took her hands as Frances wrenched the leg, twisted it and laid it flat again. Mrs. Gill screamed, her face turned red and she squeezed Gill's hands until they were white.

"Will it heal?" Gill asked. "Will she live?"

Frances smiled. "She'll be fine. Sore, but she'll live."

Gill kissed his wife on the forehead. "Hear that, Nessa? You're gonna live!"

Mrs. Gill sighed. "It does nay feel like it." She lifted her head. "Was that you blastin' down to where the devil dwells?"

Gill chuckled. "Aye. 'Twas a stubborn old tamarack stump we been working at for two days."

She let go of his hand and slapped him on the side of his head. "Foolish old goat."

Gill laughed. "Aye, you've still got your sense of humor."

Mrs. Gill asked, "How much powder did you use this time?"

"Perhaps it was a wee too much, mother," Gill said. Then he threw his head back and laughed. "Aye, but it was a mighty fine blast."

Arthur and the four miners carried Mrs. Gill to her cabin where her husband and Frances stayed with her. Back at the kitchen, Housell, Minnie, and Virginia worked to salvage dinner, and Arthur went into the dining room to double-check the stability of the building. Satisfied that it would not collapse any further, he told Wood that the men could still use the space for dinner. Then he went back into the kitchen.

"How's Nessa?" Minnie said.

Arthur said, "She will be fine. How are you?"

She smiled. "I have been through worse."

He put his arms around her. She pressed her cheek to his chest. He was glad she was safe.

"Hey, Maki," Housell said. "Do that when I ain't got a hundred mouths to feed."

Minnie said, "I am fine, Arvid."

Benjamin was sitting on the floor at his mother's feet. "Papa?" he said. Arthur picked him up and held him.

"Let us eat," he told the boy. Arthur carried him back to the dining hall. Somehow Housell had managed to save the fish stew, and aside from a new earthy flavoring, it tasted good. He and Benjamin sat at a table with Halley and Wood and Cohoe.

"How is Mrs. Gill?" Halley asked when Arthur sat down.

"She will be fine," he said. "Hip out of joint, Mrs. Halley think."

"She should know," Halley said but did not elaborate.

"The kitchen will need much repair," Arthur said.

"Lucky no one else was hurt," Wood said.

"*Joo, joo,*" Arthur said.

Virginia came out of the kitchen and wiped her forehead with the back of her wrist. A white apron covered her blue dress, the sleeves of which were wet from dishwater. Cohoe and Wood both watched her as she moved along the tables. The workers, too, were keenly interested in her. The girl smiled at the attention. In fact, it seemed to Arthur that she had come out of the kitchen solely for the looks and whistles she knew she would receive.

Wood turned back to his bowl and continued an interrupted conversation. "Who cares how much it costs? There is so much iron here that we're gonna make it all back, and then some."

Halley shook his head. "Cost is never immaterial."

Cohoe's gray eyebrows furrowed. "You've got to think about it. That's why no one wants what we've got here, ain't it? They think it'll cost too much to get out of the ground and there won't be enough ore to make it worthwhile."

"But there's enough ore here to last for a hundred years," Wood declared. "We seen it. We know it's here."

"That's what we hope, and I know that's what Lon hopes," Cohoe said. "It's what he's relying on as he gets investors."

"Borrowing money, you mean," Halley said.

Cohoe shrugged. "Call it what you will. He's just laying out a bet, is all. The future profits for the capital to make 'em."

"Neither a borrower nor a lender be," Halley said.

Arthur said, "Big fish are worth fishing, even if you don't catch one." It was something his *isä* used to tell him. The reward of failure is sometimes greater than the risk of doing nothing. But when the others just stared at him, he regretted saying anything.

Then Halley laughed and slapped him on the shoulder. "I like you," he said.

Arthur felt at ease. He was now part of the discussion, not an outsider observing it.

Cohoe waved his hands. "Arthur's right. In this business some capital must be borrowed in order to gain a profitable return. This process is cheap compared to other mines I've worked at. But it ain't easy to get all these men out here and all the supplies and the equipment. Got to have capital, and a lot of it, to get that running. It's the only way to make a profit."

"When does the borrowing stop?" Halley asked.

Cohoe replied, "When the ore starts bringing in the cash."

"It's all about men," Wood said. "With enough strong backs anything can be done."

"Back to the expense and difficulty of getting supplies up here," Halley said. "The more men, the more supplies you need."

Cohoe shook his head. "You both miss the point. The money to pay for all this is right here, below our feet. All that Lon has to do is find a way to get it out of the ground and to harbor."

Halley said, "And then he has to sell it and transport it."

Cohoe raised his eyebrows and his face seemed to brighten. "Ah, but they *don't* have to move it. They have to sell it, sure. Find a buyer or buyers—Carnegie would be first choice, but there are others. Point is, the buyers will move it. They'll want it."

Arthur was still confused. "But is Lon not borrowing from the same men he wants to sell to?"

Virginia stepped over to their table and began slowly collecting plates. She seemed interested in the conversation.

Cohoe followed her with his eyes. "No, he is selling stock. I took the stock from Lon, and now I own a piece of the company, like each of you. If Carnegie buys stock, he'll want to see it succeed just as much as I do. Just as much as any of us. Lon is offering anyone who wants to join him the opportunity to own a piece of the richest deposit of iron in the world."

"Seems risky," Halley said, doubtful.

Cohoe's tone became more heated. "You are here. You came for the risk, did you not?"

"I came because Lon offered me more money than anyone else and he said my family was welcome to join me."

Arthur wondered why he had not been offered that deal. Cohoe only shrugged, as though Halley's reasons had nothing to do with his argument.

"What about prospecting?" Virginia suddenly said. Halley glared at her as though silently ordering her to be quiet.

Cohoe turned to her. "Oh, yes, security in prospecting. If you enjoy traipsing through the swamps on mostly wild goose-chases, then prospecting is for you."

"Is there money to be made?" Virginia said sweetly, ignoring her uncle's facial pleas.

Cohoe faced her, giving her all his attention now. "If you find something. Takes a long time to find something, though, and when you do it better be enough to make up for all the time you spent looking." His tone was that of a teacher giving lessons to a student, gentle and patient. "Why, look at old George Stuntz. Spent years wandering around up here on some chase for iron. Everyone thought he was loony, figured he'd spent too much time lost on juniper juice. Sure, he wasn't wrong. If he were, we wouldn't be here. But he was only one of many, the Merritt boys being the next in the line. In between there were hundreds, maybe more, who came and looked and looked and found nothing and left."

"But there *is* iron," Virginia insisted.

Cohoe smiled. "Yes, miss, this is true. But without the eye to see it then it just lies there. The timbermen who roam these woods, they know what trees to look for. They know every type of bark and leaf, and they can tell you with one glance how many white pine fill an acre. That kind of knowing takes experience and skill. Same with prospecting—gold or silver or iron, it's all the same. You just got to know what you're looking for."

"You don't believe anyone could go into the woods and find ore?" Virginia said. She seemed to have forgotten all about picking up the plates.

Cohoe took hold of his cup to have something to do with his hands. "I am not saying that. Anyone can find the ore. But not anyone can *see* the ore. Finding it and knowing what you've found, those are two different things."

Wood scoffed. "Anybody knows a rock from a tree can recognize mineral deposits."

Virginia reached across the table and picked up Wood's plate. She looked into his dark eyes as though seeing him for the first time. "I'll bet you know what you're looking for," she said.

He licked his lips, mesmerized. "Aye, aye, that I do."

Halley seemed ignorant of her overtures. "Virginia, what are you driving at?"

She did not waver her gaze from Wood. "Nothing, Uncle. Just that it takes a man with the right pair of eyes to see what is lying right at his feet."

Halley turned to Cohoe. "Not everyone can see it?"

Cohoe shook his head, his eyes darting from Wood to Virginia. "Takes a trained eye."

"I thought so," Halley said.

Virginia finally turned to Cohoe. "Do you think there is more ore to be found in the woods?"

Wood sat up and bared his yellow teeth in a crooked smile. "Aye, there is. I've seen the maps Lon's got. There's iron everywhere 'round here, and they've only dug a small part of it. This place holds enough iron ore we could mine it for more'n a hundred years and not run out."

Virginia whistled, just standing behind her uncle with her hands full of empty plates. She was watching Wood.

"And all you got to do is find it," Wood continued, happy to have the girl's attention again. "Sell that information and you can deal yourself into a share of each ton of ore mined. If it's a big enough cache you've set yourself up for life!"

"If you can find it," Halley said, as much to Virginia as to Wood.

"Yes," Cohoe said. "If you can find it."

Virginia said, "Sounds to me like it is just waiting to be found."

Wood said, "Anybody can find it you got the right eyes helping you look." He winked.

"It would need to be someone who knows where to look and what to look for," Cohoe said, "Someone with experience, not a tunnel rat."

Wood said, "I ain't no tunnel rat."

Cohoe smiled. "Who said I was talking about you?"

Virginia laughed and the two men smiled at her. "Now boys, no need to fight." She winked and smiled at each of them, then flipped her hair over her shoulder, turned and walked back into the kitchen. Cohoe and Wood watched her go.

Halley shook his head. "She's headstrong."

"You say she's your niece?" Wood asked.

"Her father was my brother. He and his wife were killed when their wagon rolled down an embankment. Virginia was only four. We've taken care of her since."

Arthur thought of his own parents taken from him, and of Minnie's swooped away by the air itself. He put his hand on Halley's shoulder. "I am sorry."

Halley smiled. "No need. Been fourteen years. We've had time to grieve."

"You've done a nice job with her," Cohoe said hopefully.

Wood stuck a cigar between his teeth and leered at the space the girl had occupied moments before. "Yeah, real good."

The two men eyed each other. Halley, paying no attention to the two captains, stared at his empty cup as though looking through it to the floor below. Finally, Wood snatched his cup off the table and stood. "I best be getting on."

Cohoe said, "Me, too."

Cohoe darted toward the kitchen door, but Wood, already on his feet, beat him through it. Cohoe licked his palms and rubbed his hands over his hair, then followed Wood into the kitchen.

Arthur watched Benjamin push his food around his plate. Virginia seemed to be playing a game with the two captains, and Arthur hoped she knew what she was doing. Frances certainly seemed capable of taking care of herself, but had she passed that ability on to her niece? The dining room grew quiet as the men filed out after dinner, exhausted from the long day. Halley, who hadn't noticed Cohoe preen himself before entering the kitchen, turned to Arthur. "Where is this Richardson fellow? Henrik tells me he has not been seen in days."

Arthur said, "Gone."

"Oh. Will he return?"

Arthur shook his head.

Halley considered this. "Too bad. He was a skilled worker. Those Swedish brothers you sent to me seem neither skilled nor workers."

Arthur laughed. "They work when they feel it. They need direction."

Halley looked up at the ceiling. A draft whistled from the kitchen door. "You built all this?"

Arthur nodded. "With Richardson and Charlie."

"Charlie? Have I met him?"

"I think not. He left before you came."

"Will you need help repairing this place? The roof in the kitchen must be bad."

"Not so hard. The beams are strong."

"Whatever you need, my mill is at your disposal."

Arthur nodded. This was the longest conversation he had had with Halley since they arrived and he wondered how much he could talk about Virginia.

As though sensing Arthur's unease, though, Halley stood up. "I best be seeing what kind of trouble Virginia is getting to in there. She and Mrs. Halley together can be a tough pair." With that he wandered into the kitchen.

Arthur and Benjamin finished eating and then they went into the kitchen, too. Minnie and Frances were cleaning as best they could, but Housell was on the floor leaning against the stump, bottle in hand.

"When're you gonna fix my kitchen?" the drunk cook demanded.

Arthur ignored him. He told Minnie he would take Benjamin home and then he walked outside with the boy. The night air was cool and a breeze blew across the trees. The fingernail moon cast little light over the ground, and Arthur's eyes took a few moments to get used to the darkness. While he waited he heard voices.

A woman giggled. "Maybe you can show me this map and I can go look." It was Virginia.

A man answered. "Sure, honey. I got the right pair o' eyes." Captain Wood's voice was unmistakable.

Virginia laughed. "You sure do." And she laughed again.

"Tell you what," Wood said. "Come on with me and I'll show you what the maps say."

"Lead the way, Captain," she said.

Arthur heard their footsteps scuttling away in the dark. It was unbecoming, a woman going off alone with a man. At night. He considered going after her and bringing her back to Frances, but he knew it was not his place. Instead, he quickly picked up Benjamin and held him close while he carried him home.

The next morning the kitchen was cold. The hole through the roof had brought in the night air, and when Minnie and Arthur stepped into the dining cabin they found it nearly freezing. Minnie started a fire in the big iron stove while Arthur assessed the stump. It was too big to go out either kitchen door, so Arthur leveled it with a saw and filled in the hole around it, converting the stump to another worktable. Upstairs, Arthur found Housell passed out with an empty bottle on the floor next to him, wrapped in two layers of underwear, a pair of overalls, a fur coat and a woolen blanket. While Arthur took measurements, Frances clomped up the stairs.

"Good morning, Mr. Maki," she said. She stepped to where Housell was snoring and kicked him, hard, with one sharp-toed boot.

He rolled off the bed. "Ooof! Whazza?"

"Time for breakfast, Mr. Housell," she said. She turned and stepped past Arthur, smiling. "Nice to see early risers." She then went back downstairs.

Housell rubbed his eyes. "Damn woman like to break my ribs," he grumbled. As he stood he kicked the empty whiskey bottle into the hole. It crashed against the stump below.

"Watch what you drop down here," Frances shouted.

Housell laughed. "Somebody's gonna fall through that you don't git it fixed." His laughter turned to a hacking cough. He rolled a cigarette and lit it.

Arthur said, "Maybe it will be you."

"O! Your gettin' bold. Got to prove something for your woman down there?"

"Shut up." Arthur had not slept well last night, and he was in no mood for Housell. He went downstairs. Outside he picked up two wide boards from Halley and brought them back up. Housell was in the kitchen, and through the floor Arthur heard the three of them talking.

"At least this stump will be put to some use," Frances said.

"Use?" Housell said. "Maki's just too lazy to get it out of here."

"At least he's doing something, Mr. Housell. More than we can say for you."

"Bah. I've run bigger kitchens than this by myself."

"What have you done lately?" Minnie asked.

"The Finnish filly fires," Housell said. "Now I see where he gets it." Arthur dropped his hammer on the floor. "Uh-oh. We didn't make the man upstairs unhappy, did we?"

Frances said, "Either help or get out of the way."

"I'll just take a seat on this stump here. You ladies are doin' fine."

Pots clanged and the heavy iron door of the cookstove squeaked open. Arthur fitted a board over the hole and hammered it in place, imagining that the board was the cook's head.

Housell said, "Where's that little lady of yours? Virginia?"

There was no answer to that.

"Did she not get home last night?"

"Mind yourself, Mr. Housell," Frances snapped.

He laughed. "Which captain did she get on with? Hard to tell—she seemed sweet on both of 'em." He chuckled. "Maybe it was both."

Metal clanged against metal. "How dare you, Mr. Housell? My niece is a respectable woman."

"Now we have struck a nerve, haven't we. Someone should tell Captains Cohoe and Wood how respectable the fair Virginia is."

No one spoke for a moment, and then Arthur thrilled when he heard a slap. Frances could indeed take care of herself.

"That's more like it," Housell said. "Better than the boot, that's for sure."

Minnie said, "Just mind your own business, Mr. Housell."

"You want to try your hand? I've got another cheek." He laughed some more.

Frances said, "Don't pay him any mind. I've dealt with worse in my time. Why don't you do something useful and get some wood for the fire."

"If you'll slap me like that again I'll do just about anything for you," Housell said.

"You make me sick, Housell."

"Ha, I've heard that before." Arthur heard a frying pan clatter across the iron stove. He hoped Frances would use it. "All right, I'm goin'." The door opened and closed.

Arthur finished the repair to the floor and set to work sealing up the hole in the ceiling. He hated to consider that he and Housell might think the same way about anything, but he too had been worried about Virginia's behavior. He had been so worried that it had kept him awake, and he and Minnie had whispered about it before falling asleep.

Minnie had defended the girl. "She is a grown woman. Nothing wrong with a grown woman getting courted."

"She was the one doing the courting," Arthur said.

Minnie said, "I was there. Both men came into the kitchen preening like roosters, and the poor girl had to fend them off. Frances seemed to encourage them a little, actually. Finally they were taking up too much space in the kitchen so Frances told them to leave, and told Virginia to leave with them."

"I heard her with one of them."

"They will fight for her hand."

"It is not right, her going."

"I remember another young man who needed a little push," Minnie said. "It is not our business, Arvid." She put her hand on his cheek. "We have our own lives to live and do not need to live the lives of others."

"Someone must look after the girl."

"Then let that someone be Frances and Mr. Halley. They are her guardians, not you." She took his hand and placed it on her belly. "We have our own family to worry over."

Arthur felt her stomach rumble. "Are you hungry?" he said.

She said, "We are going to need a crib."

Arthur sat up. "When?"

"Soon enough," she said. "Summertime."

He was too excited to lay down. "What will it be?"

She smiled. "It is too soon to tell."

Now, as he sealed the roof repair with pine tar he felt the excitement of another baby in the house, another child in the camp. If there were more children, then maybe there would be an air of family to the place, and Arthur could stop feeling like a preacher imposing morals on a restless congregation. With the number of men working now, too, the kitchen was busy constantly, and that work required more than three cooks and a lazy drunk.

Arthur finished and returned downstairs just as Virginia rushed in through the door. She was still tying up her hair.

"I am sorry I am late, Aunt," she said.

Frances smiled kindly. "That is all right, dear."

The girl smiled coyly and winked. "Ah, but what a grand night it was last night."

Frances pulled the girl closer and said, quietly, "Not here. We shall talk later."

Virginia nodded and began cutting vegetables.

Arthur paused in the doorway, but Minnie glared at him—and the look told him to stay out of it.

⋙◈⋘

Arthur and Minnie walked back to their cabin. Benjamin ambled slowly beside his father. He had been asleep beneath a table in the kitchen when Arthur had woken him with a gentle touch on his shoulder. "Time to go home," he whispered. Benjamin blinked a few times and then put his arms around his father. By the time they got to the door he was awake and kicked his legs to walk. The cold air that had settled over the clearing had brought with it a layer of thick fog. The light from the lantern that Arthur held in front of him was reflected back in his face, blinding in the thick white mass. It felt like the three of them were exploring the clouds. The ground was stiff underfoot as they tread along maple and ash and birch leaves that littered the path between the buildings. Arthur did not need the lantern to find his way, but Benjamin had refused to go more than a few feet without a light.

"Will we find it?" Minnie said.

Arthur said, "It is just ahead."

Benjamin stopped. Arthur tugged on his hand but he refused

to budge another step.

"Come, Ben," he said. "We must get home."

In the dark fog the boy said nothing. He let go of Arthur's hand and the fog swallowed him. Arthur stepped back so the boy was in the light. He simply looked up at Arthur, his eyes slits, his mouth drawn and dour. Minnie appeared from behind Arthur, swooped the boy into her arms, and began to walk again. Arthur followed her.

"You must let the boy use his legs," Arthur said.

"He is only two, Arvid," she said. "You push him too hard."

"He is almost three. He must learn to do for himself."

Benjamin put his head on his mother's shoulder.

Arthur felt wet splotches on his cheeks and then on the hand that held the lantern. He lifted the light higher. Small pellets drifted across the sheltered lantern light. Benjamin raised his head and lifted his face to the sky. He smiled.

"Snow," Arthur said.

"It is a good omen, the first snow," Minnie said.

"Yes." Arthur put his hand on Minnie's arm. The snow was falling steadily now, but the flakes were too big and wet to stick to anything. Still, the moist snow was dissipating the fog and now he could see beyond his arm. In the darkness they heard the sound of the mine: rocks falling, shovels full of ore hitting the bottom of the carts, rust-colored wheels scratching cold, rust-colored rails.

"Arvid, what if the men come?"

"What men?"

"The ones who killed Charlie," Minnie said.

Arthur took a breath. It was not something he had considered. It was possible, after all. Men were straggling into camp every day looking for work, men who had not been recruited in Duluth. The mine needed workers, and if two able-bodied men appeared Captain Wood would not turn them away. Arthur would have to convince him not to hire them. Or somehow get rid of them. At a minimum he would have to watch them.

"I am sure they will not come here," he told her, as much to assure himself as his wife. "Let us have a sauna," he said, to change the subject.

Arthur led them past the house and to the entrance to the sauna. The fire inside smoldered and the interior room was hot. They entered the warm outer room and got undressed. Arthur helped Benjamin with his coat and overalls and underwear while Minnie settled herself on one of the benches. It had only been a few weeks, but Arthur thought he could see the bump of a new baby on her belly. He put his palm there and thought he could feel the movement of a body. Perhaps?

The inner room was hot. The rocks hissed when he poured water on them. He lay down on the long bench, and Minnie got comfortable next to him. The boy lay on the floor next to the door and fell asleep. The wood bench was wet and warm. When the water was warm Arthur wet a cloth with soap and washed Minnie, then he washed himself. Together they went to the lake to rinse and cool, and then went back to the sauna. Minnie curled next to Arthur and put her head on his chest.

Arthur said, "I am still worried about the girl."

"Virginia?"

"Yes. Something is going on. Frances knows about it, too, but I do not like it."

"She is not our family, Arvid."

"She spends time with Ben."

"Because she is a good person," Minnie said. "Worry less, please?" She took his hand and placed it on her belly again.

He wanted this place to be a home for his wife, for his children. A good home, honest and God fearing. So much that was happening in the camp seemed out of his control, seemed beyond his ability to contain. He had built this village and worked hard to organize it well, but he could foresee this peace not lasting. The waking giant would bring men looking for work. Arthur knew it was only a matter of time. And since he had taken the stocks offered by Lon he felt more and more concerned about the ore piling up around the mine. Not moving. His pay would do nothing if the ore did not sell. If it could not get out of the forest. He thought of Charlie and held Minnie and tried to let his worries rise like the heat.

They lay quiet for a while, and then they rose and cooled themselves again in the water. They dressed in the outer room and Arthur carried the still sleeping Benjamin along the path to the house. The fog had lifted, and the snow continued to fall.

⋲━◆━⋺

By morning the ground was covered in a thick white blanket, and the air was crisp and cold. Sunlight sparkled on the snowy clearing. Benjamin ran through it, his shoes marking two muddy ruts along the path to camp. In the dining cabin the mood of the men seemed to have darkened. Hardened men, experienced at working in deep, dark holes, had grown accustomed to digging in the bright, warm light of day. This snow was the first portent of the coming winter, and they wondered aloud what they would do when the ground became too cold to dig.

Minnie and Arthur followed Benjamin into the kitchen. Frances was sobbing into her husband's shoulder.

Arthur said, "What is wrong?"

Halley said, "She only had five days worth of food."

"Food?"

Halley looked at Minnie, who stepped over to Frances and took her hand. "Your wife keeps her secrets well," Halley said to Arthur.

Frances sobbed.

"*En ymmärrä*," Arthur said to Minnie. *I do not understand.*

Minnie did not answer.

"It's the snow," Frances said. "We did not anticipate the snow."

Benjamin stood by Minnie and raised his hands in the air. Minnie said, "Not now, Ben."

"Is there not enough food?" Arthur asked, looking around the kitchen. Housell was not to be seen. Probably still asleep upstairs.

Halley said, "Virginia. Against my wishes, she and Frances wanted to get a piece of the iron ore business. Prospecting, they thought, was a way to make money, so Virginia went looking for a ore."

"When did she leave?"

"Four days. She had supplies for five, but this snow, and the cold." He shook his head. "I don't know."

Frances sniffled. "She is strong. She has been through worse than this."

Halley managed a smile. "She is strong-willed, like her father was. And her aunt." Frances dabbed her eyes with a white lace handkerchief she pulled from her bodice. "We won't hear from her until she returns. If she is out there alone there is no way for her to get word back to us."

"She went alone?" Arthur glared at Minnie.

Frances said, "I thought that she would join Captain Cohoe."

Halley turned to her. "Cohoe is not an explorer. He's a miner, sure, and knows a lot about mines. But prospecting isn't his trade."

"Maybe it was Wood," she suggested.

"They are both at the mine," Arthur said. "I was seeing them this morning."

Halley hung his head. "Then she is alone."

"Len, we must look for her," Frances said.

Minnie agreed. "Arvid will help."

"We don't even know which way she went," Halley said.

"She told me. Township fifty-eight, range seventeen," Frances said hopefully.

"That is a big area," Arthur said. "Hard to search."

Frances put her face in her hands. Her shoulders shook as she sobbed.

Wood came in then, his coat wet from the snow. He stamped his feet and whisked his hat off his head. "Where's breakfast?" he said. "The men are starved!"

Everyone turned to look at him.

"Why all the long faces?" He looked around the room. "Where's Virginia?"

Halley shook his head.

"She should have returned yesterday."

Halley said, "You knew she was going?"

Wood said, "Well, I, uh, I mean, she's not here." He moved back toward the door.

Halley stepped over to the mining captain. "It was you?"

"Look, I, uh—"

"You sent her out there alone?"

"Whoa now, I didn't tell her to go alone." He waved his hands in the air like he was swatting at flies. "I offered to go with her. But she insisted. Said she could take care of herself. I gave her a map, pointed her in the right direction."

"Where?"

"South and east of here, I think. Not far."

"It is a big area," Arthur said.

"Sections four and nine," Wood added. "She can't have gotten lost."

Halley took another step towards him. "Did you teach her how to use a compass?"

Wood put his hands in front of him. "Back off. I ain't responsible for that filly. She wanted information and she asked nice for it."

Halley clenched his fists. "You son of a bitch."

"You can't blame me," Wood said. With his eyes he pleaded for Arthur to intervene.

Arthur would have preferred to see Halley punch the mining captain, but instead he reluctantly stepped forward and put his hand on Halley's shoulder.

Frances became strangely calm. "Len, it is not his fault. She wanted to go. She would have gone with or without his help."

"Listen to the lady there, lumberman," Wood growled.

"Though you could be less cavalier about it, Captain," Frances added.

"Bah, she ain't my problem."

Housell came down the stairs with a bottle in his hand. He had been listening. "All this fret over a little tart?" He took a swig and the liquid drizzled down his chin.

Arthur said, "Shut up, Housell."

"Even the Finn misses her." Housell turned to Wood and cackled. "She's the most fun this place has had since I been here. You got to bring her back, Wood."

Frances did something then Arthur had been wanting to do for months. She punched Housell in the nose. The cook dropped his bottle and put both hands on his face. Blood seeped between his fingers.

"You brote my node," he said.

"That's the last time you speak ill of my niece," Frances said and turned away from the bleeding cook.

Arthur was glad to see someone put the cook in his place. It wasn't going to bring back Virginia, though.

Halley said, "We need to organize a search." He turned to Wood. "Show me on the map where you sent her."

Wood led Halley, Arthur, Cohoe, and twenty men along the now well-traveled tote road as another blanket of snow began to fall on the mining camp. With it came the kind of wind and damp chill that would settle on the search party's bones and erase any tracks Virginia might have left.

"This way," Wood said, and pointed south. "There's the boundary marker."

Nailed to a tree was a small white sign with a grid printed on it. Cohoe, taking charge, brought the men into a group and gave instructions. The men would fan out in pairs who would each search a portion of the section. "It's just like looking for ore," Cohoe explained. "Pace off twenty steps and mark it on your map, then pace off another twenty and mark it. And keep your eyes on the ground. Look for signs of a camp or a fire. Anything." They setup a camp in a cluster of trees. Cohoe wanted everyone back before night fall.

Snow began to fall harder and faster. Wind whipped feet deep drifts which hampered their movement and obscured the ground. Arthur and Halley set out together, Halley moving in foot-shuffling silence. The air felt wet and heavy and Arthur found himself breathing hard as he slogged through the thickening snow. Any possible sign of Virginia, tracks or a camp, Arthur knew, were lost to the weather. Still, in silence, he continued to trudge forward through the snow, Halley only a few feet from him. Every few minutes Halley called out her name. "Virginia! Virginia!" But there was no answer.

The men ate around a roaring fire and then curled into their tents for a fitful night's sleep. When the sun finally cast long yellow beams through the sagging trees, their tents were covered by a snowdrift. Arthur dug a tunnel to get to the surface.

Halley looked at the snow and began to weep. "No use," he said.

Arthur thought of his own long trek to Helsinki and determined to go on. He could not end here. What if the one lost in the woods was Minnie? Or Ben? He pulled on his winter boots and then strapped on a pair of snowshoes.

"You don't know how to stop, do you?" Halley said.

Arthur shook his head.

"Look at the snow," Halley said. "We can barely see the other tents." He shook his head sadly. "If she is out here, we simply have to hope that she can survive long enough to find her way back. If she is not, we must hope that she has made her way somewhere."

Cohoe agreed. "We risk our own lives if we stay out in this. I am sorry, Leonard."

Arthur finally gave in to their objections. They packed up the camp, leaving one tent and some food in case Virginia found her way to this place—she would have shelter and something to eat. But as they made their quiet way back to Mountain Iron, no one thought there was any hope that Virginia would use it.

⟞⟩◆⟨⟞

The snow also put an end to all mining operations. The overburden was now cloaked in snow, and the ore beneath it froze into a solid mass. For two days Wood continued to work the men, but pick handles broke and shovels rang uselessly against the frozen ground. Wood finally called a halt when in the darkness of the pit, a man's partner brought a pick handle down on his arm, snapping the bone in two.

At first most of the men seemed excited about the time off from work. That changed quickly, though, when they realized that they would not be paid for time not spent mining for ore. Winter pay of one dollar per week was not enough to keep many of the miners at camp. A week after the first snowfall, the first wave of miners deserted Mountain Iron. The Irish miners, as a group, packed up without a word to anyone, walked south to the tote road, and disappeared among the swaying pine and birch. Arthur only realized it during breakfast when he noted to Halley that the room seemed less crowded than usual.

"The Irish left this morning. They had trouble with the cold, I guess." He pushed away a plate of eggs and ham and sipped his coffee, head down. His face had begun to look gaunt, his eyes sallow and sunken.

The winter shutdown of the mine seemed to hit Halley worst of all; he knew the darkest, coldest days still loomed ahead. With no work to keep him busy, he spent his days wandering the woods around camp, calling Virginia's name into the quiet snow. With each day that passed without sight of the girl, and without word of her from anywhere else, Halley's mood lowered. Frances stayed

167

busy in the kitchen, cooking and canning. She spoke little to Minnie, though, keeping her thoughts to herself.

The mood of the whole camp seemed to fall. Gone were the nights of wild talking and excited singing in the dining cabin. The men who remained in camp filed in silently, stamped the snow off their feet and then went to the big wood burning stove to warm themselves. They ate in silence, and even Housell's whiskey did not perk up their enthusiasm. They drank solemnly, slugging down the hooch as though it might warm them. Then, pulling on layers of woolen coats and fur-lined mittens, the men trudged back out through the snow to their cabins.

For Arthur this cold was unlike Finland's cold, even unlike the winters in Tower. There was a damp that crept under your skin. If you made the mistake of leaving a part of your body exposed to the air, you made the mistake only once. The wind felt like thousands of tiny ice daggers digging and cutting until exposed flesh seemed to disappear into a tingling void.

The morning after another snowstorm left another foot of snow, Gill banged on Arthur's door and told him that one of the Cornish miners had gone missing in the night. Found among his possessions was a letter from his family in Minneapolis. His wife had died giving birth to their second child. Gill feared the worst. Arthur got dressed and organized a search party. Gill and Halley, and the Cornishmen who shared the missing man's cabin, were willing to go out in the snow. From the cabin door Arthur followed what looked like footprints leading into the woods. Within fifty yards Arthur found the body sitting up against a tree, frozen solid, lips blue, eyes hard and lifeless. He had walked into the cold night in his long underwear, shoeless, hatless, gloveless. As the other miners gathered around their fallen brother, Halley stepped up to the body and covered it with a strip of canvas. The ground was too frozen to dig a grave, so they packed snow around him so animals would not get to him. Afterwards the men filed numbly back to their warm cabins. Halley stayed behind, staring into the trees. He said to Arthur, "She is gone."

Arthur said, "Never give up." But even Arthur felt there was little hope.

Arthur tried to enjoy the winter, for Minnie and Ben's sake. For a few hours every morning after breakfast, he took Ben into the woods and showed him how to find winter firewood. Using a small hatchet Arthur made for him, the boy clumsily hacked at a tree while Arthur felled it. Inside their cabin, Arthur taught his son the art of wood craft. Arthur gave him a small set of carving knives which fit Ben's small fingers. His first project was a crude boat carved from a birch branch which they placed on the mantle above the fireplace in their home.

In the afternoon Arthur took Nils into the woods where they marked trees for clearing. Halley often joined. The lumberman would wander the periphery, looking out into the woods for any sign of his missing niece. Often he would wander away, the only sign that he was still near his voice calling out her name. Arthur knew that the only chance for the girl lay in the hope that she had made her way to another settlement in the woods.

"Why does he keep looking?" Minnie asked Arthur.

"It is *sisu*," Arthur said. "He must go on."

Christmas was cold and lonely. The snow piled in drifts as high as the roofs. The only benefit to it was the extra insulation it gave the cabins when it lay on the roofs. Arthur found that they were using less firewood than he had predicted, and as a result he had to spend less time chopping wood. Instead, each morning Arthur rose and shoveled paths through the snow to the barn and to the kitchen. Eventually, the snow piled so high he could no longer see the other cabins. He took extra time and care clearing some of the snow off of the roofs, however, so that the cabins didn't cave in.

Still troubled by Virginia's loss, Arthur showed Ben how to build a shelter, in case he too got lost in the woods. Father and son traipsed through the snow to the edge of the clearing, where they were able to climb the drifts. There, Arthur and Ben dug a path through the snow to a nearby tree. They hollowed out a cave in the snow, and using a candle, Arthur melted snow over their heads to form a ceiling. He dug an air shaft opposite the doorway. The room was large enough for him to sit up in it, and long enough that he could lay flat and stretch out his legs.

"If you get lost, this is what you do to survive the cold," Arthur told him in Finnish. "Do you understand me?"

"Yes, Papa," the boy said. "My mine!"

Arthur smiled. "A good place to be just in case."

As the boy crawled out of the cavern on his belly, through the four-foot tunnel back to the path, Arthur smiled to himself. He felt a surge of pride as he remembered making snow caves with his father, and he wondered if *isä* was smiling down on him now. He lay in the cavern of snow and ice and felt the air warm with his breath. On his back, he found himself grow sleepy. Ben brought back the yarn doll that his mother had made for him. The doll's head was stuffed with goose feathers, and it had no arms. Just the head and a few strands of woolen yarn for a body. Still, the boy loved it and called it Eustis.

"Eustis home," Ben said.

Arthur nodded. "Yes, home for Eustis," he said. "And for you. In an emergency, this is home."

The sauna was a welcome respite from the cold, and Arthur and Minnie and Benjamin went there at least three nights a week. On Sundays, Halley and Frances came to their cabin. The four adults would read from the Bible together. Arthur's English began to improve during these sessions, as the others would help him learn to pronounce the words—but his Finnish tongue would never quite get the hang of the W.

After they said a final prayer, Minnie and Frances prepared dinner while Arthur and Halley set the fire in the sauna. They ate together, and then the men took the sauna first. Halley's first time in the sauna was short. He could last only a few minutes before the heat became too intense. When Arthur told him he had to roll in the snow outside, he laughed.

"You must be joking," he said.

Arthur shook his head. "It is the way."

To demonstrate, Arthur went out, his body steaming from the heat. He plunged himself in the snow, rolled until his entire body had melted a swatch of the white stuff, and then he stepped back into the sauna. He lay on the bench and sighed as the heat penetrated the cold.

Halley said, "All right." He stepped outside. "Ouch, ooh, aah," he said, grumbling as he stepped across the frozen ground. Seconds later he ran back into the sauna.

"You are dry," Arthur said.

"It is damned cold out there," Halley said.

Arthur laughed. "You are not Finnish."

"I'll take the heat."

But after a few minutes of heat, the lumberman realized that he was getting too hot. He felt himself grow weak and light-headed. Arthur took him outside. The cold air was bracing. As Halley breathed it in, the sweat on his body froze and then flaked off immediately. His body steamed, and even as he saw his sweat freeze on the ground he was not cold. Arthur left him leaning against the building while he jumped in the snow. He rolled twice and then got back to his feet. They went back into the sauna to rinse a final time and get dressed.

"We go back to the house," Arthur told him. "Give the women a turn."

Frances had never been in a sauna and she was skeptical, but she was more adventurous than her husband. When Minnie told her to go outside and plunge in the snow, she did it with a shriek of laughter—her first in weeks. From the kitchen Arthur and Halley heard her cry and ran to the door.

"Are you all right?" Halley yelled into the night.

Frances laughed. "I am fine, Len," she said. "This is exhilarating!"

Arthur amazed at how people got over loss. It came in fits and starts. Some days were better than others. Even now Arthur sometimes felt the pain of losing his parents, and the memory of Charlie still stung. Minnie, too, would cry at the oddest moments as she thought of the day her *isä* and *äiti* were torn from her. But they moved on. They continued to live because they had to, because they had Ben and a new baby on the way, because the future was a dream and the past was a memory and all they really had was the here and now. Because the alternative to living was a

Cornish miner leaning against a tree buried in snow.

⬥

January was the most difficult month. The mood in camp dropped with the temperature. The fifty miners who were left continued to receive a modest weekly wage of one dollar to stay at camp, but they became withdrawn and sullen. As the month wore on, they stopped talking. Meals remained silent affairs, the occasional sneeze echoing in the largely empty cabin.

January turned to February and the air grew colder, the snow deeper. They ate dried meat and rice, and when the meat ran out they ate fish and rice, and when the rice ran out they ate beans. The mess hall served a lot of soups because the kitchen could make the soup go further. Frances and Minnie baked bread, and Mrs. Gill, who walked with a slight limp now, taught them how to make Irish soda bread. She had a horde of raisins she used only for bread, though she shared them with little Benjamin. Minnie made *kalakukko*, a Finnish bread baked with a fish inside. As the cold grew more intense, the men consolidated to fewer cabins to make the most of their body heat, and to ensure they were as close to the kitchen as possible so they would have to walk less to get to meals. They stopped going outside except for this sole purpose, and then they sat around the fireplace until the evening, smoking and drinking and eating. Each night after dinner they returned to their cabins as the sun set so there would be no chance of anyone getting lost in the dark.

Soon Arthur noticed that the days were getting longer. The sun crested closer to the tips of the trees, and icicles began to drip from the eaves. The caverns of snow they had spent three months walking around shrank, and the ground became slushy during the day.

One afternoon Arthur and Halley were scouting for trees when Minnie let out a cry. Arthur ran back to camp to find Minnie crying outside the dining cabin. Arthur put his hands on her shoulders to get her to stop and talk to him. She sputtered something in Finnish but Arthur could not understand.

"Calmly," he told her.

She took a breath. "Ben," she said. "I cannot find him."

She had assumed he was playing upstairs in Housell's room, as usual, and had not noticed when exactly he had left, and had no idea where he had gone. Then Housell came downstairs, drunk already, and told her Benjamin had not been upstairs all morning. The cook had not seen the boy at all. She panicked and ran outside and began shouting his name, but heard no response.

Arthur imagined the boy wandering through the woods, simple curiosity compelling him along an unworn path. Now that the nightmare was happening to him, his own son lost to the giant, he told himself not to panic. All at once he understood why Halley continued to call Virginia's name to the trees. One can never give up hope, even when all hope seems lost.

Halley organized a search party: he and Frances, the Swedes Henrik and Nils, Gill and a few of the miners, with Arthur and Minnie walked along the paths of snow calling out the boy's name. The walls were only a few feet high, the path a slush of mud and ice.

Then Nils called out, "Here!"

The others ran to him. He was near the edge of the clearing, on the eastern side of the camp away from the mine. "There," he said and pointed to a cluster of trees. "I heard a voice."

"Ben," Arthur called.

There was a muffled reply.

Arthur began to dig at the snow. Here it was piled higher than elsewhere. The drifts were deeper where the wind had blown the snow into the trees. Arthur dug carefully with his bare hands, pushing the snow backwards as he moved forward. "Ben," he shouted.

The boy shouted again and his voice, though still muffled, was louder. Arthur dug a few more feet and then plunged his hand through the snow to his elbow. A warm, wet hand touched his. He squeezed it and his heart soared.

The ice cave was filled with little pieces of wood and a few rocks that Benjamin had been using as toys. He had apparently been going into the cave frequently, and spent a lot of time there. Today, when he entered the cave, he had begun to play when he heard something groan—and then the tunnel, which had grown smaller and smaller each day, collapsed. He was trapped.

"Mining, Papa," Benjamin said. "Shaft collapsed."

Arthur lifted him out of the snow and handed the boy to

Minnie who held him close. Halley smiled, and Frances, too, seemed genuinely happy since before Virginia disappeared. For Arthur, the moment seemed to signal the beginning of the end of the long cold winter.

⸺◆⸺

As the snow melted, so too did the dampened spirits of the winter residents of Mountain Iron. Soon enough, even Wood and Cohoe were smiling again. One morning in March, Cohoe left camp with five days' worth of supplies on his back, a pick, and a shovel. With him were Gill and two other Cornish miners. He returned three days later, breathless and relieved, marched up to the table where Wilbur and Cassius, who had arrived that morning, were eating with Halley and Arthur and Wood.

"We've found more ore!" he said.

Cassius sat up. "Where?"

"Fifty-eight north, seventeen west, section nine. Right there, sitting on the surface. We dug a little and beneath only about a foot of dirt we found quite a load."

Halley looked around the room and saw that Frances was not nearby. "Any sign of Virginia?" he asked, his eyes brimming with promise. Arthur wondered if he hoped they would find nothing at all, because finding nothing meant she might still be alive somewhere.

Cohoe sat down. "I'm afraid that's the bad news, Len. She was in a snowdrift leaning against a tree not twenty paces from where we found the deposit. Just sitting there. She looked so peaceful and quiet. Like she'd just sat down to take a nap."

Halley's face drooped and a shadow seemed to cloud his eyes. He turned to Arthur. "She's gone, then," he said.

"I am sorry," Arthur said.

Halley stood up. His plate of food was largely uneaten. He went through the door to the kitchen. Seconds later, they heard Frances break into fresh sobs.

Arthur said, "Where is her body?"

"Gill is bringing it back," Cohoe said.

The Cornishman arrived in camp a few hours later pulling the body on a sled made from two slim pine branches crisscrossed with rope. He had folded her hands over her chest and wrapped her in canvas.

The ground was still too hard to dig through, but Halley was determined to bury his niece. He convinced Cohoe to use the big diamond drill to bore holes in the ground. They selected a spot on the north end of town and Arthur built a fence around the area. He marked off two plots where the drill cut holes in the frozen earth, one for Virginia and one for the Cornishman who had wandered off months ago and frozen to death. Gill packed the holes with explosives, and the Cornish miners shoveled out the hardened earth.

After the bodies were buried, Wood began to drink heavily. He snuck into the storage room in the kitchen and swiped three bottles and drank one of them on the first day. On the second he slowed a little, drinking half a bottle, and by the end of the week he had finished all three bottles. Cassius advised him that since the ground seemed soft enough to bury bodies, it must be soft enough to dig for ore, but Wood was too drunk to listen.

"If you cannot get this mine started again then I shall find someone who can," Cassius told him.

"Who're you gonna get," Wood said. "I'm the only one knows how to do this job."

And after a week of entreaties and demands, Cassius finally fired him. "Mr. Cohoe will take over as head of the mine."

The next day Wood was gone.

Cohoe got the mine running immediately. It could not have been soon enough. A message came from Duluth that Lon was no longer recruiting there. The ads were listing the jobs in Mountain Iron, and men were on their way to apply.

"Get ready," Lon's telegram said.

Arthur didn't know how to prepare himself for the hordes of men coming undoubtedly to wake the giant.

CHAPTER 8

HÄN ON TULLUT TAKAISIN

The workers came. They were Norwegian and Swedish and Polish and Slovenian and German and Italian and Finn. They walked from Duluth and Tower. They came on horseback and by donkey. The came alone and they came with families. They hauled wagons carrying all their belongings, or they lugged packs on their backs, or they came with nothing at all. They came to work the mines, and they came to support the workers, to sell beer or open a grocery store or cut hair. One young Slovenian, barely fifteen years-old, walked from Duluth with nothing but the clothes on his body, a comb, a razor, and a pair of scissors. Overwhelmingly they were men.

By March the little camp that Arthur had built was not little anymore. Men were sleeping on the floors of the bunkhouses, and on the floor of the dining room. Arthur hired a dozen Finns to help with construction, sending Henrik and Nils back to the mine. Arthur no longer built log cabins that would withstand the cold, harsh winter and which took days to build; now they constructed simple framed shacks, windowless and dark, sided with boards and covered with tarpaper to keep out the damp spring rains.

Cohoe ordered that no one was allowed to set up a residence or business at the mining camp unless he or she was an employee of the Mountain Iron Company. South of camp, merchants and sellers and saloonkeepers, like Mike Griviz, the boy barber, cleared trees and organized a grid of streets. They put up a few small shacks using scraps left over from the mine, but quickly needed more. Halley offered to sell them some of the lumber he was making—there was more than enough—but at first, Cohoe would have none of it. Only when Halley convinced him the company could make extra money did the mining captain agree. Shops were put up in a day.

Arthur thought these loosely boarded hodgepodges of lumber would come down in the first stiff breeze. But they were occupied immediately, stocked with dry goods and foodstuffs, liquor, and beer, which was also sold by the glass and bottle in saloons. The first hotel—named after the owner, Daniel Marfield—was up by April, and a month later, a second hotel appeared. Soon a group of merchants met in one of the new homes and voted to form a town. They called it Marfield.

When Cohoe heard the name, he was indignant. "Do they think they would be here without this mountain of iron?" He remained busy with the mine, though, and had no time for what he called the folly of townsfolk.

From his vantage point at the head of the giant, Arthur could see that the boom that was happening here was happening everywhere. Huge swaths of trees were being razed and in their place, plumes of white smoke drifted over the bare, low valleys. As winter melted into spring and the trees began to bud, the quiet world of the Mesabi was changing. The giant had stirred.

"Maybe we should move," Arthur suggested to Minnie at breakfast.

"No," she said. "I like it here."

"This place is getting so crowded," he said. "Too many people. Too noisy." He didn't want to leave, not really, but the camp was changing. Crowded and loud, the little mining location was busy with men wandering day and night to and from the now constantly active mine. It had been a year since he'd come and he felt strangely nostalgic for the quiet woods that he had found when he first stepped out of the trees. Thoughts of those early days reminded him of Charlie and Richardson. He missed his friends.

"You are a leader here," she said. "You cannot just leave. Have you so little confidence in the place you built? In the people here?"

Benjamin finished his breakfast and ran outside with the dog. "The boy must be schooled," he said. It was a sheepish attempt at persuasion.

She had an answer for everything. "I have heard they are organizing a school in Marfield," she said. "He will go there."

Letting go the question of moving for now, he put his arms around her growing belly. "When?"

"Soon," she smiled and fell back into him.

The pit was more than a hundred yards long now, stretching north toward the low hills, and at least a hundred feet deep. Men worked around the clock throwing picks into the soft earth and lifting the heavy, red-tinted ore from the ground. They worked alongside a steam shovel, which, though it broke down regularly, still moved earth faster than ten men. The laborers had daily competitions to see if one of them could match the shoveling power of that mechanical behemoth. No one won.

The stockpile grew into a small mountain that began to dwarf the rolling hills Charlie had shown Arthur on that day a year before. He watched the pile of ore grow and wondered when they would begin to ship the ore, when it would start to sell. Was it really worth anything at all? To Arthur the grass growing atop the pile was the hair on the giant's head. He was sitting up now, glowering at them, mocking them. You might have woken me, the giant seemed to say, but you will not move me.

One night, as he bathed with Minnie in the sauna, he said, "We have nothing if the mine makes nothing. The ore sits there. Why are these men digging it out of the ground if no one buys it? If no one buys it, how can the company make any money?"

Minnie said, "You must have faith in Mr. Merritt."

Arthur thought about that. He recalled the charismatic Lon who had come to visit him in Tower and had convinced him to join the search for iron ore. He thought of the giant who had climbed down into the pit and had called on them all to believe. That Lon was a far cry from the uncomfortable business man who appeared in the fall and promised Arthur a fortune in exchange for his pay. He said, "Maybe that is the problem. Maybe I have lost faith."

On Sundays he prayed for the ore to leave the mountain. He prayed that a buyer would come, and that soon the papers that he kept in an iron box beneath the floorboards in the living room of his home would be worth more than his wage. That they would make all of this effort worthwhile.

One bright day in May Arthur was in the office with Captain

Cohoe discussing construction needs for the mine—support for walls, lights in the pit for night work, a shelter for the pit captains. There was much to be done. One of the Irish laborers came in with a letter. Cohoe tore open the envelope and read it, his lips moving as he traced the words. His eyes brightened.

"Woo-hoo!" he said. "This is it!"

"What?" Arthur said.

"A railroad is coming," Cohoe said. "Lon says they've signed a deal with the Duluth and Winnipeg. If we build a spur down to Stony Brook junction, the D&W will take the ore to Allouez Bay in Superior."

"What about Two Harbors?"

Cohoe shrugged. "I guess the deal with the D&IR fell through. No matter. Superior means we don't have to compete with Tower's mines for ore cars and dock space in Two Harbors."

"Does it say when?"

Cohoe read the message again. "No, just says a contract has been awarded to Donald Grant. I've heard of him. A fine railroad builder."

At least the ore will move, Arthur thought.

A crew arrived a few days later. They were Irish workers, most of them, led by a tough Irishman named Finnigan with wild red hair and wide handlebar mustache. He burst into the office, fell into one of Arthur's chairs, and immediately lit a cigarette.

"Let's build a railroad," he said.

Arthur said, "No smoke, please. The building will burn."

"You jokin'?" Finnigan rolled back in the chair and laughed. "The whole country's made of wood, friend."

"And if it burns, what else do we use to build?" Fire was a carpenter's worst fear.

The chair legs clapped against the floorboards as Finnegan leaned forward. He nodded thoughtfully. "Iron," he said. "'Tis what we're here for anyway."

Arthur said nothing. He was not going to back down.

Finnigan puffed and then went to the open window and flicked the cigarette out. "That suit ye?"

Arthur nodded. Across his desk he had laid a map of the mine and the surrounding area. He had marked two or three places on his map where the train could enter, and where he could build a depot. Finnegan peered over Arthur's shoulder. He reeked of tobacco and whiskey. "I have located places to build a depot."

The Irishman spread his red stained fingers across the space on the map that indicated the mine. "That the mine?"

"Yes."

"Is it that hole in the ground I saw over there?"

"Yes."

Finnigan whistled. "People have talked, sure, but to see it. It's quite a pit you've dug. This shallow grade, is that the access?"

"Yes."

"Then we bring the line to there. 'Twould serve the village, too."

Finnigan and his crew surveyed the area west of town close to the mine entrance, which was nothing more than a road leading down into the pit. The survey took two days as they marked exactly where the rail would come into town, and where the depot would have to be built.

"We ain't building the depot, though," Finnigan told Arthur.

"Who will?" Arthur said.

Finnigan shrugged. "I'm here to lay a railroad. You want a depot maybe you should find the man who built this camp. He has a good eye."

It felt good to have a stranger admire his work. Arthur liked the idea of getting back to what he loved to do and getting away from worrying about the influx of people to the camp. So he agreed to build the depot himself.

By June work in the mine had reached a fever pitch. The steam shovel was working around the clock, crunching the soft ore into piles and dumping them in ore carts to be hauled out of the pit. There was a restlessness in the mine, though, as the ore piles got larger and larger but still there was no movement of the ore. The giant just sat there, mocking their progress.

A small group of Finnish laborers who worked the steam shovel found Arthur in his office one afternoon. He was finalizing the plan for the train station when they came into the building. There were five of them, fair skinned and clean-shaven, with red dirt on their cheeks and hands. They wore rubber jackets and pants and rubber boots. One of them stepped ahead of the others and removed his rubber hat. He had piercing blue eyes and a slight smile; Arthur imagined Benjamin in sixteen years.

"Mr. Maki," the young man said in Finnish.

"Yes," Arthur said.

"I am Paavo. I work in the mine. These men are my brothers."

Arthur looked at the five young men again, and there was a similarity to their faces.

"We are working brothers. We look out for one another, protect one another. The mine is a dangerous place." The others nodded in agreement. "We need your help."

Arthur laid down his pencil and laced his fingers together.

"We have not been paid. We have only been here for two months and in that time we have received no pay. We are men. We have needs. Food to buy, supplies, clothes, shelter. Rooms in Mountain Iron cost but little, but they do cost."

"Why do you come to me?"

"You are one of us," Paavo said. "A Finn. One of our brothers."

The others again nodded in agreement. Paavo looked like he could be the oldest of the group, but all together they were probably not as old as Hephzibah Merritt. Each man looked back at Arthur with a solemn, respectful expression. They were not afraid of his response, were not afraid of what he might say, as though they were unafraid of anyone. Of anything. They had come to Arthur not because he was the meek one who would do as they asked, but because he spoke their language. Arthur both envied and admired their boldness.

"What do you want of me?"

"We want you to represent us with the Merritts. Talk to them. We need to be paid. If they want to keep us happy, they will pay us what we are owed."

"Mr. Merritt does what he can, I know this. He is not wealthy."

"We only ask to be paid what we are owed, what we have worked for. He should understand that without us there can be no iron ore."

Arthur considered this. The ore, piling up, had been bothering him, and now these men were threatening to stop digging it out of the ground. What would that do to the Mountain Iron Company certificates Lon had given him?

"The Soudan mine shut down," Paavo said.

"I had not heard this. What happened?"

"The workers have taken over the mine. They are demonstrating that they have the power. We do not want to do the same here, but if we do not receive our pay we may have no choice."

Arthur could not mask his shock at hearing this. "You will shut down Mountain Iron?"

The other men looked at the floor, but Paavo lifted his chin and pushed out his chest. "If we must."

"The other men, the other workers, they feel the same?" Arthur could not keep the concern out of his voice. If they shut down the mine…? He could not continue the thought.

Paavo's resolve faltered for a moment. He exhaled and his eyes looked left and right for support from the men with him. The others continued to look at the floor, though, their hats in their hands. Then Paavo lifted his head again and confidently said, "Yes."

Arthur did not believe that this Finn had the power to stop anything, nor did he believe that there were any more than these five who were willing to say they would stop working. Still, the question of pay was important. Arthur had agreed to stocks in exchange for some cash, but these men relied on the cash in their pockets to survive. They were sending money home to families, were saving to bring their wives and children to Mountain Iron. Arthur understood that. He had pined after his own wife for months. If they wanted his help, he would give it to them.

Arthur stood up. "I shall speak with Captain Cohoe. Perhaps there was a clerical error. I want you to get what you deserve."

Paavo smiled. "This is why we came to you."

"Because I am Finnish?"

"Because you care."

Paavo stepped forward and offered his hand across the desk. Arthur reached out and took it, and the two men shook hands. Then the five young Finns turned and, as a group, left the office without another word, boots shuffling along the dust covered floor. Arthur waited until they were gone and then he went looking for Cohoe. He found the mine boss hiding in his office.

"Are they gone?" he said.

"Yes," Arthur said.

Cohoe breathed a sigh of relief. "Thanks, Maki," he said. "I was afraid they'd come looking for me."

Arthur said, "Why is there no pay?"

"You know how it is. Cash flow. Johnnie tells me that the company's cash reserves are getting tied up in the railroad. Don't worry, though. Money's coming. They'll get paid."

"Have you heard of Soudan?"

"Terrible business, that. They've called in the militia to keep order. They'll have it sorted out in no time." He turned to the window. Paavo and his group were walking back to the mine. "They don't realize how replaceable they are."

Arthur was surprised to hear this. "Are they?"

"There's a lot more of them than they think. I can find twenty guys to shovel dirt or sort through rocks. They're out there by the thousands, each one waiting for his special chance to get rich. This country is opening up, Maki. It's a new world, and men like Paavo over there had better wise up to it."

"We must pay them," Arthur repeated.

"Bah, they'll get paid." Cohoe waved his hand like he was swatting at a swarm of gnats. "It takes time. They have no patience. And if they stop working because they have not gotten paid, then they will not get paid ever. It is simple."

Arthur was beginning to understand, and he did not like what he heard. Was this the way Lon felt? The attitude was different from that of the man who had promoted a mine to benefit all of Minnesota.

"Don't worry about Paavo," Cohoe said. "Let them keep thinking you are on their side. It gives us an in. We can keep an eye on guys like that. They make our jobs harder, you know."

"How?" Arthur eyed Cohoe warily. Was he asking Arthur to spy on the workers who trusted him?

"By stirring up trouble. They make the men think we are the bad guys. The Merritts aren't bad. We are all out here trying to make a living. Lon and his brothers want what is best for these men as much as they do, and the sooner they see it the sooner they'll realize that we are not out to get one another."

"I think they only want to survive."

"You think these men aren't surviving? Do you know they get one day off per week? That's a luxury. Most of the companies out here, they don't give 'em that. But Lon believes that the men, to be happy, should have time off. And do you know what most of them do with their time off? Do they go to church? Spend time with family? No, they go to the saloons in town, the hotels, drinking away their non-existent pay and seeking comfort in the arms of women.

"Look, Maki. We are controllers of our destiny, controllers of this place. We can and should take what we can from it. We work hard for ourselves, and we do not ask for handouts. We don't take what is given—we take what is ours. If they work hard, then they too shall have their reward."

Cohoe's face had grown red and his breathing labored. His knuckles pressed against the books on his desk. "I don't like to see men try to get more than they earn."

"But they are not asking for more than they earn," Arthur said. "They only ask for what they are owed." Arthur felt torn between the two worlds: the company making money on the one hand, and treating people fairly on the other.

"Whose side are you on, Maki?"

Arthur wondered himself. It was a question he couldn't answer.

⸺◆⸺

When he told Minnie about the incident with Paavo and the conversation with Cohoe, she was indignant.

"You must help," she said. "How do they expect people to live without pay?"

Arthur shrugged. "I have no influence over pay. What can I do? Cohoe says they will be paid."

"You must go higher than Cohoe. Go to Johnnie. Or write to Lon and tell him what is happening."

"I can ask, but I cannot force them. What if there is no money?"

"Of course there is money. Look at all the work going on? I have heard that they are bringing in a second steam shovel to help with the digging. The mine works around the clock. If they have no money how do they make it all happen?"

"People are cheap," Arthur said. "They are expendable."

Minnie shook her head. "I refuse to believe that is what Lon thinks."

But Arthur had his doubts. "He has changed."

Minnie took the dishes to the kitchen. "Men like Lon do not change," she called.

The dog, Uros, perked up his ears and began barking. Benjamin followed the dog to the front door. Arthur stood and strode across the house. It was odd to have someone visit at such a late hour. Was there an emergency? Benjamin pulled the handle and Arthur was stunned by the man who stood in the doorway.

He wore a buckskin suit, leather boots, and he had an axe tucked into his belt loop. Richardson. Arthur had not seen him since the fall, and he looked weathered from the winter, but his eyes were clear and sober.

From the kitchen Minnie called, "Who is there?"

Arthur turned to her. "Richardson. *Hän on tullut takaisin.*" *He has come back.*

"*Hei,*" Richardson said.

"*Boozhoo,*" Arthur said.

"Good to see you again."

"And you," Arthur said. Minnie appeared behind him then and he took her arm and tugged her gently forward. "This is Minnie," he said. "I wanted you to meet her."

Richardson bowed his head. "Pleased to meet you."

"This is Verne Richardson," Arthur said.

"I have heard much about you," Minnie said. "Arvid has told me how good you were to him."

Richardson smiled. "The feeling is mutual."

Benjamin hid behind his father's legs. "This is my son, Ben," he said.

Richardson knelt down. "You look just like your father."

The boy smiled shyly and buried his face in the fabric of Arthur's pants. Richardson laughed. "Your father was just as shy when I first met him."

Minnie said, "Please come in. I have *pulla* and coffee."

"Thank you," Richardson said. "I have something I need to talk to you both about."

Minnie brought coffee and the sweet bread to the living room and served it while Richardson unburdened himself. He told them that he had gone to the reservation to help put Charlie to rest and see his soul into the next world. Afterwards, Charlie's father had asked him to stay.

"'You were his brother,' his father told me," Richardson explained. So he had agreed to stay for a month to help the family prepare for winter. Charlie's father was a *medewin*, a medicine man, and relied on the assistance of others in the tribe, and his own children, for food and clothing. All the time Richardson was there, he was haunted by dreams of the two men who killed Charlie. He could not rid himself of the image of them, of what they had done.

"When I left the reservation I thought it would end. I thought the dreams would end and that I could leave it behind. But when I found my own father at his cabin the dreams continued. I knew I could not stay there as I had planned. I knew I had to find the men who had killed Charlie."

He traveled by train to Duluth where he talked to Lon and the sheriff and others who had seen what had happened that day. All Richardson had to go on were the names Minnie had told Arthur: Ned and Danny. Lon remembered, of course, but he was preoccupied with business. He couldn't be bothered with finding the men who had killed Charlie.

"So I kept looking. The sheriff told me the same story, that Charlie had stolen money and had threatened the two men. I did not try to change his mind. I told him I wanted to find the murderers. He told me that revenge was not an answer. 'We don't like that kind of stuff around here,' he told me. I assured him that I'd not be looking for revenge as much as an answer of some sort. I don't think he believed me, but he at least gave me a description of them. And a last name: Walters. He told me they were from a gang that came out of Iowa, bad men I'd do best to avoid.

"They left Duluth shortly after the shooting. Went to Tower and Ely and then disappeared in the woods. This was May. I stayed in Tower, working the mine, always keeping an eye and an ear open. I made friends in town and they stayed in touch. I heard nothing until a few weeks ago. The bartender at the Vermilion Hotel had heard a couple men talking about coming down here looking for work. They called themselves Ned and Danny."

Minnie shuddered. "That must be them."

Richardson nodded. "I left that day. Took the train to Mesaba. It's changed a lot since we were there, Arthur. Remember that? It's not run-down anymore. Now it's a busy place—at least a dozen hotels and half again as many saloons. Supplies moving in and out all the time, hundreds of men coming through every day. They have opened up this country. Then I walked along the road, our old road. It, too, has changed. Still hard to travel, sure, but at least all those old tree stumps and boulders are gone. Now it's just thick mud and thirty miles of swamp. I passed a long wagon train hauling what looked to be pieces of a steam engine. I was not sure what it was until I saw that behemoth in the pit here.

"I went to most of the mines between Mesaba and here. There are dozens, and more opening all the time. At Biwabik they have already dug a mine half as large as this one. And southeast of here is a place called Virginia where they have already voted to create a town. Half a dozen small mines are there. Missabe Mountain is the largest. They told me Lon owns that one, too. He must be doing well. The country is filling with people, speculators and operators and miners. You should see it."

"I have seen it here," Arthur said.

"I guess you have. I saw that little place on the other side of the road. What are they calling it? Marfield?"

Minnie laughed.

"Why not Mountain Iron?"

Arthur said, "We do not know."

"I worked in Virginia for a while. Wasn't that the name of that sawmiller's daughter up here?"

Minnie lowered her head.

"What of Ned and Danny?" Arthur said, impatient with all this talk of plans and riches and men's boasts.

Minnie laid a calming hand on her husband's arm.

"I've not forgotten," Richardson continued. "All the time I was there I asked about them. Especially at the saloons. I figured I'd missed them. Maybe they'd gone back to Ohio, or further south." But he had gone into a saloon in town called the Nugget and was on his third beer when he saw two men coming down the stairs with a soiled dove called Kate. He knew immediately it had to be them. They looked like brothers, with long, weathered faces and the same crooked nose. One of them was taller and when he laughed his mouth opened to reveal black teeth and gums that looked like he'd been eating tar.

"'Don't worry about it, Ned,' he said. 'Happens to the best of 'em. Right Kate?' He pushed the one he called Ned in the back, and Ned tumbled down the steps and landed on a guy sipping a beer. A brawl broke out. Kind of comical, really. Next thing you know the whole place is throwing punches and Ned and Danny have somehow slipped out of it and sidled over to the bar and are asking for another couple whiskeys. The bartender tells 'em to get out, and they each pull out these silver revolvers. The bartender slides a bottle across to 'em and then they just walk away."

Richardson followed them into the street. They wobbled and wandered like lost children until finally they slipped into a stable. He watched them from outside and when they didn't come out he knew they'd be in there for the night.

"I had my chance, Arthur. They were there, probably incoherent, and I could have walked right in and taken care of them. I sat down on the street and stared at that barn all night long and I did nothing. Eventually the sun came up, and I must have fallen asleep, because they were gone."

He went back to the saloon and found the woman the two men had been with. She said they had come in before, that they said they worked at the Ohio mine.

"By the time I got there they were gone. Captain told me they'd not come in that morning. One of the other miners said he heard them saying they was going to go further west, said they'd heard there was another outfit that was paying better money." No one liked them. They were drunk and violent men who pushed around the other miners and acted like the land belonged to them.

Arthur leaned forward. "You think they come here?"

"It's the only place left, ain't it? I know people are exploring further west, but ain't nobody found nothing out there yet."

Minnie put her hand over her mouth. "*Voi Luoja*," she said. *Oh God.*

"It's why I need you both. Ma'am, I don't want to put you through anything. I just want justice for our friend, Charlie. Seems like—" His voice trailed off.

The trio sat in silence while outside Gill's bell sounded and then an earth rattling explosion. The dog was asleep next to the fireplace and his legs scurried through a dream. Even he was used to the blasting.

Arthur said, "If they are working at the mine, Cohoe will know them."

"Cohoe? What happened to Captain Wood?"

"He is gone."

"Good riddance." He stood up. "Can we talk to this Cohoe?"

Arthur said, "Tomorrow. It is late."

Richardson nodded. "You're right." He turned to Minnie. "I'm sorry to bring worry into your home."

She smiled. "That is kind of you to say, but I know you bring more than worry." She put her hand on Arthur's arm. "Arvid has missed his friends."

Arthur slept fitfully that night. For the first time he thought about putting a lock on the door. And he told Minnie he did not want to leave her alone.

"I will be fine, Arvid," she said. "You must have faith."

That was the problem, he thought. He was losing faith in everything.

Arthur was nervous. He hadn't slept very well. And walking through camp now, with Richardson by his side, every face he didn't recognize was a face to question. "There," Arthur said, pointing to two scraggly men slumbering along the dusty street after a long night shift at the mine. "Is that them?"

Richardson laughed. "Seeing ghosts in every corner? No, not them."

"I am nervous to meet them. What will I do? What will I say?"

"What would Charlie do?" Richardson asked.

It was a good question.

They found Cohoe in the office. "Maki, look at this," he said, barely glancing up from the maps on his desk.

Arthur strode over to him. Richardson stood in the doorway. "I must speak with you."

"On the east end, over here." He dropped a muddy finger on the map. "We thought the vein stopped, but Gill loosened the rock there last night and found more ore on the other side of this thick layer of taconite. It just keeps getting better." He lifted his head and smiled, but the look on Arthur's face brought him back down. "What is it?" He glanced from Arthur to Richardson in the doorway.

"This is Verne Richardson," Arthur said.

Cohoe corked his face, studying the man, and then he smiled in recognition. "Ah, yes, I remember. The timberman, right? Tousled with Housell, if I recall."

At the mention of the fight Richardson put his hand on his shoulder.

"We need to find out about two men who may have joined the company here," Arthur said.

Cohoe looked from Arthur to Richardson. "What is this about?"

Richardson took his first step forward. "I am hunting two brothers who are wanted by the authorities in Iowa: Danny and Ned Walters."

Cohoe sat down and began stroking his beard. "What are they wanted for?"

"A string of bank robberies up the Mississippi. They killed a deputy sheriff in Dubuque."

Arthur was sure Richardson was lying, but he said nothing.

Cohoe looked confused. "How do you know this? Don't you work the sawmill?"

"I left last year," Richardson said. "My shoulder would not allow me to work. I'm a Pinkerton man now." He stepped over to where Cohoe was sitting. "Do you know these men?"

Cohoe eyed the lumberman wearily. Arthur surmised that he would call Richardson's bluff, would ask for proof, would ultimately give no information at all. Then Cohoe surprised him. "Can't say I recognize the names. But if they're on the payroll they'd be in the book." He went to the front room and brought back a large black ledger.

"This has all the men I've hired in the last two months," he said.

Richardson flipped through the pages and found the dates that matched the last time he had seen the two killers.

"Sounds like bad business," Cohoe said to Arthur.

"Yes," Arthur said. He watched Richardson scan through the names.

Cohoe continued, "The new vein means we'll have more ore to stockpile. Hope that train gets here fast."

Arthur was not really listening to the captain. He was thinking about Charlie, and Minnie, and the two killers.

"How about that depot?"

Arthur had been working on the depot every day. With a crew of men who spoke his language and knew what they were doing, construction moved swiftly. For Arthur, the quality of the building was its most impressive feature. He wanted the depot to be the nicest building in town.

Suddenly there was a crash outside, a noise like a rumbling in the earth, and then a thundering boom. It was not like the explosions Gill set off.

"What was that?" Cohoe said.

Arthur forgot for the moment about the killers and about Richardson and about the depot and bolted out the door. Outside smoke was rising from the pit, along with a deafening roar. Arthur, lighter and faster on his feet than Cohoe, arrived first. Down in the pit the steam shovel had lifted partway off its tracks and was leaning against the pit wall, the swing arm lying in the red dirt and iron ore like a broken limb. Black smoke rose from its engine, water and oil dripping out of her belly like blood from a deer. The collapsed pit wall was now raining dirt and rocks and debris down into the pit, partially burying the shovel itself and anyone who had been working around it.

Cohoe arrived and barked orders. "You men, there, dig out the shovel and get it upright!"

The men paid him no attention. Most of them stared in shock at the behemoth of a shovel that looked like it had been pushed over by a giant hand. Others were digging under the bucket and arm and ignoring the engine. Cohoe ran around Arthur and, grabbing one of the ropes the men used to climb into and out of the pit, slid down on his feet like he was skiing. He shouted as he scrambled down, "We have to get the engine up." The massive machine rumbled and creaked. The men either did not hear Cohoe shout or chose to ignore him, because as a group they continued to frantically dig the earth out from under the fallen shovel and shovel arm.

Cohoe got to the bottom and stumbled through the loose earth and rocks towards the engine, which was teetering now on two wheels. The more the men dug, the more unstable the engine became, leaning further against the unstable pit wall. Cohoe waved his arms and shouted, pointing to the engine. Finally the men stopped and looked and as a group the dozen or so that were digging stopped. Cohoe barked more orders. Two men ran to the engine and climbed on it. Two others set about straightening the tracks on which it would have to sit. Still more men came from the mine. They brought ropes and cables, tied them to the fallen shovel arm, and then threaded them through the pulleys and chains that controlled the movement of the bucket. One of the cables that held the shovel arm in place had snapped. It looked to Arthur like the weight of the bucket and arm had caused the engine to tip over.

Arthur saw something else, too: an arm sticking out from under the dirt and rubble, from under the bucket.

The men retied the bucket to the arm. The operator waited and watched the mechanics, three of them, work to get the engine operating. They opened the steam valve and released the pressure from the boiler. Steam hissed like a teakettle. The steam rose higher than the trees, and the sound of it was deafening. Even from the top of the pit Arthur could feel the heat. He wondered how the men working down there could handle it. With the pressure down, the men filled the fire pit with coal and stoked the flames. Water was added to the boiler and then it was sealed. More coal was shoveled in. Flames shot out of the firebox. Then the engine rumbled to life. It was like hearing something come alive, like a body that had been killed and suddenly had arisen.

Arthur watched, fascinated. He knew trees, he knew wood. He could build a house in a day, add a second story in two days. But when it came to mechanical things, he was lost. The men who got the steam shovel started seemed like miracle workers.

One of the mechanics gave a thumbs-up to the shovel operator, who then pulled a lever. The great arm creaked and the bucket rose into the air. The operator pulled another lever and the arm swung left, toward the middle of the pit. It seemed that the little engine strained under the effort of lifting its own arm, groaning and creaking as it swung away from the wall of the pit. Then, as though exhausted, the arm fell again, landing heavily against the floor of the pit, dust and debris bouncing from the impact. The shovel was the hand of the giant, active and angry. The miners rushed back to the collapsed wall of the pit and began to dig. Within minutes they pulled a body out from under the rubble. Arthur couldn't see the face, but he recognized the clothes. It was one of Paavo's brothers who had visited him yesterday.

The giant had taken its revenge.

They found two bodies beneath the rubble. The Finn, it turned out, was Paavo's real brother and had been working in the mine longer than Paavo. He had been in charge of the line crew that ensured the steam shovel tracks were aligned with the ore deposit. The engineer working the shovel reported that when the cable broke, he had rushed between the engine and the pit wall yelling for everyone to run.

"'Twas because of him they weren't more men killed than they was," the engineer said.

The second man was an Italian laborer who had arrived in Mountain Iron only two days before. When he had signed on he had presented a letter from a brother of his who worked in Tower. He seemed to know no one else at the mine and spoke very little English. It was believed that he simply came to the wrong place looking for his brother. Cohoe had put him to work shoveling ore that fell out of the steam shovel bucket. When the cable broke he had been killed almost instantly, crushed by the falling debris and the bucket itself.

The bodies were buried in the little cemetery next to Virginia and the Cornishman who had frozen to death over the winter. Arthur fashioned crosses from an ash tree, and the blacksmith burned their names into the wood. Paavo was alone next to the mounded dirt of his brother's grave when Arthur approached.

"I am sorry for your loss," Arthur said.

"He was my only brother. He was three years older than I. He was the smart one; I followed him. He brought me here and taught me how to work in a mine, what to look for in the ore. He was the only family I had left." He put his face in his hands. "It is my fault."

"It was a terrible accident."

Paavo shook his head. "No, that is not what I mean. It is my fault he was there. He should have been somewhere else. He was working for me while I spoke to the men."

Arthur thought for a moment. "God chose him," he said. "We cannot understand His will. Your brother is in a better place."

Paavo turned to Arthur. "Do you think that God cares about us? We who are tearing apart his creation? Do you think that He looks down and takes pity on us? He does not care. He does not watch. He has abandoned us here to suffer as fools." Paavo kicked dirt onto the grave of his brother. "God is dead," he said, and walked away.

Afterwards Richardson found Arthur to tell him that the two men's names were not in the payroll ledger. "Doesn't mean they're not here," Richardson said. "Could be using other names."

"They will come," Arthur said. He was beginning to have faith in fatalism. "We lost two men, so two more will come to replace them. We must keep watch." Richardson agreed. So Arthur hired the lumberman again and had Cohoe put him on the payroll. Though technically part of Arthur's crew, Richardson spent most of his time around the pit watching the workers. He rented a room in town and avoided the dining hall. He didn't want another run in with Housell.

Cohoe liked having him around. "He's like our own security force," Cohoe said. "I tell the men we've got a Pinkerton man watching 'em and they don't slack off a bit."

Paavo left the day after the funeral, rucksack on his back. Arthur watched him stop at the edge of the clearing, pick a stick up off the ground, and begin to whittle it as he disappeared into the woods. Later, Arthur asked Cohoe why he had left.

"I fired him," Cohoe said.

"Why?"

"He was stirring up trouble. He was off getting the men riled up with that babble about their pay, but had he been with his brother, the men would have seen that the cable tension was too high. They would have caught it before it snapped and nobody would have died."

"Is this true?" Arthur asked. He found it hard to believe.

"Aye, 'tis true. The men were distracted."

Arthur was no mechanic, but he knew an accident when he saw one. Paavo could no more have predicted that cable breaking than Cohoe himself could. "You fired him over pay," Arthur said flatly.

"He was disruptive to my mine," Cohoe said, and went back to his desk. He was finished with the discussion.

Arthur had no stomach for staring at maps again today so he stepped outside. The trees surrounding the camp were growing thin. To the north Arthur could see the swell of low hills rising over the exposed land. The red earth met a pale horizon under a sky of wispy clouds. Arthur thought of Charlie and began walking towards the old *waaginogaan*.

So far, he had been able to keep that wooded area safe from the axe, but he did not know how much longer he could. The mine was expanding fast, and the whole operation devoured wood. Ultimately, Arthur knew, the mine would go where it would go. The steam shovel had started again, churning and crunching through the earth. The clearing was filled with smoke from the fires of the steam engine and the dinky train engines pulling the ore cars out of the pit. This place, when Arthur had first seen it, was pristine, even holy. Now it was a place taken over by men, transformed by men. It was not what he had expected or hoped for, but he had to support his family, and it was all he had.

Arthur hadn't gone forty yards when he heard a yell. He turned and saw Halley, his round body bouncing over the camp road, with Richardson by his side. He thought the worst: Ned and Danny had found Minnie.

"Arthur," Halley called. "Arthur, come, come!"

Arthur ran towards the two men. Richardson caught him first.

"It is Minnie," Richardson said, out of breath. "It is time."

"Time?" Arthur said.

"The baby," Richardson said. "She's having the baby."

And for the second time in two days Arthur ran across the camp.

Frances was in the house with Minnie. His wife waddled back and forth in the living room, mumbling in Finnish, hands on her back, her body hunched.

"If you would lie down," Frances urged, but Minnie kept pacing. "Why will this woman not listen to me?"

Minnie saw Arthur and smiled. "*Saunaan,*" she said. *To the sauna.*

Frances saw him for the first time. "Thank goodness. She keeps saying something about the sauna, but I do not know what. I've been trying to get her to lie down so I can help her deliver the baby, but she refuses. Would you talk with her?"

"You have not delivered a Finnish baby?"

Frances shook her head.

"She will walk. I will put a fire in the sauna."

Benjamin walked with Minnie. "Mama?" he whined. "Mama! Okay, Mama?"

Arthur took the boy's hand and together they went to the sauna. Arthur gave the boy a pail and told him to fill it with water from the lake. Arthur lit a fire in the sauna stove and then took another pail, and together he and the boy carried the two pails of water back to it. Richardson and Halley brought rags from the house. Soon the air inside grew warm. The sauna was ready.

He took Minnie's hand and helped her along the path. Cats scurried out of the way as the group hurried back to the heated hut.

"We deliver in there? But it's so hot!" Frances said.

"It is the Finnish way," Arthur said.

Minnie was already undressing in the anteroom, so Frances followed her inside. Outside, Benjamin waited eagerly.

"Papa?" he said. "Where Mama?"

"Go play, Ben," Arthur said. But the boy walked alongside his father.

The sun burned through a thin layer of clouds. Halley, sitting on a bench, asked, "Why the sauna?"

Arthur said, "It is our cleanest place."

Halley nodded. "I hope Fran can handle the heat."

There were muffled cries from within. Arthur waited, but no one emerged.

The bell sounded the mine shift change. The steam engine stopped whirring and rumbling. The sky, filled with smoke and steam and exhaust, could have been the sky in any city, in Duluth or Minneapolis. The mine was dangerous. Even the people were dangerous. This was not the place he had wanted to raise his children. And yet here he was, and he had to stay. He was part of this place, part of this company, and where the Merritts went, he followed; just like Benjamin following his father. The boy was looking for guidance, for a lesson. He searched for understanding in a confusing world. Arthur looked for peace and for the opportunity to make a difference. To raise his family where they could breathe clean air and smell clean earth and where the trees would surround them.

Benjamin said, "Papa!"

Arthur stopped pacing. He turned his ear towards the sauna. A muffled cry gave way to a louder one, and then a high-pitched squeal. The mine bell sounded and the steam shovel started wailing again and the sky again filled with smoke. Frances came out of the sauna wiping her hands with her apron. Sweat dripped from her forehead, and her clothes were soaked. She took a breath as though it were the first breath she had taken in her life.

"My goodness it is hot in there," she said.

"*Miten ne?*" Arthur said, beside himself with anticipation.

"What?"

"How are they?"

"Oh, yes. Mother and daughter are fine. Are you allowed to go in now?"

"*Joo*, yes," he said, already rushing past her.

Inside he found Minnie with the baby on her chest. The baby was wet and pink, and she was beautiful.

"What will we name her?" Minnie said.

Arthur reached out and took the girl from her mother. Her eyes were closed and her fingers were balled into fists and then she opened her eyes and she raised her shining eyes to him. Arthur smiled.

"Margaret," he said. "Margaret Riiski Maki."

Minnie smiled. "A good name," she said.

Arthur gave the girl back to her mother. "A good name," he said.

With a new baby in camp, Arthur was more anxious than ever. He implored Minnie to stay home, but she would not hear of it.

"Frances and Nessa need me," she told Arthur. As usual, Minnie had the final say. Frances told Arthur to bring his wife a stool for the kitchen, where she and Mrs. Gill did much of the work. Housell, as usual, sat on the floor in the corner, drunk. He seemed to have discovered that the last swallow from the bottle was as easy to get as the first.

"Feed the troops," he said, sloshing whiskey onto his shirt.

"Ignore him," Frances said, and they did.

The dining hall was crowded before and after the shift change. Up to a hundred men would stand in line and wait for a plate of venison steaks or fish stew or some of Minnie's now-famous rye bread. The few who had families went to their homes to eat, to town, or to their houses in camp. After eating, most wandered like ghosts back to their shared cabins and slept for a few hours before they got up and did the whole thing over again. Those who were heading to their shift would take a small lunch bucket filled with sandwiches or soup, prepared by Minnie and Frances and Mrs. Gill.

More workers arrived, swarming out of the woods like mosquitoes. Richardson did his best to watch them all, but he was only one man. He stayed near camp, wandering the outskirts, keeping tabs on the new men. And they eyed him warily. They didn't like being watched. He reported back to Arthur daily: no sign of the two men.

When pay finally came, a month late, there was not enough cash to cover the back wages each man was owed. Lon Merritt had, however, included a stock certificate to be handed out to each worker on the payroll.

"You are now a part owner of the company," Cohoe told the men as he distributed payroll in the dining cabin. "The harder you work, the more value your stock will have and the higher your pay in the long run."

Each man also received a shot of whiskey. For many of them it wasn't enough. They took their meager wages and vanished into town. The noise from the southern side of the pit was raucous. For others, the lack of back pay was a sign that the Merritts were more interested in lining their own pockets than in paying their bills.

One of the Irishmen stood up. He had red hair and a scraggly red beard that looked like he had glued a squirrel tail to his chin. "Don't make much difference what we do," he said. "If the ore does nay move our labor's for naught."

Housell shouted, "Just be glad you've got work, Mick."

"Be glad you've got legs," the Irishman said.

Housell laughed. "My pay depends on you digging the ore. When the train comes, the ore'll move so fast you won't know it was ever there."

"*When the train comes, when the train comes.* That's all we hear. All I see is the sweat off me brow and a couple piles o' dirt. I don't see no train."

The stockpile had grown so large that workers, using shovels and horses, graded a narrow road that wound around the stockpile so that wagons full of ore could ride to the top. While the dump pile of overburden did not grow as fast, Arthur used what Cohoe called wasted dirt to level the foundation for the train depot. The rest of the dirt went to Marfield, the town, for grading beneath the new buildings. This name seemed not to stick, though. When people found out that a railroad was being built, they began to call the town Grant after the man who would build it. Arthur wondered if the townspeople were considering the railroad man the hero who would bring civilization to their little community. But had they even heard of Leonidas Merritt?

Arthur stood to take his plate and cup to the kitchen. "Train will come," he said, as much to assure himself as to assure the men.

"See?" Housell said. "Even our faithless Finn knows."

CHAPTER 9

ARMOA

On a clear day in August, the mosquitoes were out in force, attacking everyone. Arthur was slathered in yarrow paste but still had to swat them from his face. He was supervising the construction of the rail depot when he happened to turn for a moment and spotted a lone horse and rider coming up the hill from the tote road.

The rider stopped at the headquarters office and went inside. Arthur walked over to meet him, since he knew there was no one in the office.

The man came out as Arthur approached.

"Hello," the man said. He was well dressed in a shiny riding suit, leather riding gloves, and long leather riding boots. He wore a tall hat and an absurdly long handlebar mustache. A red and white sash, decorated with blue stars, stretched across his chest, proclaiming *Harrison*. The man pulled off a glove and extended a smooth hand to Arthur.

"How do you do, sir?" said the dandy. "My name is Henry Oliver. I came to see this famous ore I've heard so much about."

Arthur ignored the offered hand.

Oliver dropped his hand. He turned to face the pit. "That's quite a hole in the ground."

"Yes."

"Is that pile iron ore?" He seemed genuinely curious.

"The big one," Arthur said.

"Doesn't look like more than a mountain of dirt." He turned back to Arthur. "I've heard the ore you are taking from the ground is upwards of sixty-five percent pure. Is that right?"

Arthur shrugged. "I know nothing about the quality of the iron. Are you another mineral man?" Arthur was thinking of Harvey Lewis, the last lone rider who had appeared in Mountain Iron.

Oliver laughed. "No, no. I am not a mineralogist, if that's what you mean." He pulled off his other glove and dropped both in the pocket of his riding jacket. "I am simply a business man." He was friendly and outgoing, and though he seemed over dressed for riding, he could just as easily have been on the crew that was putting the finishing touches on the train depot. "What is your role here?"

"I am in charge of the camp. I am Arthur Maki."

"Pleased to meet you, Mr. Maki. Is this what they are calling Mountain Iron?"

Arthur nodded.

"And is Mr. Merritt himself here?" Oliver seemed hopeful.

Arthur shook his head.

He nodded thoughtfully. "Can you tell me who is in charge of the mine?"

"Captain Cohoe."

"Is that John Cohoe? His reputation stretches to Pittsburgh. May I speak with him?"

Arthur pointed at the office building. "Wait here." The visitor went inside and Arthur went to the pit where he found Cohoe supervising the construction of a new system of girders for a trestle that would carry men in and out of the pit—which would be easier than climbing ropes hand-over-hand. Arthur told him there was a man in the office looking for him. "He is well-dressed. His name is Henry Oliver."

Above the din of the steam engines Cohoe said, "Who in Sam Hill is that?"

Arthur shook his head.

"Dammit."

At the office Oliver stood when they entered. Cohoe remained in the doorway and yanked off his gloves. "Who the hell are you?" he barked.

"I am Henry Oliver," the man said. "From Pittsburg. Are you Captain John G. Cohoe?"

"Aye," Cohoe said. "State your business. I've a mine to run."

Oliver took a small card from inside his jacket and held it out.

"Steel, Captain. My business is steel."

Arthur could see it was slickly embossed, a nicer card than the one the mineralogist had given him. Cohoe ran a finger across the face of it. Then he looked up and his expression changed. He smiled broadly. "A pleasure to meet you, Mr. Oliver. Would you like a tour of our mine?"

Cohoe and Arthur took Oliver on a tour of the pit. They walked to its far side, following the path of the narrow rail tracks that led down onto the mine floor. "We are extracting everything by digging it out of the ground," Cohoe explained. He pointed to a pile of rocks and dirt on the south side of the pit. "That's the overburden. It's mostly rock, hard stuff, and some dirt. The rock has some ore in it, though it's not as pure as what we are piling up south—there—and what we are taking out of the ground right now."

"What's the iron content?" Oliver asked.

"Testing shows sixty-five-percent pure."

Oliver whistled. "What about that?" He pointed to the debris pile.

"We have not tested it. There is enough of the rich ore just beneath our feet to last for a hundred years."

"You've dug that deep?"

"We've drilled fifty feet below the mine level and the samples are all the same," Cohoe said. "It's all around. Everywhere you look." He spread his arms.

Oliver shook his head. "It's hard to believe."

"Believe it," Cohoe said.

"Two companions and I hired a buggy to take us to the Missabe Mountain mine near what I believe they are calling Virginia," Oliver said. "They refused to travel any farther. They claimed the road was too rough. It was, but well worth it to see this. This is more spectacular than any mine I've ever seen." The steam shovel hissed and clanked as it tore into the wall of ore, lifting a bucketful and dumping it into a waiting car on the tracks. "How many men are working here now?"

"Around two hundred all told. We are mining around the clock."

Oliver squatted and grabbed a handful of dirt. He squeezed it and the damp ore formed a ball in his fist. "It's heavy," he said.

"That's the iron," Cohoe said.

"You seem to have two towns growing here. Looks like more

than a couple hundred people."

Cohoe said, "The town's not part of the mine. It just kind of appeared there."

"Do you have a sawmill?"

Arthur said, "Yes. There is a mill to the north. We have a big supply of trees as you see. What we don't use for the mine we sell to the town."

"I have seen pit mines before," Oliver said. "But this is massive."

They began to walk back up the hill. "How are you going to get the ore out of here?"

Cohoe pointed to the half completed train station. "See that building there? Maki here is building a train station. We expect the track to come through within a couple months."

"That soon?"

"We got a deal with the Duluth and Winnipeg. Our line will connect to theirs in Stony Brook and they'll take it the rest of the way to Allouez Bay."

They walked around the perimeter of the pit. Oliver walked upright, his hands clasped behind his back, his fine hat perched high on his head. By the time they got back to the headquarters office his black boots were covered with red dust. He removed his hat and the Harrison sash and sat down in the offered chair.

"This place was all the talk in Minneapolis this week. Seems some people think you've found another Vermilion up here."

Cohoe smiled. "This is better than the Vermilion range. Our ore's just as pure and cheaper to get. You've seen the operation. All we must do is dig it out of the ground. No drilling shafts or tunneling or shoring up drifts underground. It's just lying there."

"Can it be that easy?"

"You bet."

Oliver thought for a moment. "I want this ore for my plants. I'm prepared to pay seventy-five thousand now for the right to all the ore you have here. In addition, I shall offer sixty-five cents a ton if you can guarantee annual tonnage for the next shipping season."

Cohoe whistled. "I sure wish I could take that offer," he said.

"Why can't you?"

"I'm just the mining captain here, Mr. Oliver. For a deal you'll have to talk to the men in charge. Lon Merritt, I'd imagine, or his nephew Johnnie."

"Where are they?"

"I'd guess down in Duluth."

Oliver stood up. "Then I shall ride back down and find them. My mills need your ore, sir. If you can guarantee me two hundred thousand tons next year, and that it's as pure as you say it is, then my pig iron will be the envy of the industry. Hell, the world. I'll have Andrew on a rail."

"Andrew?"

"Carnegie. That old goat'll eat his hat when he finds out."

Outside Oliver shook hands with Cohoe and offered a hand to Arthur who stared at it like it was the hoof of a stuffed deer. Oliver shrugged and mounted his horse. "I know you shall hear from me again," he said as he rode away.

After he was gone Cohoe whipped his hat off and threw it into the air.

"That could be just what we need, Maki!"

Arthur wanted to share Cohoe's enthusiasm, but he couldn't. He would only believe it when he saw the ore move.

"Look at that stockpile. We got four or five thousand tons there, and that's just from the last couple months with only one shovel. We get another couple steam shovels up here, more men, another dinky engine and the railroad, we've met his quota! It's guaranteed!"

"Guarantee?"

"It means we can't lose. Don't you see? All those worries about selling the ore have just gone. We've got a buyer!"

That night, as he thought about the certificates under his floor, he told Minnie, "I will believe it when I see it."

Minnie cradled baby Margaret. "But this is the answer to what has worried you. The ore will sell, Arvid." She was more positive than Arthur, and her faith that, in the end—somehow—things would work out never faltered.

"I hope you are right," Arthur said.

Two days later a message came from Lon in Duluth. It was short but to the point:

> Have signed agreement with Mr. Henry W. Oliver
> of the Oliver Steel Company for 200,000 tons of
> orc at 65 cents per ton in 1893. Railroad to arrive
> within a month. This is a cause for celebration.

Housell broke out his whiskey—Cohoe gave away the company's stash—after Cohoe agreed to pay him for it, and in the dining hall that night the men celebrated. Frances put a bottle on each table, while Housell made sure he saved two bottles for himself. The men who came off their shift were given one cup full each so as not to disturb the running of the mine itself. After all, Cohoe determined, if they were to meet the demands of the new contract with Oliver, then a round of hangovers would do nothing to accelerate their work tomorrow. Still, the celebration ran into the night. Four Irishmen took the bottle from the Finnish table and after emptying the last of it into their cups, stood on the table and began to sing:

> *I met my love by the gas works wall*
> *Dreamed a dream by the old canal*
> *I kissed a girl by the factory wall*
> *Dirty old town dirty old town*

There was no music except the Irishmen's song. While Minnie worked the kitchen, Arthur held Margaret, and Benjamin danced with the workers. Despite the loud voices singing and the boots thudding against the tables, his baby girl slept peacefully, her small eyes closed and her little fingers curled into fists on her chest. Arthur watched his son dance and laugh and thought that maybe all his worry was for nothing. That maybe all the work he had put into this place would mean something.

Earlier Richardson had told Arthur that he believed Ned and Danny must have moved on. "Farther west, maybe. Or south where there might still be a lawless frontier."

Things were falling into place.

Minnie came out of the kitchen wiping her hands on her apron. She looked tired. It had only been a month since the baby was born and she had been working almost daily since, her only respite being Sundays. Still, there was no time for complaints, and when she came over to Arvid to take the baby from him, she smiled.

One of the Finnish miners grabbed Arthur's hand and pulled him up to dance. Benjamin laughed and skipped around his father's legs. Arthur laughed, too.

Moments later Frances burst out of the kitchen and rushed to Arthur. "Come quick," she said. "It's Minnie."

Arthur followed Frances into the kitchen. Minnie was pacing just inside the door with Margaret clutched to her chest. She had a wild, frantic look in her eyes.

"What is wrong?" he said.

She grabbed his arm. "Get Richardson," she said. "Tell him. I have seen them, Arvid. They are here."

⟫◆⟪

Arthur didn't want to leave Minnie. "You cannot stay here with the two of them out there."

Minnie said, "I am not alone. Frances is here. The room is full of people. Go."

As usual, she was right. Still, as he rushed out the back door, he felt a pang of horror. She had seen them, but he did not know where. In his rush to convince her to get to safety, and then get out the door and find Richardson, he had neglected himself to see them. They must be in the dining hall. Would they cause trouble there? Would they find Minnie in the kitchen? Arthur ran as hard as he could past the pit and across the tote road into Marfield. He found Richardson sitting in front of his boarding house. There was no hesitation from the timberman when he saw Arthur approach. Richardson did not give Arthur a chance to even catch his breath before he began to run toward the mining camp.

Men were stumbling along the main street that connected the camp buildings and spilling out the door of the dining hall. This was not the kind of celebration that Lon would have wanted, Arthur thought. He brought Richardson into the kitchen and found Minnie sitting on a stool quietly rocking Margaret. She seemed to have calmed. Mrs. Gill was washing dishes while Frances was cleaning up the pots and pans from dinner. Halley was there, too, leaning against a wall. They all looked anxious. The noise from the dining hall was deafening.

"I do wish Cohoe had taken it easy with the bottles," Frances said.

"*Oletko kunnossa?*" Arthur asked Minnie. *Are you okay?*

She nodded. The baby was asleep.

"*Jossa on Ben?*" *Where is Ben?*

Minnie looked up. The boy was asleep upstairs, then.

"You must go home," he pleaded. "Take the children."

She shook her head. "I will not leave you."

Arthur turned to Halley. He was a big man, but not a fighter. Still, Halley would keep his family safe. "Please, take her home."

Halley nodded. "I agree. Things could get bad in there."

Frances dried her hands. "Come, Minnie. Let's get you and those little ones home." She went upstairs.

With her eyes, Minnie pleaded with Arthur. He said, "I must do this."

She stood up, cradling the baby. Frances reappeared carrying a sleeping Benjamin. Arthur touched the boy's head, then kissed baby Margaret.

"*Olla varovainen*," Minnie told him. *Be careful.*

"I will," he said.

She held Arthur's eyes and implored him, "*Sinun täytyy näyttää heille armoa.*" *You must show them mercy.*

Arthur smiled but said nothing. It was a promise he could not make.

When the others were outside he turned to Richardson. "Are you ready?"

Richardson nodded.

In the dining room men danced on tables, singing and shouting. There were competing songs going in five different languages. Richardson scanned the room. They hadn't gotten more than a few feet before Housell appeared from the shadows.

"What have we got here?" He sneered. "Look what's come back from the reservation."

"Hello, Housell," Richardson said.

"Last time I saw you you was being carried outta here. Let's see if we can make that happen again."

Arthur turned to the cook. "You have done enough."

Housell laughed. "Not by far, Maki. Not by far." His meaty fist clutched the neck of a brown bottle.

Richardson was trying to ignore Housell. "It's all right, Arthur. He's drunk."

Housell refused to be brushed off. He put the bottle he was holding on a table. His beard was flecked with fish and dirt and grease, and he reeked of dead fish and whiskey. Still, his eyes were clear and he moved toward Richardson as steady as a tree come to life. "Drunk or not, I'm going to beat you."

"We have no time for this," Arthur said.

Housell rolled his shoulders and cracked the knuckles on his right hand. He cackled. "I ain't had any fun since you left." He stared Richardson in the eye.

"I said enough." Arthur put his hand on Housell's chest.

Housell turned his cold, hard eyes on Arthur. "Take yer hand off me, Finn."

"You will not do this," Arthur said coldly.

"Are you gonna stop me?"

"This is not your fight," Richardson insisted.

Housell grabbed Arthur's wrist. "It is now."

Arthur kept his eyes locked on Housell's. "It is my job."

"I'm gonna break you, Maki."

Arthur planted his feet. Like a stubborn tamarack root, he was not going to move. "No. This will stop."

Housell tried to twist his arm, but Arthur was stronger than the cook realized. Arthur pulled free and then landed a right hook square on the cook's nose. Housell was almost lifted off his feet. He fell on his back, blood drooling from his nose. The room erupted in cheers as the singing miners realized there was a fight. They formed a half circle around the three men.

Housell put his hands on his face. "I'll fucking get you, Maki."

Richardson stepped forward as though to land another kick, but Arthur stopped him.

"No. He has had enough." Arthur looked down at the cook. "You will not get anyone. You will cook. That is *your* job."

A man stepped out of the circle of workers and grabbed Housell's bottle off the table. He was tall with a narrow, wrinkled face and a mouth as black as pitch. "You gotta keep kicking him else he'll get up and kick you back," the man cackled. He took a long swallow from the bottle and then stepped over to Housell.

"Then you give him a little salve for his wounds." He poured the rest of the whiskey onto the cook's head. When some got in his eyes, Housell howled and rolled out of the way. Some of the gathered men cheered, but most of them grew suddenly quiet.

Richardson snatched the bottle from the man's hand. The man looked up, startled. Slowly his mouth turned into a smile, lips cracking over black teeth.

"I know you. Seen you in Virginia. You and this cook here friends?"

Richardson said, "He's not a friend of mine."

Realization dawned on Arthur. This was Danny, the older of the two brothers. Arthur turned and stood next to Richardson. His fist hurt from the punch, but he pushed the pain away. He felt his heart beat fast and he flexed his fingers. He was ready to punch again if necessary.

"That's inneresting. I generally only get killed for my friends," Danny said.

Richardson overturned the bottle and let the liquid pour onto the floor. There was a mumbled hiss from the crowd. "I understand you do a lot of killing," he said.

Danny smiled. "Glad to see somebody's takin' notice."

A shorter man stepped forward, younger than the first, with the same crooked nose. This was the other brother, the one who had killed Charlie. "Don't let him take yer whiskey, Danny."

Arthur clenched his fist. He wanted to jump the man, wanted to beat him until he was as bloody as Housell's apron. Anger raged like a fire inside him. But the circle of miners, most of them drunk, were watching. Arthur did not want to start a brawl. It was one thing to punch the cook; no one liked him. But Arthur did not know how the other men felt about Ned and Danny. They were members of the crew, after all. The best thing to do would be to get the two men out of the dining hall without creating a scene.

Danny eyed Richardson's buckskin jacket and pants. "Brother, I think we got us a Injun."

When the bottle was empty Richardson tossed it against the wall where it shattered.

"I thought they's supposed to all be up at the reservation," Ned said.

"This un's a wanderer." Danny smiled like he had an idea that would solve all their problems. "Hey, we ever get our discharge papers from the army?"

Ned shook his head.

"That means we got us a duty to put this one back where he belongs."

Arthur stepped up then. "Are you Danny and Ned Walters?"

Ned faced Arthur. "Who the fuck're you?"

"I am Arthur Maki. I run this camp."

"Well then, thanks for the whiskey." The circled men cheered. "Unfortunately, it is our duty as soldiers for the U.S. Government to take this Injun back to his reservation. They ain't supposed to leave 'em, you know. These savages are dangerous."

Arthur tried to remain focused. He wanted to get them out of the dining hall. "Do you work here?"

Danny laughed. "Listen to that accent, Ned. 'Nother one of them foreigners. Country up here's full of 'em."

One of the big Irish laborers stepped out of the crowd. "I'd be careful what ye say about the men here." He had a shock of red hair and a scraggly red beard. He couldn't have been more than twenty-five, about the same as Danny, but he was bigger with shoulders as wide as a door and hands like rocks. Arthur did not know his name, but knew his face. He had been one of the ones to help carry Mrs. Gill out of the kitchen.

Danny smiled at the hulking Irishman. "Oh, I weren't referring to you lads. I come from fine Irish stock meself." He pointed to Arthur. "It's the others here, the less savory ones. These pasty-faced buggers from the North Sea. They've come here to take our land and our work."

"How long have you been here?" the Irishman asked. "I don't know you."

"Two days. Long enough to see that you boys are doing all the work, while Pasty-Face over here orders you around."

The Irishman glanced from Arthur to Danny to Arthur again. And then he swung his fist at the side of Danny's head. The latter was knocked into a table and then crumpled onto the floor next to Housell. The Irishman turned to Ned. "How do you feel about it, brother?"

Ned shook his head and backed away toward his brother.

Arthur did not want anyone else involved. "That is enough," he said. "We'll take care of them."

The Irishman smiled. "As you say. If you need any help call out. We take care of our own in Mountain Iron." He turned back to his table and grabbed a drink.

Arthur looked at the rest of the men who had gathered. "Go back to the celebration," he said. "The fight is over."

There was grumbling, but they dispersed quickly, went back to drinking. The noise returned to its previous volume. Arthur turned to Richardson.

"We must take them out."

Richardson turned to Ned. "Get him up. Carry him out."

Arthur turned to the men celebrating. It was late, and the mine needed to start operating. He made a decision. He found Cohoe at a table, drink in hand, talking to a couple of German miners. Arthur took the cup from him. Cohoe looked up, startled.

"Captain, this party must end."

Cohoe looked around the room. "It's just getting started."

"The mine has stopped. The men are all here, drunk. But they must work. Lon would not like this kind of celebration. It must end. If they want drink, they can go to the saloons in Mountain Iron on their day off. But not here. Not anymore."

Cohoe reached for his cup. "You let me worry about the mine."

Arthur emptied the whiskey onto the floor and took the bottle from the table. "I am sure Lon can find other men capable of running this mine."

Cohoe stared at Arthur, his mouth closed in a hard line. He was gauging how serious was the threat. Arthur had no intention of backing down. Finally, Cohoe nodded.

"All right," he said.

He stood up on a table and let out a loud whistle. The noise in the room stopped. "The party's over, boys. Everybody get to a bed and sleep it off. Let's get back to work. The sale won't mean a thing if we ain't got no iron to sell."

Arthur helped Richardson with the two men. Richardson had taken their guns and, using a stretch of rope, had bound their hands behind their backs. Arthur pushed them into the kitchen.

"What is this about?" Ned asked.

"You ain't got no right to tie us up," Danny added.

Arthur pushed them against a wall. He locked eyes with Ned.

"You killed my friend."

Danny laughed. "We killed a lot o' people."

Richardson said, "This was a Chippewa, on a street in Duluth."

Ned's eyes widened. Danny saw the look of recognition in his brother's eyes and quickly said, "We don't know what yer talkin' about."

Richardson put the muzzle of one of the revolvers into Ned's face. "How about now? Do you remember better now?"

Ned nodded. "Yeah, yeah, I remember."

"Shut up, Ned," Danny said.

Richardson lowered the gun.

"It was a accident," Ned said. "I didn't mean for the gun to go off. Honest. I ain't killed nobody before. Not up close like that."

Danny kicked his brother. "I said shut it."

Ned stepped away. Richardson kept the gun pointed at Danny.

"Danny's the one took the money. He said weren't no way an Injun could have a stash like that. Said if he stole it then we could steal it from him."

Arthur grabbed Ned's shirt. "He was my friend." He felt the anger rise up. His arm shook as he balled his hand into a fist.

Richardson lowered the gun. "What do we do with them, Arthur?"

He wanted to take them to the woods and shoot them. He wanted to leave their bodies to be eaten by bears and wolves. He wanted them to feel the same pain and anguish he felt when he lost his friend, his brother. He remembered the Russian soldiers beating him and locking him away for refusing to fight. He remembered the old man who told him his parents were dead. And then he remembered seeing Margaret for the first time, her little feet, her little hands. And he thought of Ben. What would he tell his son? He recalled Minnie's words.

It took a force of effort to let go of Ned Walters, but Arthur did. He pushed the man away and turned to Richardson.

"You must take them to Duluth. They are wanted men. The sheriff will know what to do with them."

Danny shouted, "You ain't the law! You can't take us nowhere."

Richardson eyed him coldly. "I can take you into the woods and put bullets in your legs and let the animals feed on you."

Ned began to cry. "Please don't do that, mister. We'll go with you."

"They gonna hang us, Ned."

"I'll take my chances with the law before the wolves."

Arthur took two horses from the stable and sat the two men facing each other on the back of one. He tied their hands behind their backs and then wrapped the ends of the rope around the horse's belly. He then tied their feet together. Richardson got on the other horse. "I'll not stop until I reach Duluth," he said to Arthur. "Only a two-day journey. We go slow enough the horses will be fine." He turned to the two men. "You boys decide to slow me down by falling off that horse, I'll shoot you where you land." He winked at Arthur.

"Good luck," Arthur said.

"You, too. Tell Minnie I was sorry to have missed her. I think she'll understand."

He kicked the horse and rode off in the darkness toward the mine, disappearing into the trees.

Arthur went home. Margaret and Ben were both asleep, but Minnie lay awake. He laid next to her and told her what happened. She put her arms around him.

"You did the right thing," she said.

He closed his eyes. "It is what Charlie would have wanted."

Despite the celebration of the agreement with Oliver, the men working the mine were still discontented with the pay situation. And now that there was a buyer for the iron ore they had been piling up, they were worked harder than ever. To provide a further incentive for faster work, Cohoe implemented a new pay system whereby workers would be separated into small groups, and each group would earn their pay based on the amount of ore they added to the stockpile. There was grumbling about it at first. The Cornish miners accepted it right off—that was the way the business of mining was done, they said. Some of the others, especially those with less experience, thought it unfair that their pay might drop if they did not work as quickly or as efficiently as the others.

Still, work at the mine continued unabated and the stockpile grew.

Arthur and his crew finished the train depot before the advance rail crew arrived. It was the nicest building in Mountain Iron—both in the camp location and in town, two stories tall and constructed entirely of milled lumber. Lon had sent stained glass windows from Duluth packed heavily in straw. The eaves were finished with a patterned design that to Arthur looked like the pattern of the low hills to the north of town. He was trying to mimic the sleeping giant. And the walls themselves were lacquered in green and brown paint to mimic the trees from which the lumber, and the town, had come.

It was Cohoe who insisted they have a celebration marking the day. Arthur and his crew stood on the steps of the newly finished building while Cohoe praised the work to a gathering of twenty or so men, most of them from the town.

Daniel Marfield—of the Marfield Hotel and after whom the town had currently been named—wore a tall silk hat. He smiled broadly. "Nicely done, sir," he said and offered Arthur his hand. Arthur ignored it. Benjamin stood next to his father, tall and proud. When Cohoe introduced him to the gathered crowd, Benjamin said, "Papa!" Minnie had wanted to be there but she was in the kitchen, cooking. Everyone had jobs to do, Arthur told her. The men must be fed.

While the depot building itself was finished, the platform had to wait for the laying of rail lines. The advanced train crew arrived in late September, and men worked around the clock piling overburden as foundation for the ties, laying rails, and hammering spikes. The whole of Mountain Iron, and Marfield, was alive with excitement.

Within a few weeks the track was laid, and in October the engine arrived. Benjamin, holding his father's hand, jumped up and down as the steel machine whistled up the shallow incline to the end of the tracks beyond the depot. Four stacked rail ties braced by iron struts acted as an emergency stop to prevent the train from tumbling into the mine. The engine stopped just short of this barricade and a thin balding man with a white chinstrap beard stepped down from the cab. Ash and soot covered his blue striped overalls.

He tugged off a leather glove and held out one hand, which Arthur ignored.

"I'm Don Grant," he said.

"I am Arthur Maki."

"Ah, Mr. Finnigan told me about you." He pointed to the depot behind them. "That must be your handiwork."

"Yes."

Benjamin ran to the engine and pointed at the big steel wheels which were as tall as him. White steam hissed and Arthur grabbed the boy and pulled him away from the heat. For a week he had excitedly listened to the *chink-chink* of sledgehammers pounding iron spikes. He had asked about it every day. "When will the train come, Papa?" Arthur had grown tired of both answering the question and ignoring it.

"It's a big engine," Grant said.

"Blow the whistle?" Benjamin asked.

Grant smiled. "Sure."

A crowd gathered around them; men in woolen suits and hats introduced themselves to the engineer who was bringing civilization to their little mining town.

But Arthur was disappointed. He said, "You have no cars to take the ore?" He was still being paid in stocks, and those sheets of paper were beginning to stack up under the floorboards. What good were they if the ore didn't go to market? It was already early October and the weather was beginning to turn cold again. Within a month the stockpiles would freeze and the mine would become unworkable. If ore did not move to market now, everyone would have to wait until spring to get paid. Arthur was no accountant, but he knew that another winter without moving ore meant another year before the mine began to make money. Before he began to make money.

Grant smiled. "This is the advance work engine. I'm riding through to make sure the rail is set," he said. "We worked faster on this track than on any other that I've ever been involved in. Got to make sure the rail holds up."

Along with the train came another connection to the world outside of the woods: a telegraph. Two days after the arrival of the engine, a message came from Lon in Duluth. The first official train car would ride up from Duluth on October 17. Cohoe worked the miners feverishly for a week, cleaning up the stockpiles and the mine. The people in town, too, swept debris, buried trash, and graded streets. This was to be the biggest day in Mountain Iron history, the first shipment of ore from the Mesabi Range.

Arthur heard of a vote in the village to incorporate the town. The first unofficial vote was to call the place Grant after the man who brought the train, and for a few days that's what they called it. The day before the train was due to arrive, the town held an official meeting which Gill attended. He came back incredulous and pleased with himself. He found Arthur and Cohoe in the office and told them that he had spoken to the three men spearheading the incorporation campaign.

"Grant's nothing more than a hired hand, I said. Might as

well call the town Gill for all the good that name is. That put a thought into their thick skulls." Outside the two steam shovels were churning through ore that Gill and his crew had blasted clear during the night.

Gill continued. "By the time I left they'd decided to name it Mountain Iron. Now that's the name of a town."

Pencils danced as Gill slapped Cohoe's desk.

"About damned time," Cohoe snapped. "Damned town better get right who's in charge around here."

Arthur had grown so accustomed to the sounds of activity at the mine that the noise blended into the background. It was Gill who noticed that it seemed to have grown quiet outside.

"What's that?" he said.

Cohoe sat down and began making notes on his maps. "I don't hear anything."

Gill said, "That's just it. Nothing."

Arthur went to the window and looked toward the mine. Normally a trail of white smoke drifted up from the shovels in the pit. Right now the air above the pit was clear. Beyond Arthur could see the golden colors in the trees. The rumble and whine of the buckets, the crumbling of rock, and the whistle of the steam engines, all had ceased. Outside the window was silence. "The steam shovels," he said. "They have stopped."

Cohoe stood up. "What?"

Gill said, "Listen to that. You give an order to stop shoveling?" he asked Cohoe.

"Damn if I did anything of the sort," Cohoe shouted.

Before any of them could go to inquire the door opened and a group of about fifteen miners marched into the office. Paavo, the Finnish miner who had been fired after his brother's death, led them.

"What are you doing here?" Cohoe said. "I told you to never come back."

Paavo strode across the room and faced the two men. Laborers and workmen filed in behind him, filling the small room. "The men have not been paid in two months," he said. "They demand their wages."

Cohoe threw up his hands. "Payday's next week," he said. "You boy, get out of here. You don't work here. And you other boys need to get back to work or there ain't gonna be no pay for any one of you, next week or ever."

Paavo turned to Arthur and spoke in Finnish. "I come to you as a man and as a Finn. What is happening to our brother workers is not fair. While Lon feasts on caviar and oysters, these men suffer the bonds of servitude, suffering the hazards without compensation. These men sought me out to come here and plead with you to give them what is rightfully theirs. For if you do not, they have sworn to me they will take it by force."

Arthur looked at the faces behind the young Finn. They were Finn and Irish and Cornish and German and Italian. They spoke different languages, ate different food, and outside of the mine they spoke not a word to one another. But here they were, united and angry. These were rough men used to a fight, and Arthur saw they were prepared to start one now.

Paavo turned to Cohoe and spoke perfect English. "You know what happened in Soudan. That is what is happening here. This place, this mine, from this moment, is closed. There will be no more ore taken from the ground, no more track laid, no more shovels moved, until these men receive their pay. Tomorrow the Merritts will see their mine shuttered. The men will stand together and block the arrival of the train. We shall see to it that this mine moves no ore until we receive our pay."

Cohoe stood. "How dare you come here and threaten us? This is a mine. If you want to work, then you work. If you do not, then leave now. We pay well here, you all know that."

"We know that we have been promised good pay. But so far these men have not received it. All they get are partial payouts and promises. Promises don't pay rent. Promises don't bring families from England and Germany and Italy and Finland. We demand what we have been promised or this mine will cease operations."

Cohoe stammered. "I give the orders around here, not you."

Someone produced a long knife, and then more steel was unsheathed. Paavo said, "We just want our pay."

Cohoe was indignant. "Will attacking us get your money? One telegraph to Lon and the state militia will be here in a day and run all of you off. There'll be no job for any of you. How will you be paid, then?"

Arthur spoke to Paavo in Finnish. "Violence is not an answer. If we fight then you achieve nothing.”

Paavo replied, “Neither do you.”

“What did you say?” Cohoe said.

The two Finns stared at each other for a long moment. Cohoe was impatient.

“What did you tell him, Maki?”

Finally Paavo nodded and motioned for the men behind him to put away their weapons. The men grumbled but the knives were sheathed.

Arthur said, “I tell him we will pay.”

“God dammit, Maki, this is not your mine.”

“Nor is it yours, Captain,” Paavo said. He turned to Arthur and said in Finnish, “They will not wait long.”

Arthur said, “They will not have to.”

Cohoe objected, but Arthur took out the work ledger and began calculating pay. He wrote a pay slip for each man who had come that day, and for every worker who was still outside, waiting for word about their future. They were scared, Arthur knew, because deep down they knew they had no power. That the company could replace them at any time. But, while Arthur was here, he would make sure that did not happen. He sent a telegram to Lon explaining that when the train came the next day, there would need to be payroll on it. “These men have worked for months with only the promise of pay,” he told Lon. “You must fulfill your obligations to them if to no one else.”

The following day, Arthur received his answer.

⸺◆⸺

That next day a cool breeze drifted through the swaying trees, carrying with it the faint smell of pine smoke. An explosion echoed in the distance from one of the newer mines springing up around what everyone had begun to call the Range. Miners and laborers alike, along with the village, dressed in their Sunday finest. Three hundred men, women, and a few children lined the rail line and stacked themselves on the slopes of the stockpiles and overburden to watch the train arrive.

Arthur, uncomfortable in a stiff collar, watched the tracks expectantly. Beside him stood Cohoe, Gill, Halley, and Wilbur Merritt on the platform of the wooden depot building. Behind them were Minnie, Frances and Mrs. Gill. Minnie wore a yellow gingham dress hand-stitched from fabric she brought from Duluth. In one arm she cradled Margaret and the other held the hand of a bobbing Benjamin. The boy wore a gray suit and matching gray tie, inadequate to dampen his spirits, or his constant motion.

"Still," Minnie told him, but he continued to bounce.

Black smoke plumed above the tree line as the train wound caterpillar-like around the final bend in the line. The whistle screamed. The tracks rumbled and the ground seemed to shake.

Captain Cohoe leaned over to Arthur. "I hope the men stay in line."

Arthur replied, "They will cooperate." He had made them a promise, and they looked to him to fulfill it. Paavo was out there watching him. When Arthur saw from Lon that the money had arrived to pay wages, he would give a signal to Paavo who would make sure the men did not attempt to revolt. Anything that marred this day, Arthur knew, would leave a black mark on not only the Merritts but also on the stocks that he was relying on for his own future.

Wilbur snickered, "I hope the rail lines hold together. They put it together so fast, I'd not be surprised if it collapsed beneath the weight."

But hold together they did. Engine, coal car, and two passenger cars pulled into the station at just past eleven in the morning. An empty wooden ore car, freshly painted black and labeled number 342, rode between the coal hopper and the passenger cars.

Lon Merritt stepped onto a platform at the back of the rear passenger car. He wore a long black wool coat and a black bowler. He appeared to have aged even more since last Arthur had seen him. In his face were etched the deep lines that months of worry and financial haggling had wrought. His eyes, once bright pools, were now dark as though a giant were casting a long shadow over them. As the train squealed to a stop, Lon looked at the assembled men and women on the platform. He smiled weakly at Arthur and nodded. Then he turned to face the crowd.

Arthur did not know what to do. He waited and watched. Paavo stood on the slope of a pile of overburden and watched, too, waiting for a sign from Arthur.

Lon flashed a broad smile. Arthur could see the effort it took to show enthusiasm. Maybe the gathered miners and townspeople sensed it, too. The men needed the Lon of old, the firebrand who could rouse them. They seemed to know, too, that he needed them, for they erupted into frenetic, cathartic applause as though encouraging Lon. Maybe for the workers they simply knew that their payday had finally arrived. Wilbur yelped and miners from across the tracks echoed the yell with their own cries.

"Hip, hip," someone shouted.

"Hooray!" the mass of men emoted at once.

"Hip, hip!"

"Hooray!"

The wild cheering lasted for a few minutes while Lon held up his hands demurely, but no one seemed to care that he refused the accolades. They continued to applaud. Finally, voices tired, the applause faded on its own. Lon cleared his throat.

"Thank you all for coming. This day represents, for my family, the culmination of years of dedicated searching. Twenty years ago my father came out of these hills and told his sons wild tales of the rich red earth and how it spun his compass in wild circles." He gestured to the other men behind him on the platform. "My family and I have spent many long years seeking to realize the fulfillment of my father's discovery. Each of you has helped to make this dream possible, and we thank you for your hard work and dedication. While this place may mark the terminus of this railroad, this day marks not the end but the beginning of the journey for all of us. Not just for you and me, but for all of the Mesabi Range, and for all of Minnesota. Today we send to market the first load of ore that will ever be shipped from what will come to be known as the greatest reserve of iron ore the world has ever seen."

The speech was all Lon Merritt, extemporaneous and motivational. The crowd erupted in applause. They cheered from the heaps of overburden, whistled from the rooftops of the saloons and hotels in Mountain Iron, and hollered from the edge of the great yawning red pit itself.

And Leonidas Merritt stood on the platform beaming.

Arthur applauded politely, not for the words but for the sentiment behind it. That this was the beginning of the venture, and the end of the financial worries. Still, he wished he had felt motivated by the speech. Despite the work he had done and the home he had built, he saw in Lon a man desperate to show that he has accomplished what he set out to accomplish. But his promise of a mine "for all of Minnesota" fell flat when Arthur thought of the workers who were only there because Arthur had made his own promise to them.

From inside the passenger car emerged the figures of Lon's brothers and cousins. There was his older brother, Alfred, whom Arthur had met only once. He was taller than Lon and quite a bit leaner. Cassius emerged next, followed by Johnnie and then two men whom Arthur had never seen. He assumed they were Andrus and Napoleon. These last two were helping Hephzibah Merritt emerge from inside the car. She stepped slowly, supporting herself on either side. Lon reached out and took her arm and when he did she looked up and saw the crowd of workmen looking back at her. Her legs seemed to crumble beneath her. The brothers all reached out to support her. Lon put his arm behind her knees and carried her down the steps of the train through the parting crowd to the platform.

When they reached the group Lon set her on her feet again. Hephzibah turned to Minnie. "Hello, Minnie. Is this the new baby?" To Arthur she looked older and more frail. The worry of her sons had been passed on to her. "What's her name?"

"Margaret," Minnie said awkwardly. She, too, felt the discomfort of the moment. Lon seemed to have suddenly taken on the role of supporting son, as opposed to leader of the largest mine in the state of Minnesota.

Hephzibah touched the child gently on the forehead. "What a sweet child," she said. "And this must be Benjamin. He has grown so much!"

The boy held up three fingers and proclaimed, "I'm three!"

"You look well," Minnie lied.

Hephzibah shook her head and smiled. "No need to fool an old woman," she said.

Wilbur Merritt gave Hephzibah a hug.

Lon turned to Cohoe and Gill. "You have done marvelous work, Captains." His voice was big and he exuded confidence as he shook their hands. The two men smiled as they took the accolades of the man of the hour. For Arthur, there was something empty still in his words, something hollow. As though for Lon the work of digging out the pit had dug out a part of himself as well.

When he reached Arthur he lowered his head. His voice was whispered and serious. "We'll talk shortly." Then he lifted his head and flashed his big smile again and turned to Hephzibah. "You must see the mine, Mother." He swept the old woman in his great arms, resuming the role of dutiful son.

Minnie put her hand on Arthur's back. "I'm proud of you," she said. "You have built a place we can call home."

Arthur shook his head. "We call it home, yes, but what of the others? They have not even been paid for their work."

"It is not your worry," she scolded. Minnie generally had a way of soothing his fears, but today even she could not allay his concerns.

"It is not Lon who has made the promise," Arthur said. "I have given my word."

Margaret began to cry and Minnie took the baby and Benjamin into the depot to warm by the stove. Benjamin whined that he wanted to stay outside with the train, but Minnie insisted and the boy followed his mother.

Lon stepped carefully along the wooden platform to the pile of overburden that stood on the southern end of the pit itself. Wilbur, Cohoe, Gill, and Arthur all followed him. The grade was steep but Lon demonstrated the strength he still had in his legs as he climbed that pile of overburden. Shale and rocks slipped beneath his feet but he never faltered, kept climbing until he reached the top where the ten or so workmen there fanned around him. Hephzibah looked out over the mine. "There it is, Mother," Lon said.

From the bottom of the pile, someone yelled, "Three cheers for Mother Merritt!"

The crowd roared, "Hooray! Hooray! Hooray!"

Lon climbed carefully down the giant of overburden, still carrying his mother. He was followed by his brothers and cousins, as well as a few reporters writing in small notepads. The captains, too, followed him down, but Arthur stayed on the top of the mound. The giant steam shovel rumbled slowly out of the mine. It was coming up to load the ore into the waiting train car. In the distance the low hills that Charlie had shown Arthur, the sleeping giant himself, was now a flat, treeless prairie. The giant, it seemed, had woken and moved on. Before Arthur spread the great pit itself, the culmination of all Lon's promises: vast and empty.

A group of neatly dressed train workers setup tables along the rail cars. They brought out sweating ceramic jugs. The workmen grew excited when they saw cups being handed out. But when they discovered nothing but cold, fresh milk being offered, the men who did not work the mine made their slow way back to the saloons in town. Cohoe and Gill followed them, as did Halley. The rest of the men, miners and workers, clustered in groups around the train. They were waiting for their pay, and Arthur wondered if they would fulfill Paavo's promise of not letting the train leave. Paavo was nowhere to be found. Lon, too, seemed to have forgotten about his promise to talk with Arthur.

Arthur could wait no longer. He scrambled down the small hill of overburden and ran toward Lon talking with three newspapermen at the edge of the pit. The other Merritts stood behind them, set pieces for the Leonidas show.

"Yessir," Lon was saying. "Sixty-five percent pure."

Arthur was breathless when he came up behind Lon and said, "I must speak with you."

Lon put on his big smile and said, "Ah, yes." He put an arm around Arthur. "Gentlemen, this is Arthur Maki, the leader at camp here. He is the one who built that fabulous depot building you see here, and he built our entire mining camp over on the eastern side of the pit there."

Lon pointed and the three men's faces followed. Lon nodded approvingly. "Yes, Mr. Maki has been invaluable to our work. He saw this crew through a harsh winter up here."

Arthur shifted uncomfortably. Lon squeezed his shoulder tight. Lon was using him to promote himself, and Arthur did not like it.

One of the men said, "Mr. Maki, how cold did it get?"

Arthur turned to Lon and said again, "I must speak with you."

Pencil hovered as the reporter waited for an answer.

Lon patted him on the shoulder. "All in good time, my boy. All in good time." He smiled broadly.

"What was winter like?" another man asked. "Are you able to dig the ore during the cold months?"

"Now, please," Arthur insisted.

The look of confidence on Lon's face faltered for a moment. This was his big moment, and he wanted nothing to ruin it. The world would watch what happened today, would record it for history, and he wanted it known that he was in charge. He recovered quickly, though, and reapplied his broad smile. "Gentlemen, if you'll excuse us for a few moments. There is a business still to run, even on a glorious day like this." He laughed. "I'm sure my brother, Alfred, can continue to answer any questions you may have." He directed the three reporters to the men standing a few feet away, the other Merritts. Alfred was the tallest of these, and the most distinguished in a wool overcoat and pince-nez.

"Gentlemen," Alfred said. "If you'll come this way I'll show you some of the other features of the pit mine."

Lon took Arthur's arm and pulled him away from the crowd. "I told you we would speak later," he growled under his breath. Arthur had never seen Lon Merritt angry.

"You must pay the men," Arthur said flatly. "I have promised them. As have you."

Lon walked briskly toward the depot as though trying to get as far from prying ears as possible. "Yes, yes, I have the payroll on the train. The workers will get paid before we leave."

"They must get paid now," Arthur said. "They will revolt. They will stop the train. They will not load the ore."

Lon waved his arm as though swatting at a swarm of blackflies. "They will not," he barked. His voice was tinged with something hard, rough. He seemed no longer the gentle giant in the pit exuding confidence; instead he was the steam shovel barreling through the earth, clawing at it without a care as to who might get in his way. "They have no power to revolt. Each of them is expendable. Each of them can be replaced tomorrow. There are hundreds of men coming off the train each day for every one of the men that work up here. If they want to start a fight, I'll show them how to win."

They stepped up onto the wooden train platform. A small group of Cornishmen maneuvered the steam shovel in place between the pile of ore and the train. Paavo, surrounded by his Finnish brothers, watched from the other end of the platform.

"I shall fulfill my promise and pay their wages," Lon continued.

"I am a man who keeps my promises." He looked out at the men clustered around the train and snarled, "But if they attempt to get out of line, to disrupt this glorious day, then there will be no pay. There will be nothing but the summary discharge of every worker in the mine."

"You would not?" Arthur said, shocked. He had never heard such talk from Lon Merritt before.

Lon smiled. His old confidence seemed to return and his voice changed instantly. "Of course not, Arthur. I would not want to do this. You tell the men they will be paid. I'll have the money brought to the office, and Cohoe can start giving out pay. It will be done, don't worry." He patted Arthur on the arm.

Arthur stared at Lon. His eyes darted about and for a moment he seemed unable to meet Arthur's gaze. Then their eyes locked and Arthur saw in the giant's eyes cold fear. Lon had the money, that Arthur knew, but there was something else looming that seemed to frighten Leonidas Merritt. It was as though the shadow of another giant were clouding him, and as he spoke he seemed to shrink in size.

"We have the chance to make something grand here, Arthur. By this time next year the Mountain Iron Company will be the most profitable company in the world. We have enough ore here to build a thousand ships, and then some. Add to that our other mines, Biwabik and Missabe Mountain, and we control the greatest reserves of iron ore in the nation."

He was trying to sell his iron, but to Arthur the words were meaningless.

Arthur heard a laugh and he turned to see Housell. He clomped along the wooden platform to where Lon and Arthur were standing, smoking a thin, hand-rolled cigarette. "It'll never work, you know." He let out a long stream of smoke.

The cook seemed uncharacteristically sober. He had combed his greasy hair and beard and for once did not smell like rancid meat. His suit was clean save for a patina of red dust. When he spoke his neatly waxed gray mustache seemed stuck in place. He held a cup of milk in his hand.

Lon held onto his air of invincibility. "What do you mean, Mr. Housell?"

Housell laughed. "This place is a dream. You've hocked your

boots to pay for it. Ever'body knows you ain't got enough money to pay for this railroad, much less the men who're shoveling the ore onto it."

"You know nothing—" Lon began to protest but Housell cut him off.

"Look, none of us want to see this place go down." Milk spilled out of his cup as he swept his arm toward the steaming engine. "Ever'body out there's got a stake in this thing. Ever' miner, ever' mechanic, ever' engineer. Hell, half of Minnesota owns stock in the Mountain Iron, or the Biwabik, or even this damned railroad itself." He laughed. "The stock we've all got ain't worth a savage scalp when there's so much of it out there."

Lon protested, "Your stock has tremendous value!"

Housell laughed. "Don't blow smoke." He swallowed the rest of the milk and dropped the cup onto the platform. "The D&W ain't gonna haul that ore. They don't believe any more'n anybody else that there's anything worthwhile up here. They ain't gonna risk their bread and butter timber contracts for the sake of a few screwy teetotalers who think millions of dollars of ore is just lying on the ground." He turned to Arthur for the first time. "Think about it, Maki. If the ore was really that easy to get, don't you think some-body would have done it by now? Somebody with more money? Or more experience in building up a big operation like this?"

Arthur wanted Lon to say something, anything, to counter the cook. But for the moment, Lon seemed struck mute, his mouth hanging open. Arthur half expected a swarm of flies to buzz out of the darkness.

Arthur blurted out, "Mr. Oliver. He will buy the ore."

Housell snorted. "Oliver's a quack like the rest of 'em. Made his money on a bet. Next year he'll be broke because this year he bet on this. Look around you. This place is filled with the rejects from the world. We are the ones no one else wanted, and we came to this Godforsaken place where winters are colder than a penguin's tit to dig holes in the ground. Open yer eyes, Maki. Ain't nothing here but dirt."

The massive steam shovel began to dig at the stockpile of iron, filling car number 342 with ore. Lon pointed at it indignantly. "That is iron. Look at it, and see."

Housell laughed. "How long we been here? More'n a year. And

we got one car of ore. We'd need another forty-nine cars and sixty years to meet Oliver's order." He puffed on his cigarette and shook his head sadly.

"What do you know of mining?" Lon hissed. "There is ore here for a hundred years."

"Okay, let's say we do manage to meet the quota," Housell continued. "This train goes to Superior. But the D&W ain't gonna take the ore anywhere. They're moving this one, sure, but this is all for show. They ain't got enough cars to take that much to Allouez, and they ain't gonna buy more just for this. For nothing."

Lon smiled triumphantly, as though he had already won the argument. "We have always known this would be a short-term solution to a long-term problem. That is why we are building our own line into Duluth."

"And connect to what?" Housell countered. "Duluth ain't even got any ore docks."

"We shall build them," Lon said, as though putting up a railroad and building ore docks into the bay were as easy as building a house.

"That Oliver contract ain't enough to even pay for a railroad," Housell said.

The talk of expenses and costs and the difficulty in getting all this ore to market was overwhelming for Arthur. He only wanted to see the men get paid their due. But the more he listened to Housell, the more he began to think that this venture was not as sound as he had hoped it would be. That maybe those papers under the floorboards in his house were worth as much as the paper itself: good enough to start a fire.

Lon said, "The mine will pay for itself." For Lon this seemed a foregone conclusion. "This place is valuable beyond measure."

Housell was not going to back down. "Where's the money comin' from?"

"We have investors," Lon shouted, startling both Arthur and Housell. He looked around quickly to see if anyone heard him, then lowered his voice. "Men with money who see the value in what we are trying to do here. They have agreed to finance the venture."

"What men?" Housell said.

Lon narrowed his eyes. "Mr. Housell, I have no reason to be

under this level of inquiry from my cook."

Housell shrugged. "I got a trunk full of paper up in my room that says I own a part of this company. Far as I'm concerned you work for me. So maybe I got a duty to ask." He twisted his head around. "Maybe if those men from the newspapers asked, you'd answer."

Lon gritted his teeth. "Mr. Housell, these deals have not gone through. For word to get out about them before they have been finalized might ruin them."

Housell scoffed. "You think Minnesota is that big that you can keep something like this a secret?"

"It must be kept quiet for now," Lon said defiantly.

Housell jabbed his thumb toward Arthur. "Just tell Maki here. Tell him how you ain't got a red cent to your name and you're hip-deep in debt paying for all of it."

Arthur gaped at Housell. How did the cook know all this?

As though sensing his question, Housell said to Arthur, "You'd be surprised the stuff people talk about when they've gotten a little hooch in 'em. I may be just a cook, but I ain't the village idiot." He drank a swallow of milk.

Lon turned to Arthur as though imploring him to understand. He seemed to deflate. "These are things one does in the normal course of business. Few men have the capital and resources to accomplish what we are trying to accomplish here. Resources in Minnesota have been tapped but the sap has run dry. And so we must extend our reach."

He shook his head and stared at the cook. "You say that no one believes in us, Mr. Housell? Don Grant, the man who built this railroad, believes, and so strongly in fact that he is trying to wrest control of the company from my family." He turned and looked at the engine. For the moment, Housell was silent, letting the giant have his say. Arthur was anxious to hear how Lon would answer Housell's claims. After a few seconds Lon turned back to the two men. He lifted his chin and thrust back his shoulders, crossing his hands behind his back. Some of his old confidence was returning.

"I'll not lie," he continued as though he were a child confessing a transgression. "Building a railroad is expensive business. We put up a lot of capital to construct this spur line down to Stony Brook, and we know it will not be enough. The docks at Allouez Bay are already working to capacity. They will not be able to handle the extra tonnage that will come their way from our mines. We have known all along that something more would need to be done.

"Housell is right. In order to ensure that we retain control of the company we shall need backing. Tomorrow I leave for New York where I shall meet with John D. Rockefeller. You know who he is?"

Arthur shook his head.

Housell whistled. "That's big money."

"Rockefeller is one of the richest men in America. He's got no interest in iron ore—he's an oilman. But his rival is a man named Andrew Carnegie—"

Arthur's eyes lit up. "Oliver's man!"

"That's right. Only Carnegie turned Oliver down flat. Which gives us an opening. If I can get Rockefeller to give us backing, in exchange for some stocks, then he'll have Carnegie over the ropes and we'll have the money to build our railroad our way—with ore docks in Duluth that we own. Don't you see? It'll be ours. Not just mine and my brothers' but yours and Housell's and Cohoe's and Gill's." He turned to face the railroad and the men loading the ore car, his back to Arthur and Housell. "It'll belong to every one of the men out there. It'll belong to all of Minnesota." He spread his arms as though he could embrace the state. But to Arthur, even with arms outstretched he seemed to shrink. Lon was reusing words from his earlier speech, still trying to convince everyone that he was right.

Housell was not a believer, either. "Say you get Rockefeller's money. Then what?"

Lon dropped his arms and turned around. His face wore a mask of dejected resignation. The fight in him was gone. "I cannot make you believe, Mr. Housell," he said. "If you wish to resign your post I'm sure we can find someone to replace you."

Housell guffawed. "I ain't leaving. I'm having too much fun!" He flashed a broad, yellow-toothed smile.

Lon took a breath and squared his jaw. "Mark my words: History will prove me right."

As the steam shovel loaded the last of the ore into the car, Arthur looked for Paavo. The Finn stood in the same spot, rooted to the pile of overburden as though he were a birch tree planting roots around the rock. Arthur removed his hat, and Paavo removed his.

Then the young Finn clambered down the hill and talked with the men assembled below. Word spread quickly and they nodded approvingly. Arthur saw smiles spread across their faces and a wave of relief spread over him.

Alfred appeared at the end of the platform followed by the other guests—the rest of the family, Hephzibah, Wilbur, Cash, the men from the newspapers, even Cohoe and Gill. The train crew brought a small satchel to Lon, who handed it to Cohoe.

Lon turned to Arthur. "That is the pay. This promise is fulfilled." He took a breath. "Thank you for all you have done," he said. "This place could not have been built without you."

Alfred passed them. "Time to go, Lon."

A group of Finnish miners came from the trees then, carrying a six-foot-tall pine tree. They were led by Paavo. "What is that?" Lon said.

Paavo and another miner climbed on top of the ore car, while the others lashed ropes to the tree. The two miners on top of the car then pulled the tree up onto the ore. They laid the tree flat and tied it down then climbed back down the car. Paavo waved to Arthur.

Arthur said, "It is a Finnish custom, to bring good fortune." He had cut the tree himself that morning, and had hoped that the men, once they found out about their pay, would follow through on their promise to install it atop the ore car.

Lon smiled. "It is the start of a new tradition. The first shipment of ore from every Merritt mine will be accompanied by a pine tree to represent the promise of future wealth. I like it!"

He clapped Arthur on the shoulder, grabbed Arthur's hand and shook it. And Arthur, almost without realizing it, shook back.

Jo and I attended the funeral, and all Arthur's surviving kids were there, including Uncle Ben and Aunt Margaret, neither of whom remembered the early days in Mountain Iron. Uncle Ben was tall and lean and even with a shock of white hair he didn't look older than fifty, though he was pushing sixty. I showed him the rock that Pappa had given me, and he remembered seeing it on the mantle in Virginia. I told him I wanted to give it back to Pappa. "Isä would like that," he said. So I laid it next to him in the coffin.

Jo and I stayed in Virginia for another few days. I visited some old friends, and got some fishing in on the lake. Before we left we took a drive over to Mountain Iron to see the place where it all started, and, for Lon Merritt anyway, where it kind of ended.

The old mining location was gone, taken over first by the Oliver Mining Company and then by U.S. Steel officially. They had the place fenced off and wouldn't allow us to even walk up to see the spot where that first drill was sunk, or where those first cabins were built. Even the train depot, which my grandfather had been so proud of, was gone. The mine itself was shuttered and full of water. In the 1940s granite was quarried out of it, but once that was gone there was nothing left but a hole in the ground.

The rest of the story Pappa didn't talk much about, but it's a story I learned in school. For Lon Merritt and his brothers, that triumphant day in October, 1892 in Mountain Iron marked the culmination of years of hard work. But it would prove to be the high point of the Merritt mining venture. Other successes would come, sure, but with each one came more setbacks.

A few days after car 342 left Mountain Iron, ten more cars were filled with the wet, dense iron ore from Mountain Iron and sent down the tracks. The train connected with the D&W line at Stony Brook and in early November arrived at Allouez Bay. The ore was loaded onto whalebacks—long, narrow, hollow, and flat-bottomed barges—and hauled to Pittsburgh. There the furnaces, unused to the soft, rich ore, clogged and stopped production at the steel factories. Once again, word spread about the uselessness of the iron from the Mesabi, and once again money began to dry up.

Lon continued to believe, though, and made his deal with John D. Rockefeller. The oil titan gave the Merritts enough capital to extend their railroad into Duluth where they built two huge ore docks that jutted out into the bay. By the time the shipping season started in 1893, they had fulfilled their dream of owning the iron mines and the means of getting the ore to market, and had managed to make it all happen within Minnesota.

The first train on the Duluth, Missabe and Northern Railway, carrying ore from the Mountain Iron Mine, arrived into Duluth in early 1893. There the ore was poured directly into waiting whalebacks that would take it to the steel mills in Cleveland. The Merritts were not in Mountain Iron to watch the train depart, nor were they in Duluth to see their ore docks put to first use. Lon was in New York trying to save the company he had worked so hard to build.

Because in early 1893 the stock market had begun a steady decline that by May had reached its lowest level in more than a decade. A financial panic set in. Two million tons of ore from the 1892 shipping season sat unsold at the docks of Erie, Pennsylvania. The price of ore plummeted. The contract with Oliver was not enough to pay expenses, and the declining demand for ore meant layoffs at the mines. But the Merritts didn't have enough capital to meet even a scaled-back payroll. Lon's ambitions were still bigger than his pocketbook.

The problems for the Merritts mounted. Unable to pay off the debts incurred in building the railroad and the ore docks, the Merritt family was forced to give up the collateral they had put down on the loans: their ownership of the railroad and the mines. Three years after they started what was briefly the largest mining operation in Minnesota, they lost it all.

John D. Rockefeller, the industrial giant, took over.

It was February of 1894. The bleak financial picture had left only the barest of staff in Mountain Iron during the frigid winter, and those men who remained were left feeling low and depressed. Just a month before, one despondent worker had walked into the drifting snow with a pistol and had not returned.

Arthur was eating alone in the dining cabin. On the table lay the stack of twenty stock certificates he had been given in the last two years. A telegram had arrived that morning informing the employees of the mine and the railroad that John D. Rockefeller was now in full control of the new Lake Superior Consolidated Mines. Any stocks they had in the Mountain Iron Mining Company would be purchased by the new owner at one penny per share.

Housell came out of the kitchen with a bottle. "Hear the news?"

Arthur nodded.

"Worthless." Housell drank from the bottle and winced. "Well, worth less than it was supposed to be." He offered the bottle to Arthur.

Arthur had not touched a drop of liquor in his life, but that day he briefly considered it. The stock that Arthur had so relied on to make his fortune, to bring well-being and comfort to his family, was worthless. This was what he had gotten for taking a risk, for taking chances. When he arrived three years before he was full of promise and hope for a bright future. Now, snowed in for another winter in Mountain Iron, ore piled up with no place to go and no one willing to buy it at a price that would bring half what the company needed, those hopeful ideals seemed less and less real. Seemed like foolish hope.

Housell dropped a stack of the certificates on the table. "They're good enough to wipe your ass," he said.

Pappa laughed.

Housell said, "What are you going to do with them?"

My grandfather stood up. "I do not know."

"Here." Housell fished pennies from his pocket. "I'll buy yours.

Nostalgia. Two cents each."

Each certificate was signed by Lon Merritt. Arthur had at one time given more credence to the stocks because they were signed by Leonidas himself. He hated Housell for all that he stood for, and there was a part of Arthur that hoped that the cook would be stuck with a bunch of paper only good to burn. He could buy Ben some candy for forty cents. Housell was offering him double what the stocks were worth. Arthur pushed the stack of paper to Housell.

"I'm going to tack them to my wall," Housell said. "Maybe use them as kindling." He counted out the correct number of coins and dropped them on the table. "Or maybe I'll keep 'em. They don't have much value now, but I get the feeling Rockefeller's gonna make this place work."

"From now on I take cash," Arthur said. "Only cash." He meant it. My grandfather would never invest in stocks, spent his life deriding the market. Maybe that was one reason my father became so obsessed with money himself.

Housell shrugged. "Suit yourself."

Outside the cold bit into him. Snow drifted under an overcast sky, green pine branches, like his spirit, weighed down by winter's burden. He walked to the office which was his alone now, Cohoe having left a week before. The mining captain had received a telegram from Duluth informing him that a new mining head was coming to Mountain Iron. "Your services no longer needed. Arthur Maki in charge of operations in the interim."

"I don't know who you know back East," Cohoe had told Arthur. "But you made an impression on somebody." He thrust out his hand. "No hard feelings."

"I know nothing of this," Arthur had said.

Cohoe had grabbed Arthur's hand and shook it. "If you are going to be management you had better learn how to shake hands," he had said. "Watch out for that Paavo. Men like him are trouble."

Arthur made a pot of coffee and sat down at his desk. In the distance he heard the whistle of a train and then checked the schedule. No trains were due to arrive until tomorrow. He put his coat back on and walked down to the depot. Steam and smoke billowed across the platform in the blustery winter wind as the engine and a single passenger car rolled into the station. The Mountain

Iron sign hanging from the depot's eaves squeaked as it swung. A lone figure stepped off the train. He wore a tattered fur coat and a heavy woolen muffler, his hat pulled low on his head. His black mustache quickly became covered with white from the snow and frost in the air. His sallow cheeks sunk against his pale face. He walked slowly, shoulders hunched forward, and he seemed smaller somehow than the last time Arthur had seen him.

When he saw Arthur, Leonidas Merritt smiled. "Is there a place we can go?"

Arthur led him back to his house. Now that Lon no longer owned the mine, Arthur didn't know if it was appropriate to take him to the office.

Inside his house, Arthur put another log on the fire. Minnie brought the men coffee as they sat in the living room.

"I wanted to come up and see it one last time," Lon said. "It was good while it lasted."

Arthur nodded. "It was."

Lon sipped his coffee and stared at the fire. After a moment he said, "Cassius is dead. He was always a sickly child and an even sicklier man. His heart, I think, couldn't take the strain of it."

"I am so sorry," Arthur said.

Lon shook his head. "We must persevere," he said. "It is what we have always done. What is it you call it?"

"*Sisu*," Arthur said.

The two men drank their coffee. Then Lon reached into his pocket and removed a rock. He held it in his hand. It was a dark rock, gray with stripes of red and silver. It was as big as Arthur's fist, but in Lon's big hand it seemed like a child's toy. "Cassius found this, way back in '90. This is what started it all," he said. "We've kept it in the office in Duluth since then, sitting on a shelf on the wall. Kind of a reminder of all the potential that exists here, and all that we had to live up to. To somehow serve the land this rock represents, and to allow the rock to serve us." He tossed the rock in the air and caught it like a ball. Then he leaned forward and held it out to Arthur. "I want you to have it," he said. "You are all that remains of what we had here. I put in a good word for you with Rockefeller. Hope you don't mind. It was all falling down around us, and they asked who was the best man back here and yours was the first name that came to mind. If anyone will keep the spirit of what this rock represents alive it will be you, Arthur. Please, take it."

Arthur held out his hand. The rock felt heavy, denser than most rock. It was like the earth around here: heavier, denser. Suddenly Arthur thought of Charlie. He hadn't thought of his friend in a year. "Sleeping giant wakes," he said, his memory of that day as vivid as ever.

"We did wake a giant," Lon said. "Rockefeller. He'll be bigger than ever now. I didn't see what that meant before." He looked at Arthur as though he were looking through him to the low hills outside. "We woke the giant, and I don't think he'll ever get back to sleep."

Lon finally stood. "I had better go."

He found his coat and pulled on his hat. Outside the day was turning to night and a new snowfall began to drift across the town of Mountain Iron. Arthur stood on his front porch next to Lon and looked out at what the town had become. He remembered when he had first arrived and seen the one rudely built cabin and thick stands of white pine trees that seemed to stretch into infinity, seemed to block out the world. At the time it seemed to Arthur that this could never be a place where anyone would want to live. All that had changed.

Arthur had built a home here, not just for himself and Minnie and Ben and Margaret, but for all the workers that came before and after. He built not only houses but also a community, and for that he was proud.

"Maybe none of it was worth it," Lon said.

Arthur turned to him. For Arthur, it was never about the money. The stocks, the promise of a future free of worry—it had seemed a fantasy. He had gotten caught up in the excitement of it, sure, in the promise of it. But when the red dust settled, when the train had come and then gone again, when the excitement was over, he turned to find Minnie standing beside him, her warm smile comforting him. He was right where he was supposed to be, he realized. Home. "It must be," he said.

Lon smiled. "Goodbye, Arthur."

"Goodbye," Arthur said.

My grandfather said he watched Lon walk away through the snow then stepped back into the warmth of his home. My grandmother Minnie put her arms around him. "*Tämä on loppu,*" she said. *This is the end.*

Arthur pulled her close. "No, love. This is the beginning."

Not long later Arthur heard the train whistle fade into the distance. After it was gone the only sounds remaining were the crackling of the fire and the soft patter of snow on the roof.

This book is a work of fiction. However, in telling of the story of the early days of mining in Mountain Iron I have attempted to be as historically accurate as possible. While some character names are real, any similarities to actual persons, living or dead, is coincidental.

I took fictional liberties with many of the stories in the book. There is no historical record that the real Housell cooked for the Cavalry, or that Lon Merritt came to Mountain Iron to rouse the men against the findings of those "scientific squirts." The real Captain Cohoe took over supervision of the Mountain Iron Mine in April of 1892, replacing Captain Wood. That a girl named Virginia was the cause of the change, or that there ever even was a girl named Virginia who was found near where the town of Virginia was itself founded, is one of the Range's tall tales. Mountain Ironers might wonder how two lakes east of town could magically form, or how a sawmill was in operation two years before the historical record says there was a sawmill. The answer lies in one word: fiction.

The Iron Range is full of great stories—and great story tellers. Paul de Kruif in his enlightening book *Seven Iron Men* recounts the tale of the rocket stump that crashed into the camp kitchen, wounding the wife of the man who set off the explosion. Wilbur Merritt, by his own account, stumbled into Mountain Iron in the middle of the night and led a group of men to Biwabik. Newspapers from October 18, 1892, reported that a white pine tree was laid across the top of the first shipment of ore that came from the Mountain Iron Mine, and it remains tradition to this day for a pine tree to accompany the first shipment from any new mine on the Iron Range.

Stories abound about how the town of Virginia got its name. Walter Van Brunt in his seminal work *Duluth and St. Louis County, Minnesota: their story and people* mentions that the town was named after the state from which David T. Adams haled. I have taken considerable liberties with that bit of history. Virginia, as the Queen City of the Mesabi Range, will play a more prominent role in future books in this series.

Marvin G. Lamppa's book *Minnesota's Iron Country* and David A. Walker's *Iron Frontier* have both also been excellent sources of information. If you want to read more about the history of iron mining in Minnesota, those fine books are a great place to start.

What is not fiction is the true grit and determination—the *sisu*—of those first Rangers. In very short order these men—most of them immigrants with little education and speaking only their native language—transformed the thick forest into an industrial factory. In writing their story, I hope I have captured some truth to the story of all the men and women who came after them.

J.S.
BERLIN, MD
AUGUST 2014